CW00920006

THE FLATLANDS DIARY

By Martin Burrows

DEDICATION

This book is dedicated to the loving memory of my mother

Dorothy Jane Burrows, a wonderful, funny lady

That's greatly missed by all who were blessed to know her.

Acknowledgements

Many thanks to family, friends and everyone

who encouraged me to write this drivel ...

it's your fault. A huge thank you to Ann

Harrisskitt of Ann Harrisskitt Photography

for providing the cover photograph

Copyright © 2017 Martin Burrows

All rights reserved.

ISBN: 9781520755212

ISBN-13: 9781520755212

CONTENTS

INTRODUCTION

Welcome friends, welcome one and all to my Flatlands.

What follows is an account seen through my diary, scrapbook, social media and local media, of the day to day existence of Flatlands folk. This will be a snapshot, a journal through a year of my life and all my adventures, and in particular my involvement in a series of events which changed Flatlands forever.

This tome is about an area of the United Kingdom that is very often, quite rightly, overlooked. Flatland District is an abandoned region that is steeped in old rituals, traditions and customs that date back to the beginning of time or even older. It is an area that can only be described as very, very rural, it is populated by folk who can only be described as very, very rural. Flatlands is very, very rural.

Flatland District is a remote part of the East Anglian *'cundreysoid'*, and is an unusual, backward trending fen community, in an odd district within a strange region. Despite its relative close proximity to civilisation - Peterborough - it still possesses an antiquated outlook and many bizarre characters and traditions. It has its own calendar, its own currency (*mostly root crop based*), its own dialect, its own separate internet and even its own unique, indigenous wild life. It's a kind of Madagascar of the Fens. The currency is based on the variable root crop exchange rate to the local coinage. Local money is referred colloquially as a 'Dave' for notes or 'Davey's for coins'. This is because the Mayor of Flatlands, David Devilman, is particularly vain and insisted he has his face on the coins and notes used in the district. This can be exchanged into UK currency on the very rare occasions people leave the district and venture into what Flatlanders call the UK of Great Britain.

The landscape of Flatland is, as its name suggests, flat. Flatland District is incredibly flat, flat like a snooker table, even for the Fens, Flatlands is amazingly flat. The area mostly sits well below sea level in a sort of inverted plateau. Due to this inverted plateau-ness of Flatlands it has a micro climate of cloudy, drab, uninteresting, grey, drizzly weather. It's a weather system that lends itself to a tiresome existence, and is often cited by many rural scholars and statisticians as a possible, in fact very likely reason, for the areas unusually high rates of incest, madness and suicide.

Flatlands it's safe to say, is dank. This reflects in its inhabitants grey appearance and overall demeanour. The sun seldom shines in a micro climate that almost defines the perimeter area of the District. That golden globe of scary heat rarely manages to pierce the low level clouds but when it does shine through it frightens most of the local folk who view it as a portal of doom. Many of the regional traditions and ceremonies are avoided during daylight. Skin cancer is not an issue in Flatlands or the Fens … or East Anglia in general.

The river Kumber runs through Flatlands and along the outside edge of the village of Chumpton, giving it the name Chumpton-by-Kumberly. The river however is a somewhat misleading description, it's actually just an arterial branch of the many drainage dykes found throughout East Anglia. This drainage dyke system was created by the Dutch when they drained the Fens in the 1650s (or the 1251s as it's known in Flatlands). Legend has it that Cornelius Vermuyden, the man largely attributed as the 'main drainer' of the Fens actually insisted his men were protected by the kings soldiers when draining Flatlands because the 'swampfolk', (*as they were known*) scared the navies half to death with their webbed appendages and unintelligible marshland talk. As you will see nothing has changed much since then.

This dreary and unremarkable area has several villages and one market town that is all part of the Flatland District Council remit. They're places that time (*and the national grid*) has forgotten. The district has a small market town called Ropey, two large villages and a number of small satellite villages. One of the villages is the aforementioned Chumpton-by-Kumberly, which is where I live, and the other is called Chatterby. The small satellite villages are dotted randomly about the area, but never far from a dyke. Although these 'villages' are usually nothing more than a few small dwellings and the occasional pumping station used to regulate the water table. All this constitutes what is known as the Flatland District.

This is Flatlands main Compoota console; it's held at Ropey Town hall in the 'Chamber of the Elders of Flatlands' and has complete control of all of the 25 compoootas located throughout Flatlands. It acts as a kind of "Survva" which allows contact with other compoootas throughout the district and all of the known living world area via tefelone lines. It is known as a 'state of the arrrt' compoooting machine that has some 'software' as well as 'hardware'... so it has both kinds of 'ware'. It also has a steering wheel but our "IT" expert (IT means Intelligent Talk) isn't too sure what it's needed for yet. It could be that our big Compoota/survva needs Compoota wheels.

This is one of our 25 Compoootas in Flatlands. Our compoootas help connect us to the rest of the world, UK and even Peterborough. It has things called Mega Bites and helps us to "download" and view photographs of ladies tuppences and breasties. Our 25 compoootas are very popular among the men in our communities of Flatlands keen on mastybayshun.

What follows will be a look at my life in a community that has its own unique, and often disturbing, news and views. It's a closed community that's best described as 'tight knit', based around family values … very 'family' values. These values mean the district has an extremely limited gene pool and subsequently, a very limited selection of surnames.

Inbreeding is a constant within the area and is a commonly accepted practice or hobby in a community where people still point at aircraft. Of course the outside world is more than aware of the Fens sexual practices with insinuations about the indigenous folk of East Anglia having webbed fingers due to the inbreeding mutations. The truth about Flatlands folk however, is that locals seldom have webbed fingers. They do have numerical variations of digits compared to what hoooman people would view as the 'normal amount' of fingers and toes per limb, or indeed a normal amount of limbs. Many of the Flatlands females, known as 'dyke donkeys', do have webbed breasts though. This additional flap of skin between their 'breasties' has evolved over many, many years of un-selective breeding and is utilised by the Flatland dyke donkeys to swim the drainage dykes from village to village. They strap a reed basket to their backs filled with their villages produce and, when the tide is right, swim the dykes in a sort of butterfly style. Similar to the man from Atlantis (*who did have webbed fingers*), the breast webbing is used as a method of propulsion to sell their wares and sexual favours to other villages. It's a sort of local commerce that's conveyed by F5 generation mutated 'vehicles'.

This diary's objective is to view this strange little community through its limited media outlets and a few personal accounts of mine during its most turbulent year, in order to give you the reader (*and potential, but unlikely visitor to Flatlands*) a good idea of what living in a rural area in deepest, darkest East Anglia is like. A sort of travellers rough guide if you like. From a personal aspect this project has helped me chronicle an incredibly eventful year of my life.

That is all!

INTRODUCTION PART 2

I'm sure you'll probably be asking yourselves "so who the fuck are you"? Unless of course you don't use coarse language in which case you will probably be just asking "so who are you"?

Incidentally, if you are offended by F'ing and Jeffing then you may wish to source alternative reading material, perhaps something slightly less abrasive. One good, rude word free book is called 'The Bible' by God. Although the Bible deals with some fairly saucy topics it doesn't use the word 'cunt' quite as often as I do … if at all maybe.

So then, back to the question you'll no doubt be asking, so who the fuck are you?

My name is Morton Babeldom, I am very much a local celebrity and sort of 'linchpin' within the community. I have many amazing skills and several job roles. My primary job used to be as a local sex worker/erotic drag dancer/glass collector at 'The Peppermint Hippo' (*Chumptons best lap/pole dancing bar and adult entertainment complex*) although prior to this I was one of Flatlands better Elvis impersonators. Had Elvis ever appeared on stage naked in the fens in the latter, fatter part of his career then I would've been a dead ringer.

I am not originally from Flatlands, not born and bred here … or born inbred here so to speak. Although I'm called Morton Babeldom I know this is the name the Flatlanders gave me on my arrival. I recall my hoooman name was originally Martin and my surname began with 'B' but it's such a long time ago now I can't really remember. I was kidnapped, stolen as a child aged 10, by a small herd of nomadic dyke donkeys (*or swamp mules are another term often used*) that had misjudged the tides and drifted out of Flatlands and into the UK of Great Britain. They took the opportunity to drug me with a hallucinogenic substance extracted from various root crops and distilled into a concoction called 'the devils prolapse'. I was taken with a view to being ransomed back to my kin for some chickens' beaks and a comfy rocking chair, but my parents said "they would not give into terrorist threats" and subsequently never coughed up the ransom. I was kept in a pen at the local petting zoo (*like most Flatland childers are*) and I became something of a local curio due to my equal number of digits and limbs, not to mention my strange use of language. As the years have progressed I have adopted some of their customs and odd little ways but I still like to believe, at heart, I am that same little boy from 'the right side of the A1'.

I was schooled in Chumpton village, at St Jethro's Primary School for the Criminally Insane on Upper Fen drove yon Lower drove Fen. I was a pupil for several weeks before it was deemed that my understanding of numeracy, literacy and general knowledge considerably outweighed that of any of the teachers at the school and subsequently, I was classified as a child prodigy (*or braaneylilbugga as it's called in Flatlands*). At the age of just 10 hoooman years, I was inducted as a teacher at the school and became its headmaster several days later. The position of responsibility was nice and it came with a house, that I still live in to this day, and it also fitted nicely around my duties at the petting zoo as technically I was still owned by them until I hit poooberty.

This is the Flatland District stretch of the A14 and is due to be made into a two lane road allowing more auto vehicles into and occasionally out of Flatlands. The A14 is mostly used for tractoring root crops to places outside Flatlands. Mayor David Devilman of Flatland District Council has said that they will be investing as much £753.26 in Hoooman money in its modernisation program.

In more recent years Flatlands has seen a considerable increase in outsiders (*or hooomans as locals call them*). They are not really welcomed but are tolerated, and along with their fancy ways have come more motor cars on our already deserted roadway (*a seldom used branch of the A14 called the A14/1. Outsiders call it the A141*). The hooomans have different language skills and fancy ideas of 'toleration and acceptance of differences in others'.

This does not sit well with the locals. What does sit well with the locals however is the introduction of new technologies and gadgets such as electricity and tefelones. Personally, I like the hooomans as I was once an outsider myself. I have some fading but fond memories of my life before my abduction and would one day like to revisit the other side of the A1 perhaps, but I've managed to forge quite a nice life for myself here. I have plenty of hobbies and of course my beloved Peppermint Hippo (*Chumptons premier pole/lap dancing adult entertainment venue*).

Last year I took an online doctors test comprising of 19 questions of varying difficulty from the highly regarded seat of learning, Chatterby University. Chatterby University is noted for its 'medicality' learning for people with the poorly bodies, and 'psychiality' learning for people with the poorly brains. I decided to specialise in both. By doing two, three hour courses in cosmetic surgery and trepanning, I can do a breast augmentation and simultaneously release demons or brain tension. I know of no other trepanning cosmetic surgeon locally … or unlocally. I have recently opened my own clinic again as it was closed down by the authorities due to me not being suitably qualified … or qualified at all. I'm happy to say since taking the doctors test online it has recently re-opened and see this as a possible future source of considerable income.

fenbook | Surch for peeeple and othur things tooooo 🔍   📷 Morton   Hoome   Foind frends   👥 💬 🔔 ⚙️ ▾

Chumpton-by-Kumberly Cosmetic Surgery & Trepanning Emporium

I am certain all of my Fenbook pals will be delighted to see I have reopened my cosmetic surgery and trepanning clinic once again. Despite numerous attempts to close me down by Flatland District Council and the local Police Brigade, my legal team found an ancient loophole that allows me to drill holes in peoples (or cats) skulls allowing demons and headaches to escape. I can also do cosmetic surgery and gender re-assignment, I have taken an online exam and now have a "certificate of being a doctor" issued by none other than the prestigious seat of learning the 'University of Chatterby'. This is a sort of legal document (*as far as I'm concerned*), that allows me to practice my doctoring and mediaeval surgical procedures in the dioceses of Flatlands and surrounding parishes. So if any of my Fenbook buddies need a nip n tuck or a quick trepanning I am now taking bookings again and I'm sure I can do mates rates ... especially if there is any kind of breast work needs doing ... I'll do it free ... but not blokes!

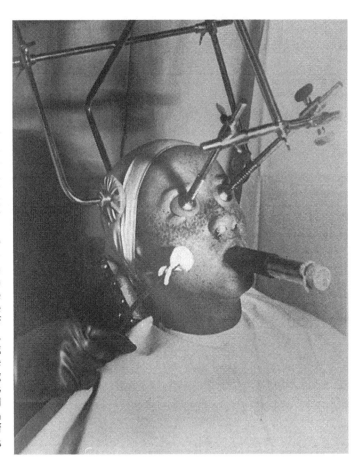

I have remodelled my kitchen into a state of the art operating theatre, using the sink to clean some of my surgical instruments every other week or so to avoid infection. I enjoy many hobbies but my most fruitful (*and hopefully, also financially lucrative for future projects*) is my inventing. I hope one day to invent something really useful that will make me famous and wealthy. Failing that, maybe invent something that can peel root crops a bit quicker than the sharp sticks currently used. I have my own page on Flatlands very own social media site called fenbook, which I update regularly at Chumptons compoota in the library. I also collect many adverts and stories from local newspapers to give an insight into local daily existence and commerce. I have religiously and meticulously kept a diary for the whole of the year and I shall be using these entries to best illustrate my life and community. This will be shown in all its glory in my diary.

I will segment this book into 13 chapters (*one for each month of the year + one special chapter*) which will, I believe, make it a chronological order of events for the readers ease, comfort and delight.

This is me ☺

SEXXXYYYYYYY

Here I am posing for Flatlands Calendar Boys at Chatterby Sands when the tide was out earlier today. The Calendar will be available at Chumpton Happy Pauper and at Peppermint Hippo. I think all my Fenbook friends will agree I look fantastic. As this photo was being taken a freak wave moved my tummy up exposing my rather fetching spaedos.

Sadly my watch wasn't waterproof and didn't fair well. It hadn't worked for some years anyway so no great loss there.

Talk is already underway of next years calendar being shot in the town of Ropey ..... Ooooohh get me, Mr. ~~cosmipolitns cosmapliatine comsapolitic~~ globe trotter.

CHAPTER ONE

A New Year commences

Janeundmary 1896

The beginning of every Flatlands year always starts on Thrisdeee 1th of Janeundmary. The year number will differ to and fro, back and forth, with each second leap year, alternating back to the previous decade and only proceeding forward again once the fifth trimester of the first pregnancy of the last month has been successfully achieved and logged. This particular system is known as the 'Fen-Lunar-C' and has been used since 1752, but not fully incorporated into the calendrical requirements of Flatland District Council until a year later in 1948.

Thrisdeee 1th Janeundmary:

I awoke at the crack of daaymiddlin having enjoyed a noyght of New Year celebration at Peppermint Hippo (*Chumptons leading lap/pole dancing venue*) with a glass or two of Turnip Pochine. My recollections of the noyght's events are hazy, but I awoke wearing someone else's underpants and discovered a dead cat, next to me in my bed. The cat had some kind of head trauma, I may have tried some New Year celebratory trepanning on the stray feline when I returned from the club. It's never a good idea to release demons and/or cranial bonce pressure after drinking wildly hallucinogenic root crop based cocktails. This is a lesson I'd hoped I had already learned, as only months earlier a similar incident occurred when returning home from 'The Hippo' full of beverage. I encountered a demon riddled homeless person that I ended up drunkenly trepanning. He ended up living in my basement. He later became known as 'Barry the tramp'.

After I had peeled the cats limp, seemingly lifeless body from my groinal area and cleaned the blood out of my pooobic hair, I laid Mr Tibbins (*that's what I'd decided to call the dead cat with a hole in his head*) out to rest in my basement next to Barry the 'almost dead' tramp. Barry the tramp isn't completely dead but sometimes looks that way after bonce procedures, anyway I thought it would make a nice companion for him the next time he momentarily regains consciousness. Although it's virtually pitch black in the basement I've heard Barry feeling about in the dark to try and explore his surroundings (*or as far as his chains will let him*). It'll be a nice surprise if he gets chance to introduce himself to Mr Tibbins before its buried it in my garden … with the others. I laid the perforated pussy to rest for 3 hours (*as per Flatland customs for deadness*) and during that time Barry remained unconscious. I decided to make a start on Mr Tibbins' journey to the next life. The ceremony was a short one, as I like to keep all of my animal burials/cremations/embalming/christenings nice and simple. I made a prayer up as I went along and sang a hymn (*a medley of Kyle Minogue songs*) for Mr Tibbins, shed some tears for 7 seconds and left his blood soaked, lifeless cadaver to stiffen next to my sleeping vagrant friend.

I remained clothed for the rest of the day. Yay me!

Frydims 2th Janeundmary

I made a tefelone call today. Apparently there is **NO** form of compensation for people who have had accidents of an underpant/faecal nature. Flatland Lawyers 4U should perhaps provide a bit more information with their advertisements about what constitutes an "accident". The lady from the call centre was quite abrupt.

Edith, my next door neighbour, popped round at daaymiddlin to ask if I had seen 'Sprinkles' her pet cat. Bless her, I told her the only cat I had seen lately was Mr Tibbins. I went on to tell her how he had met with an unfortunate accident. Edith looked alarmed, a bit sad, and went to leave as I changed into my bikini. I decided to cheer Edith up before she left, by showing her my latest dance routine I had choreographed myself for my next stint at Peppermint Hippo (*Chumptons leading lap/pole dancing venue*) for when/if I should get my Flatland sex workers licence back. I felt bad that she had lost her beloved pet; it really struck home when, with tears in her eyes, she showed me a photo of Sprinkles. Her cat reminded me so much of Mr Tibbins, same colour and markings … you would swear they were twins.

It was then when it hit me, like a brick wall. I am almost certainly Chumptons finest inventor. Surely the simplest thing I can do to help Edith become reunited with her beloved Sprinkles is to get her to retrace her memoryness back to the last time she saw her cat. I could simply invent a time machine, go back in time to the moment she last saw him, and investigate where Sprinkles went to next.

The rest of the day was spent partially clothed and inventing my cat finding device/time machine.

SatD 3nd Janeundmary

This mawnin I began sourcing the equipment for my cat finding time machine invention. I may have underestimated the complexity and viability of constructing such a contraption. Luckily though, when I went into the cellar to try and wake Barry up and give him his weekly food supply I was met with a howling and screeching, it was a very much alive Mr Tibbins, who sprinted past me and scarpered out of the basement. He ran twice around the kitchen and crashed through the closed kitchen window to complete his dramatic exit. Animals must have an uncanny 6th sense. Mr Tibbins must have 'sensed' that Edith had lost Sprinkles so he made his way to her house.

The physical similarity of the two cats convinced my elderly neighbour that Sprinkles had been in an accident and had somehow limped its way home. She believed Mr Tibbins was in fact Sprinkles and all was well once more in Edith's world, who was I to say different. This meant I no longer needed a cat finding time machine. However, I couldn't quite shake the concept of a device that allowed me to travel through time. I have made a prototype this aftynune and posted the outcome on my fenbook page.

Another Invention

Another of my magnificent inventions. This one is not, as I'm sure many of you assumed, a home recording studio or a one man band contraption. It is in fact a time machine. It's mainly constructed from old musical instruments I acquired from fenBay. As yet I haven't managed to get it to work but once I locate a fux capacitator (looking on fenBay) I am very hopeful I will be able to travel through time "willy nilly".
My Fenbook friends will of course be welcome to join me.

I think all attempts at time travel may be problematic to begin with but I don't envisage any issues I can't cope with once I get going. What could possibly go wrong?

Sunty 4rd Janeundmary

I have, in the past, been at the very forefront of local music and movement. Mainly in the guise of an interpretive dance group/workshop I started and still occasionally do. Not only is interpretive dance great fun and keeps you fit and healthy but, it is also a superb alternative form of communication. My only concern is I might be spreading myself a little too thinly. I already have many activities and clubs I am involved with, ranging from my interest in trepanning to an enthusiasm for prostate milking. I am also part of several committees locally. These include the committee for getting Chumpton-by-Kumberly to host the next Olympic Games and the committee hoping to make Flatland District a centre of culture, although to be honest I think the Olympics are more likely.

My involuntary flatulence was problematic whilst practicing some interpretive dance in my garden today. I fail to see why passers-by found it so funny. It is a medical condition. I'm sure they wouldn't laugh at a person with genital warts or cancer … or cancer of the genital warts. It's this kind of intolerance to my medical condition that lead to me being sacked from my role as an erotic dancer at the Peppermint Hippo.

fenbook   Surch for peeeple and othur things tooooo   🔍   Morton   Hoome   Foind frends

Yours truly ☺

Here is a photo of me doing my thang at Peppermint Hippo, Chumptons premier adult entertainment nightspot.
This was taken only minutes before I did one of my erotic lunges where I seductively touch my toes whilst shaking my little booty.

Unfortunately, it was precisely at that moment I suffered a bout of involuntary flatulence, passed wind and had a full anal prolapse which put me out of action for a while. Life as a sex worker/pole dancer/glass collector is a tough one from time to time.

Moondee 5th Janeundmary

Sadly, I have been reported to the local police Brigade for the feral screaming coming from the basement of my house. Apparently 'passers-by' have become concerned at the cries for help. On another, more pleasurable note, I have recently discovered, courtesy of the Fen Wide Web, that stimulating the anal beard surrounding ones sphincter with an Ostrich feather is an extremely pleasurable experience. This mawnin though, I was asked to leave a local Ostrich farm near Chatterby following complaints from passers-by and farm employees alike regarding my conduct. This is a huge shame as although it was my first and last visit I liked the Ostrich farm. I am beginning to find 'passers-by' somewhat bothersome though.

Toosdi 6nd Janeundmary

Chumpton-by-Kumberly Informer

CHUMPTONS MONASTIC FIRE BRIGADE WANTS YOU!!!!
Chumpton-by-Kumberly's Monastic Fire Brigade are on a recruitment drive to enlist the help of any local persons (male or partially male) who wish to join this legendary Flatland Rescue service.

Ever wondered what it would be like to live the dangerous and heroic life of a Fire Officer or maybe you hanker for the tranquillity and peace of a monk? Well now you can do both in Chumptons Monastic Fire Brigade. If you are aged between 9-87 and are fit enough to tackle a blazing farm building or simply enthusiastic enough to turn up every now and then, why not join Chumptons Monastic Fire Brigade. A belief in God or any superstitious/ethereal/heavenly or celestial being is not necessary but an interest in perverse sexual practises is essential.

I have received some new (*or new to me at least*) trepanning equipment I won in an auction on fenBay. I was looking forward to trying it out on a very lucky demon riddled individual as soon as is practically possible. As incredible luck would have it there was a lady who joggs past my house each day that, as of this mawnin, currently lives in my basement with Barry the tramp. She cries a lot because of her head demons, so I'm hoping to help her with some gentle trepanning (*or trepanning lite as it's known in local trepanning circles*) with one of my smaller cranial bonce drills. I'll give her some more sleepy drink soon. I have the song 'Living Doll' in my head now. There was a small fire outside the Happy Pauper shop just over the road from my house, but neither I nor the Flatland Monastic Fire Brigade are entirely sure it was me who started it, so I'm going to give myself the benefit of the doubt.

Winsti 7th Janeundmary

I have named my new housemate 'Jemimah', after the doll off the famous children's TV programme Playschool. I still have that Cliff Richard song screaming around my head. "I got myself a crying, screaming, drugged up, dreaming, living doll. I got to do my best to release her, demons cus she's a living doll".

I have been short listed by the maternity ward at Ropey Town Hospital for the Genetically Impure as the Flatland Districts official new-born baby toe/finger counter. The competition for the role was fierce but I was the only one of the six people that applied that could count beyond thirty five, a regular requirement when counting fingers and toes in these parts so I'm quietly confident. I think that taking on the additional responsibility will be a huge plus sign on my CV. It should also help alleviate any concerns or misgivings future patients of mine may have about my competency as a professional cosmetic surgeon, or enthusiastic amateur trepanner when they can see I work in an actual hospital. Very comforting I'd have thought ☺

Thrisdeee 8th Janeundmary

Great sadness dearest diary, I awoke this mawnin to discover that Jemimah had escaped from my basement, not even a goodbye. Jemimah has left the building. Barry the tramp was devastated … perhaps … or he would have been if he were alive to experience the whole thing. That's right diary, I think she may have killed Barry, he displayed no signs of life so I pronounced him dead at the scene. Jemimah must have allowed her bonce demons to talk her into leaving the sanctuary of my basement and find another dwelling. I may see her again if she continues to aimlessly jog around the village in a ridiculous quest to live longer. I think that the large glass of Devils Prolapse I gave her had worn off, allowing the demons to talk her into leaving. If I do see her running past my house again I'll have a word and just make absolutely certain she doesn't want trepanning.

The house seems empty without her … I know she's only been gone a few hours and was only living here for just over a day but we grew close. Dare I say it, but maybe we were in love. I would dance gaily around the basement in just my underpants, while she slept. I would read her adverts from the Flatland District Weekly News while she slept. I would sniff her hair and stroke her ears … also while she slept. She slept a lot. We only made love the once (*while she slept*) but I felt the connection, the desire, that singular understanding of purpose that lovers share together.

The majority of our relationship was conducted whilst Jemimah slept but I'll never forget the one, brief moment in time that our eyes actually met. I don't know who screamed the loudest. Jemimah, when she momentarily awoke from her slumber, to discover me mastybayting and about to do a shuddering of sex juice all over her face. Or me, because I honestly thought she was dead. A strange, sad day. I shall miss Jemimah.

Frydims 9nd Janeundmary

Still no fires … major fires. The Ropey police Brigade came around this mawnin to ask if I had any information on a young lady who had gone missing a couple of days ago and was found yisdee aftynune wandering around Chumpton in her soiled jogging outfit, semi-conscious, with a vacant expression, dribbling profusely and unable to speak. Of course she blended right in with locals at first, but once she had regained some of her faculties she recounted a tale of kidnapping and drugged torture. PC Jack Wormer of Flatlands Police Brigade wondered if I had seen anything suspicious. I informed him that I hadn't seen much as I had spent most of the last two days in my basement. I told him I would of course co-operate fully, I love assisting the police with their enquiries, and I'm very good at it. It makes me feel important. I assured him I'd help as much as I could as this was a subject close to my heart. I went on to say that I too had lost touch with someone very dear to me, a hoooman girl, similar in description to the one the PC was on about, but mine was called Jemimah. PC Wormer very kindly said he would keep an eye out for Jemimah and return her to me if she was found.

I have won a Krakorbang feather off the fenBay auction site. It's a curly wing feather from the indigenous flightless Flatlands bird called the Krakorbang. It is used mostly for stroking and teasing the sphincter immediately prior to "familee toime". I was unable to locate an Ostrich feather and all contact with the local Ostrich farm is to cease immediately according to the court paperwork.

I'd like a Girlfriend. Jemimah's brief stay at 'casa Babeldom' bought this home to me. I sometimes nip into farmer Grunty Crowboilers field nearby and pay him 15 Davey's for a chance to visit the very sexy Rowenta for some 'naughty time' at noyght but I'd prefer a lady friend if possible. I sometimes call Rowenta my life partner but if I'm honest I think my feelings are unrequited, I know she see's other men.

This is Rowetta my pet sheep and life partner

I named her Rowenta after my electric kettle. Both are nice to look at and both contain large amounts of my sperm.

That is all

SatD 10rd Janeundmary

My daily newspaper, the 'Flatland District Weekly News', was delivered this mawnin and the front page was all about Mayor David Devilman calling for a District referendum about whether Flatlands should remain within the UK of Great Britain. Many folk are concerned about the immigration of too many more "Hooomans" from places outside the Flatland District such as Norfolkshire and even Lundun. Many Flatlands folk believe that the introduction and continued influx of outsiders or immigrants is a bad thing because it may dilute our culture and bring in disease and illness.

Others, myself included, believe it's a good thing as it may increase the gene pool and improve the economy. It's a very complex argument but luckily we have our local politicians and media outlets to point us in the right direction and help us make our decision come polling day with their unbiased, non-agenda driven and impartial, factual advice about such an important and influential decision for our community. Of course there are rumours that many more trying to leave Flatlands rather than trying to get in. I heard on the news the other day that there are great encampments of Flatland folk who are entrenched at the district border looking to escape to make a better life for themselves in Peterborough. Peterborough is an almost mythical, magical place to many Flatland folk, and when the tide is in the correct moon phase, lots of people will make the effort to escape to Peterborough by drifting along the dykes out of the district.

A famous tale is often told of Jebediah Felcher's favourite daughter, Mengele` who, as legend has it, once drifted not just to Peterborough but as far as Wisbech. She was promptly returned by the Peterborian police brigade and an injunction was made against her from ever entering any branches of MacDonald's food shops (*a place popular with the Hooomans of Peterborough and Great Britain for the procurement of non-root crop based foods*). This injunction was taken out against Mengele` because she had wandered into the gents WC in error and she used the hand drier machine to dry her swollen labia. The lips to her lady garden baby squeezer had become engorged with dyke water due to the large amount of time she had spent floating about, lost in the drainage dykes and Wisbech estuary. Mengele` spent many hours recounting the tale to locals and tourists alike for drinks of Turnip Pochine in The Jolly Sphincter public house in Ropey Town centre. She quickly became an old lush and a well-known Police informer and recounted so many different versions of the same story that her account couldn't be relied as true.

The local police in Ropey town have continued using her as a star witness for some quite high profile trials though.

Mengele`Felcher was not the prettiest of local lasses but she told many exciting yarns about her crazy travels and the exploits of local criminals. This picture was taken shortly before she was taken into the Flatlands Witness Protection Program and secreted into a safe house in Chatterby, No.15 Lower Fen fen at Yon end where she still resides today, fearful of reprisals from the criminal fraternity keen to know her whereabouts. It's interesting to note that Mengele's facial hair is not a disguise.

Our Mayor, David Devilman is something of a mystery man. He was made the Mayor of Flatlands at the tender age of 6 years old. He wasn't schooled in the district but outside Flatlands. He lives in a monstrously large house just outside Ropey town, it's believed to have five bedrooms and a swimming pool. There are rumours his father used to be the Mayor of Flatlands previously but had to leave urgently due to some dishonest goings on. Locals are not encouraged to speak of this openly and to do so can result in on the spot beatings by the Police Brigade. The Mayor has recently won the Mayoral election campaign to continue as the Mayor of Flatland District.

FLATLAND DISTRICT WEEKLY NEWS

.... Breaking News .....

MAYOR DEVILMAN RE-ELECTED AS MAYOR OF FLATLANDS DISTRICT IN A TIGHT FIGHT WITH HIMSELF.

Mayor David Devilman (pictured roight) has been re-elected as Mayor of Flatland District despite a gallant effort from his opponent in the election race, namely himself. David Devilman has been Mayor of Flatland for the last forty two years, first elected to the office of Mayor when he was just six and a half years old. As outgoing Mayor one of his last Mayoral duties in chambers was to pass a law, initiated by himself, forbidding anybody else to run against him in the forthcoming elections. It was then pointed out to him shortly before he was due to start his campaign tour of Chumpton and Chatterby that there needed to be at least one other person running against him to make the election legal under Flatland District laws. Mayor Devilman decided to take a huge and unprecedented political risk by putting his name forward a second time and fight the campaign by running against himself. The election battle was hotly contested with some very unsavoury and personal slurs made against himself, about himself, by himself, but this evening, democracy spoke loud and clear and votes poled placed Mayor Devilman just ahead and first over the finishing line.

The Mayor accepted the daisy chain of chambers and the staff of supreme power throughout the Flatland region in an archaic and terrifying ceremony at 87 minutes after noyghtmiddlin.

When asked about her husbands achievement Mayor Devilman's wife, V'Gina, said nothing but smiled a lot and nodded, occasionally waving when prompted with a loving swipe around the back of the head from her attentive husband the new Mayor of Flatlands District.

Votes poled for Mayor David Devilman for Mayor of Flatland = 12
Votes poled for Mayor David Devilman for Mayor of Flatland = 10

Sunty 11nd Janeundmary

To my utter surprise and amazement 'Barry the tramp/homeless person' wasn't as dead as I thought he was. I heard some unusual screaming sounds coming from my basement but I assumed it was the screaming in my head. So soon after experiencing the disappointment of Jemimah leaving me I thought the wailing sound I heard could be the cries of utter dispare from the lonely abyss of darkness and horror inside my noggin.

The screaming I heard then turned into sobbing, but sobbing of a much lower pitch than I recall Jemimah or my imaginary friends having. Had Mr Tibbles returned? If the wailing was real I needed to investigate before more bothersome passers-by became alarmed. I entered the basement to investigate the source of the noise and to my utter amazement I found Barry slumped against the wall in an upright-ish position. I hurriedly gave him some water and a Jacobs cream cracker I had found some weeks earlier in the car park of the Peppermint Hippo, and once he had received his sustenance I bathed him. As luck would have it I had actually had the foresight to chain him to a bath when he first moved into my basement. He looked frightened and confused and shivered as I bathed him, despite it being very warm in the basement. I put a blonde wig and some make up on him (*to make him feel pretty*) as being dead for a bit can be a grubby time for anyone, being deceased can lower ones self-esteem and sense of self-worth too. Barry's uncontrollable sobbing became quite tiresome after several minutes, so I dried him with some hessian towels and set about ridding him of the demons that were quite clearly troubling his brainal area with a quick trepanning.

I'm sure he must have thought all his Chrimstaaas's had come at once when he first moved into my basement and discovered I was Chumptons foremost trepanning expert. It was going to take some serious procedures though to get rid of these demons. One of Barry's demons revealed itself and claimed he was not Barry but "Neil" a travelling agricultural fertilizer salesman. The demon went on to say he had a wife and three kids and "Neil" was from a place called Northampton. As it was a difficult trepanning I unveiled my new skull drill (*well it was new to me and largely free of bone and bonce matter*) and set about trying to save Barry's life and sanity. I made seven large drills into his noggin and began to release his demons (*the worst being Neil, constantly insisting he was a real person and pleading to "let him go"*) and any residual pressure that had built up inside his cranial bonce cavity (*technical term for the brainal internals of a head*). Sadly, despite my best efforts, Barry the tramp is dead again. This time I am fairly sure his deadness is a bit more permanent than the last time he was dead. So confident was I that he was much deader this time, that I buried him in my garden when it was dark. I held a short but moving service and sang a hymn. I wasn't sure what hymn to sing, there are so many, so I chose "hit me with your rhythm stick" by Ian Dury and the Blockheads.

The uncontrollable flatulence that has been the bane of my adult life and has put a successful career as an erotic drag dancer on hold returned with vengeance when I decided to funk up the service with some interpretive dance. My rendition of the post punk/new wave classic was cut short by a fanfare of farting and a hint of anal seepage.

I got changed out of the latex vicar's outfit I previously used during my aforementioned career and went indoors. If any of the neighbours had seen me I'm sure they'd think I'm bonkers. This has been a tough year for me so far. I have lost a pet, a girlfriend and now my homeless person I lovingly called Barry the tramp. After a few minutes grieving at my loss I decided to stop feeling sorry for myself and change my life.

If there was going to be an influx of even more hooomans from the outside world then this would be an ideal time for me to take in a lodger. The more I thought about it the more sense it made. Despite being a renowned local trepanner of some considerable skill, I couldn't help feel a tiny bit responsible for Barry's demise. My confidence as a healer has been shaken at this latest loss and yet … and yet I could clearly see what a senseless waste of surgical doctoringness it would be if I were to turn my back on the medical profession. I stayed up until well after laasloyght and then the penny dropped like a massive penny dropping.

My cosmetic surgical abilities could also incorporate gender re-assignment, an area of my expertise I have previously neglected. Just think of all the people who are simply born in the wrong body that I can help. Now Barry's gone I can use the basement as a recovery area. It's quiet (*sound proofed with egg cartons since the complaints*), it's very, very warm and snug, it doesn't have any windows to distract patients from concentrating on anything but their recovery and rehabilitation … it also has a bath.

My lucky new housemate could be my surgical assistant/helper … PERFECT!

This was Barry and I in happier times, the photo was kindly taken by PC Jack Wormer of Ropey Town Police Brigade as they came to talk to me about the screaming. Once I explained about my trepanning business and the releasing of demons he was satisfied all was well at Casa Babeldom.

fenbook | Surch for peeeple and othur things tooooo | Q | Morton Hoome Foind frends

Trepanning fun

Here is a snap of me performing an intricate trepanning procedure on Barry my captive tramp.

This photo is courtesy of the Police library and was taken as they entered my house during one of its many raids. So called neighbours had alerted the authorities after concern at the screaming noises from my operating theatre/kitchen.

That is all!

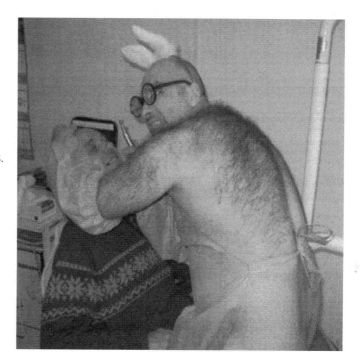

Moondee 12thth Janeundmary

This mawnin I am absolutely buzzing.

As I write this entry in my diary it is only the daaymiddlin and I have completely rearranged my basement to accommodate patients in my recovery area for Chumptons newest, premier gender reassignment clinic. I have burned what remained of Barry's possessions and some of the bloodstained hessian sacking he used as bed linen. I have cleaned most of his brain matter out of the bath (*the place of his demise during his last, emotional trepanning*). It was a poignant moment for me as I cleaned the stale vomit from his restraining chains, but I know that a little piece of Barry will always be with me.

This is because I placed some of his pubic hair in a locket he had around his neck that I confiscated, it just had a useless photograph of a woman and some children in it so I burned the photo and replaced it with his pubic hair. Sadly due the amount of trepanning Barry needed to exorcise his demons his head was pretty well devoid of hair. With the number of holes in his noggin I will always think of Barry whenever I see some Edam cheese. The pubic hair was plucked from around his sphincter, so I only have to open the locket and the smell of Barry will greet my nostrils like an old friend … an old friend that smells of faeces … like a tramp … a captive, shit smelling tramp.

I have been down to the Happy Pauper shop to place two adverts in the shop window. One is for a new housemate/surgical assistant and the other advert is for anyone who is unsure about gender identity and may wish to have bits snipped or bits added. I gave the added incentive of stating on the ad that all gender reassignment will be half price whilst I am still learning the techniques involved in reassigning someone's gender. If that doesn't entice someone to change sex what will?

The time is now laasloyght and since my last entry in my diary earlier today I have had absolutely no enquiries about the gender reassignment from nervous parents unsure about their childer's preferred gender identity. This is surprising, due to the ambiguous genital mutations experienced by some of the more 'established' families within Flatlands community, I'd have hoped for a better response. Another slightly negative note is my 'no major fires started' abstinence came to an abrupt end today when I set fire to one of the classroom at St Jethro's primary school for the criminally insane on Upper Fen drove yon Lower drove Fen fen. Luckily none of the childers inside were too seriously injured and the ones that were a bit crispy or in any way disfigured by the blaze were fairly ugly to begin with. Thankfully the Flatland Police are none the wiser regarding the fires beginnings. I feel ashamed.

Toosdi 13th Janeundmary

Today I received my krakobang feather in the post. It arrived from Flatlands most popular online auction site 'fenBay' so I have spent most of the mawnin rinsing it under the tap to wash out the previous owners anal detritus prior to teasing my own sphincter. I shall pop upstairs for a touch of 'botting' with the rare birds' feather later on. This one was a lot more used than the seller had stated in the item description and had not been cleaned as thoroughly as I would have hoped. I shall be leaving negative feedback. Because of the aforementioned fun I was having with my botting feather I completely forgot to go to the Happy Pauper shop to see if there'd been any responses to my window ads regarding housemates and potential gender reassignment patients. The day wasn't completely wasted though; I scrubbed my kitchen ready for its use as my operating theatre. It is now very sparkly and free from bacteria thanks to my 'deep clean', taking almost 20 minutes and two Jay cloths. Just prior to writing these words in my diary I also prepared the potential new housemates room, or other side of the room I sleep in to be slightly more precise. All is looking spick and span in Casa Babeldom.

Winsti 14nd Janeundmary

Joy of all joy's, I have just returned from the shop after learning that I have no less than 4 potential housemates. I will write out some questions I may want to ask them concerning their suitability regarding, not just living with me, but how they'll fit in within our community. I will of course ask the relevant questions such as; do you have a job? Are you a smoker? How would you describe your drinking habits? Can you talk in Flatland Ingulish? (*actually, I shall probably ask this one first*), and finally if it's a lady person I shall politely enquire whether or not they have an interest in anal bleaching (*or changing your ringtone as it's known locally*), as well as noting the size of their breasties and sexual availability. Oddly these are precisely the kinds of questions that people were so offended by when my chum Drake Furryhands had a brief career as a professional hypnotist travelling over the Flatland borderline to Peterborough He now resides in a place of incarceration. As I am anticipating 4 potential housemates obviously only one will be lucky enough to live with me. This means three disappointed people leaving with possibly nowhere to live. This has been weighing heavily on my conscience so my final question to the housemates will be "are you happy being a boy/girl (*delete as applicable*) and if not, would you consider gender reassignment as an option?" It is laasloyght now so I am going to bed to mastybate for 7 minutes 22 seconds before drifting into a peaceful slumber. Noyghty noyght one and all. ☺

Thrisdeee 15lbs Janeundmary

I have a crusty sock now as I used one from my only pair to catch my sex wee after shuddering during last noyght's mastybayshun. The shuddering at the end always results in a messy time so I have discovered that socks help catch the rude juice/sex wee (*or hot creamy ejaculate as it's called in doctoring circles*). I had previously sneaked a pair of tights off Edith's washing line and placed them on my winky (*or penis it's called in doctoring circles*) and it worked great for a few times but I developed a nasty yeast infection from the gusset of Edith's tights. I have seen Edith's tuppence (*or Vagina as it's called in doctoring circles*) when I have crept into her house some noyghts when I've been lonely, and needed to sit by her bed and watch her sleep. Edith needs to clean her tuppence a bit more often, it sometimes smells when you get close to it. It's no wonder I had difficulty having a pee for a few days afterwards.

After firsdocky this mawnin I had a knock at the front door. On opening the aforementioned front door I was confronted by Finnders Dastardly, the owner of Peppermint Hippo. He has realised that my unique form of erotic dancing was sorely missed by the regulars at the Hippo and many, many people had requested my return. Both of the customers requesting my return praised me very highly indeed. I had previously been asked to leave by Finnders following a couple of flatulence incidents (*that involved a small amount of faecal splattering*) during my world legendary erotic lunges. Of course I apologised profusely to the recipients of my flatulent propelled stool, but they were mostly inconsolable. After much legal wrangling and plenty of media attention I was asked to cease performing my erotic dancing within the Flatland district and subsequently had my sex workers licence withheld. Finnders informed me that he was extremely confident that my licence would be reinstated. He went on to say that Mayor Devilman himself would sign my licence if I did a personal dance for him in his office tomorrow mawnin at the crack of firsloyght. No worries then.

I treated myself to a carrot baguette before the carrots turned any mouldier, they gave me smelly belches. The rest of the laasloyght was spent scraping some of the mould and love stains from my lucky dancing thong ready for my solo performance in Mayor Devilman's office the following mawnin. Imagine how impressed my new housemate and potential patients will be when learning that I'm once again a locally celebrated erotic dancer.

Frydims 16th Janeundmary

My day began well with no fires. It then went from okay to very bad, very quickly … or so I thought at first, either way I had a better day than a certain crow did! I shall elaborate. I arrived at Mayor Devilman's chambers to perform one of my routines from my considerable repertoire of erotic dancing. My licence depended on me giving the performance of my life so I decided to go "balls out" as it were to ensure that I was quickly back at Peppermint Hippo as a dancer and not a glass collector, as is the current situation. I entered the room and found Mayor David Devilman himself sitting jammed firmly against his desk. He was smiling and sweating, his left arm gripping the desktop, his right arm under the desk moving rhythmically. I introduced myself and he asked me to begin. He went on to say that he was "stroking his dog under the desk", it was called Growler. The lucky dog was getting a good rough stroke but I couldn't help thinking about all the dog hair it would dislodge. I can imagine that there's quite a mess under the Mayors desk. I placed my ghetto blaster on the floor and switched it on with an air of the Irene Cara's about me.

I began dancing to the mighty Jedwards mash up of Queens 'Under Pressure'. I was spectacular; the Mayor was groaning with enjoyment, I was moving freely and sexily in my skimpiest of costumes. When I started to reach the climax of my routine I moved over to the Mayors desk and slowly gyrated my hips before lunging seductively in front of the eager dignitary. I had mistakenly overstretched myself during my world famous erotic lunge, mistake number one. Mistake number two was last noyght's carrot baguette as the carrots, it would seem, were well past their best. My powerful lunge combined with my delicate constitution resulted on a loud fart followed by a small yelp from our esteemed Mayor as a considerable quantity of loose, carroty, liquid turd flew through the air until it met its journey's end on the Mayor's chin and chest-al vicinity, thusly spoiling his shirt, and I assumed, his enjoyment of my performance. I was asked to leave the office and wait outside by Mayor Devilman's assistant. I hurried out embarrassed and worried. I sat in the waiting room. History, it would seem, like my bottom, was repeating itself. The door was slightly ajar and I could hear the conversation between the Mayors aide and David Devilman. Cranshaw St. John, the Mayoral aide who had been wiping my pooh of the Mayors chin and chest-al area, came out and informed me that not only was the Mayor happy to sign my licence but wanted me to be his own "personal, private dancer", it turns out that the faecal incident was "not a deal breaker" and reminded him of his old school apparently. Cranshaw St. John used the Mayors faecal covered shirt to wipe the stool from the stool I had briefly sat on (*do you see what I did there* ☺), he looked at me sternly and said in a fairly intimidating way that all information I may hear or see in the Mayors chambers are to remain secret. I readily agreed, knowing full well I had no chance of keeping it to myself. I'm a right blabber mouth me.

On my return home I was greeted by a courier crow from the Happy Pauper shop in the village, with a message tied to its leg informing me that people needing to be interviewed about becoming my housemate (*or surgical patient*) were all attending the interviews. This thrilling news prompted me into a quick 3 minute mastybayshun in the kitchen/operating theatre. Sadly I was still holding the courier crow at the time and I accidentally crushed it whilst shuddering my sex wee. I will need to buy the Flatland Postal Service a new courier crow. It still didn't ruin my day … it may have ruined the crow's day though.

SatD 17rd Janeundmary

I have been on the Tefelone all mawnin, in fact since firsloyght, making arrangements for the interviews to become my flatmate. I have chosen the blouse I would like all the candidates to wear during the interview and decided that they may wear clotheses of their own choosing during the 10 minute period it takes for me to prepare the sleepy drink for the candidates that failed. All the people I spoke to have funny accents and say they come from a places called Africa or Eewrope… or something like that (*They're the ones that kindly come and help us pick our root crops for us*). Once they have answered the questions and I have ascertained which ones are unhappy with their gender I can begin the final interview for the preferred candidate. I will be wearing a chiffon robe (*slightly see through teehee*) with no under garments. I am going to conduct the entire second interview through the medium of interpretive dance.

Sunty 18st Janeundmary

Today is the Lords day apparently. I have begun drawing up the plans for my 'time machine'. I have most of the parts but I will need some nails, some cardboard boxes, some Selotape and some weapons grade plutonium. Not sure where I'm going to get Selotape from though. I have prepared my underwear for tomorrow's interviews (*I shall be wearing my old "lucky pants" from my days as an Elvis impersonator*) and made the final preparations for the restraining harnesses (*to stop them from scratching their wounds…*) for my gender reassignment patients when they are in recovery. I read a bit more of the vet's book I took out of St.Jebediahs Library on how to neuter cats. I figure it can't be too different to gender reassignment.

fenbook   Surch for peeeple and othur things tooooo   Q   Morton   Hoome   Foind frends

Stinky the cock

This was taken back in the day, when I was a professional Elvis Impersonator before Peppermint Hippo (Chumptons premier Pole/lap dancing nightspot) had opened. Here I am on a photoshoot for Radio Flatland with the stations mascot 'Stinky the cock'. When the photographer first mentioned he wanted a shot of me holding a cock I completely misunderstood and a very embarrassing incident ensued, one I'm sure we'd all like to forget.

All these years later I still have those underpants and even use them from time to time when doing "private dances" for some of Chumptons elite businessmen and town officials. They are a slightly different colour these days and have a few holes (or battle scars I like to call them) and could probably do with a wash sometime soon but still serve me well.

The cock is now dead .... Sadly.

Me in my lucky red pants ☺

<u>Moondee 19jr Janeundmary</u>

This mawnin I was feeling very fruity so I managed a 3 minute 75 second mastybayshun. I was surprised at my sudden libido … so were some of the other shoppers. I can only put my extra fruitiness down to the excitement of having my interviews today. I think the management of the Happy Pauper are becoming tired with my mastybayshun shenanigans during my shopping trips although they did compliment me on my lucky red pants.

Horse sniffing my genitalia

Back in the day I was something of a local personality, primarily noted as an Elvis impersonator. Some of you may remember the photo I posted recently on Fenbook from way back when I posed for the Radio Flatland Calendar. The photo featured me and the stations mascot "Stinky the Cock" posing in a farm yard setting with me looking gorgeous in just my tightest, sexiest thong.

Here is another photo from that day that didn't make the calendar showing me posing with the Radio Flatland 'reserve mascot' and primary source of transport for their OBU transmissions. It is of course "Licky the Horse" but once again a huge misunderstanding and horrendous incident occurred between myself and the make up girl when I was asked by the photographer if he could get a shot of me "feeding the pony". I apologised numerous times to the make up girl but she still pressed charges and a protracted and well publicised court case ensued ..... happy days.

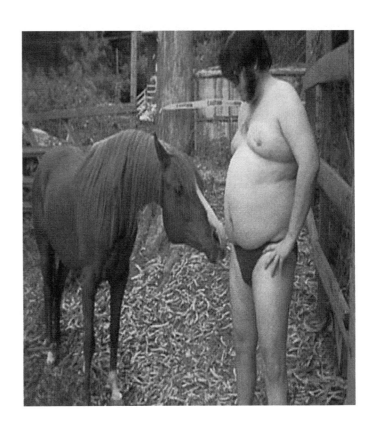

One more of me in my lucky red pants

The first interview: Early mawnin – **Dimitri Kalashnikov**

Dimitri was very nice and he looked great in the blouse but became somewhat confused when I asked how he enjoyed his life as a chap. Dimitri started to become a little agitated when I began to sniff his armpits and groinal area for compatibility reasons (*it's not the most scientific way to cross match for organ donoring perhaps but has never let me down yet*). He asked if he could leave and started making his way to the door but he had already had a sip of sleepy drink. I had anticipated some interviewees needing more persuasion so I prepared a very potent batch of Devils Prolapse. Dimitri made it is far as the hallway. Well done Dimitri. He is now asleep awaiting prepping for the theatre. As lovely as Dimitri was he was not housemate material.

The second interview: daaymiddlin – **Ngala Mindossa**

Ngala was a nice gentleman with a skin colour that was seldom seen in Flatlands. He was from a place called Kanye West or West Kenya, it was difficult to understand what he was saying because he was speaking in tongues, and kept clicking his mouth, similar to our cleric, Reverend Cedric Von Ringstinga. Ngala was altogether much more receptive to armpit and groinal inhalation but alas it was not to be. He appeared very confused during questioning about how happy he was with his life as a chap. He drank three good gulps of juice and now sleeps next to Dimitri in the theatre prep area.

The third interview: Aftynune - **Nigelle F`Rage**

Nigelle was a very unpleasant man. He never even got to the end of the first question let alone get to the groin sniffing stage. He will be my first patient and will be trepanned rather than reassigned a new gender. I firmly believe he would make an equally horrible fucker as a lady, and it would seem, he needed some pretty awful demons releasing. He never had a slurp of sleepy drink so I utilised my "Vulcan death grip". That didn't work so I hit him with a milk bottle. I don't mind admitting that by this stage of the day I had lost all hope of finding a new housemate, as the ones I had interviewed so far were inappropriate as living companions. But, they did seem very suitable subjects for either being aggressively trepanned or spending the rest of their days as a member of the opposite sex.

The final interview: Late aftynune – **Nina Chopyakokov**

I didn't think my day could get worse but it did. Because Nigelle had not had time to drink his complementary cup of hallucinogen it was still on the table after the interview. I inadvertently picked it up and took a swig before realising my error. Moments later I drifted off into a deep slumber. I awoke an hour later to a vision of pure beauty greeting my eyes. As the haze cleared and I started to focus it was then I saw Nina for the first time. Her face was a picture of purity and unsurpassed gorgeousness.

"arrrrre you okayyyy" she said in a voice I can only liken to Mikhail Gorbachev … but sexier.

"I'm fine … now" I replied, blushing slightly.

"I think you must hev follen aslip you poor man, you have woorrked very hard for such slippings, yes?"

"yyyes" I stuttered like a nervous schoolboy as I sat up, somewhat wearily. She willingly changed into the interview blouse and began telling me all about herself. About how she wanted to become a nurse like her sister and send money back to her family in Lithuania who she loved and missed very much. When I told her that I was something of a local celebrity and mentioned my doctoring skills as well as my plans to open my own clinic here in my home, she became very excited. I told her about my days as an erotic dancer, about The Peppermint Hippo and my role as chairperson of the Chumpton Prostrate Milking Association she was positively ecstatic. When I mentioned my interpretive dance and gave her a brief demonstration she laughed hysterically. I'm certain this hysterical laughing is an eastern bloc tradition to show sexual availability.

The interview went from great to fantastic in a very short period of time. I told her of my current client base in the prepping area. She tentatively entered the basement/prepping/restraining bay. As her eyes adjusted to the low lighting conditions she saw the collection of previous interviewees and she smiled with delight. She ventured closer to each one and even squared a decent kick in the ribs at Nigelle. She was clearly a good judge of character. She said that my surgical and recovery area was almost to the same standard as her local hospital back home. I can only assume she was into medicality as much as I am. She helped me read some of the bigger words in the vets' book I was going to use as a sort of 'instruction manual' for the gender reassignment. Nina taught me all about ejaculation (*sex wee … already knew it*), doing the orgasms (*shuddering … already knew it*), Penis (*winky … already knew it*) and that a ladies tuppence was a Vagina (*again, already knew it but just loved hearing say "Vagiiinaa"*). This kind of medical terminology will be handy when talking to paramedics in the unlikely event I need to call an ambulance. I taught her about interpretive dancing for the next hour. The noyght flew by with laughing, chitchat and liberal swigging of Turnip Pochine. Nina was very good at drinking the Pochine I noticed. She told me that where she comes from the community was very similar to Flatlands but much poorer (*hence her venture to foreign shores for a new career*). There was very little else to do but in Lithuania except drink something called Vodka and eat root crops. You can imagine how in love I was by now. We retired to bed and we made sweet love for 2 minutes 87 secunds (*properly … whilst she was awake*). We made love again a bit later for 32 secunds … but she wasn't so awake for this one.

I slept soundly, with my new housemate/girlfriend/surgical assistant, Nina.

Toosdi 20mr Janeundmary

As Nina and I enjoyed our firsdocky of dried bread, beetabix and parsnip sprinkles washed down with a nice Carrot smoothie I could hear groaning from the prepping area. It would seem some of the patients were stirring so I administered some more sleepy drink, apart from Nigelle, both Nina and I returned him to his previous state of slumber by hitting him over the noggin with a chair leg. Nina had agreed to watch over the patients while I went to the Mayor's office to collect my licence and do another private dance.

The Mayor was in a fine mood today and became very breath panty during my dance. He gave me my licence and I took it straight to The Peppermint Hippo ready for me to resume my career as an erotic entertainer. Finnders placed it in a picture frame and put it behind the bar with the others. It was a proud moment.

I spent the laasloyght sharpening my surgical kit ready for a busy day of surgerying tomorrow. Nina kept on top of keeping the patients sedated and calm; we were making a great team Nina and I.

No major fires.

Winsti 21th Janeundmary

Nina and I got up early ready for the many hours ahead of us both.

I started with a trepanning on Nigelle. He was very struggly but once I had drilled several holes in Nigelle's noggin and the demons were released he became quite limp. He was returned to his area of the basement for recuperation.

Next was Ngala. I removed his winky with some garden sheers and fashioned the remaining parts into a ladies tuppence of sorts. Nina very kindly showed me hers as a sort of plan to go by. Several times I found the sight of Nina displaying her most joyous of places too much for me to bear. I managed to do a couple of mastybates whilst surgerying. Nina says I'm 'crrraazeeeee' and she laughs at me, apparently the surgeons in Lithuania don't mastybate during surgery time.

Finally we did Dimitri. He unfortunately regained consciousness during the surgery. It was at the penis removal stage when he awoke, this served as a timely reminder how important it is to ensure that as a surgeon, my patient is not awake when I'm cutting their penis off. As traumatic as it was at the time I'm sure Dimitri will look back and have a good laugh about it all one day. Probably sipping tea with other ladies of leisure, all of whom unaware that this dainty beauty was once a fella, a chap, a bloke with all the bits associated with blokes. Nina washed the operating theatre/kitchen down with water and cleaned the utensils with a cloth whilst I was tending to our guests in the recovery bay. Nigelle sobbed and dribbled a bit so I made certain he was as asleep as possible. To be honest his groaning and saliva dribbling everywhere was a bit nauseating so I made absolutely sure he would remain unconscious for a few days at least with a combination of devils prolapse and additional head beatings. Considering I had never done gender reassignment surgery before I was pleased with my efforts. Nina and I went to bed happy and proud how I had changed these people's lives forever …. and for the better.

Thrisdeee 22rd Janeundmary

Today whilst Nina helped keep the patients sedated I went and started my first ever shift at the Ropey Hospital for the Genetically Impure to count some new born babies fingers and toes. As I had shown such an aptitude for accurately counting the digits of Flatlands latest arrivals, I was also put in charge of disposing of the used, bloody, dirty bandages. This couldn't have possibly worked out any better as I needed bandages for my patients, and funds were limited. Instead of throwing the old bandages away for incineration I would sneak them out and rinse them under the tap, ready, recycled and rejuvenated for a second life for my own patients.

In the aftynune I called into Mayor Devilman's office for another private dance. I overheard him having a tefelone discussion about the forthcoming referendum. He was saying how he was hoping to have a very successful campaign but wasn't sure what side he was going to lead. The Flexit campaign was all for leaving the UK of Great Britain and becoming an independent state, whilst the Flemainers wanted things to stay as they were. I was surprised to learn that the Mayor wasn't sure which side to be associated with. Mayor Devilman was stroking his dog very aggressively during my dance routine. He started sweating profusely and was so moved he cried at the end. The dog remained quiet throughout, as always. What a great dog. On returning home Nina informed me there was a problem. Dmitri's tuppence had fallen out and needed sewing back up again. During the tuppence sewing procedure Dmitri awoke again, he really wasn't having much luck, but once again it served as yet another reminder to ensure that patients were asleep during any kind of genital surgery, even tuppence sewing. Nina used the small amount of turnip Pochine she hadn't drunk during the procedure to pour on the tuppence wound to stop infection. This is possibly what woke Dmitri up. Once he had been re-sleeped with the chair leg I completed the operation by selotaping some of the bandages I had sneaked out of the hospital to him/her. I hadn't had chance to wash them but Nina's use of the turnip Pochine had ensured there was no risk of infection. She is a gem.

Frydims 23th Janeundmary

Tonoyght was going to see me resume my career as an erotic dancer at the Peppermint Hippo. My creative juices (*and a few other juices too*) were flowing as I began to limber up in the garden in my latex star troopers outfit. There were no signs of the involuntary flatulence that had previously blighted my career as a sexy dancer. I noticed the curtains twitching upstairs next door at Edith's house. I bet that's not the only thing that's twitching, I thought to myself as I started lunging more freely and erotically. I caught a glimpse of Edith's face just before she darted behind her bedroom curtain again. I could see an expression of lust, desire, almost quizzical and startled in appearance but was quite clearly the face of a woman who had long since forgotten the tender embrace of a fine specimen of manhood such as my good self. I went on stage at laasloyght and began driving the crowd wild within a couple of minutes of my routine getting underway. There was a sell-out crowd of 9 people, 11 if you include the bar staff, 14 if you include me and the other turns. This made it a club attendance record for a Toosdi. Unfortunately though, it was a Frydims but either way I was thrilled, the club owner Finnders Dastardly was thrilled, the punters were thrilled and Nina was thrilled. Her fella (*me*) was once again an erotic drag dancer of some considerable note … once again a sex worker. I had plenty of tips too. I had 3 turnips, 11 carrots and one cheeky bugger called Mahatma Bojangles of Lower Fen Drove, even tried to put the wedge end of a beetroot in my thong. The root crops were coming thick and fast and so was I when I got home and made love to Nina on the sofa (*whilst she was awake* ☺) then on the kitchen/operating table (*awake*) and then finally in bed (*she started off awake for this one but gently drifted off to sleep half way through*).

SatD 24lb Janeundmary

I was awoken at the crack of firsloyght this mawnin, by the sound of sobbing and wailing. It was not Nina so I went down stairs to the recovery suite to check on the patients. To my amazement they were all asleep/comatose too, which is not surprising considering how much devils prolapse Nina had given them for their bedtime treat. Once again the only thing I could think it would possibly be is the endless screaming of utter pain and despair of my inner mind. I was just about to return to bed when I heard it again, this time clearer, louder. It sounded like it was coming from the garden or maybe even next door. I quickly put on my noyghtgown and went to grab the chair leg that we use to help Nigelle F`Rage get back to sleep if his demons wake him up but couldn't find it. I found a butter knife and slowly crept outside into my back garden but the noises stopped. I spent several minutes looking about my garden but found nothing. There was no evidence of anything that could possibly have made the awful wailing and groaning. Very, very strange.

Sunty 25st Janeundmary

The smell was unbearable in the kitchen/operating theatre when Nina and I came down for firsdocky. As we tucked into our beetrootflakes soaked with Gimbles Dyke Clunger's milk I told Nina about the unusual happenings in the small hours. My tale of strangeness was falling on deaf ears, Nina was finding it difficult to concentrate on my conversation piece, and she was too engulfed in the foul aroma filling the air. The lady patients "new genitals" were not the source of the unpleasant pong either. Nina and I spent almost half an hour sniffing the patients groinal area and also Nigelle F`Rage trepanned bonce hole (*although that did have an aroma all of its own*).

No fires ☺

Moondee 26th Janeundmary

My noyghtly slumber was once again interrupted by the sound of groaning and wailing, as if someone, something, was in the most incredible pain. I checked the patients, as I did the noyght before, as they were most likely source of painful sobbing. Once again they were all asleep. The noise was closer to firsloyght this time but it was the unmistakable sound of outrageous discomfort followed sometime later by the horrendous stench. It was a stench of death, a stench of decay. I even dug Barry up again to check he was as dead as I originally suspected but there was definitely no life there. The mystery continues.

Tonoyght when I returned from my shift at Peppermint Hippo Nina was teaching the ladies to feed themselves again. I had decided to trepan the ladies, partly as a precaution to ensure they were demon free and partly because I was bored and I'd lost my Krakorbang feather. As a result of the trepanning, the part of the brain that knows how to operate feeding utensils had been erased. Nina was relearning the ladies these essential skills. I say essential, there are many, many people in Flatland District unable to feed themselves with knives and forks. There are many who become fearful at the site of these utensils. These are skills the ladies will need as we are hoping they will be socialising in Chumptons 'polite society' very soon. Tomorrow Nina plans on role playing aftynune tea in the garden with the ladies. As Nina and I gave the ladies and Nigelle there noyght time sleepy drink the noise began again.

This time it was very intense and very near, a rhythmical banging and feral grunting. It was also very quick and it stopped as soon as it started, sadly before we had time to investigate where it was coming from.

Toosdi 27th Janeundmary

I returned from counting toes and fingers at Ropey Hospital to find Nina and the ladies in the back garden having mid-mawnin tea and carrot cake (*which is actually just grated carrots moulded into a cake shape*). Nina had set a small table on the lawn near Barry's grave and put out some deck chairs. The ladies were dressed in flowery dresses and adorned with wigs made from some of their left over pubic hair. Ngala was now known as Cinderella, a name she chose herself from a book that Nina was reading to her at the time. She chose it by pointing at the picture of a character called Cinderella and dribbling saliva on it whilst giggling. She looked very lovely in her dress and the wig Nina had fashioned covered up some of the unsightly trepanning holes. Dmitri was now called Pocahontas which was chosen with a very similar method to Ngala … just a different book. Nigelle can keep his name as it is. Also, we don't read him any books. Nigelle's rantings are becoming more and more obscure. Partly due to the demons (*which my noyghtly trepanning seemed to be helping*) and partly due to being hit on the head with a chair leg to render him sleepy if we run out of the devils prolapse, but we still couldn't find the chair leg. It was a picture to behold, seeing them all sitting there, when all of a sudden PC Jack Wormer appeared from nowhere. He entered the garden from the back gate and removed his helmet as a matter of respect for the ladies.

"Mawnin all" he said in his nasally policeman's drone as he bowed slightly.
"My apologies for interrupting your mawnin tea party but I'm here regarding reports of wailing and groaning noises coming from this vicinity. Given the previous reports relating to your trepanning services I wondered if you heard anything".
"Yes oddly enough, we have" I said as PC Wormer sat down on the large mound of earth that I now call the rockery but is in fact Barry's grave.
"They happen most noyghts" I continued "and it varies when and how long they can be heard for".
PC Wormer had a concerned look on his face as he placed his helmet next to him on Barry's final resting place. He then turned to the ladies and asked if they had heard anything. Cinderella smiled coyly and dribbled as she tilted her head away and Pocahontas sneezed a small amount of carrot cake onto PC Wormers leg. She then smiled coyly and tilted her head away in an almost identical manner.
"And what about you?" he said to Nigelle.
"I think you'll find it's the immigrants … murderers, drug traffickers and rapists … the fucking lot of em" Nigelle replied. PC Wormer, frowned, stood up from the mound of earth he had been sitting on and returned his helmet to his head.
"Well I have taken up enough of your time" he said whilst smiling at the ladies. Pocahontas reached out and began stroking PC Wormers groinal area as she released a big globule of saliva from the side of her mouth. Un-phased, PC Wormer smiled once more, and looked at her with a slightly humbled grin and a semi erect winky.
"Madame" he said before turning to leave. As he moved towards the garden gate Nigelle F`Rage leapt up and screamed "FUCKING MURDERING IMMIGRANTS" at the top of his voice. Reaction from the policeman was swift and brutal. In one quick

movement PC Wormer punched Nigelle square in the face, sending him quickly to the lawn. The slightly alarmed, the policeman apologised immediately and explained it was his training that meant he responded in such a manner. I told him he had nothing to apologise for and that Nigelle had been receiving some of my trepanning treatment but was a thoroughly unlikeable character anyway. To my surprise and relief the PC merely said "okay then" and then stuck the boot into his ribs for good measure. I did the same and we both laughed as Nigelle lay on my garden semi-conscious and bleeding. It was the first time I have ever been involved in police brutality where I wasn't the recipient and I have to say I hope it isn't the last.

Winsti 28rd Janeundmary

Well dearest diary, yet more noises from who knows where, late last noyght and again first thing at firsloyght. This mawnin whilst the ladies have tea in the garden and Nigelle nursed his broken jaw and sore ribs, I treated them all to some of my interpretive dancing. I was dancing to Black Lace Greatest Party Hits and the ladies were happy, smiling and very dribbly. Once again PC Wormer appeared, this time without any apparent reason and stood in the garden for a while, grinning at the ladies.

He kept thrusting his groinal parts towards Pocahontas and smiling at her. She seemed to be ignoring him and after a few minutes the bobby left with a look of sadness on his face. As he left he managed to give Nigelle a little dig in the tummy but nothing too bad. I told him I usually used a chair leg but had lost it a few days earlier. PC Wormer kindly let me have a go with his truncheon. It was brilliant and better than a chair leg for making Nigelle sleep. The friendly bobby said he would let me keep his truncheon if he could take Pocahontas out for a drink next week. I readily agreed … or agreed readily, I can't remember which, but all I knew was I had a policeman's truncheon in my hand (*and not for the first time if you know what I mean Teehee*).

Thrisdee 29nd Janeundmary

Nina caught me doing a quick 2 minute 96 second mastybayshun this mawnin. I was sniffing the gusset of her underpants at the time so we were both a little bit embarrassed by the situation. So were some of the other shoppers in the Happy Pauper.

It all got a little awkward and it nearly put me off finishing but I managed to do the shuddering before I was asked to leave by Horatio Horatio, the shop manager.

On our way home from the shop Nina told me it was okay to smell her lingerie, that she would only change them once every two weeks instead of once a week for some extra lady smell. She also said that I could take some with me for when I go out in case I ever have another 2 minutes 96 seconds to pass. It would be useful for me if I need to become genitally engorged during private dances at the Peppermint Hippo or for the Mayor. I get extra Davey's or root crops when my winky becomes inflamed (*inflamed without an infection that is*).

Frydims 30nd Janeundmary

This mawnin I thought I had it, the noise that is. I thought I was about to find out where it was coming from. One minute it seemed to be coming from the basement/recovery bay, the next from the garden near the fence. The ladies were out with Nina learning how to socialise with the Chumpton community.
Frustrating.

No fires

SatD 31th Janeundmary

A busy day today. I was counting toes at the maternity ward in Ropey until daaymiddlin and then I had a matinee dance at Peppermint Hippo. By the time I arrived back home at laasloyght I was shattered.

As I entered my home I was immediately struck by the wailing and groaning noise. I knew Nina was out with the ladies introducing them to the women of the Chumpton WI, so apart from the sleeping Nigelle F`Rage the house should be empty. Once again it seemed to be coming from two places but this time I managed to narrow it down to the basement/recovery bay. As I entered the dark, dank room I noticed some movement out of the corner of my eye in the far left end of the room. It was difficult to make out what it was due to the darkness but I was able to see enough to approach. The wailing got louder as I approached and then stopped as I got very near. So did the movement, but I had seen it long enough to realise it was coming from underneath a pile clothes near Nigelle's part of the radiator. As I gingerly removed the top layers of hessian sacking I saw to my utter disbelief Sprinkles, Edith's cat.

It was rather damaged and battered but it was definitely Sprinkles. As soon as Sprinkles saw me it began wailing louder than ever, I think it liked me. It reminded me it was actually Mr Tibbins and sadness crept over me. I went round to Edith's house to return the noisy cat and very happy that I had discovered the source of the wailing sound that had been driving us all batty for days. As I approached Edith's back door I heard the groaning sound coming from her bedroom. I stealthily entered her house and crept along the stairs with her battered cat lying limply in my hands. Nothing prepared me for what I saw when I opened Edith's bedroom door. Edith was naked on the bed, surrounded by pictures of Barry Manilow and she was on all fours, sucking her own tits and tickling her sphincter with MY Krakorbang feather whilst bouncing up and down with MY chair leg up her tuppence. Her groaning was incredibly loud but it was plain to see what she was doing. She was doing some mastybayshun.

At that moment Sprinkles mustered the strength to jump out of my arms and scrambled over to Edith. Sprinkles wailed loudly and Edith jumped and screamed when she saw the cat. Then she noticed me stood in the doorway and we both screamed at each other at the same time. It was a moment neither will forget in a hurry. I didn't realise that ladies could mastybate too. When ladies do mastybayshun the shuddering part didn't involve lots of Tissues, sex wee and crying, like us chaps, but it did involve lots and lots of shouting and groaning.

A rather embarrassed Edith apologised for stealing my feather and chair leg and thanked me for returning Sprinkles. Nigelle had 'borrowed' Sprinkles for some company it seems and Edith pinched my stuff when she came around looking for her cat. I remembered she had seen me doing my interpretive dancing in the garden and it must have awoken something primal, deep inside of her. It was only understandable; I am after all one of the main attractions at the best adult entertainment complexes in Chumpton-by-Kumberly. Before nicking my chair leg Edith had used a partly decayed arm for mastybayshun and the smell was awful … awful but familiar. The arm lay on her bedroom floor, severed at the elbow … smelling the same smell that first permeated our house when the noises started. It was then when I realised that Sprinkles may have 'sourced' and dug up an arm from Barry's grave. I took the arm and returned it to its rightful owner.

Today has been a great day. I counted some childers toes, danced a sexy dance at the Hippo and best of all I discovered that ladies mastybate too which subsequently lead to me finding out what the noise was that had kept us awake all this week.

Sunty 32ⁿᵈ Janeundmary

Finnders Dastardly came round and asked if I could do an extra dance for the Mayor tomorrow. I happily agreed and said that I would be at his office in the mawnin. Finnders curtly told me not to go to his office this time but to his house. It had to be after daaymiddlin as well. He seemed quite strict about the time, most definitely not before daaymiddlin. Not a problem but I couldn't figure out what his wife, V`Gina would make of me prancing around semi clothed about the place. Maybe she'd join in … maybe she wanted me to teach her the art of seductive movement.

Moondee 33st Janeundmary

As requested by Finnders, I arrived at the Mayor's private dwelling at just after daaymiddlin. It was everything that the rumour mongers said it was, and more. He handed me a glass of fine whiskey (*the sort that classy immigrant hooomans drink*) "to get us in the mood". I followed him into his living room and he closed the door behind me, I removed my coat to reveal my latest outfit. It was a latex school girl's outfit I had made myself from reconstituted tractor tyres and some white wash. Mayor Devilman's eyes lit up as the music played on my system. It was none other than the Latest offering by the Bay City Rollers, 'Bye Bye Baby'. I asked where his wife was and he informed me she was visiting friends in Peterborough. I was impressed, Peterborough eh! As I started to get into my moves I noticed the Mayor's hand slip inside his dressing gown. He seemed to be once again stroking Growler the dog (*what an odd place to keep a dog I thought, but then I've heard that ladies in high society in Peterborough keep small dogs in handbags*), he was grinning and sweating the same as he does at his office. I concluded that Growler must be the smallest dog in Chumpton … about six inches long at a guess, but very well stroked. I hitched my skirt up around my hips and lunged, erotically, right in front of him. As I looked up I could see my reflection in his patio door and I could see that the Mayor was struggling. Growler was getting quite a severe stroking poor dog. I then felt his hand squeeze my bum, not something I would normally tolerate at the hippo but this is the residence of the Mayor of Flatlands. This time I'd let it go.

The Mayor the leaned forward a bit and began licking and kissing my bottom, quite feverishly actually. He pulled my thong to one side and inserted his tongue into my bottom hole, normally just used for pooing. I would've trimmed my anal beard if I'd known he was going to do that. He let out a loud gasp opened his gown and stood up. As he stood up I could see there was no dog in his gown at all. There was however, a very large winky and he squirted his sex wee all over my back. I have had similar responses to my routines at Peppermint Hippo so I wasn't bothered but then the Mayor screamed "come on gorgeous, show me your cunny". I hadn't heard this expression before, "eh"? I exclaimed.

"Your cunt, show me your cunt … your flange" the Mayor said excitedly.

"I don't have a tuppence" I replied.

"WHAT" the Mayor expolded.

"I don't have a tuppence … I have a winky like you do", I pulled down the front of my thong and showed him my groinal parts. The Mayor vomited immediately and started sobbing. I tried to console him but he seemed really, really upset that I wasn't a lady. The vomiting continued for a few minutes in between the uncontrollable sobbing.

"Why did you think I was a lady"? I asked.

"You dance at the Peppermint Hippo … is the … are you … a …" he stuttered.

"A drag act? Yes I am. I thought you knew that, I thought everyone knew that" I said. He had one more wretch and asked me to leave. I felt quite disheartened. I started towards the door and he asked me to wait. "What do you want"? Enquired the Mayor.

"I don't know what you mean" I shrugged.

"To keep this quiet … what do you want? Do you like the Peppermint Hippo"?

"Of course I do, I work there"

"Then it's yours, but you never mention this again to anyone" he said.

"Do you want me to carry on dancing at your office for you?" I enquired tentatively.

"NO" he yelled "No … no … y … yes … yes okay but I'll have to make you one of the campaign advisers though. I can't have it known that a drag dancer performs privately for me' I haven't done anything like this since school, you understand? I don't want those feeling awakening again … daddy was so disappointed. I can't go through all that again … you understand don't you"

"I think so" I said, not really understanding.

I was confused now. I reminded him that the club was already owned by Finnders Dastardly. The Mayor just looked at me and smiled a fiendish grin and told me not to worry about that.

I don't really understand what has happened today.

Toosdi 34rd Janeundmary

Terrible news this mawnin. I received a knock at the door from PC Wormer who informed me that Finnders Dastardly had committed suicide by shooting himself in the back of the head with his shotgun late last noyght, Cranshaw St.John found him. He had blown his brains out with both barrels apparently. Obviously I was shocked but I wasn't sure what this had to with me. Jack Wormer went on to tell me that by his side was a suicide note saying he been "quite sad lately" and that he wanted to leave all his stuff to me, including the Peppermint Hippo. After yisdee's odd aftynune at the Mayor's house this had left me feeling much happier. It was a shame that Finnders was sad but hey ho, he's not sad anymore, that's the good thing about deadness, it stops you feeling sad. Later Today I received a courier crow telling me to attend the Mayor's office on Thrisdee, more dancing I suspect. Didn't even think about fires Today.

Winsti 35th Janeundmary

Most of today Nina has been getting Pocahontas ready for her big noyght out with PC Jack Wormer of Ropey Town Police Brigade. Just as it was approaching laasloyght there was a knock at the door and PC Jack was stood there, clutching a bunch of flowers (potato stalks), eagerly awaiting his beautiful companion. Some of the pubic hair had dropped off her wig so I shaved some of mine off to make up the deficit and coloured other bits with a black marker pen.

My pubic hair managed to give her some highlights. She looked lovely …and confused … confused and lovely as she wandered off down the street with our local bobby. Nina had a tear in her eye as Pocahontas left. She soon cheered up when I agreed to let her have a go on my truncheon that Jack had given me. Nina loved the truncheon. She spent nearly an hour hitting Nigelle F`Rage around the ankles and knees with it. She was quite out of breath from exertion, and asthma … asthmatic exertion.

The happy couple returned just before noyghtmiddlin. Pocahontas still seemed confused so we put her to bed. After PC Wormer had kissed her goodnoyght he quietly took me to one side and said that they hadn't had coitus as she was experiencing her monthly cycle.

I asked how he knew this, I knew I was possibly the best gender reassignment surgeon in all of Chumpton but I didn't think I was that good that I could actually give a chap, recently turned into a girl, real periods. It was after all my first attempt at this complicated surgical technique.

Jack then went on to inform me that he tried giving her a good fingering in the fields at Upper Fen drove at yon end and she was bleeding everywhere. I gave him my condolences but he shrugged it off and said he'll give her a "right good fuckin next time" and winked at me as he left. I will try and purchase some feminine hygiene products from the Happy Pauper but they may be reluctant to let me in after the embarrassment experienced with Nina's mildly soiled underwear a few days ago.

Thrisdee 36lbs Janeundmary

Today, at toe counting in the maternity ward, I managed to procure some feminine napkins for the ladies. They weren't the standard shop bought type, these were ones I made myself, fashioned from yet more bandages being thrown away and some partially used cotton wool. Waste not, want not.

After toe counting I attended the Mayor's office as requested. It wasn't to dance, as I thought, but to hear the last will and testament of Finnders Dastardly being read out, I felt slightly underdressed as I sat there in just my thong. I would have left my nurses clothes on if had known. The tension was tense due to lots of tenseness between Mayor Devilman and myself, creating tension following our tense 'situation' that occurred tensely at the weekend.

He could barely look me in the eyes as he read out the will. Oddly it was signed and dated with yisdee's date on it. I laughed quietly to myself Finnders was never very clever, always getting things mixed up. As Mayor Devilman concluded the meeting and signing the booze licence for Peppermint Hippo over to me, he asked me to remain behind. As the elders of the Flatland District council shuffled out of the Mayor's office he sat next to me in a vacant commode and said "you now have ... own, what we discussed, the weekends confusion is not to be mentioned again. Do you understand me"? I nodded. David placed his hand on my knee and told me to return tomorrow for more dancing.

I got home and had several showers and three baths.

CHAPTER TWO

TO OWN A PIECE OF FLATLAND

Feberee 1896

SatD 1th Feberee

This mawnin did not start well. I have had a very lengthy and angry tefelone call from Hermione Guttersnipe, the president of Chumpton-by-Kumberly Women's Institute. Her concerns were regarding one of the many hobby clubs I belong to. She was complaining specifically about the Chumpton-by-Kumberly Prostrate Milking Association, which I'm president of, and in particular the condition the WI hall floor is left in after our weekly meeting.

It transpires that the Chumpton Line Dancing Club use the hall immediately after our meeting and subsequently a number of injuries have been incurred by some of the line dancers, due to slipping on deposits of gentlemen's sex wee following some very heavy prostrate milking sessions recently. Hermione reminded me that we had been warned before about hot creamy ejaculate being left willy nilly, and as a result she feels she is left with no choice but to not allow us to hire the use of the facility from them. Hermione has even sold the story to the press (*well 'local' press*) for an undisclosed quantity of potatoes.

It was only a couple of years ago that one of the line dancers, called Jizzelle Kelptugger, claimed that after slipping over and landing on the deck she not only sprained her ankle but she was also impregnated by some of the floor bound ejaculatory deposits. Most people, including Hermione, felt this was a fall of convenience that covered up an extra marital indiscretion with her father and possibly brother. To end the argument Flatland District Council took the unprecedented action of taking DNA samples from all the members of the Prostrate Milking Association (*mostly collected from the floor of the WI hall*) who were present that day and one from Jizzelle herself and from two of the five triplets when they were born. The samples were sent to Peterborough, were such marvels of science are readily available to determine the biological father, but the results proved inconclusive.

The DNA results showed that almost all those sampled sent to the laboratory was too closely related to give a definite outcome. Most folk of Flatlands don't hold much regard for DNA results anyway, which is ironic considering large sections of the community share the same DNA. After the call I was left feeling very annoyed. Thankfully we had PC Jacks truncheon and Nigelle F`Rage's noggin to help release some of my pent up frustration. A small fire happened, that destroyed Edith's shed and some of her fencing. I have apologised. She showed little emotion, a little bit of fear maybe.

I had the great idea of explaining to Edith the shed and fence fire incident using only the medium of interpretive dance. I quickly stripped down to my underpants and nipped through the smouldering gap in her fence, knocked on her back door and adopted a crouching position whilst waiting for her to answer her door. When she opened the door and I leapt into the air and began my dance routine of fire explanation.

The impact of my interpretive dance on Edith's senses caused her to drop her mug of tea and to start shaking. I noticed during my dance that the shed door had begun to reignite so I extinguished the flames by urinating on the door but, cleverly I incorporated it into my dance routine. Edith and several of my other neighbours disturbed by the commotion and smoke were amazed at my interpretive dance skills. All they could do was stand and shake their heads as they admired me.

Edith had done a little bit of wee too, but sadly she hadn't managed to direct it towards the shed fire. My only regret was not checking my underwear was clean prior to my performance.

Chumpton-by-Kumberly Informer

Chumptons Parish Council are proud to announce that the star of screen and stage, Dame Judy Dench will be visiting the Flatland district and in particular Chumpton WI hall to help promote her new production of Shakespeares lesser known play "Nazi Kung Fu Sex Bitches From Venus".
Dame Judy is probably better known for her role as M in some of the James Bond films and also as Madame Ranevsky in Chekhovs The Cherry Orchard. Further information of her visit will be available once her visa has been cleared by the Flatland Council of the Elders which will allow her in to the Fens from the human city of Lundun.

On another note, but still to do with Chumptons WI hall, can the Chumpton Prostate Milking Society please ensure that the floor has been thoroughly mopped after their meeting. Chumptons Line Dancing Association uses the hall straight after and there has been some near fatal accidents involving line dancers slipping on residual body fluids from the previous meeting.

Possibly Dame Judy Dench possibly not

Sunty 3rd Feberee

Not turning into a very good weekend. After yisdee's sad news that the Chumpton Prostrate Milking Association is no longer allowed the use of the WI hall another hammer blow beset the household.

Nina took the ladies to the Happy Pauper shop for some provisions earlier today. On returning she was distraught, she informed me that whilst in the shop Pocahontas's vagina dropped out and fell on to the floor. I think it was probably due to the aggressive finger blasting she received during a romantic liaison with PC Wormer last week. His thick, pudgy finger must have dislodged some of the internal stitching and Selotape I used to keep the vagina in situ. This is a man most noted for the extreme brutality exerted on people he has arrested, so a delicate ladies tuppence, recently surgeryised stood little or no chance against such aggressive manipulation. I should have thought this through better. Luckily Horatio Horatio, the shop keeper (*confusingly, his middle name is Horatio too*) assumed she was attempting to shoplift some guided bus route road kill from the deli counter.

Moondee 3th Feberee

I went to peppermint Hippo this mawnin for the first time as the new official owner. I opened it up and took a long, lingering, look around, surveying all that I owned. The hassles of the weekend seemed to drift away as I gazed, all dewy eyed, at **MY** club with a great big smile on my face. It was then when a thunderbolt hit me. Now I owned the Peppermint Hippo I could hold the weekly Chumpton-by-Kumberly Prostrate Milking Association meetings here. I could even charge some of the locals to come and watch the milking of prostrates, charge them extra to join in and be milked. I called the Flatland Ambulance Cart Service to collect me from the club and went to Ropey Hospital A&E to be treated for my thunderbolt wounds. Once the roof had been fixed from the thunderbolt strike there were many attractions that the club could host, and I would never have to rely on other venues to assist me in my interests again.

Ironically the fire I started today was due to my clothes setting fire to the club courtesy of the thunderbolt and this was another first, a genuinely accidental fire caused by me. Otherwise it had been a good, no deliberate fires day.

Toosdi 4nd Feberee

Yisdee's fire from the thunderbolt had caused a bit more damage than I first thought, but it would be repaired by the end of the week apparently.

The Mayor asked me to his office to be sworn in as a campaign adviser and to do a private little dance for him afterwards. I think I'm right in saying I am the only advisor sworn in to the Mayor's office dressed in a latex Star troopers uniform. Once again Growler lucked out on the stroking as it was all over before the second minute of my music (*Ant and Dec's "Let's get ready to Rumble"*).

Before I had a chance to put my troopers helmet back in my carrier bag Mayor Devilman asked me to come over to his desk. As I approached he began sweating and stroking Growler again.

"Turn around and do that special lunge thing again and this time make an oinking sound" he asked.

I reluctantly did as requested and straightened my left leg and seductively ran my hands down its entire length. I was desperately trying not passing wind this time but alas, I forgot about the outcome of sneezing as I tried to make an oinking noise or I must be allergic to Growlers fur. I sneezed a massive sneeze, immediately braking into liquid bumsong.

"Oooooh yessss" Mayor David Devilman exclaimed in sheer exhilaration at my bottybursting sexy leg lunge. I can't be sure, but I thought I heard Growler yelp, it was either Growler or my sphincter … it's a good job I didn't get a chance to oink. If it was Growler I heard then the Mayor must have been really stroking him hard. As he cleaned a small amount of my loose liquid stool from his forearm he playfully smacked my arse cheeks before saying "You've awoken old demons within me … reminds me of my days at boarding school … Eton y'know …" I have no idea what he was talking about or what an 'Etonyinno' was, but I'm sure it was very nice and if he wants ridding of his demons I'm your man. He asked me for another dance tomorrow, I agreed.

I arrived back home to find that Nina had sewn/selotaped Pocahontas's tuppence back into place. Hopefully it'll hold out for her first proper sexual encounter with Jack later this week.

Winsti 5rd Feberee

After a busy mawnin toe counting I went to the Peppermint Hippo to see how the repairs were coming on and to get changed into my thong and bra ready for the Mayors dance. Today I shall be gyrating to "Mawnin has Broken" by a cat called Steven. I have decided to dance to a much slower song to show the Mayor I'm not just a one trick pony, it's also something I'm hoping to try out in my routine at the Hippo. It would hopefully cut down on the number of flatulence incidents that, I've heard through the grapevine, is putting some people off coming to the club, especially childers.

After I arrived at the Flatland District Council office I was moved into the waiting room outside the Mayor's chambers by Cranshaw St. John. He informed me that the Mayor had overdone it with the Turnip Pochine at The Jolly Sphincter last noyght and was spending some quality time on the toilet. After a few minutes Cranshaw asked me to go and set up in the office. I cued the song up and waited for Mayor Devilman to grace me with his presence. As I wandered around his chambers I walked past his Mayoral desk and on it I noticed a piece of paper. It was headed with two columns. One column had the words 'Real reasons to Flexit' the other with 'Campaign reasons to Flexit'. Under the heading Real reasons to Flexit it was left blank but under the heading Campaign reasons to Flexit it was well populated by some very bizarre claims. Obviously this was something to do with the forthcoming referendum to decide whether or not to remain in the UK of Great Britain. As I started to read down the page I heard David Devilman approaching the chambers so I quickly scooted over to my music machine. He went straight to his desk and briskly waved me to start my routine. As the music began echoing through the spacious office I began slowly swaying to and fro, fro and to, back and forth, forth and back. As I turned to face the Mayor I saw him reach for his mouth and run from his desk in the direction he'd come from only seconds earlier.

My curiosity got the better of me so I nonchalantly strolled back over to the desk and continued reading the document. The heading 'Campaign reasons to Flexit' was full; all the way to the bottom it was full. It was full of lies, untruths and exaggerations on an industrial scale. It ranged from no longer having to give the UK of Great Britain governance people money right through to alien abduction or the possibility of triggering the next world war if we remained in the United Kingdom. I was astounded and somewhat shaken at what I'd read. My dazedness was jolted by the return of footsteps; footsteps I assumed belonged to David Devilman. It was Cranshaw though, he marched into the chambers and informed me I "should leave now", quite tersely. I arranged to return to dance early next week.

Thrisdee 6st Feberee

Nina has introduced the ladies to the Chumpton-by-Kumberly Women's Institute as part of her on-going process to ingratiate them with Flatland District polite society or "Ladies what Docky" as it's known locally. Sad news though dearest diary, after discovering that my flatulence/anal seepage can be off putting for some of the clientele at Peppermint Hippo I have decided that to increase local interest and subsequently improve the revenue of my club I will need to look at making the club a cultural mecca and beacon of highbrow entertainment of refined diversity. I have therefore been in touch with Yawk Haaaall in Ropey town to supply me with Lady Boxers to appear at both The Hippo and Yawk Haaaall for some female fight club action. I also have to acknowledge that maybe it's time for me to hang up my thong and concentrate on making the club a success. Apart from the private dances for Mayor Devilman where seepage and flatulence appears to be a plus, I think I shall only dance at the Hippo on very special occasions. If my flatulence really is affecting takings then it's time to call it a day even though I have just got my licence back ☹ Flatlands TV news reported today that David Devilman had tefeloned the UK government of Great Britain and said that he wanted some more compoootas for the district, at least ten, otherwise we would leave the UK. He informed them that we are having a referendum about whether or not to remain in the UK of Great Britain. I'd imagine they are very worried as we supply them with lots of root crops. During the interview he assured everyone he would be spending lots of time in Lundun and was brokering a deal that would benefit the district in ways none of us simple folk could imagine. I think the threat of the UK of Great Britain losing its main supplier of root crops would be enough to make any government think twice about not giving it more compoootas.

---

fenbook   Surch for peeeple and othur thinqs tooooo   🔍   👤 Morton   Hoome   Foind frends   👥 💬 🌐 ⚙▾

Lady boxing

Back by popular demand 'lady Boxing' will be returning to Yawk Haaaall in the east end of Ropey every ninth Thrisdee of the month. Marquee of Kingsdyke rules will be strictly adhered to and Flatland etiquette is expected by all attendees. All boxers will undergo a rigorous medical examination before the pugalism commences in order to establish that the contenders are medically female (*thus avoiding the controversy surrounding last months title defence by big cock McGee*).
Lady Boxing is an ancient Flatland sport and tradition and as such clothing is required by all those wishing to attend.
I am holding auditions for ladies not wishing to box but carry the card in between rounds. Should any of my Fenbook lady friends wish to apply then contact me via courier crow stating your intentions.

Frydims 7jr Feberee

Tonoyght is the noyght that Pocahontas will be losing her virginity again (*assuming of course she ever lost it as a man*). Nina and Cinderella spent most of the day making Pocahontas look irresistible. Nigelle mentioned they looked like immigrants, so we all took it turns to hit him with the truncheon, what a spiteful bastard. Several well aimed hefty blows later he soon calmed down and had a sleep.

At laasloyght the door sounded with the, by now recognisable firm knock of a Police official. It was time for Pocahontas to go and finally complete her transformation and 'become a woman', a worldly woman. I opened the door to find Jack clutching a bunch of flowers and the small amount of money we had agreed as a "finder's fee". It was to help cover the costs of all the expensive treatment and care I had given my patients since having their procedures. He also gave me a bottle of turnip Pochine as a personal thank you to me for being a good pal and assisting the Police with their enquiries as often as I did. As they left the house I couldn't help thinking they made a sweet couple, and it was all down to me … and Nina, me and Nina, but mostly me.

Nina and I snuggled up on the sofa and began sipping the Pochine that PC Jack had left behind. Tomorrow noyght the Hippo was opening its doors to the public again after its brush with the elements a week or so earlier. It was an exciting time. There was going to be Lady Boxing fight club, unfettered prostrate milking and The Ropey Town Dogging Club asked about using the car park every second Sunty. Things were starting to come together.

Sadly however, the same couldn't be said for poor old Pocahontas and her quest to become a real woman. As Nina and I were just settling down to a second mug of turnip Pochine our laasloyght tranquillity was interrupted by a desperate and persistent banging at my front door. A low pitched, scared and panicked howling was just the other side of my threshold. I hurriedly opened my door to have PC Wormer fall through the doorway, terrified and screaming, whilst attempting to hold his trousers in place, "Help me" he begged. "Help me, I'm sorry, I'm so sorry … I don't know how it happened".
Nina ushered a confused but calm Pocahontas through the door, closed it and sat Pocahontas down.

"What's happened Jack" I asked but he had no reply. I asked him again "What's happened" but he just sat there shaking and repeating how sorry he was.

I placed both my hands on Jacks shoulders and shook him slightly to try and jolt him into some kind of coherence but not enough for his policeman's 'instincts' to kick in. It worked. Jack calmed momentarily, long enough for me to ask again what had happened. Jack removed his hands, previously holding his trousers in place, to reveal an unsightly lump of rotting, purulent, festering flesh between his legs. Jack of course was confused as to how this could happen but I knew immediately that Pocahontas's tuppence had once again fallen off and became stuck on the policeman's penis.

"I didn't … couldn't, go to the hospital with this. Not with my job and everything" Jack said, struggling to hold back the tears. "We were … you know … at it … and when I'd finished I pulled away to find I had shagged her that hard that her tuppence had welded itself to my winky. I'm so sorry, what are we going to do?"

Fear not I informed my policeman pal as I slowly twisted Pocahontas's vagina free from Jacks flaccid member. I reminded him of my brilliant surgical abilities and reassured him all would be well. I handed him the bottom of the living room curtains to clean the blood and sex wee off his winky with and turned my attention to Pocahontas. She seemed fine, just missing her genitals, but other than that fine. I instructed Nina to clear the kitchen table of the docky plates and "prepare for surgery my dear". Jack looked more confused than ever but helped Nina prepare the kitchen/theatre.

Jack waited with the worried look of an expectant father in the living room whilst Nina and I went about our task repairing this young ladies dignity. A full 25 minutes later the operation was complete and Pocahontas once again had a vagina fit for purpose. This time I used stitches (*lots of em*), Selotape (*lots of it*) and sooperdooper rabbit bone glue (*lots n lots of it*) purchased only that day from the Happy Pauper.

Jack was as relieved as any man I'd ever seen when I told him the operation had been a complete success. He assured me that my surgical expertise would never be forgotten and if I ever found myself in need of assistance from Ropey Town Police Brigade then I need look no further. I'll remember this promise as I may need to hold him to that one day but an emergency was averted. Nina and I snuggled up on the sofa again as Pocahontas slept peacefully as her vagina started its healing process.

SatD 8th Feberee

Today saw the grand reopening of Peppermint Hippo after its small reparation. I opened the noyght with the great news that the 'legend' that is Floella Nipsy will be performing at this year's Klungefest, this was met with much enthusiasm by our club members.

As I have had issues with involuntary flatulence, Floella has struggled with dance related incontinence. It's because of this she, like me, only performs on special occasions these days and only ever at venues with professional cleaning services noted for their mopping capabilities. Now I'm the owner of the Peppermint Hippo I had toyed with the idea of retirement from dancing but the prospect of performing with Flo was too much … maybe just one last time. I placed an ad in the Chumpton Informer.

Chumpton-by-Kumberly Informer

Peppermint Hippo is proud to announce that the Chumpton-by-Kumberly erotic dance legend Floella Nipsy will be performing at this years 'Klungefest'.
Pints of Badgerspizzle will be flowing freely and thongs will be snapping.
For those who miss my sexy dancing and exotic lunges you will be thrilled to discover that I will be knocking the dust off my trusty old G string and coming out of retirement just for Klungefest.

Floella proving a big draw to customers at the Peppermint Hippo. Incontinence cut short her promising career. As seen above she is performing the "fart sniffer", her signature move that became perilous once her bladder issues took hold.

<u>Sunty 9th Feberee</u>

Mayor Devilman came round and visited me this mawnin whilst the ladies were out and about socialising and eating creamed parsnip scones at the WI hall. This meant only myself and Nigelle F`Rage were in the house when the Mayor arrived. I prepared some devils prolapse earlier for Nigelle to drink, so I didn't have to listen to him talking about immigrants whilst the ladies were out. I dusted down my latex vicars' outfit, as I was assuming that the Mayor had come for a private dance. As the Mayor sat down I offered him a cup of onion cosh tea and gave Nigelle a little head beating to keep him quiet whilst the Mayor spoke.

Mayor Devilman started by saying that he wanted me as a local celebrity and pillar of the Chumpton community, a much respected man throughout Flatlands (*he didn't actually say any of this but I knew what he meant*) to be the co-ordinator for his campaign to Flexit/Flemain. He didn't know who was going to lead the campaign yet though. I readily agreed, somewhat flustered at being offered this most prestigious of roles.

Unfortunately, I once again accidentally picked up Nigelle's cup of sleepy drink and took a sip. I awoke some time later to discover the Mayor was still there on my sofa. To my utter horror he had spent the whole time talking to Nigelle. Before Nigelle could say anything more I sprung to my feet and clumped him across the bonce with the truncheon and rendered him sleepy for a bit.

"I'm so sorry, please ignore everything that complete moron said to you, he has many brain issues for which I am treating him with some hefty trepanning" I said to the somewhat bemused dignitary. To my absolute amazement the Mayor began to tell me that Nigelle was perfect, just what he was looking for. He went on to say that an enormous weight had been lifted from his shoulders and he instructed me to stop trepanning F`Rage and get him ready to begin his role as the leader for the campaign for Flexit. Now I was really confused. The Mayor informed me whilst I was having a nap, Nigelle had been telling him all about his distrust and deep set hatred of immigrants, foreigners and all things not local to Flatlands. Odd considering until a few weeks ago he was not local to Flatlands either I thought. I reminded Mayor Devilman that Nigelle was an odious, fuckwitted cuntbucket and not to be listened to. The Mayor looked me straight in the eyes and beamed "I know he is … he's perfect". With that he got up and left. I hadn't even had a chance to dance for him.

Moondee 10th Feberee

Flanders, our cloakroom attendant from the Hippo is giving a talk soon. That is all

I'm still dazed from yisdee's events so this is Today's diary entry. The concept that I was going to be co-ordinating Nigelle F`Rage in the forthcoming referendum was now beginning to worry me. What did the Mayor have planned?

Alright so it wasn't the only entry for Today in the diary … fuck off … It's my diary.

Chumpton-by-Kumberly Informer

Flanders 'The Tash' Goatstrangler, naked wrestler and part time cloakroom attendant at the Peppermint Hippo (Chumptons premier lap/pole dancing venue) will be appearing at Chatterby University to deliver a lecture on sexual deviancy in rural communities.

The talk is expected to last three days, no refreshments will be served or allowed in the auditorium.
Entry is free however attendees will be expected to sniff Flanders' inner thigh at several times during the lecture and immediately prior to exiting the university. That is all!

Toosdi 11rd Feberee

I went and visited the Mayor in his chambers this mawnin. This time however, it wasn't to dance whilst he stroked his Growler. This time I had Nigelle with me. The Mayor asked to us to sit and then the Flatland Council of the Elders, all four of them, entered the chamber. I was a little bit nervous now.

"I want Nigelle here to run against me in the forthcoming referendum" Mayor Devilman announced to all present. "I will be leading the campaign to remain part of the United Kingdom … the Flemain campaign … I like it, it even rhymes, Nigelle F`Rage here will be leading the campaign to leave it, the Flexit campaign" he continued. "I'd really rather not leave the UK as it suits me to remain in it. To be honest I only agreed to a bloody referendum to keep some of the locals happy to guarantee success at the recent Mayoral election".

At this point I couldn't help thinking that he actually passed a bill to allow him to run against himself in the Mayoral election and therefore couldn't possibly have lost, I kept quiet though.

"I can't have a credible opponent that might perhaps win, I can't allow that … I must win. I had no idea who could be inept enough to mount a credible campaign against me but then … but then I met Mr F`Rage here. I spent several tedious hours at Morton's house on Sunty listening to this grinning halfwit tell me how much he hated immigrants in such a fuckwitted way that all became clear to me. This was the man that is so vacuous, so incredibly unpleasant, and so unbelievably stupid that only the dimmest of people could vote for him, I can't lose … I don't like losing".

"So where do I come into it" I asked.

"You, you will be his campaign manager, he lives in your house, you occasionally … erm … you know, attend to my entertainment needs so we can liaise about what has to be done to ensure this dribbling goon does not, will not, under any circumstances win. If you manage this right then it will be very beneficial to the two of us … but mostly me".

Once again on my return home after a meeting with our esteemed Mayor I had to have a few showers and a couple of baths.

Winsti 12nd Feberee

This mawnin I crafted a wig for Nigelle ready for the start of his campaign. Due to the amount of trepanning he has undergone recently and occasional punishment beatings he looks a bit of a mess. He looks like he has just stepped out of a plane crash to be honest so I shall be taking him out to get a suit and Nina is mixing up a fresh batch of sooperdooper gloo to fix the wig in place. The wig has once again been crafted from the abundance of pubic hair around Nina's anus and a fair amount I harvested from Edith's tuppence while she slept. It certainly is a fine looking wig, making him a more than passing resemblance to Bamber Gasgoine from the brainbox Hoooman quiz show University Challenge.

The wig looks fine but smells a bit pongy so I gave it a good wash in the sink in case anyone wishes to kiss Nigelle's head during the campaign. It washed up well but the water left in my bowl was like a chocolate coloured puddle of bum and genital whiffing soup.

There was a knock at the door so I dried my hands and went to answer it. To my surprise I saw Cranshaw St. John in front of me. I invited him in and offered him a seat but he but he refused saying he wasn't stopping long. He wanted a quick chat about the forthcoming referendum campaigns.

He followed me into the kitchen where we discovered both Cinderella and Pocahontas drinking the stinky wig water from the washing up bowl. All conversation stopped dead. Cranshaw wanted to tell me that the campaigns will start in earnest next week and I needed to devise a timetable for the Mayor to look at so he can plan his strategy. As he imparting this information I could see he was struggling not to vomit so I ushered him out of the kitchen and into my front room.

He asked if I had any idea what my strategy was going to be. To lose I replied.

Thrisdee 13lbs Feberee

Chumpton-by-Kumberly Informer

FENWEAR CLOTHIERS of Chumpton

The Spring catalogue from **FENWEAR** is now available from our shop at Lower Fen drove by-yon end as well as Chumpton Happy Pauper and St Jebediah's Primary School for the Criminally Insane, for the perusal of local dandy's and fashionistas. If you're planning a special occasion and want to look your best or you're simply wanting to look good sipping a turnip Daiquiri at the Jolly Sphincter then **FENWEAR** has it all at reasonable prices.
Rural chic is this seasons must have (as it was last season and all seasons since the Dutch invasion) and as you can see from the picture below, we stock a huge selection of styles and colours ranging from brown to black. These latest outfits taken from the very best high fashion designers from as far afield as Chatterby and Ropey are really pushing the boundaries. If you want to feel Glam when either standing about at a social gathering or standing in a field of root crops then visits **FENWEAR CLOTHIERS** of Chumpton

Advertisement

The sooperdooper gloo worked a treat but not only have they glued his wig on but some of it got onto his face skin which has given Nigelle F`Rage a kind of gormless frog expression. He seems to be smiling at everything.

I whisked Nigelle off to Fenwear Clothiers of Chumpton to complete the look of a man on the campaign trail. It's rumoured that Fenwear Clothiers have been providing the finest threads to Flatlands well healed since they days of the Dutch invasion. Some of the cloth and designs were also dated that far back, good quality never goes out of fashion.

Frydims 14mr Feberee

CHATTERBY MONTHLY ADVERTISER

MASON DICKSYLINE Hairstylist to local farmers and the stars of Flatlands.

Flatlands premier hair creation artiste` Mason Dicksyline is currently taking bookings. If you want a new look, a new style, a new image then mason can offer you his 'haircut' and you can leave with his style.

Mason trained at The Ropey School of Hair cuts and now owns the foremost haircut place in Chumpton-by-Kumberly. If you want a cut like Masons very own, or even something very slightly different Mason can and will cater for you.

MASON DICKSYLINE ADVENTURES IN HAIR

Nina has taken the ladies to get their hair done at Chumpton's premier salon today. When they saw how dandy Nigelle was looking in his fancy threads and new wig they became a bit jealous so off they went Masons. I spent the alone time in the house with the Krakorbang feather and a box of tissues.

SatD 15th and Sunty 16rd Feberee

This weekend saw the start of Klungefest at Peppermint Hippo. There were no real issues but we did run out of Badgerspizzle beer. The main attraction, Floella Nipsy, pulled out all the stops to ensure that the temporary lack of beer didn't damper the ardour of the punters and regular club members, keen on seeing the ultimate in lap/pole dancing. I too dazzled them with my Mawnin has broken routine, the one I almost got to try out in the Mayor's office. Several people complimented me on not spraying them with faeces during the performance. Once a fresh batch of Badgers had been squeezed and the beer had been brewed in cask conditions and left to mature for 20 minutes things got into full flow. The turnip Pochine was in great demand too, especially when we were treated to an impromptu performance by our very own Jebwould.

fenbook   Surch for peeeple and othur things tooooo   🔍   Morton Hoome   Foind frends

JEBWOULD

Jebwould are Chumptons latest pop sensation. Their latest hit "mulled wine around my ringo" reached number 16583 in the pop on hit parade. Anyone wishing to book them for parties, weddings, festivals or obscure Flatland religious ceremonies please contact me via here on Fenbook courier crow or tefelone me (016547642776427754std) 31.

Jebwould relaxing casually near an open fire with their cat called "Darren Hinchcliffe"

The whole weekend went without a hitch and made me realise what an absolute goldmine this wonderful club could be. Even the Ropey Town Dogging Club turned up to give a special demonstration in the car park. Hermione Guttersnipe from Chumpton WI had a face like a plasterer's radio after 20 minutes. I don't think she was impressed as she was only walking past the club to go to the Happy Pauper for some Beetroot wine, but later she commented that it left her hair and face feeling great and it would save her money on hair conditioner and a face mask. She went on to say she would be asking Mr Guttersnipe for the occasional spraying of "gentlemen's life essence" to assist her complexion. Let's hope she doesn't try out her homemade beauty regime in the WI hall … someone might slip on her face mask.

It was a truly wonderful weekend that wonderfully showcased some of the wonderful, wonderful talent we have in our wonderful little district … wonderful. We should think about future events and perhaps even a festival. A lot of the local Flatland talent could do much worse than have me as their manager, someone who has done the circuit a few times as an erotic entertainer and celebrated drag artiste of some reckoning.

Moondee 17th Feberee

Today came the announcement on Flatland Radio that the Mayor of Flatland District David Devilman was going to head the campaign to remain in the UK whilst "The unknown" Nigelle F`Rage was going to lead the Flexit debate. Pocahontas was out again with Jack Wormer. As ever, she looked radiant and this time they returned without incident. Jack understood Pocahontas's lady parts would need to be treated a little bit more carefully this time, so we both agreed prior to him leaving that full penetrative lustings is off the cards for the time being. Jack said in that case he would just stick his head up her dress and lick her tuppence for an hour or so. Pocahontas looked blankly at the wall, dribbled a bit, grinned and then farted.

Toosdi 18st Feberee

FLATLAND DISTRICT WEEKLY NEWS

Advertisement

Lundun ladies may have the Chippendales but the lucky lasses of Flatlands have these hot hunks of inbred male beefcake the 'Chumpton Wood Butchers'.
They will be appearing next weekend at Peppermint Hippo and tickets are on sale for 12 human pences or equivalent value in root crops.
Come on ladies, get your party gear on and get yourselves down to Peppermint Hippo (Chumptons premiere lap/pole dancing facility).
Bring plenty of sugar beet to slip into the guys skimpy outfits, they may do "extras".
If the last time we had these boys on is anything to go by then some of the more sexually promiscuous ladies are in for a treat … so don't forget the sugar beet.

The Chumpton Wood Butchers striking a pose. Teehee, the little one on the end has trouble finding his genitals. Possibly because he is obese.

Toosdi noyght is ladies noyght at the Peppermint Hippo and tonoyght we have the Chumpton Wood Butchers doing their thang for the Flatland lovelies. I made certain that the Prostate Milking was done early so that none of the local ladies attending tonoyghts gash frothing performance by these local beef cakes could possibly lead to any more seminal fluid slipping incidents and subsequent accusations about floor based impregnations.

Winsti 19st Feberee

A cracking noyght at the hippo last noyght meant I had a bit of a thick head this mawnin. I could have done without a hangover today as it was the day I introduced the world to Nigelle F`Rage, the leader of the campaign to persuade the residents of Flatland District to leave the UK of Great Britain and becoming independent. The launch was at the club and I decided that the best way to start the day was with a quick livener of turnip Pochine to steady the nerves and help shift the hangover. Nigelle started drinking some of the dregs from the slops trays from last noyght and unbelievably started talking even more incomprehensible drivel than before. This was perfect. Imagine that, talking even more shite than he did previously just with a pint of slops down him. This I could see was going to be a mainstay of this campaign. Wherever Nigelle and the press was I'd make sure he had a pint in his hand and just let him talk his rubbish. This was PR gold, if your aim was to lose that is.

Thrisdee 20st Feberee

Yet another milestone see's the re-opening of my interpretive dance school. It's something that's close to my heart, but has sadly taken something of a backseat just lately following all of the shenanigans and going on.

FLATLANDS DISTRICT ADVERTISER

Finally, Chumpton School of Interpretive Dance is open for business.

From Moondee 17th Feberee, Chumpton will be known throughout the Flatland region as the hub of interpretive dancing and all interpretive dance related subject matter.

Improve your chances with that dream job interview by answering your questions with a mixture of Jazz freestyle and improvised ballet moves.

Unrequited love issues? Then admire from afar no more, by simply learning a few interpretive dance moves to woo the heart of your potential suitor.

Make your life a total success through our experimental dance workshops at Chumpton School of Interpretive Dance

From Childers to adults, all welcome at Chumpton School of Interpretive Dance

I placed an advert in the Flatland District Advertiser to try and drum up some new customers and even used a lovely old picture I had of the first 'Barry the tramp' before he became too demon filled and rather un-cooperative. The second Barry the tramp was much more docile.

Nigelle F`Rage had his first proper press call Today and did superbly. He accused several members of the gathered press and Flatland paparazzi of being "Fucking foreigners" and telling people how he was going to build a wall around the Fenland District to keep the Hooomans out as they were all murderers and rapists and then went on to say it was going to be the UK Government … yes the UK Government that would be paying for it. It was comedy gold and the press were lapping it up. At one point a gust of wind got up and blew Nigelle's wig about the place but it remained firmly attached to his skull and only showed a few of the scars from his trepanning sessions from earlier in the month.

This was a tribute to my wig making abilities and Nina's gluing skills. When I called into the Mayor's office later this aftynune and told him. He was pleased although I thought he'd be thrilled, he didn't seem that bothered about the referendum. David informed me that he was going to announce that the day of the referendum was going to be 23th Jism, the last day of the month.

CHAPTER THREE

POWER TO THE PEOPLE

MUNCH 1896

Frydims 1st Munch

The Flatlands Weekly News had run a story on both campaigns and sure enough they featured a lovely picture of Nigelle spewing his poisonous tirade at rather bemused local news reporters. I took Nigelle into the pub and the reporters duly obliged by following us in there. I started giving Nigelle beer and cigarettes as this was considered very unprofessional and politically incorrect. It would almost certainly portray him as an incoherent old lush. Sure enough this mawnin's papers printed the pictures this mawnin of Nigelle standing there looking very austere and was bizarrely blaming the unusually sunny weather outside on the "fucking immigrants".

David Devilman, Mayor of Flatlands and leader of the 'Flemain' campaign, even made a call on the tefelone (*very unusual for him*) to pass on his delight at my master stroke. It was a cracking start to the campaign.

FLATLAND DISTRICT WEEKLY NEWS

This week saw the announcement from Mayor Devilman's chambers that the long awaited referendum will be held on 23th Jism. He also announced that he would be leading the campaign for Flatlands to remain (Flemain) within the UK and the campaign for Flatlands to leave the UK (Flexit) will be lead by the unknown Nigelle F'Rage. Oddly enough Mr F'Rage is believed to originate from the UK but has spent at least a month in Flatlands and is therefore a naturalised citizen of our beautiful district.

Mr F'Rage feels strongly that most things wrong with Flatlands are primarily because of immigrants coming into Flatlands from the UK and trying to change things with their funny ways and cosmopolitan ideas and strange talking sounds. Mr F'Rage smokes heavily and drinks to excess most days, we were reliably informed by his campaign manager, local erotic dancer and interpretive dancer/cosmetic surgeon, Morton Babeldom.

During his press announcement Mr F'Rage drank several pints of Badgerspizzle beer whilst ranting incoherently about "f@%cking foreigners" whilst lighting cigarettes one after the other.

The Mayors office was unavailable for any comments about their strategy for the forthcoming campaign. Cranshaw St.John said that the Mayor was on holiday and later would be busy tending to 'Growler' his dog but would inform the inhabitants of Flatlands at some point in the future why they must vote to remain in the UK. When pressed when the Mayor would become involved in the campaign Mr St.John assured us it would almost certainly be before the 23th Jism, polling day.

Nigelle F'Rage 36, leader of the Flexit campaign.

SatD 2rd Munch

Today has been a slow day.

Nina has been sewing Cinderella's nipples back on after an accident with the cutlery drawer. Pocahontas's tuppence seems to be holding out. She went out this aftynune with PC Wormer for a stroll around the witch's pond. On their return she had a noticeable amount of sex wee on her dress and Jack informed me it was where he had wiped his 'old man' after some slap n tickle. Not really sure why he took his dad on a date with him especially if they were having some slap n tickle. We gave the ladies some sleepy drink and took Nigelle over to the Peppermint Hippo for some Turnip Pochine and Badgerspizzle beer. Nigelle was wonderfully embarrassing and accused many of the locals of being immigrants. I expected some of them to take offence at this accusation but it transpired most of them were unaware of what immigrants actually are.

Sunty 3lbs Munch

We awoke this mawnin to find that Pocahontas had pooed on the kitchen floor again. Considering this is where I conduct many of my operations it is not very hygienic to have her pooing there, I thought about rubbing her nose in it. Nina said she will teach her to use the toilet today. No fires, some public nudity though.

Moondee 4th Munch

Today I had a meeting with the Mayor in the local pub nearest the Town hall called The Jolly Sphincter. He was pleased with the way things had been going with the F`Rage/Flexit campaign. I asked him when he was planning on divulging his strategy to remain within the UK of Great Britain. He didn't seem particularly bothered with it, hinting that he was hoping that the Flexit campaign would make such a mess of things that he wouldn't really need to "worry himself too much with campaigning", he went on to say he had much bigger plans to worry about. Odd, what could be bigger than leaving the UK of great Britain. Hopefully Nigelle will continue making such an almighty fuck up that the Mayor was right. The people of Flatlands couldn't be that dim that they would ever vote for Nigelle, I'm certain of it … certain of it. Cranshaw took me to one side as I left the pub and informed me he would arrange some kind of local press release within the next few days and a couple of personal appearances by Mayor Devilman to start the Flemain ball rolling.

Toosdi 5st Munch

A warning went out this mawnin on Flatlands Radio that a Theltwells Dykebumma has been seen on the outskirts of the village. I made sure everyone knew of this by putting it on my Fenbook page and by standing outside my house shouting "Theltwells Dykebumma, beware everyone" over and over again for half an hour until someone pointed out to me that my noisy warning cries might actually attract the scary bugger into the village. I thought maybe we could capture the beast with a decoy but my Fenbook chums were less than forthcoming. The last I heard today was that the Theltwells Dykebumma was still at large.

Flatland   District   Welfare   Warning

A **Theltwells Dykebumma** has been spotted lurking in ditches between Chumpton and the Chatterby timeline, it has been confirmed today. These creatures are known for sneaking up and brutally sodomising Dyke workers (sometimes without their full consent) and disappearing again into the flatland undergrowth without as much as a peck on the cheek. The one pictured here was captured and domesticated before being hired out for childers birfdee parties and occasionally appearing at the legendary Peppermint Hippo. As you will see from this photo, violation from a Theltwells Dykebumma is a painful and humiliating experience. The lady that appears in this photo was mostly consenting during consciousness . In an attempt to capture the Theltwells Dykebumma currently at large, it is proposed to lure the creature from the Flatland with a decoy. I am therefore asking if any of my buddies in Fenbook land would be willing to be the decoy? The reward for this brave and selfless act will be bag of carrots and a free pass to Chumptons World of Adventures (*the best rural/root crop based theme park in the district ... possibly the area*). If you are willing to help please contact me by either Fenbook or courier crow.

Winsti 6th Munch

I discussed with Nina the possibility of using my loft as a campaign headquarters. Today has involved the arduous task of cleaning it out and getting it 'office ready'. Had some fun going through some old photos and posted some on my Fenbook page later.

Halcion days

Whilst serving a short custodial sentence at her majesties pleasure in Ropey Prison, following a small misunderstanding with some Selotape, a sink plunger, a small amount of Semtex and a Poodle called Stephanie, I would often wile away the cold dark winter evenings with my other cellmates and chums by standing around in our underwear while looking at divers flippers and other aquatic sportswear. Occasionally one of us would try things on for size as the others watched .... marvellous times. As the picture suggests, not all the time spent in prison is bad, it's not all inedible food, beatings, buggery and bullying. Sometimes spending time trying out diving equipment with like minded people could help blot out all the negative things about incarceration.
But generally not!

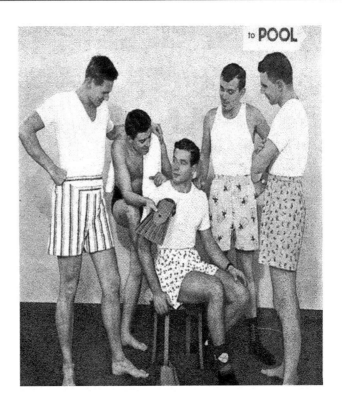

Thrisdee 7nd Munch

The loft is now a fully functional campaign headquarters. It has a desk, a chair and several pieces of paper and a pencil. I am feeling like a proper executive and it means I don't have to revert to plan B which was running it from the Peppermint Hippos office which is full of various types of lubricant and significant amounts of pills and potions to assist anal sphincter dilation used mostly for private parties such as weddings and children's Birfdeee parties. Nigelle was subdued today and seemed out of sorts. I managed to give him a trepanning lite at the back of his head under the hairline of his wig for discretion. He spent the rest of the day sleeping it off. Early laasloyght was spent watching Flatland TV and sipping potato flavoured coco with Nina. We are both pleased that there have been no more pooing accidents or nipple loss mishaps from the ladies. Pocahontas's vagina seems to be holding out really well. Next week I shall possibly start giving the ladies some breasties to complete the transformation.

Frydims 8nd Munch

Last noyght's TV perusal has given me some ideas for events, competitions and festivals that we can hold at Peppermint Hippo or the WI hall (*as long as there's no seminal excretion involved of course*) or even in surrounding villages. Watch this space. I have begun inventing various breast implants ready for next week's operations and any future requirements for breast enlargement. The best so far seems to be plastic bags filled with mud and sand. Very realistic. ☺

Don't even think about fires these days …. Well not too much.

SatD 9st Munch

Today we decided, on something of a last minute whim, to visit Chumpton World of Adventures with the ladies and Nigelle. It advertises itself as possibly the best root crop based theme park in the district, possibly the area and do you know what? I think it might be.

Even Better than Chatterby Towers where you have to que for hours, sometimes days for the rides (*mostly tractor based rides*) and pay a small fortune for onion orientated products. The ladies had tremendous fun at one of the attractions called "Gleaning the fields" where the visitors get the chance to enter a real live root crop growing field that has grown it's produce and pick the product to hand over to the owners of Chumptons World of Adventure and guess what? It's all included in the entry price so you don't have to shell out more money to go on the attraction like you do at Chatterby Towers.

I treated everyone to a nice cooling Parsnip Smoothie afterwards and even had a punnet of carrot and onion ice-cream, endorsed by our very own celebrity chef Nigella Cokesnorter, although word around the camp fire says she stole the recipe from our other celebrity cook Heston Bailer. Heston is renowned for his unorthodox approach to cuisine, which in Flatlands is saying something.

Advertisement

CHUMPTON WORLD OF ADVENTURE

(The best rural/root crop based adventure theme park in the district ... possibly the area)

Are you looking for something to do at the weekend or during the long summer holidays? Are you looking for somewhere interesting and exciting to take the childers that can feed their minds as well as their tummys?

Then look no further. Come to <u>Chumpton World of Adventure</u> and discover the joy of root crop based entertainment. Sample the harsh rasping burn of our world famous Turnip Pochine in the comfort of ~~one of~~ our ~~several~~ bars whilst the kids play in relative safety at the award winning playground of terror.

Enjoy the delights of our Root Crop cuisine in one of ~~two~~ one restaurants as the kids are shown the joys of picking root crops straight from the field. What can be more satisfying knowing the cuisine you are about to eat has been hand picked by one of your own offspring?

Above is our restaurant and bar before last years tragic fire

Kids can never get bored at <u>Chumpton World of Adventure</u>. We have the most haunted barn in the area, Dare you spend more than 6 hours in it? No? then you can leave the kids there whilst they await Transportation to the 'Fields of plenty' where they learn the basics in root crop extraction prior to their field picking/gleaning experience. As your childers learn how to pick root crops you can relax in our world Class luxury spar. Sip a carrot smoothie whilst having your feet massaged by some of the childers that didn't quite make the grade extracting root crops from the 'Fields of Plenty'. Lounge about like a film star at the Hollywood place in Merica. Wear one of our complimentary dressing gowns made from the finest hessian.

Above is our world class spar before last years tragic fire

Just when you think you've had it all, just when you've had the best, most exciting time of your life you get to take home a complimentary sack of Turnips or Carrots *(you choose ... depending on availability)*. Either take them with you or alternatively, they can be given to your childers to take home with them when we return them to you 4/5 days later.

Above is our turnips before last years tragic fire

Sunty 10th Munch

We all spent most of the day on the toilet passing very runny/liquid poo's. When Chumpton World of Adventures says you can eat as many raw onions and consume as much Carrot and Potato stew as you can, they aren't kidding. We definitely over did the Turnip Pochine (*their own secret recipe with a hint of red diesel*). Nigelle made a fool of himself insisting that all non-birthed Flatlanders will need to go on a register (*he seems to have overlooked the fact that he is a non-birthed Flatlander*) and the ladies enjoyed lots of attention from some of the local lads keen to show them how hairy and long their winky's were. Cinderella seems to have caught the eye of one young gentleman called Finbar Knuckleshuffla who is something of a local celebrity. I remember him from a short spell he had dancing at Peppermint Hippo, but these days he's known as a local Lothario and is currently hotly tipped to be the winner of the hit TV show Flatlands Next Top Model.

Moondee 11nd Munch

Chumpton-by-Kamberly Informer

The indigenous folk of Chumpton would like to wish Finbar Knuckleshuffla the very best of luck in his attempt to become Flatlands next top model, the hit TV series on local access channel 'inbreed-indeed TV'.

Finbar hails from Upper fen drove on Yon end Lower Fen fen and is the son and half brother of local acting legend Buck Knuckleshuffla (*he famously stood in as a body double for Paul Henry, who played Benny in Crossroads, in some of the shows more blood thirsty scenes*).

Finbar was noted for his striking good looks and was quickly enrolled in the 'Flatlands Academy to Performing Arts and Root Crop Cultivation' but was equally as quickly removed again when he was considered too much of a distraction for his fellow lady students. His boyish charm and sexy allure won him a short stint at Peppermint Hippo (*Chumptons premier lap/pole dancing night spot*) but other performers at the nightspot became jealous of his appeal to the clientele and noticed he was leaving each noyght laden with root crop based gifts and strange bite marks on his buttocks (a well known Flatland sign of amorous intent).

Finbar then performed for several nights at the infamous Klunge Klub in Chatterby before being spotted by Fenland rural PR guru and well known child catcher, Max Triffid. Max saw Finbar in his office and suggested he removed some of his clothing and walked up and down his office for twenty minutes before Max groaned and told him he would take him under his wing ... so to speak.

I'm sure all from Chumpton would like to wish Finbar the very best of luck in the competition and his future success in becoming the 'poster boy of the Flatlands'.

I contacted Finbar via Max Triffid, his agent, this aftynune and he was very keen to be associated with Mayor Devilman. As he was busy with the modelling contest he was also keen to portray himself as a one girl guy and having Cinderella as his steady girl was not going to hurt his celebrity persona one bit.

I had already started planning for more vaginal mishaps and hoped that Finbar wasn't quite as sexually aggressive as Jack is. What could possibly go wrong?

Toosdi 12th Munch

FLATLAND DISTRICT WEEKLY NEWS

A Grubblers Pisser has been spotted wandering between Witches Fen and fen drove Fen yesterday (Moondee 11nd Munch) by a local courting couple, Blodwella and Blodwin Scablicker. Blodwella explained that she and her brother, Blodwin were dyke swimming and about to engage in an amorous encounter when an unearthly smell engulfed the couple. Initially they thought it was nothing more than a Granville Bush Flapper or possibly Blodwins flatulence gland inflaming again but as the pair swam to the bank edge to investigate they were sprayed with a warm, thick, orange/green liquid. Blodwin suspected he and his sister/fiance' had been covered in urine from the mythical Fenland creature known as the Grubblers Pisser, thought to have been extinct for nearly 3 months. It was then when his suspicion was confirmed when Blodwella saw the creature, although at first mistaking it for their father Jebadiah, she quickly realised it was the indeed a Grubblers Pisser lurking on the side of the dyke.

A local wildlife expert, who wished to remain anonymous for legal reasons, said the creature was probably marking its territory, ready for the mating season. During this time the Grubblers Pisser will spray bog oaks with its rancid urine and attempt to procreate with the ancient tree stump. This strange activity largely explains why they were believed to be extinct, that and they are a Flatland deliciously and hunted for their meat and fur (used to make Swampies shoooooooos, a sort of Uggboot for rural folk).

If anyone sees a Grubblers Pisser they are advised to not approach the creature and also strongly urged to avoid putting fingers or genitals near the animals mouth and to notify somebody that owns a shotgun.

More indigenous animals reaping havoc among the rural folk of Flatlands this week. The dyke people run many risks swimming and working on the outskirts of the populated areas. Some of the creatures found around drainage dykes are extremely dangerous others merely life threatening. The swamp mules can often sense the danger with special glands found in one of their numerous nipples.

The inverted plateau of Flatlands has acted as a kind of evolutionary segregation zone and subsequently many of the Hooomans that have migrated into the district over the last few years have been puzzled and alarmed by the animals of Flatlands.

Winsti 13rd Munch

Nigelle had more press interviews this mawnin. He held them in our garden near Barry's grave, it was quite poignant really. As Nigelle stood on the mound that was Barry's head he addressed the press, holding a pint of Badgerspizzle and a cigarette whilst grinning inanely. He maintained that Flatlands was paying the UK of Great Britain 350 tonnes of root crops each week just to remain in the UK. Of course this was absolute garbage but to my amazement the press were busy scribbling away the quotes without questioning where Nigelle got this ridiculous figure from.

There was nothing for it but I had to intervene.
"Erm … can you substantiate any of these figures that you're giving us Today Mr F`Rage" I blurted.
"Well yes of course I can, I don't make things up to suit my argument" he said "that's the kind of thing that immigrants do quite frankly".

I looked around and to my amazement not a single derisory comment or question was posed by the gathered press. Just fevered scribbling, fantastic I thought. They are going to quote every word. I was just about to pose another question which would lead to more insane responses but Nigelle beat me to it.

"If we didn't send this 350 tonnes of root crops to the UK each week we could give it to our hospital in ropey town for the making of lovely broth. We could give it to our people in Chumpton, Chatterby and surrounding satellite villages … quite frankly" he continued. Again, nothing from the local journalists. Some were even nodding as they wrote their version of what was being said. "Finally I would just like to add that … quite frankly … if we manage to vote for our independence from the UK then we can finally take control of our borders and keep the Hooomans from flooding into our beautiful, slightly below sea level and very flat district. These rapists, murderers and terrorists can stay within the UK where they belong. I say again, I will build a wall around Flatland District … and the UK will pay for it. We can make Flatlands great again".

Nigelle stepped back off the mound of Barry's head with his hands clasped in front of him grinning inanely again and nodding his head as if people were applauding his rant. The only sound that could be heard was the sound of pencils busily scribbling on note paper. I stood, almost shell shocked at the insanity that was just uttered from the leader of the Flexit campaign. This was perfect. A great day.

Thrisdee 14st Munch

This mawnin I gave the ladies there sleepy drink and Nina prepared the kitchen for surgery. The previous noyght I had prepared the ladies implants by mixing the organic 'jugfiller compound' for the 'tittysac bags' (*hopefully not blinding you with doctoring language*) which basically means I filled four Happy Pauper sandwich bags with my special mud and sand mix.

When doing my toe counting duties at Ropey hospital I had heard from some of the nurses there, that lots of wounds were being closed up with staples so this is how I intend to close the boobywounds whilst doing the breast augmentation procedure. I had acquired the stapler from Mayor Devilman's office when nobody was looking as I thought it might come in handy for when I build my time machine but now it was going to have a secondary use.

My first patient was Pocahontas. I made two incisions where I thought the bottom of the breasties was going to be with a bread knife and began stuffing the tittysacs into the fleshy pockets I had created. I stapled the boobywounds up with the stapler and began to manipulate the breasties around. Once my winky went hard I knew I had achieved surgical perfection. I had a quick 1 minute 15 second mastybayshun and repeated the procedure for Cinderella. My doctoring work was superb and after a few days recuperation the girls would be ready to entice and fulfil all the carnal desires that PC Jack Wormer and Finbar Knuckleshuffla could possibly dream of.

Frydims 15nd Munch

What a crazy week it's been, looking forward to a bit R&R at the Peppermint Hippo tonoyght.

FLATLAND DISTRICT WEEKLY NEWS

Frydims noyghts is Fetish noyghts at Peppermint Hippo (Chumptons premier lap dancing/adult entertainment emporium) so bring a bottle, domestic pet or farm stock creatures and indulge in your darkest desires.
Ladies (or men dressed as ladies) get in free but a surcharge may be applied for any animals bought into the club to assist in cleaning bills and veterinary fees.

Wellington boots are advised and a poor sense of smell is very much a positive. A selection of "special creams" are available at the bar and private dance booths can be adapted for members should privacy be required for those more 'intimate moments'.

SatD 16th Munch

The Flatlands Weekly News landed on my floor this mawnin with a big front page spread with Nigelle F`Rage plastered all over it. His frog like grinning mug was hardly what I wanted to see first thing this mawnin, especially after the drink filled noyght we had at fetish noyght over at the Hippo. The picture may have been annoying but the story wasn't. it quoted him literally word for word, which is unusual for any newspaper but particularly for a Flatland newspaper as often the journalists forget what was said (*sometimes what the actual story was about*).

Nigelle was portrayed as the nutter he was. The plan was coming together. Hopefully by 23th Jism I can put all this behind me and we can continue as normal and carry on being part of the UK, trading and reaping the benefits of being part of the great realm.

Sunty 17nd Munch

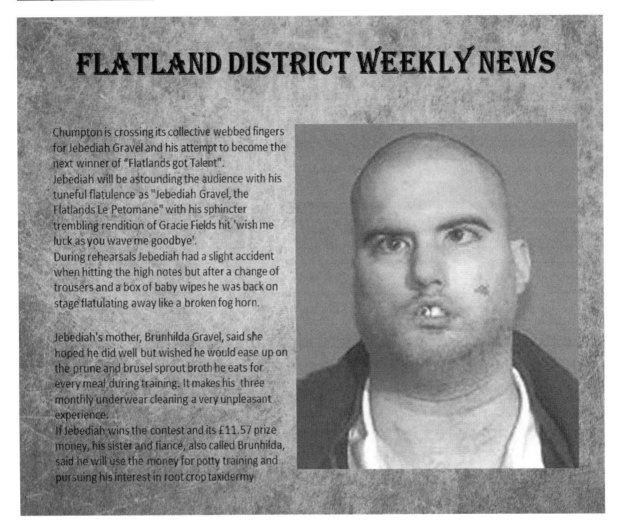

FLATLAND DISTRICT WEEKLY NEWS

Chumpton is crossing its collective webbed fingers for Jebediah Gravel and his attempt to become the next winner of "Flatlands got Talent".
Jebediah will be astounding the audience with his tuneful flatulence as "Jebediah Gravel, the Flatlands Le Petomane" with his sphincter trembling rendition of Gracie Fields hit 'wish me luck as you wave me goodbye'.
During rehearsals Jebediah had a slight accident when hitting the high notes but after a change of trousers and a box of baby wipes he was back on stage flatulating away like a broken fog horn.

Jebediah's mother, Brunhilda Gravel, said she hoped he did well but wished he would ease up on the prune and brusel sprout broth he eats for every meal during training. It makes his three monthly underwear cleaning a very unpleasant experience.
If Jebediah wins the contest and its £11.57 prize money, his sister and fiancé, also called Brunhilda, said he will use the money for potty training and pursuing his interest in root crop taxidermy

Sunty is traditionally the noyght we stay in and watch various talent shows and reality competitions. Currently running is my personal favourite Flatlands Got Talent. Because of my awful affliction I will always lean towards preferring the many flatulence based acts but Jeb Gravel is a cut above the rest. If only I could control my farting with such skill I could see a new hobby/career for me but my anal seepage also had a negative effect on my even attempting this.

Moondee 18th Munch

Today the Mayor appeared on Flatland TV on the Firsloyght program called Firsloyght

Flatlands today. It's TV for people to watch when having their Beetabix or Beetflakes and carrot and potato smoothies. David Devilman was interviewed by Flatlands presenting legend and news anchor Hillbilly Billy Hill who was noted for his unusual skin complaints and persistent dribbling. The Mayor was asked a few questions about his forthcoming campaign and he duly responded with reasonable answers. He informed the watching public that for us to continue trading with the UK we needed to allow the Hooomans to come and live in Flatlands. It was good for trade and it was good for improving the gene pool. Put quite simply, the more Hooomans we had in Flatlands the fewer fingers our children would have. All was going nicely and then right at the end was his killer blow. My heart leapt as Mayor Devilman declared he thought it would be a good idea to have a head to head debate between himself and Nigelle F`Rage. This would be the final nail in the coffin of the Flexit campaign. Genius.

Toosdi 19lbs Munch

Nina has been tending to the ladies needs since the increasing of the breasties operation (*or breast augmentation procedure as it's also known in doctoring circles*) and she was doing a sterling job. The ladies were causing quite a stir in the village and their absence would be noticed. The quicker the healing process the better so I made a special healing cream out of concentrated Swans tears, clock parts, a small melted rubber washer from a domestic electrical appliance … and also a small amount of sex wee I had left over in a milk bottle after doing some mastybayshun this mawnin. I have smeared the special cream all over ladies boobywounds and before you know it they'll be out and about socialising willy nilly. Not sure who willy nilly is but I didn't start any fires today and stayed clothed nearly all day.

Winsti 20st Munch

This mawnin I spent with Nina. With all the hullaballoo that's been going on lately we have only been able to spend 11-15 hours a day with each other. We had sex two and a half times and after firsdocky we watched a few auditions for the Peppermint Hippo "Open Pole Noyght", one of my new initiatives I was thinking about. It would help bring on new talent and bring off new customers. A win/win in anyone's book.

Thrisdee 21ˢᵗ Munch

Well dearest diary, I'm back to Ropey Town Hospital to do a bit of serious toe counting this mawnin. I have access to the Hospital compoota and when nobody was looking I decided to do a bit of research to help the Mayor in his campaign with some facts and figures. In his interview the other mawnin on Firsloyght TV with Hillbilly Billy Hill he mentioned about the positive effect that the Hoooman immigration has had on trade and the gene pool. On my way into work this mawnin I wondered if there were any statistics to back this up. The Hoomans have been migrating from the places like Peterborough and beyond for a quieter, more rural and peaceful way of life. For decades now they have been mingling with the indigenous folk of Flatlands and quite a few inter-racial relationships, even marriages have happened. My investigations using the Hospital Compoota showed that there are more and more babies being born with equal numbers of fingers and toes. Some with as few as 6-7 toes or fingers on each limb. Several babies had been born in the last three years with 5 fingers on each hand and 5 toes on each foot. This is generally considered to be the norm outside of Flatland District and also proof that the influx of the Hoooman immigrants, with their fancy sex wee, has reduced the toe count. The Hooomans TV programs and different talking sounds were also proof how we were evolving as a District, evolving for the better.

Frydims 22st Munch

Here is an advertisement for my friend's, Lesley and Lesley Lesleyson's new shop called Guns N Parrots, perfect if you need a gun or a parrot. I have pointed out to lots of my chums on fenbook that Chumptons gun owning laws are some of the strictest in Flatlands. You're not allowed to carry them about after Firsloyght and people under the age of 7 years old are not even allowed them at all. There are very similar laws regarding the owning of Parrots too, however this tends to get overlooked by Flatlands Police Brigade as there are fewer Parrot related deaths each year than guns. In fact I think there were only 3 parrot related deaths last year, a dramatic reduction from previous years.

There was absolute furore late last year when it was suggested that anyone wishing to own a parrot had to have a five day cooling off period as well as background checks to ensure that the person wishing to own the parrot was mentally stable enough to own, look after and maintain the beautiful colourful birdies. That was unless they wanted them for eating, then they could have them straight away.

Some residents from Flatlands that were already parrot owners said you can take my parrot when you prize it from my numerically excessive dead fingers. Knowing as I do PC Wormer and his band of merry policers I don't think this would be an issue to them.

Chumpton-by-Kamberly Informer

GUNS 'N PARROTS of Chumpton

Need a parrot? need a high calibre weapon?
Then look no further than **GUNS 'N PARROTS** of Chumpton. We can cater for ALL of your gun and parrot requirements.
Not just parrots either, we can provide access to many more birds of paradise, birds of prey and even some species previously believed to be extinct.
Whether looking for a family pet, a change from chicken at Sunday lunch or a tasty snack *WE CAN HELP.*
Once you have selected your parrot you may be looking for something to kill it with, *WE CAN HELP.*
We stock a wide range of rifles and handguns perfect for despatching your recently purchased parrot.
If you love parrots or you love guns then come to **GUNS 'N PARROTS** of Chumpton.

Advertisement

SatD 23st Munch

Most of the day has been spent in my campaign headquarters (*loft*) collating the information I gleaned from the Hospital Compooota the day before the other one. It was becoming abundantly clear that the migration of Hooomans was a good thing and that improving the local DNA structure was only ever going to be a good thing. It would prove that building a great big wall around Flatland District was not only expensive and unnecessary but actually harmful to our development.

Sunty 24st Munch

I have been quite restless today. Nina has the ladies to look after and Nigelle is out in the garden again doing interviews with the Chumpton Monthly Informer and I was a bit bored.

Digby Klakavalve and his Ferrets of Fire are on over the Club tonoyght so I shall have a wander across for some first class rodent stunts and erotic dance entertainment. What could go wrong?

Moondee 25nd Munch

Disaster has beset me. It is as though I'm not destined to own the club of my dreams. It's as though as soon as one problem at the club has been solved another one comes crashing through. Today dear diary, I am almost inconsolable with grief. Today I feel I have nothing, nothing to offer anymore.

Last noyght my wonderful Peppermint Hippo caught fire. The fire took hold and has gutted the building. The Chumpton Monastic Fire Brigade were on the scene within three hours but even with that kind of lightening quick response nothing could be done.

Early indications are that one of Digby Klakavalve's Ferrets of Fire escaped whilst ignited and set the building alight. Because of all the lubricants stored at the Hippo it went up like a tinder box. I now appreciate why I myself shouldn't start fires as they are not things of sparkly beauty and hypnotic sizzling wonderment, but actually forces of destruction and sadness to those I have fired. All I can say to the places, people and swans I have set fire to in the past is I am so terribly sorry. I have nothing else I want to write in this diary as I am too emotionally distraught. It is all I can do to record this event in this book. I will go to bed now, a broken man, to sleep, if I can. I may do a bit of mastybayshun first though.

Toosdi 26nd Munch

The Chumpton Monastic Fire Brigade this mawnin confirmed it was the Ferret of Fire that burned my beloved Peppermint Hippo to a crisp. The good news is that it's structurally sound and can be refurbished. The bad news is that it's not covered by the insurance. I foolishly opted out of the 'fire by burning rodents' clause when I completed the online application form to save a bit of money.

Unfortunately this wasn't the first time that small, ignited creatures had caused fire damage at the Hippo. In fact, when I went through the clubs old log books it had occurred on no less than fifteen separate occasions in the last decades. All of these occasions involved Digby Klakavalve and various incendiaried animals.

I think if I ever get The Peppermint Hippo up and running again then I will need to stop Digby Klakavalve turning up and performing stunts with ignited creatures. A sad day but now I need to go and think how I can make some money to save my wonderful pole/lap dancing emporium. And I need to do it quickly before all my custom starts going to Chatterby, and to our arch rivals The Klunge Klub.

Needless to say … no fires today!

Winsti 27th Munch

The last day of the month and a noyght contemplating how I will get the money together to save the club. I was at a loss all day. I had very little sleep the previous noyght.

Nina was out with the ladies and re-introducing them into Chumpton-by-Kumberly's polite society now they had breasties. I took some of my frustration out on Nigelle F`Rage with Jack's truncheon (*careful to avoid the face now he was appearing on magazines and in papers*). But even hitting a fascist with a truncheon wasn't making me feel any better. It wasn't helping me arrive at a solution.

Just after Daaymiddlin there was a knock at the door. It was Zachariah Katkiller the Chumpton postal service person with a parcel for me to sign. It was some weapons grade Plutonium I had purchased from fenBay weeks ago to build my time machine to look for Edith's cat, Sprinkles …

… to build my time machine … **BINGO**

That was it. I would simply finish building my time machine and go back to the time before Digby Klakavalve was at the club and stop him from performing by beating him with Jack's truncheon or setting him on fire … no, no I won't set him on fire.

When Nina arrived home with the ladies she could tell by my mood and general demeanour that something had happened to cheer me up. When I told her of my plan, to my huge disappointment she was less than enthusiastic. This took the wind out of my sails a bit, she said that inventing a time machine is very hard, and although she had faith in me the fruition of such a massive leap in world technology might be several months away, and we didn't have several months. She also pointed out to me my referendum obligations too.

Nina then suggested that perhaps I could do lots and lots of other, easier inventions and business plans to generate quick money instead. Nina had re-inflated my sails fully again now. I was very, very excited now. I went to the toilet for a poo and also did a quick mastybayshun and set about getting some ideas down on paper. But not the paper I had just wiped my botty and winky on. That paper had to be thrown away … Nina insisted on it.

I had several ideas to be getting on with and more importantly I had the tools and bits to build them with. I had my shed at the bottom of my garden that was already called my inventing shed so I didn't even have to rename my shed, what a stroke of luck. Nina was going to be my head of marketing and, I'd imagine, before you know it I would have all the money required to refurbish Peppermint Hippo.

CHAPTER FOUR

THE MOTHER OF ALL INVENTION IS NECESSITY

AVON 1896

Thrisdee 1st Avon 1896

fenbook   Surch for peeeple and othur things tooooo   Q   Morton   Hoome   Foind frends

I am proud to show and announce my latest invention here on Fenbook to all my FB buddies.

It's called the J6 and is designed to extract tears from Flatland Racing Swans captured by myself and other members of the Flatland Swan Fanciers Association.

Concentrated Swans tears are used in many household appliances locally and can also be distilled to produce a popular Fenland alcoholic beverage so potent that it has no name ... a bit like Gin in that respect.

My new invention will automate the process which originally involved squeezing Swans heads until they cried and mopping the tears up with a sponge. As you can imagine although great fun, this was very labour intensive and would drive the cost up.

The J6 will hopefully increase productivity and reduce overheads making this product cheaper.

Originally the J6 was one of my early attempts at creating a time travelling machine but when I realised that time travel was quite specialised and some of the components for my time traveller had not yet been invented I felt this may become problematic. I therefore adjusted the machine to simply make Swans cry in an automated fashion.

I am hoping to go into mass production of the J6 Swan Milker and take concentrated Swan tear production into the next centuries.

The J6

Today was a busy day designing stuff. I wrote plenty of sums and inspirational ideas to start my money making ventures. I popped into Ropey Town Hospital and did a quick bit of toe counting before borrowing their Compooota to do some equations. I have completed several designs and actually built my first invention today called 'The J6'. The J6 is a fantastic new Swans tear extractor device which has been designed on commission by the Flatland Swan Fanciers Association. I personally use concentrated swans tears for many of my inventions so considered it prudent to invent this first prior to other contraptions that may be require some Swan tearage. I have posted it on Fenbook to advertise my inventions and show off a bit.

Frydims 2st Avon

I am proud to announce that I have almost completed my very own Hadron Collider. My fantastic machine (pictured here) that I have made has taken me almost an entire day to construct and is a compact version of the Large Hadron Collider that has been built abroad somewhere. I will let CERN discover the existence of dark matter as I am hoping to discover some grey matter in the Flatland district.

I am also hoping to find the elusive Biggs Hoson (the Dog particle) which will help explain the Big Banger (an enormous ancient sausage believed to hold the genetic structure of all Flatland creatures and inhabitants).

All I have left to do is make it work some how. I am planning on making sub atomic particles whizz around very very fastley at 186 miles per hour, or the speed of thought if you a scientist/inventor like me. These particles will crash into each other and create a tiny black hole.

Hopefully my Small Hadron Collider will not trigger the end of the universe but if all known matter does collapse in on itself I would like to take this opportunity to say sorry.

Fingers crossed

Today I have upped the ante a bit. Yisdee I completed a bit of toe counting and used the Hospitals Compooota. I read about something called the Large Hadron Collider in an abroad country by a company called CERN. I have decided to make a more compact, travel version.

SatD 3st Avon

The ladies have been helping Nina with some publicity photos for Nigelle's Flexit campaign. I did some stretching exercises in the garden and tried incorporating some of my Kung Fu moves into my interpretive dancing. Unfortunately I experienced a small amount of anal seepage. The ladies became very upset when Nigelle started shouting at them (*the usual thing about immigrants*) so I decided to calm everybody down and made us all a nice carrot and turnipcolladas from some old root crops I had knocking about in a small pile in the garden. Pretty quickly everyone had considerable anal seepage. Poor old Pocahontas had so much anal seepage her vagina dropped off again. This time I re-affixed her tuppence with Selotape, sooperdooper gloo, stitches and some left over staples from the breast augmentation surgery I had done a few weeks ago. I'd say in my professional opinion as a doctor that bugger's going nowhere now. Even PC Jack Wormer pudgy, brutal fingers won't pull that off. ☺

Sunty 4st Avon

fenbook Surch for peeeple and othur things tooooo   Morton Hoome   Foind frends

My latest invention is this wonderful machine I call the "Flatulator".
It converts overnight under-duvet flatulence into warm air ideal for ladies to dry their hair with, in the ongoing quest to make themselves look beautiful and sexually available for their husbands.
Of course gents beware, although it may make your lady look a hundred dollars you might want to give romantically sniffing her locks a miss for an hour or two after using the "Flatulator".

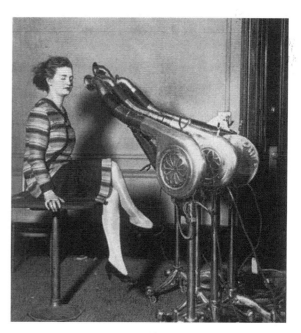

THE FLATULATOR

Today's marvellous invention has already raised money from several interested parties and Mason Dicksyline adventures in hair, Chumptons very own Vidal Baboon. A good, financially lucrative day.

Moondee 5th Avon

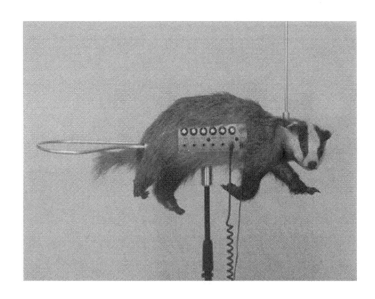

Finally I have managed to incorporate the best things in the world. I have invented the worlds first Badger/CB Radio which is part solid state electronics, part nocturnal burrow dwelling wildlife.

Want a CB radio, want a Bagder, why not have both with my Badger CB ..... come back good buddy

You're welcome

My artistic bent is shining through like an incredibly shiny thing holding a torch ... on a very murky day. I am lucky enough to know the whereabouts of a Badgers set nearby. I have lured one into a cage with some Beetabix firsdocky cereal and humanely despatched it to the next life with a shovel. I then removed some its internal organs to make way for this wondrous incarnation. I have already sold it to the Flatlands Wildlife Preservation Society so they can keep in touch with each other when they are out and about preserving wildlife. Obviously they'll need more than one so I shall be returning to the secret location (*at the yon end of Fen drove fen next to the brook by the stile just outside Chumpton*) to acquire some more Badgers. I am delighted with my quick sell to the Society but I really need something more, something to really take off. I had a full 9 minutes 3 secunds mastybayshun to try and help me concentrate and think of a block busting idea. It didn't work but I had a great mastybayshun and thought about Nina and also Jemimah whilst I was shuddering (*or ejaculating as us doctors call it*). As the

Chumpton Informer was thrust through my letterbox by one of the local disinterested 'yoofs' and flopped onto the floor a brainwave passed through my cranial bonce. A paper aimed at youngsters. Yet more ideas are bouncing around. Maybe a mooosicul paper … perhaps festivals or concerts to help put Chumpton on the map… and make lots of money. ☺

Toosdi 6lbs Avon

Today I had a day off inventing and started to get quotes in for the repair work to the club. I also went and visited Mayor Devilman and we discussed how badly the Flexit campaign was going. David was delighted at its shocking lack of direction. I was pleased when Cranshaw St.John joined the conversation and said he had drawn up a very extensive list of ridiculous lies and vile insinuations that Nigelle F`Rage can incorporate into his doctrine which could be easily disproved. Cranshaw has made certain that nobody but the dullest fuckwit could possibly conceive of voting for Flexit come referendum day. This was reassuring to me and Mayor Devilman as it meant I could continue with my invention and fund raising for the club reperation and the Mayor could carry on with lavishing plenty of attention on his beloved Growler. All we had to do was continue with our daily activities and let Nigelle scupper any chance that Flexit may have come referendum day on the 23th Jism.

Winsti 7nd Avon

Today I found some more of the parts of body left over from the gender reassignment surgery and a considerable amount of hair left over from trepanning. Not to mention a large wad of pubic hair from the times I have sneaked into Edith's bedroom to watch her sleep and shaved her tuppence for her. I would imagine this would be quite confusing for her thinking about it now. I have decided to start making wigs for dogs with alopecia. This is a specialised market but I'm sure it'll be quite lucrative. After my rather heady and complex collider invention yisdee I have decided to design something a bit more down to earth and closer to my heart. I therefore have introduced to the world my portable love dolls. They are ideal for the young executive on the go or the average Jeb root crop picker busy in the field and feeling fruity or just a bit saucy.

I have decided that my dog wig business was possibly a bit too ahead of it's time.
I am therefore diverting what little funds I have left into my latest start up company that is assured to interest many of my Fenbook chums. I have designed and built this fableearse 'portable love doll' for sexually active yet incredibly lonely people. The wheel mechanism is specially crafted to allow the owner of this wonderful love toy to move it from one location to another with ease whilst still maintaining congress.
One minute you can be making love in the Happy Pauper carpark whilst chatting to friends, the next minute you can up sticks and find yourself grinding away in somebody's garden.

The model shown in Fig1 is 'The Roaming Ram' but my movable sexual partners are also available as the Porta Pig, the Mobile Moo, the Shift-able Sheep and the Amorous Adventurous Aardvark.

Make up and underwear can also be made to measure at request.

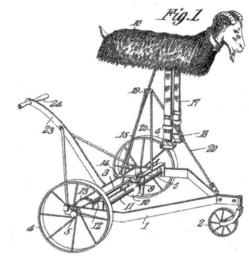

Fig 1

Thrisdee 8st Avon

I don't ask Fenbook friends for help but I have a request. I have recently started my own business providing balding dogs with wigs and toupees and I'm amazed to say that it is not doing as well as I had hoped. If anyone has a dog that requires a canine hairpiece to rebuild your pets confidence please contact me and I will of course give you my fullest attention.

I also have some goldfish bikini's left from my last business venture if anyone is interested.
The camels underwear will soon be available again once it has been returned by the police.

The dog wig business is struggling I have to say. I may have underestimated the financial viability of this particular part of my grand plan to get the money together to refurbish Peppermint Hippo. I shall have to ask my Fenbook chums to help out. I have also spent most of the aftynune completing a project I've been dabbling with, in and out of other projects, and it's a compact tortoise based time travelling machine, Hector the time travelling Tortoise. After a brief visit from Edith next door for some light sexual tension relief (*I was lonely, she was lonely … and asleep*) I confiscated Hector from her nephew and set about making him into a time traveller as a sort of experiment/prototype. I am pleased with the results so far. I set him for Frydims 4st Maayye drank a pint of Turnip Pochine and when I awoke he was gone. Could it be that I have actually invented an actual time travel machine?

Frydims 9lbs Avon

fenbook   Surch for peeeple and othur things tooooo   Q   Morton Hoome Foind frends

As if time travelling tortoises wasn't enough I have also had enough time to knock up this Child Walking Frame (or the CWF v1.0 as I shall call it for copyright purposes) this aftynune.

Ably modelled by young Jimmy Crakstroker from Fen fen at Yon end, we can see how by attaching the apparatus via some skull screws and head harness, young master Crakstroker can be placed into the contraption safely for up to 11.3 hours enabling his parents to do other more enjoyable things.

The CWF enables the child to move forwards or backwards and if going around corners is a must then the CWF is light enough so the child can lift the contraption to point it in the right direction. The rigid industrial strength skull screws will ensure the child will not be able to escape. Jimmy's parent's intend to try him in it overnight to realise it's full potential.

I am currently working on the CWF v1.1 which will incorporate an enclosed sound proof cab to help avoid inquiries from nosy neighbours/passers by.

That is all!

Following a quick shopping trip to the Happy Pauper I overheard two ladies talking about how bothersome it was to look after their offspring while enjoying alcoholic/hallucinogenic beverages. PING!!! That ping was me having an idea. This will be my last invention of the week.

SatD 10rd Avon

Did I say last invention of the week? What a lying cunt I am. I'm currently working on another one that is quickly edging me towards the target of Chumpton-by-Kumberly's premier Adult entertainment complex being re-opened for business and continue my dream. I had some spare parts left over from making the CWF v1.0 and began the CWF v1.1 but it quickly became apparent I was missing some parts to complete it to my professional standards and total satisfaction.

I have continued working on a childers dream catcher. It was abundantly clear I had enough bits to make another sturdy childers head harness but not enough parts to improve v1.0. Childers dreams are precious things … apparently. I intend to harness their little head thoughts and lovely dreams to sell and make money from. What better, purer way to become rich than making kids wear a special harness, screwing it to their heads and harvesting a few of their innocent and fluffy dreams.

Sunty 11nd Avon

This mawnin I popped down to borrow one of the Sunty school kids from the church to try and fit my dream harvester to. I found one but sadly heard that our very own Reverend Von Ringstinga is retiring. On a more positive note my dream harvester fitted an absolute treat. Utterly thrilled.

fenbook   Surch for peeeple and othur things teoooo   🔍   Morton   Hoome   Foind frends

I am delighted to announce that my week of invention is continuing with some considerable aplomb.

Pictured here is my Patented "Childers Dream Harvester". The dream harvester is simply placed onto a childers head and secured with skull screws and Selotape, plugged into the USB port of any compooota and you're ready to harvest your childers dreams.

It's plug and play capability makes it a market leader and possibly the most user friendly Childers Dream Harvester out there.

It will be available from most Q&B shops and Happy Pauper's in the area.

That is all

We now have the technology to harvest Childers dreams and sell them to large corporations for resale to adults unable to dream

Moondee 12th Avon

More news is starting to immerge about the sad plight of Reverend Cedric Von Ringstinga the top clergyman in the Chumpton/Chatterby district maybe even the Diocese of Flatlands itself. He was an unusual vicar in many respects but was undoubtedly the fulcrum of Chumpton-by-Kumberly's religious community.

From a personal point of view I have many fond memories of the 'Rev' as we called him at the Peppermint Hippo. He was always happy to help out and smear a special balm he made from stinging nettles and stagnant pond water all over us erotic dancers. He was the first person I ever trepanned. Well I say the first, he was the first who actually volunteered to be trepanned, he was up for anything was the Rev. Not sure who will replace someone who is essentially, irreplaceable. Who will take the call to be our new Reverend? Who will respond to become someone who is essentially, irresponsible? Here is what our local press had to say about this legend.

Chumpton-by-Kumberly Informer

CHUMPTON PARISH NEWS UPDATE

It is with a heavy heart and great sadness that the Chumpton Parish Council announce the early retirement of Reverend Cedric Von Ringstinga from his role as clergy to St.Jeremiah's Church, Chumpton-by-Kumberly, due to poor mental/physical health.

Reverend Von Ringstinga (or Madame Gigi as he was also known in and around Chumptons Dockland area) was noted for his colourful language, nudity, drunkenness and rambling sermons, notable as they were often spoken in 'tongues'. The Sunty sermons occasionally lasted minutes, sometimes several hours, though rarely given on a Sunty as per Christian tradition. Toosdi's were a favourite day for the church to be actually open but importantly, the Reverend always believed it was Sunty.

Cedric was probably most famed for demonstrating teachings from the Bible by swallowing live mice and rats whilst dancing to a tape recorder, playing music from the legendary Flatland pop music duo Jebwould ... a method that was never fully understood by his congregation or religious peers and regularly frightened the children of his congregation into a state of incontinence.

Reverend Von Ringstinga and Pickles the cat

It was Reverend Von Ringstinga's passion for spreading the good word through the medium of religious pest control that lead to his current health issues. He contracted Weil's disease from consuming the vermin as well as liver cirrhosis and several forms of venereal disease too, which he claims, he also got from the mice. Until a suitable replacement can be found Sunty service and all religious ceremonies at St. Jeremiah's Church will be conducted by Cedric's cat, Peter.

<u>Toosdi 13nd Avon</u>

This mawnin I spent mostly at the club, overseeing the start of the refurbishment work. So far the money from the inventions I have managed to sell means I have got enough dosh for about 50% of the work to be done, so more than enough to get started.

The local press were doing an article about Nigelle and his unpleasant ramblings. They had noticed some of the bruising and when the photographers took a light meter reading one of them noticed what appeared to be several holes in his skull. I didn't want the press to know I had trepanned Nigelle so I told them that the bruising to his body and the holes in his skull had happened after a plane crash, in which he was the only survivor. It wasn't until afterwards that I realised I had missed an opportunity. If I had stated that I had been trepanning him to release his demons it would've possibly made people think "demons? Hang on a minute". Never mind, there was no way that the Flatland population was going to be stupid enough to vote for such a bigoted Nazi fuckpig.

Winsti 14st Avon

Today I did some more inventing and building whilst the delightful Nina took the ladies to the WI hall to look at a demonstration of kitten strangling by Ropey Towns Official Kitten Strangler, Otto De Hamstringtinkler. Afterwards she had kindly agreed to take Nigelle to Radio Flatland for an interview about the forthcoming referendum and Flexits pledges. Cranshaw St.John had come through with these pledges and although, strictly speaking I should have been there with him to assist with any questions, but Nina kindly offered. And I needed to crack on with my inventing. Some of my inventions were really starting to take off. Literally, I blew a medium sized hole in the kitchen ceiling this aftynune as I was trying to assess the combustion rate of Swans against the explodabilty of rabbits. Rabbits won, they are both extremely combustible as well very explodable. My kitchen lost however. I think judging by the speed with which the money is coming in and the ease with which I can knock my inventions out this will be a hobby/career I must pursue even after the Hippo has been re-opened.

Nina, the ladies and Nigelle all came home at the crack of laasloyght and full of excitement too. The ladies had actually managed to strangle some kittens themselves and they loved every second of it. Nina went on to tell me that Nigelle had been on Flatland radio and it had been a huge success, they loved him with lots calls coming in and many saying they will vote for him at the referendum. It didn't register at first what Nina had just said but when it did I was mortified, my knees went weak so I sat on a chair. Clearly shaken. Nina asked "worts wrrrong, ay throoorght you'd be pleeeeeashed" she said in her wonderful Lithuanian accent. I was far from pleased, this was a disaster.

"how many people said they'd vote for Flexit"? I enquired
"I don't know 50 – 60 mayyybe" she replied.
I flinched at the thought, fuckity fuck … David Devilman will be livid if he finds out. As if on que the tefelone rang and it was the Mayor's chambers. They'd heard the radio program.

I managed to deflect some of the flack by saying that I had made some carrot and turnipcolladas the noyght before and I was suffering terribly from flatulence and more anal seepage. I heard the Mayor groan when I mentioned anal seepage and heard a rhythmical knocking sound which could only mean that Growler was getting stroked and tussled. We ended our conversation abruptly as Cranshaw St.John took over the tefelone duties and assured me that we must step up the campaign to discredit F`Rage and the Flexit campaign. He will start to galvanise the Mayor into action once he has finished stroking Growler and if Mayor Devilman makes elaborate promises he can't keep and Nigelle F`Rage can be made to look foolish and a liar then hopefully we can resolve this dreadful situation.

It was a fraught and rather tense tefelone call but it went some way to reducing my anxiety and fears. As soon as I put the tefelone down it rang again. I picked it up half expecting the Mayor's office again but no, it wasn't, and instead it was Scratch Mattingly wanting more Badger CBs for the Flatland Wildlife Preservation Society. He went on to say that if I run out of Badgers to use then he can tip me the wink to the whereabouts of more Badger sets in the vicinity. I collected my shovel and set off in search of more creatures to insert radio sets into. The money from this order alone was almost enough to pay for the restoration work to be completed at the Peppermint Hippo. This was going to be epic, I hadn't even started on my yoof paper for the yoof of Flatlands or my concerts, and I still had a mountain of inventions flying around my cranial bonce cavity ready to become real.

Thrisdee 15st Avon

This mawnin I contacted Scratch to let him know that when I got to the Badgers set late last noyght it had run out of big Badgers and only had the baby ones left. I thought they'd make really neat handsets, he heartily agreed and I was delighted that the 10 baby Badgers I had bought back with me weren't going to waste. As I had used a trowel to despatch them rather than the bloody great big shovel I used on mummy and daddy, a couple of the baby Badgers were just stunned and not as dead as I'd hoped. Luckily Nina's angels (*as I sometimes call the ladies*) were now fully trained kitten stranglers and jumped into action as soon as they noticed one of the baby Badgers was moving. It bought a tear to my eye as I watched my little Pocahontas and Cinderella squeeze the life from the baby Badgers. As the last gasp of existence drifted away from the smaller of the two baby Badgers Cinderella smiled and a considerable amount of dribble escaped from her mouth as she farted.

Frydims 16nd Avon

My order of baby Badger handset radio's for the Flatlands Wildlife Preservation Society was finished by daaymiddlin so I took them to Scratch Mattingly and he was astounded. He paid in full the agreed price and put a bit extra on top as an early delivery bonus. This was an unexpected but very welcome bonus which meant that I could pay the workmen in full now and get my club up and running within a few weeks.

SatD 17th Avon

This mawnin's post arrived and it contained detailed campaign structure for the Flexit referendum from Cranshaw St.John. At last it was no longer going to be left to chance and hopefully no more performances like last week's interview with Nigelle on Radio Flatland. The note was structured thusly:

1. Leaving the UK will free up the toll we pay the UK Governance people. This equates to 350 tonnes a week of root crops and root crop based products. We could distribute this 350 tonnes each week to the local hospital for use in root crop stews and unusual poultices for rare skin conditions and exotic sexually transmitted diseases.
2. Leaving the UK means we no longer have to allow unrestricted access to our delightful inverted plateau by the Hooomans from the UK and places even further away like "abroad". We can build a wall around the perimeter of the District and make the UK pay for it.
3. Leaving the UK means we no longer have to listen to the Hooomans speaking their strange and unusual words and having differences to the rest of us Flatland folk.
4. Leaving the UK means fewer of the Hooomans automobiles on our road systems; this can mean that there will be more room for tractoring root crops from one place to another.
5. Leaving the UK will mean we will be less likely to be invaded by aliens from another planet, this is because they'll find the Hooomans, by now quite rightly repatriated back to the UK, far more annoying than us.

6. Leaving the UK means we can return to our old ways again. The influx of immigrant Hooomans has affected the amount of loving 'Familee Toime' we have together.
7. Leaving the UK means we can be the masters of our own destiny and not be bullied by some faceless b'yourocrats in Lundun city/town.
8. Leaving the UK will give untold wealth and untold amounts of root crop expenditure allowances. Instead of giving root crops to Lundun we can give it to ourselves.
9. Leaving the UK means we can all have brand new tractors and safe in the knowledge that no aliens from out of space are going to come and take them away like the Hooomans might do.
10. Leaving the UK will 'Make Flatlands Great Again'.

All this utter nonsense can be easily dispelled as absolute lunacy. All I have to do is drill Nigelle to spout this garbage when we attend various functions and interviews throughout the remainder of the campaign and hopefully no more fuck ups such as last week's radio noyghtmare.

Sunty 18th Avon

Church didn't seem the same without the Rev giving it large in the pulpit, speaking in tongues, removing clothes, scaring the kids, eating live mice. Well God, I hope you're proud of yourself, you've shot yourself in the foot there God. You've lost one of your best preachers there. Although to be fair, if you have shot yourself in the foot it would probably heal pretty quickly because you're God.

This mawnins sermon was delivered by Pickles, the Rev's cat, and some argued it was more coherent and understandable than Cedric's sometimes confusing words of the Lord. Rumour has it that next week would see the announcement of a new clergyman. We very rarely went to the church to be perfectly honest but we thought it would be nice to take the ladies and introduce them to Chumptons flock of faithful. We also took Nigelle to try and stir a few of the congregation up but it soon became clear that, just like God, I had shot myself in the foot. Some were spellbound by Nigelle's startling appearance and even roused by his ridiculous, bigoted, fascist rambling were striking a chord with the faithful few of Flatlands. I guess if you actually believe in the existence of God then the inane gibberish from a half crazed Nazi dullwit like Nigelle F`Rage is easy to swallow in comparison. We won't be coming to church again for a while me thinks.

Moondee 19th Avon

Today I went over to see how the work was coming on at the club. The workmen assure me it'll be ready by the end of the month or first week of next month at the latest. This is partly because I sourced good local reputable builders but also because as part of the deal I offered them all a years free membership if they get the club ready on time. When I told them about the dogging club, the annual Klungefest, Floella Nipsy and I occasionally appearing together, the prostrate milking association, lady boxing, Frydims Fetish Noyght and all the other fantastic activities we have they seemed very keen to get the place back on its feet as soon as possible.

Nigelle spent most of the day learning his pledges, or 10 commandments as he calls them since his church visit yisdee. A good day today.

Toosdi 20rd Avon

With my wonderful success making stuff I shall continue with my inventing and entrepreneurial spirit and can see me amassing a small fortune and possibly buy out my rivals in Chatterby the 'Klunge Klub'.

The Klunge Klub does good business and I have danced there myself when work has been sparse for an erotic drag dancer, but it's rather down market in comparison to the Peppermint Hippo and is owned and run by the golden maned wonder man Pedro Mellowring. Pedro was noted for his long flowing locks and his taste for cheap bubbly carrot wine and even cheaper bubbly dance girls/men. I could really turn that place round.

All this procrastination about the Klunge Klub got me all reminiscful. I even dug out an old photo of me and wistfully posted it on Fenbook so I could get lots of likes, shares and lovely comments on my beautyfullness.

fenbook Surch for peeeple and othur things tooooo 🔍   Morton Hoome Foind frends 🔍

Memories of days gone by

Here I am back in the days when I was a skinny little pole dancer at the Klunge Klub in Chatterby.

It was a sharp learning curve and before I knew it I was topping the bill at Peppermint Hippo. Who knew then that only a few years later I would be a Trepanning/Cosmetic Surgeon par excellence`, an inventor or some considerable repute, an interpretive dance teacher, a Kung Fu expert, a local celebrity and a former erotic dance legend and now owner of The Peppermint Hippo. I am always learning new skills though, never let the grass grow under your feet I always say. I'm currently learning to be a ladies breast masseur/manipulator/implanter and hope to begin practicing and developing my own breast implant products very soon.

I look at this photo and reflect on what a rounded person I have become.

Winsti 21st Avon

fenbook Surch for peeeple and othur things tooooo 🔍   Morton Hoome Foind frends 🔍

Here is my latest invention modelled by the beautiful Pocahontas. It is a DT5000 fart inhibitor, specifically designed for the unfortunate souls who suffer from excessive flatulence.

If like me, you always seem to have unwanted attention when in restaurants or lap dancing clubs due to involuntary gaseous distention of the lower colon this contraption could be just the thing for you. No more nasty remarks or staring from uncouth members of the public, the DT5000 Fart Inhibitor will stop all unwanted attention when out and about.

The DT5000 Fart Inhibitor will be available for sale at Chumpton Happy Pauper and some less reputable branches of Q&B DIY stores, just in time for Christmas.

you're welcome

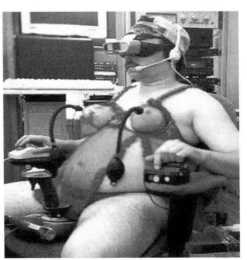

DT5000 Fart Inhibitor

Today has been back to the drawing board and more inventing. I got Pocahontas to model this for me this aftynune, it's my fart inhibitor machine and in the words of Ted Moult "it works an absolute fuckin treat" (*although this bit was cut out of his double glazing televisual advert*).

Thrisdee 22st Avon

Chumpton-by-Kumberly Informer

CHUMPTON PARISH UPDATE

Following last months sad news that Chumpton clergyman Cedric Von Ringstinga had to be retired from his role at St.Jeremiahs Church, due to very poor mental/physical health we are delighted to announce the appointment of the new Vicar of Chumpton.

will be officially taking over the position on Winsti 24rd Maayye. He learned about god at the University of Chatterby, a much revered seat of theological study. He will be talking a lot about god and other related god based subjects but has also agreed to continue with some Flatland spiritual traditions such as blessing the Flatland drainage system, Moon worship and burning witches. The new reverend assured the selection panel that his drinking is under control, he hasn't caused any of the recent spate of major fires in Flatlands District and that he fully intends to learn the English language at some point in the near future. He also expressed an interest in performing the occasional guest slot at Peppermint Hippo, I'm sure that the local people of Chumpton will welcome the reverend with open arms and legs.

The Reverend Adolph Horatio Ferdinand Globule

The Happy Pauper is pleased to sell my fart inhibitor as long as I stop the mastybayshun in the shop as it upsets other customers. I have to say the only people it really bothers are the Hoooman immigrants from the UK of Great Britain. Without wishing to sound too much like Nigelle F`Rage the immigrants definitely have a rather prudish outlook when it comes to mastybayting in shop queues. Shop queues are boring so what else are you supposed to do … just stand there and wait your turn? Some of the immigrants live in Flatland District but still emigrate every day to work in places like Peterborough or even Cambridge. Are you seriously telling me that people don't occasionally mastybate when waiting in line at a department store in Peterborough? Of course they do. Anyway I digress, the Happy Pauper chain are keen to stock the fart inhibitor as long as I can 'inhibit' my queue time mastybayshun. It's a deal.

Although not officially taking over the duties of local clergyman until next month the Diocese of Flatlands and Chumpton Parish are announcing their new man for the job. He looks like a very pious and holy man indeed.

Frydims 23st Avon

Nigelle has been learning his 10 commandments and has them firmly locked into his hole riddled bonce. He seems to have much better memory recall since Nina and I have cut out all the punishment beatings to the head with the truncheon. Also, since I have stopped trepanning him, he has become much more coherence with his speech now.

This is almost certainly due to the build-up of demons inside his head taking over his speech process. I will of course need to give him a very rigorous course of trepanning once the referendum is finished and we can go on with our daily lives happy in the knowledge that we are still very much part of the UK of Great Britain and enjoying all the benefits and trade agreements that go with it. My quest for making money continued today when I stumbled across some road kill on my way back from Ropey Town Hosptial. I also found some spare body parts knocking about at the hospital when I went delving into the skip looking for used bandages near the incinerator. Waste not want not I say. I got home feeling very artistic and with some bits I had left over from some of the various complex cosmetic surgery procedures I got to work being arty. Here are the fruits of my days labour. They are essentially "works of art" but can also be used as ornaments, pets or sex toys, depending on your personal inclinations or how lonely you are.

My ingenuity knows no bounds it seems, I have made a very life like sex doll with my surgical skills out of local road kill and the contents of my cosmetic surgery left over parts bin. Any of my Fenbook chums, let me know if you want a lend and I'll rinse it under the tap.

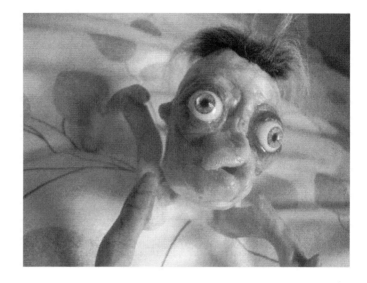

I have made good use of the parts of the bodies I have removed during some of my cosmetic surgery. Instead of just eating them I have made them into works of art. I still have plenty left over so anticipate lots of future orders from all my buddy's on Fenbook.

I quickly realised that a designer vagina wasn't Lawrence Llewelyn Bowen and was, in fact, a form of cosmetic surgery specifically to improve the aesthetics of a ladies tuppence. I soon cornered the market in and around the Chumpton area and became known as the "The Bush Master", although only by myself.

The remaining amounts of fleshy labia and pubis cuts make delightful works of art, perfect for any living room and happily grace your dinning room table and a great talking point during dinner parties.

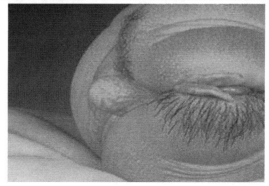

SatD 24st Avon

SatD is a busy day in Chumpton. Today sees the Chumpton-by-Kumberly annual Bring & Buy sale in the Peppermint Hippo's car park. It's only a shame that I couldn't have the club open to welcome one and all but it'll be a lovely day anyway with local legend Spongebob Delfine practising his Pig Rodeo for the Flatland Games. It will also give me an opportunity to sell some of my inventions to the general public. Nigelle and Nina and the ladies are all on hand to help out. The ladies have been talked into doing a demonstration showing off their newly acquired skills in the art of strangling kittens to some of the local childers.

It was a lovely day ☺

Spongebob riding a pig

Last years reigning champion Spongebob Delfine` already out practicing for the Pig Rodeo event in this summers Flatland Games.

Snapped practicing earlier today in the car park at Peppermint Hippo Spongebob said he had never been in better shape.

Pig rodeo is similar to cowboy rodeo as seen in Merica USA. The primary difference is that pig rodeo is much slower subsequently safer and considerably duller.

We wish him well.

Sunty 25nd Avon

I am beginning to agree with some of Nigelle F`Rage's mutterings about immigrants. Yisdee was a fableearse day at the annual Bring and Buy with a great turn out.

Some of the people present were immigrants from the place called Cambridge in the UK of Great Britain. They have officially complained to the RSPCA about Pocahontas's kitten strangling demonstration to the Childers saying it was awful and cruel. They went on to state it was not for the eyes of childers to see. Ridiculous nonsense, how are childers supposed to learn about the best ways to strangle kittens if not shown at local Bring & Buy sales? What are they supposed to do, leave them un-strangled and eat them alive? That hasn't been done for years. If the Hooomans don't like the cundreysoid ways then maybe they should go back to their Cambridge's and Peterborough's … I suppose the childers don't strangle kittens there do they, fucking immigrants … oh dear I am actually starting to sound like Nigelle F`Rage now. Oh cuntbubbles.

On a more positive note I sold several of my contraptions, most notably I took several orders for the CWF v1.0 and a few for the J6 swans tear extractor machine. I have made a considerable surplus of wealth.

Moondee 26lbs Avon

Nina and I have been constructing more of our excess flesh ornaments and road kill sex dolls today. The ladies have been having a day of leisure drinking parsnip smoothies and soaking up the ultra violet rays as today was one of the very rare days when there was some blue skies to look at.

Nigelle was out on the campaign trail talking about the 10 commandments of Flexit at the Ropey Old Folks Home for the Sexually Frustrated. He was shadowed by someone from Mayor Devilman's office called St.John (*pronounced 'Sinjun'*) Cranshaw; he was Cranshaw St.John's (*pronounced Saint John*) house buddy/sex friend. It was his job to report back to the Mayor concerning the state of the Flexit campaign. When Nigelle had returned from Ropey he was dropped off in one of the councils official cars by St.John Cranshaw. He came in for a minute to tell me how it went. It was clear that St.John had been drinking Badgerspizzle beer and by the looks of it quite heavily with Nigelle, probably in the Jolly Sphincter. What St.John kind of managed to tell me was that Nigelle had recruited another couple of people to help him campaign. I would meet them at a later date but apparently one was called Micky Dove, and by all accounts was even more unlikeable than Nigelle and even more untrustworthy. I found this difficult to believe but I guess I'll find out when I eventually get to meet him.

Nina and I had sex twice today, once whilst she was awake and once whilst not. Now things had settled down a bit we could maybe look to start going out a bit more often as a couple instead of one having to look after the ladies of Nigelle. I mentioned this to Nina and she agreed it was a good idea. I will arrange something special for either tomorrow or the day after then. She was happy as she drifted off to sleep, I was happy as I sexed her whilst she was dreaming.

Toosdi 27th Avon

Unfortunately, our plans of a noyght out together tonoyght were put on hold. Nina was a bit disappointed but she was okay about it when I told her that we'd be definitely be out and about tomorrow noyght as I had asked PC Jack Wormer, Pocahontas's boyfriend, to come and look after the girls and Nigelle tomorrow noyght while Nina and I spend a noyght fine dining with none other than my nearby neighbour and local celebrity chef Nigella Cokesnorter. The reason we couldn't go out tonoyght was because the Mayor contacted me and requested my presence at his chambers for a meeting. He sent the message via courier crow so it was a bit garbled as it would appear the crow carrying the message was coming towards the end of its working life. A considerable amount of bird poo had blotted out a chunk of the message but it said at the end to wear my latex school girl outfit. This gave me a pretty good idea of the kind of meeting it was going to be and I wasn't wrong. I danced to Jebwould's version of Ferry Across the Mersey whilst the Mayor vigorously, predictably stroked Growler. As the Mayor was wiping Growlers saliva off his hand he mentioned he would be going on Flatland TV in a series of live debates with Nigelle. He was convinced that this was going to be stroll in the park, so to speak, I agreed but warned him that although Nigelle was a fascist nutter he did know all the 10 commandments that Cranshaw sent him, off by heart. I told David to make sure he had his arguments sorted prior to going on TV as I left. Not sure he heard me as he was busily getting some of Growlers saliva off his tie. I'm not sure how it got all the way up there but I'm sure I heard his trusty dog shake his head as I could hear his jowls slapping.

Winsti 28st Avon

What a fantastic noyght that was. Nina and I went to Nigella's house just around the corner for some wonderful cuisine. Jack was looking after the house whilst we were out on the understanding he could help himself to food, drink and Pocahontas's willingness to assist the Police in their enquiries as it were.

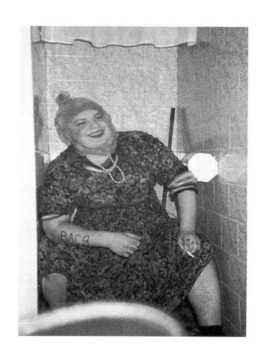

An evening with Nigella Cokesnorter

After an evenings locally made Badger and Muntjack curry with ingredients purchased from Chumpton Happy Pauper, one of my neighbours, creator of the curry and Flatland celebrity chef Nigella Cokesnorter was happy to pose whilst enjoying a good clear out. Nigella began opening her bowel at Sungomooncum and didn't finish until a full 2 hours later, excreting an eye watering 11lbs stool.

As you can see from the photo she was more than comfortable and even during some of the more difficult moments of the marathon bowel movement she remained positive and conscious.

On our return to our house we discovered that PC Wormer had indeed helped himself to our food, helped himself to our drink (*3 bottles of Parsnip and Beetroot sour mash*) and in his drunken stupor helped himself to Pocahontas and Cinderella's affections and, it would seem, a rather ashamed looking Nigelle F`Rage too. Nigelle was cowering in the corner with his trousers and pants at half-mast, with what looked like Growlers saliva in his wig/hair. Nigelle looked at me with a tear welling in his eye and asked if he could "have a shower please?".

My heart broke, for the first time I had actually felt sorry for the bigoted halfwit so I led him upstairs and let him have a shower. I even let him use my special potato shampoo,

I'm such a softie☺. It reminded me of the way I felt sometimes after returning from the Mayor's chambers. Jack swigged the remainder of the 3rd and last bottle of Parsnip and Beetroot sour mash and staggered of to his Police car in and drove himself home to Ropey.

Thrisdee 29nd Avon

Today has been a day of profuse apologies from Jack and being nice to Nigelle. Jack took Nigelle out for a ride in his Police Brigade car, which after a lot of persuading to get him to go, Nigelle went and came back all smiles. The ladies were a lot more attentive to PC Wormer, especially Cinderella, which was causing friction between them both. Nigelle is still a bit traumatised but the ladies are positively frothing.

Frydims 30st Avon

After a month of political intrigue dearest diary, amazing money making ventures (*to be continued, without a doubt*) and the ups and downs of a local entrepreneur, I was going to turn my attention today to something that had taken a back seat in my plans lately. It was time to bring it to the forefront once again. My passion for interpretive dance had been re-awoken this mawnin when I flicked onto a Hoooman channel on my TV set and saw some people called "Pans People". I was enthralled and enraptured, enraptured and enthralled, both at the same time if that is at all possible. Here were some attractive young ladies who were talking my kinda talk and walking my kinda walk … except they were dancing … not walking … or talking. The Chumpton School of Interpretive Dance was once again going to be an actual thing and not just an advert placed in the local paper a few months earlier I asked PC Jack Wormer of Ropey Town Police Brigade if he could help me by finding some people wanting lessons in interpretive dance. He readily agreed to devote as much time as possibly to this task. He could hardly do any otherwise given his rather boozy and rapey behaviour lately. His first port of call was the people who'd recently made complaints to the RSPCA about the ladies kitten strangling demonstration at the annual Bring & Buy. They all agreed to come but some of them struggled with some of the moves as they had oddly fallen down some steps … four of them … all at once. The least bruisey one, called Gary, was going to be my model.

Chumpton School of Interpretive Dance

I am pleased to announce that I am now taking bookings once more for my very own Chumpton School of Interpretive Dance.

Any of my Fenbook chums wish to discover the joy of experimental music and movement and free expression through the medium of dance then I will do mates rates for a limited time only.

Below you can see my special dance outfit being modelled by a reasonably terrified Hoooman. I am sure you will all agree there could be no finer sight than seeing an expert, such as myself, engaging in my interpretive dance workshop in my fancy leotard.

So come and join me at the Chumpton-by-Kumberly School of Interpretive Dance

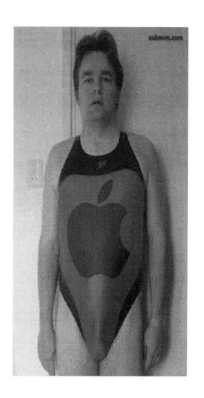

Here is how I announced my wonderful new venture in self-expression. I thanked Jack for his help and smiled his Policeman's smile and said "if any of these buggers don't turn up without a fantastic excuse … you let me know" as he looked at the students one by one.

SatD 31th Avon

SatD is another industrious day. I now have the money in place to start my newspaper for the Yoof of Flatland District. It is going to be called New Mooosicul Expressions and it will feature many of the hip and happening mooosicul acts that the modern Yoof culture of Flatlands. Along the same theme, I am also looking into staging concerts at the WI hall and various fields around the region. There is a wealth of talent just waiting to be discovered. My interpretive dance went well today. I popped into Chumpton library on my way home and used there compooota to look into how best to get the above ventures up and running. When I got indoors Nina informed me that the Mayor had been on the tefelone wanting a meeting at his chambers tomorrow mawnin to discuss the TV debates for the referendum.

"okay, will do" I said cheerily,
"oh … and caaan you wear the shhhkoool guurl outfeet again" Nina continued.
Oh, another one of those meetings again.

Sunty 32th Avon

It was barely past firsloyght as I plugged in my music player. I was going to dance to Gary Glitter's 'Wanna be in my Gang'. As I waited for the intro I wondered what ever happened to Gary Glitter. He played at Ropey Town Hall a few times some years ago but not a peep out of him these days. As the song started "Come on, Come on …" I stretched forward and wiggled my bottom. I heard Growler groan and as turned round I was confronted by Mayor Devilman slumped in his office chair with Growlers spittle all over his tummy.

"Do you want me to carry on dancing"? I asked.
"No … no I couldn't manage any more …. Erm … stroking, I mean Growler has had enough petting this mawnin" he replied.
"How's your club coming on"? He continued.
"Pretty good actually, it should be opening next week of maybe the week after"
"How's our mutual friend getting on with his Flexit campaign" … "do you have everything you need to make me the victor?" he went on.
"Yes … yes although I could do with access to a compooota, I use the Hospitals or the Library currently" I said. Then the Mayor amazed me with his response to my enquiry. "Are you in all day tomorrow?" he asked, "Yes" I replied. "Good, in that case I shall get one put into your house". I couldn't believe my ears; I was going to get my very own compooota. Wow. I told Nina and she was ecstatic.
This was a very, very good day.

Moondee 33th Avon

First thing today there was the great news that the Peppermint Hippo was going to have its refurbishment completed by Thrisdee, Frydims at the latest. This means I can open my club for business again this coming SatD

Then just after daaymiddlin there was another knock at the door and there stood Cranshaw St.John with his living partner and fellow Mayoral employee St.John Cranshaw holding the boxes that contained my compooota. I got them to put it in my living room and connect it to my tefelone line. They switched it on and hey presto I was connected the FWW … the Flatland Wide Web. Now I could do my Fenbook page in my own living room, go on fenBay in my own living room; look at pictures of ladies breasties and tuppences for some mastybayshun in my own living room. I would hardly ever have to leave the house ever again. I switched it on and tried out the mastybayshun mode, it worked perfectly. No more upsetting the Chumpton librarians any more.

Here it is in all its glory hole.

The day then got a little bit more fantastic when Jack came round to let me know that one of the students he had brutalised into attending my interpretive dance school was from a place known only as 'Newport Pagnell' and new somebody in Lundun who worked for the BBC. At Jack's insistence he had got me an audition to appear on Hoooman TV as an interpreter for hoooman people with no ears or something. They use something called sign language but Jack reckons I could wang it with my interpretive dance skills.

I have nothing to lose. Whatever else, I will always have my dignity.

CHAPTER FIVE

WE'RE ON A ROAD TO NOWHERE

MAAYYE 1896

Toosdi 1th Maayye

This mawnin I got on the tefelone first thing and contacted the Ropey exchange to book an outside line for the UK of Great Britain to call the BBC of Lundun later on and arrange a visit. Just after daaymiddlin the tefelone rang and it was the operator informing me my call to Lundun was available. I dialled the number that Gary (*my model student with the contacts at the BBC had beaten out of him by our local PC*) had given me and I spoke to a gentleman called Bill Draper (*strange name*) who was in charge of the specialist services for the disabled hooomans. He went on to inform me that a vacancy had opened and they were looking to employ the services of someone that could inform people with hearing difficulties about current news events and also some work for one of their channels called CBeebies. The latter of these two channels, CBeebies, is aimed specifically at Hoooman childers that don't have root crops to play with, or couldn't even be bothered to play outside with sticks. What a great idea.

My call was completed and I had arranged to visit on Thrisdee of this week. I needed to get a wiggle on then, as I would need to learn something called BSL (*British Sign Language, using your hands to talk with, which is how Hoooman deaf people speak*). I would also need to arrange all my visa papers and travel arrangements to visit Lundun. Gary the dance student had very kindly agreed to drive me in his autocar all the way to Lundun and drive me back again. Once this was done PC Wormer would give him his daughter back. Of course, if I get the job and had to travel to and from Lundun regularly then I would have to make other arrangements and probably need to learn how to drive one of these autocars myself. It would be a tad unfair to keep kidnapping Gary's little girl in order to get me transported to Lundun.

Winsti 2th Maayye

This mawnin I went and exchanged some Davey's, some root crops and hens beaks for Hooomans money ready for my trip to Lundun. Word had already got around Chumpton about my journey tomorrow. It had turned me into even more of a local celebrity and now I was getting the notoriety of a globetrotting jet setter.

I did a short dance for the Mayor, after which he personally signed my visa to leave Flatlands and more importantly let me back in again, he advised me not to read the papers or watch the TV and wished me good luck. I had arranged for Gary to collect me at the clock tower just before firsloyght.

I popped over to the Peppermint Hippo to see how the work was coming on ready for the big opening and was thrilled to see it was just about finished. I used the time over at the club, on the new stage, to practice my moves for the audition. The workmen looked on in amazement, literally open mouthed at my interpretive dance/BSL moves. I am pleased to say that although I haven't actually learned any of the BSL needed for the job, I have however, managed to pull off several lunges without any flatulence or anal seepage. I will ensure that the only food I shall eat between now and the audition is sustenance that's not mouldy or unlikely to cause an upset tummy. I am so looking forward to tomorrow's journey as it will be my first time outside the District in years, and then only the occasional trip to Peterborough. Tomorrow would see me going to the great big city of Lundun within the UK of Great Britain. I have seen photographs and it looks really busy. I saw some pictures on my new compooota last noyght, in-between looking at ladies tuppences, and it looks huge … Lundun, not the ladies tuppences … although …

On a slightly sadder note a Grimbles Dyke Clunger has been spotted locally, it could be a wild one or somebodies pet. They are gentle creatures and often get mistaken for hairless bears so given a wide berth but my experience is they are perfectly fine, as long as you don't venture too close. If you remain beyond 1-2 miles away it is very unlikely that they'll attack.

FLATLAND DISTRICT WEEKLY NEWS

Chumpton-by-Kumberly LOST & FOUND

A Gimbles Dyke Clunger has been found between Upper drove fen and Yon End of bottom field last week on Toosdi 1th Maayye. Anyone wishing to claim the creature needs to contact Blodwella Fannibatter and arrange collection. If the animal hasn't been claimed soon it will be inhumanely destroyed.

On a different note the aforementioned Blodwella Fannibatter would like to announce the possibility of a BBQ some time in the very near future. Further details will be available on the Flatland Wide Web or by carrier crow as soon as a things have been finalised.

Thrisdee 3th Maayye

Dear Diary, I would ordinarily start an entry on a special day like today, by stating how early I got up, but the truth is I didn't actually go to bed because I was too excited. Jack came round with a photo of Gary's daughter and a lock of her curly blonde hair to give him to help keep him focused on today's driving task. I set off shortly after Jack left. I met Gary at the clock tower and showed him the photo of his daughter. Apparently she's called Emily, as Gary so dramatically told me when I showed him the picture. "Emily, Emily" he screamed, all teary faced. What a drama queen, honestly. I was kept in a petting zoo and the local headmaster of the primary school when I was her age, she'll be fine. Once Gary had calmed down we made our way to the Flatland District border control with my expert directions, after we left Flatlands we were in Gary's hands. I was surprised to see the patrol officers on the other side of the district border checkpoints. When I asked why one of the officers informed me it was to stop people from escaping from Flatlands. I was confused, surely it was the other way round, and surely their role was to stop people from illegally entering the district. Never mind, I'm sure it was just a slip of the tongue. Gary appeared bemused by it all.

As we drove towards Lundun I was amazed how many of the Hooomans had autocars too. And when we got into Lundun I discovered two things. Firstly, Lundun is actually called London by the locals and secondly everybody was looking at their hands. Gary told me they were all too busy on Facebook or twitter to notice what's going on in the world. Facebook, it seems, is the Hooomans equivalent of Fenbook (*which they have clearly stolen from Flatlands*) and they have it on their transportable tefelones called smart phones, which is why they stare at their hands. None of their smart phones have baby Badgers covers though, so they're not that smart. We're one up on the Londoners then. I arrived at the BBC with Gary and went to check into reception. The BBC had some amazingly beautiful ladies sat behind a desk. I mentioned I was here to audition for the BSL for News24 and CBeebies and lady gave me a badge to wear. She said she wished she knew how to sign for the deaf, I thought so did I.

Gary waited down in the lobby and I was escorted to the office by a young man called Darren. Darren's trousers seemed to be falling down around his bum. There's lots of lads whose trousers appeared to be around their bottoms, London was a very modern, metropolitan city but it could clearly do with a decent belt retailer. Darren was a very pleasant young man and was telling me all about someone called Zach, who was his "life partner" as we strolled through the labyrinth of corridors. I told Darren we had lots of people called Zach in our village and he smiled at me. Eventually we arrived at an office where the audition was going to take place.
"Here you go then" said Darren cheerily.
"Will you be here when I get out"? I asked
"Nooooo" Darren replied, "No I'm wwayyy tooo busy sweet cheeks, you'll be fine" and he gave me a wink. I was a tad concerned that I wasn't going to be able to find my way back to Gary in this massive building.

On entering the office I was greeted by Bill Draper and a few others called 'the panel'. I asked him if there was somewhere I could get changed into my deaf signing outfit. Bill looked very confused but they agreed to leave the office for a few minutes whilst I put it on. When they all returned I was fully changed into my deaf signing clobber that I had made especially for the interview. I could tell by the look on everyone's faces that they were amazed at all the effort I had gone to. I then told the panel that I was going to recite part of a bicycle repair manual I had memorised from Chumpton Library and I was going to do it in BSL (*although actually, I was going to communicate with interpretive dance as I didn't remember much BSL*) he didn't say anything but just waved me to start. I took several deep breaths and started to do interpretive dance like I'd never done interpretive dance before. Like the workmen at the Peppermint Hippo the day before, my audience were left opened mouthed. Bill Draper clearly wanted to give me the job there and then as he asked me several times to stop, but I was in the groove, I was magnificent, I was killing it (*that was a phrase Darren taught me on the way up*). I danced interpretively for almost 10 minutes and for my finale` I attempted the splits. The splits are something I'm not good at, but I was feeling confident, Bill Draper looked on as I slowly sunk down as far as I could go. Just then a very considerable and echoey fart escaped, but luckily no anal seepage … Yay no anal seepage. I was sweating quite profusely as I stared at Bill Draper and the panel of others. The look on his Bills face told me all I needed to know. I strolled over to my clothes bag and tossed them the bicycle repair manual I had just recited to prove I wasn't just making it up as I went along. Obviously Bill Draper couldn't say too much but he did tell me "I hadn't been successful this time" and called security for me so I could find my way back to the lobby. The security guys were quiet but they helpfully guided me by my arms and took me to the lobby, helping me out the door. Gary came scurrying out after me. "What the hell happened?" he asked. "I just showed the BBC the way to communicate bicycle maintenance to deaf childers" I bellowed confidently. The journey home was great, I couldn't wait to tell everyone how well it went. Once we got through the Flatlands checkpoint and made our way to Chumpton's clock tower we were greeted by Nina, the ladies and PC Jack with Emily, Gary's captive daughter. It was an emotional reunion for all concerned, especially Gary. A great day.

Here I am in Lundun (*which is the capital of UK of Great Britain*) auditioning for the BBC as one of their British Sign Language people for CBeebies and News24.

Sadly, I didn't get the job despite being very exuberant with my interpretation of the word 'Flange gasket' and utilising my skills in interpretive dance for some of the more difficult words I wasn't sure of in BSL.

The man from the BBC, Bill Draper, was very positive though saying my performance had left many of the audition panel "confused and concerned".

I shall be keep on keeping on.

Frydims 4st Maayye

Many of my inventions are what some other great inventors would term as 'experimental'; subsequently some of my more experimental inventions are occasionally flawed. Some of my inventions however are so far beyond modern day scientific thinking that occasionally the workings baffle even me. My time travelling tortoise is just such an invention. I obtained Hector from Edith's grandson Jebediah Skunk. Jebediah was so pleased at me using his much loved pet tortoise as my test subject for time travel he cried solidly for almost two whole days outside my front door. Needless to say I was as amazed as anybody when Hector vanished without a trace into an unknown time travelling dimension. But my amazement was doubled when I came downstairs this mawnin and saw he had re-appeared on the kitchen table, exactly where he was last seen.

fenbook | Surch for peeeple and othur things tooooo 🔍 | 🄼 Morton Hoome Foind frends 👥 💬 🌐 ▾

I am now the proud inventor of the worlds first Time travelling Tortoise called Hector ..... the time travelling Tortoise.
Due to an oversight on my part I have released this ground-breaking invention a day after the celebrations for Back to the Future day. This partly because I had set the dates wrong on Hector *(much like Doc did in back to the Future)* and partly because I was incapacitated from drinking a pint of Turnip Pochine after Audrey from next door asked me to ...... well lets just say I needed something to take the taste out of my mouth. Hector was the result of hours of dedicated research and took almost a week to build/reconstruct. I surgically removed some of Hector's non vital organs like his Liver, intestines, urinary tract, Kidneys and the entire content of his thoracic cavity to make way for the the time travelling parts. These time travelling parts were carefully constructed from clock parts, concentrated swans tears (of course), puppy dogs dreams and some Lego bricks.

Before any animal lovers get too concerned at Hectors fate, fear not. I have kept the part I took out in the frezzer (yes you read it correctly, we call them frezzers on the Fen) and once the time travelling experimentation is completed I will be returning Hector to his former glory if he so wishes.

If any of my Facebook chums have a copy either the Penguin book "How to surgically reconstruct your Tortoise" or the Tortoise book "How to surgically reconstruct your Penguin" I would be grateful for a lend.

That is all!

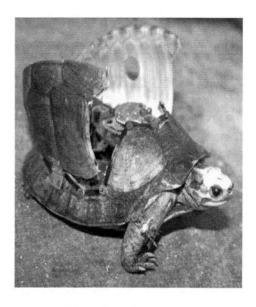

Hector the time travelling Tortoise

SatD 6st Maayye

Today is the day I have been looking forward to for several weeks now. Today I am reopening the Peppermint Hippo after fire swept through the building due to unruly ignited rodents. I have placed a new rule board on the wall in the foyer and the new rule board has a new rule on it. Rule 1623.3 Subsection 4 now states for all to see that "Under no circumstances are club members, performers or members of staff to ignite rodents, rabbits, ribbits or robbits … in fact anything that may scurry about in a state if dangerous alightedness".

I received word from Gary at today's interpretive dance class, he had heard from the BBC and asked him to tell me that not only was I not required but they had taken out an exclusion order against me. Gary seemed almost happy, in fact he seemed to gloat at my failure. I asked Gary to be sad for me and I stroked Emily's hair … she flinched. Gary looked sad straight away. After the class I was straight down the Peppermint Hippo.

The club was packed to the rafters with locals, builders who helped refurbish it and many friends and colleagues from the Ropey Hospital Maternity ward where I calculate the digits of Flatland District new-borns and a few old-borns too. After a few pints of Badgerspizzle and some fancy root crop based cocktails all was going very well. Even Mayor Devilman turned up with Cranshaw St.John and his chum St.John Cranshaw. Nina arrived with the ladies just before noyghtmiddlin; all were looking radiant and even Nigelle turned up with his new 'Flexit' pals Micky Dove and Morris Poncen. Morris is regarded as the village idiot, which in a village full of idiots is an achievement indeed. The ladies were lavishing lots of attention PC Wormer and he seemed to like it. Nigelle however, was altogether more cautious around our esteemed police person and when he made a move to go to the toilet Jack also headed towards the WC. Nigelle stopped in his tracks and Jack continued, as he walked past Nigelle he winked at him. Nigelle looked startled and decided against going for a wee but oddly, he must have needed to pee more than he thought as by the time Jack had entered into the toilet Nigelle had a large wet patch around his groinal area. Nigelle looked at his wet patch, blamed the immigrants and popped back to our house to change into some fresh, un-pissed trousers. The remainder of the noyght went well.

Morris Poncen kept everyone entertained by comically pretending to walk into things and tripping over things that weren't there. Every now and then you'd see Morris's mop of blonde unkempt hair disappear from view as he pretended to fall down or he'd walk into closed doors. Sylvia Sylvia (*who is married to Horatio Horatio the Happy Pauper owner*) my chief barmaid, later informed me this was not an act, and actually this was in fact a fabulous example of his unbridled stupidity. He comes from posh folk so it is possible his inbreeding is not as ingrained as many who were present … so we can't even blame his idiocy on that. It is just as Sylvia said.

Micky Dove and Morris Poncen's involvement with the Flexit campaign lifted my heart. All of this wonderfulness has made me completely forget about my failed audition for the BBC earlier this week.

FLATLAND DISTRICT WEEKLY NEWS

IMPORTANT NOTICE

There is great news that I'm sure all purveyors and connoisseurs of high culture and fine adult entertainment in and around the Flatland District will be thrilled to discover.

The refurbishment to Peppermint Hippo, the finest lap/pole dancing facility in the Flatland area, has been completed and the club will once again re-open it's doors very soon.

The refurbishment was needed following a fire after a much publicised and tragic incident with one of Flatlands favourite erotic acts "Dibgy Klackavalve and his Ferrets of Fire", last month. Unfortunately none of the Polecats survived the incident but Digby is out of Ropey Town Hospitals Intensive Care Unit. However the Police Brigade, the Monastic Fire Brigade and the Flatlands branch of RSPCA have all initiated investigations for possible prosecution against him and Chumpton Happy Pauper (who once again illegally supplied Digby with lighter fluid despite court orders not permitting such transactions).

I'm sure you will all agree from the photo posted that the club is now looking very sparkly and posh. It is indeed a focal point of the Chumpton village and Lower Fen Drove Fen at Yon End in general. It now places Peppermint Hippo as a centre for Flatland culture and sexually expressive artistic Dance/theatre.

The club will open its doors again tomorrow night at laasloyght and entry fee is Threpence Daveys and 4 bits or equivalent monetary value in root crops or some mice.

Peppermint Hippo looking sparkling new

Sunty 7st Maayye

There is very little I want to say about today as most of it has been spent in bed feeling very poorly. There has been, at times, a somewhat fraught battle for control of the toilet. Nina has had to poo out of the window twice today. On reflection maybe she should have used the rear window overlooking the garden and not the front window next to the path outside my house but I guess when you gotta go, you gotta go. Last noyght also saw me sign a new act for the club called Fiona Bloatstraddler. Exciting times are ahead.

FLATLAND DISTRICT WEEKLY NEWS

CHUMPTON LOCAL ANNOUNCEMENT

Peppermint Hippo is proud to announce that to mark the clubs refurbishment and Grand Re-opening it has a new artiste on its books. She is none other than Fiona Bloatstraddler previously of Peppermint Hippo's local competitors from Chatterby "The Klunge Klub".

Fiona was best known for her vaginal flatulence and her somewhat obscure Stoat/fish swallowing act. She will be the Star of Peppermint Hippo's new attraction "Dogging Winsti which will happen every Moondee in the car park at the rear of the building. The dogging events will be replacing the Dominoes and Cribbage evenings which had started to become very poorly supported prior to last months fire. Fiona said she was hoping the Dogging evenings would become a success and a regular feature for the club. She went on to say she was expecting to "have a barnet like a decorators paste brush" once word got around locally of her new act. I'm sure all of Chumptons inhabitants will wish Fiona and Peppermint Hippo every success for the future.

Moondee 8st Maayye

Still felt a bit rough today but happy the club is open again. I went out into the back garden to put some rubbish in the dustbin and noticed Morris Poncen, Flexit's bumbling blonde bozo standing in the middle of garden scratching his bonce and looking very confused.

"What are you doing Morris"? I enquired.

"Errrmm … I followed Nigelle home from the club and ended up here. I'm not sure where I am but I'm reasonably sure it's not where I live" he replied in his deep, posh tones.

I took Morris into the kitchen, sat him down and gave him a drink of water as I'm quite sure he would have been there for several hours. Morris's dullwittedness is surprising as he went to the same posh school that David Devilman went to. It was a selective school that was paid for by many, many Hoooman pounds. After Morris had a drink and walked into the kitchen door, twice, I escorted him home and called into the club. It had been a record for bar takings, obviously I was very pleased but overheard the cleaner Jebediah Shaftstroker (of the Chatterby Shaftstroker's) speaking about the referendum.

"I'll definitely be voting in this ere referee-indum an oilbe voting for that there Nigelle wot was tellin us aboooot them blerdee immigrants" he said. "Apparently one of the reasons people were strugglin to get served at the bar laaaaast noyght was becuss them blerdee immigrants were taykin over the blerdee place" he continued.
My blood ran cold for a moment, but then I reassured myself by rationalising what I'd just heard. Of course there would be some people, maybe even quite a few who would agree with Nigelle, but as long as it was just a small minority we were fine.

Toosdi 9rd Maayye

Today I received a huge delivery of parsnips, turnips, carrots, onions and potatoes from the club. It was some root crops that hadn't been used as currency in time and ended up not being taken to market in time. They needed to be consumed or thrown away. Well instead of them being thrown away Nina and I spent most of the day making root crop soup, root crop stew, root crop smoothies, root crop ice-cream and root crop wine. We had enough food to last us for a while now and it meant we used up vegetables that were otherwise going to be wasted.

Some were only a month or so past their best. We had plenty of carrot stew, and turnip ice-cream washed down with parsnip smoothie. For laasdocky we had parsnip soup, onion stew, and potato ice-cream, all finished with a nice drop of matured carrot wine that had been brewed for almost 3 hours.

We all had rumbling tummies later though.

Winsti 10rd Maayye

In between noyghtmiddlin and firsloyght I went for a poo. By daaymiddlin I was still there doing the same poo/fart. I have spent most of the day not daring to venture further than 10 feet from the toilet as poo feelings come very quickly and change from 'poo feelings' to 'poo doings' in virtually no time at all. Nina kept me sustained with warming up some more of yisdee's lovely stew and some meat (possibly chicken, not sure) to help keep my strength up. She made sure that the chicken wasn't too hot for me to eat by just warming it through to a bit above room temperature. I managed to stay off the toilet for a while but an hour or so after my possibly chicken meal, the poo feelings came back very badly. I also had sick feelings too, which also rapidly turned into sick doings. I was feeling feeble and tired so Nina helped me out by doing my mastybayshun for me. I believe when you do a shit and a fart at the same time it's referred to as a 'shart' these days. Well, as I strained to do a shuddering at the end of my mastybayshun I did a poo, a fart, a sex wee and a sicking everywhere all at the same time. Not sure what you'd call that but Pocahontas and Cinderella thought it was very clever as they both clapped and cheered as I exploded.

As I write this entry into my diary it is between laasloyght and noyghtmiddlin and I'm still on the toilet doing pooing. I have poo'd lots today.

Thrisdee 11rd Maayye

By daaymiddlin I finished the last of my poo. Even though it's Maayye the house is quite chilly as Nina has had to open all the doors and windows because of the smell of poo, sick and fartings. Nina thinks it might be something to do with all the mouldy root crop food I have been eating. Although everyone had quite a lot of the mouldy vegetables cooking I had more than most. I also was the only one to eat the 'possibly chicken' meal by which time I was the only one really ill.

I decided therefore to insist nobody in our house touches any of the food Nina and I cooked on Toosdi as it was certainly the reason for my pooing.

We took most of the food we cooked down to St.Jebediahs School for the Criminally Insane for the children to have. I decided to leave some in the house for Nigelle and the "gang of three Flexiteers" as they were starting to become known as. Nina even agreed to go and warm through the root crop based food and even show the school food dispensing ladies (*if only they had some kind of job name*) how to warm through the 'possibly chicken' meals to slightly above room temperature for the kiddies to enjoy.

It gave me great satisfaction giving all that mouldy food to the childers, I am quite the philanthropist me.

Frydims 12th Maayye

I have started booking local music acts and organising concerts hoping to promote local bands and artistes. It could be quite lucrative and I shall be advertising on Fenbook page, in the shop window and in my new Yoof paper called New Mooosicul Expressions, which starts going to print next week.

Lanita Eversole

Lanita will be playing Chumptons World of Adventure (possibly the finest root crop based theme park in the Flatland District) in the near future.

She will hopefully be playing numerous tracks from her hit album "No crippled Girls in Heaven" and will be supported by our very own local pop dou Jebwould unless anyone else can be found.

All details will be updated on the Chumpton Wide Web or here on my Fenbook page.

Lanita's parent's wish to make it clear that their daughter is not for sale, either for sexual purposes or scrap metal value and respectfully requests people stop asking.

SatD 13th Maayye

Today Micky Dove the village liar, Morris Poncen the village idiot and Nigelle F`Rage the village Nazi began their campaign in earnest. They have decided to embark on a district wide tour travelling the length and breadth of Flatlands to spread the word of Flexit. I have provided them with a bus to do it with from the profits from my re-opening noyght of the Peppermint Hippo.

Here is the Flexit Battle bus that Micky Dove, Morris Poncen and Nigelle F`Rage will use to spread the word of Flexit. Unfortunately it has no engine as none of its occupants are either qualified or capable of driving a real bus. This one will be horse drawn which means it will make slow progress throughout the Flatland District but that won't necessarily be a bad thing. Morris is going to be in charge of opening and closing doors and is hoping to have a go on

It was a cheery farewell to the Flexit team, albeit a somewhat slow one as the horse that was pulling the bus, called Shergar, was very old and needed lots of coaxing.

Once the Flexit team had gone Nina, the ladies and I, all made our way over to the Peppermint Hippo for a cooling and refreshing glass or two of Turnip Daiquiri. My arrival at the club was fortuitous as one of the acts hadn't turned up. I quickly got changed into my latex nuns outfit (an old favourite made out of some melted down tractor tyres and some bin liners) and did my stuff.

I was careful not to include any sexy lunges what so ever considering my delicate constitution earlier this week. Halfway through my routine I noticed a crowd had gathered around Cinderella. I jumped down off the stage and as I approached I could see she was having some kind of convulsive fit on the floor. The club members that were stood around her were throwing money and root crops on her. I realised they thought she was dancing. I had a brilliant idea. Once Cinderella had finished convulsing and was taken home by Nina I went back on the stage and pretended to have a fit myself. The punters loved it, within minutes I was drenched in money, root crops and sex wee. Sadly, I had forgotten about my delicate tummy and the exertion of thrashing about on the floor caused the inevitable fanfare of flatulence and faecal extravaganza that was quickly becoming my 'signature move' so to speak. Not to worry though, I had made some more profit from dancing and had a great money making idea to boot.

Sunty 14th Maayye

Nobody puts baby in a corner

Here is local choreographer and my great chum Dinsdale O'Flattley recreating the famous scene from the Hollywood blockbuster 'Dirty Dancing'.
Dinsdale recreated the legendary lift using his swampdog (also called Baby and coincidentally, rarely put in a corner) in the drainage dykes at Lower Fen drove at Yon end.

Today I met up with Dinsdale O'Flattley, a fellow dancer, pal and much sort after choreographer. He has agreed to stage a version of Dirty Dancing to be opened at the Chumpton WI hall once it has been written, choreographed and rehearsed. Dinsdale reckons it'll take him a day and a half to do all that. I have offered him all the assistance he needs from my own interpretive dance school to ensure its brilliance.

I gave him a quick demonstration of my interpretive dance without any music and he was spell bound. He had exactly the same look as Bill Draper at the BBC earlier this month. He was mystified and a tad jealous and yet chose to show this by laughing at me. I popped out a tiny bum trumpet during my dance demonstration, it was only a small squeaker but it was enough to make Dinsdale howl with laughter … in a kind of nervous "god I wished I could dance as well you" sort of laugh. He assured me he wouldn't need any help but my offer still stands.

Moondee 15th Maayye

Today has mostly been spent getting ready to start the print run for my new venture into the media of yoof culture. It is of course my newspaper paper for young uns called the "New Mooosicul Expressions".

There is an absolute wealth of talent currently circulating around Flatlands, especially the "Ropey Scene" and also a number of big acts that had made it big in the UK of Great Britain and also Merica of the USA that actually originated from the District. The first print will run on Thrisdee and will feature interviews, competitions and adverts, lots and lots of adverts which will help the yoof decide what to buy. I also get advertisers revenue; it's what's known in the Hoooman world as a win/win.

Toosdi 16lbs Maayye

Mayor Devilman was on the tefelone today wanting to know how the Flexit campaign was going on. I told him it was going brilliantly; he became startled at this until I explained it was going dreadfully, which is brilliant as far as he should be concerned, brilliantly dreadful. He calmed down a bit and intimated that he would like to book me for a private dance at his home again.

I remembered the last time this happened and how it all ended somewhat disastrously and with some considerable embarrassment for all parties concerned. David sensed my reluctance and mentioned that once the referendum was out the way and he had won, he could arrange for me to be the owner of the Klunge Klub in Chatterby in much the same way as I did the Peppermint Hippo. I was a bit confused at this as Finbar had committed suicide. Klunge Klub's owner Pedro Mellowring was far too bubbly to commit suicide.

So Winsti it is then for my private performance. I shall be wearing my skimpy cowgirl costume and dance to 'Mawnin has Broken' again by some cat called Stevens. I am assuming that Growler will not be there (*like last time*) and the Mayor will be doing some mastybayshun. I have finished off the last of the onion broth we cooked last Toosdi but didn't take to the school. This will hopefully give me the right amount of flatulence/anal seepage ratio that the Mayor likes.

Winsti 17lbs Maayye

As the words "mawnin has broken" began to fill Mayor Devilman's living room I began feeling the music course through my body and completely take over. In much the same way as it did at my BBC audition I started swaying dramatically, running my hands over my chestal area stopping momentarily at my nipples, just long enough for them to go all pointy. I turned to face the Mayor and saw he wasn't even trying to hide his mastybayshun this time. It didn't bother me as I had this sort of thing all the time at the Peppermint Hippo … well twice … but it was definitely me they were looking at both times. I could tell by the look in David Devilman's eyes that he was close to the shuddering time. I produced my Krakorbang feather from my garter and stroked it all over my legs and groinal parts. I forgot the extent to which I had been using the feather to tickle my sphincter and that I hadn't rinsed it under the tap for quite a while. Unfortunately I only realised this when I tickled the Mayor with it and wafted it under his nose and stroked it across his mouth.

The look in the Mayor's eyes changed from the onset of the shuddering to the immediate look of someone about to start sicking. He began to wretch then he quickly raised his hand to his mouth to stop the sick coming out. He swallowed his sick and regained his composure before waving me to continue with the Krakorbang feather again. What a strange man. As I wafted the feather again with much the same results as a few seconds earlier I noticed a framed photograph of Mayor Devilman laying semi clad in a pigsty with his arm around a pig. What a strange man.

As I began winding up to the climax of the song (*and presumably the climax of the Mayor*) I positioned myself in front of him and started my lunge. I felt my stomach grumble and I think the Mayor heard it above the music. It was now or never, I simultaneously lurched forward and down and as my sphincter dilated slightly it released the most enormous of farts I have ever done. The air was thick with the smell of last noyghts onion broth and shortly afterwards, the Mayors vomit. David Devilman, the Mayor of Flatland District was covered in his own vomit and sex wee, not to mention a significant quantity of my seepage. He was truly spent, and very, very grateful. What a strange man.

My attention kept being drawn to the photo of Mayor Devilman in the pigsty, cuddling the pig. It seemed where ever I was in the room the pigs eyes seemed to be following me. I never had the Mayor down as a pig enthusiast but this photo intrigued me.

As David left the room to clean himself I strolled over to the table that the picture resided on. As I approached the table I heard a strange humming sound, it was coming from inside the table itself. I went to pick up the pig picture to have a closer look and couldn't lift it far as it was a fixed to the desk by a wire. The strange humming noise appeared to be coming from underneath the picture. As I investigated further I could see that the wire coming from the back of the photo frame into the desk. It then dawned on me that the photo was actually a hidden camera that had been filming everything that had been going on in the room. **What a strange man!**

Thrisdee 18lbs Maayye

I went on the compooota this mawnin and had a look at security cameras and CCTV. Unfortunately I accidentally scrolled onto a site that showed ladies tuppences again. When Nina came down stairs she found me slumped over the compooota with a sock over my winky. As she made me some Beetroot coffee I had a look at some of the cameras that could be fitted in the picture frame. This would explain why the picture frame was as thick as it was and making a humming sound. The humming must have been a recorder inside the table.

The ladies room needed a quick hose down, as I was hosing under their bed I noticed a small object. On further investigation it transpires that the object I observed was none other than Hector the Time Travelling tortoise. I assumed he had gone off on his time travels again but it seems that it was just Pocahontas taking a shine to it. I'm now worried that the major breakthrough in time travel that I have recently announced on Fenbook was in fact nothing more than Pocahontas looking after him for a few days. Time will tell … literally.

The big news today was my yoof paper was on its first print run today. The main article was about an old Flatlands band that went on to great things in the UK. I'm hopeful this will be a major success.

NEW MOOOSICUL EXPRESSIONS

Carl Barratt on keyboard and Pete Doherty on Sax and Edward Kent on percussion were The Edward Kent Trio.

Pete and Carl were disturbed by Edwards (or Teddy K as he was known to the fans) use of recreational class A drugs and his well documented love affair with a German Shepard dog called Rascal so Edward was asked to leave the band. The Edward Kent Trio left Flatlands to live in the UK and shortly afterwards became known as a band called The Libertines. The rest is history.

Frydims 19lbs Maayye

It would seem that the epidemic of terrorism that's currently growing throughout the UK of Great Britain and rest of the world has finally made its way to Flatland District. In today's edition of The Flatland District Weekly News I read with some concern about Jihadi Jeb. The fundamentalist Turnip fanciers have always been on the fringe of acceptable root crop fancying and it's not a huge leap from being a decent root crop enthusiast to becoming radicalised and cutting the heads off vegetables in videos on YoooTooob. Worrying times.

FLATLAND DISTRICT WEEKLY NEWS

BREAKING NEWS

The identity of the Flatlands District terrorist known as Jehadi Jeb has been released by the press office at the Fenland District Council this evening. Jehadi Jeb, or Zebedee Glans as he is known round these parts, has posted numerous videos of himself cutting the heads off carrots on YooooTooob claiming he is doing it to highlight the plight of fundamentalist Turnip fanciers.

The Chatterby Association of Turnipers are believed to behind a campaign of terror in the Flatland district which has left wheely bins pushed over and windows knocked loudly after sundown.

Flatland Police Authority have advised members of the public if they see Jehadi Jeb to kick his head in

Jehadi Jeb, described by local Police as "an absolute cunt"

SatD 20lbs Maayye

On the Flatlands TV news yisdee's newspaper story of jihadi Jeb was being covered. We were all sat down to eat our food and saw none other than Nigelle, Micky Dove and Morris appear on our TV screen. The interviewer asked Nigelle what his views were regarding the wanton pushing over of dustbins in and around Chumpton and his views on the extremist faction currently associated with turnip fancying. Nigelle went into a rant about how it was almost certainly due to the influx of immigrants, Micky stood behind Nigelle squinting his piggy little eyes and sneering and agreeing with everything Nigelle said but not actually contributing to the interview.

Morris smiled with a puzzled expression on his face and ended the interview rather abruptly by walking into the cameraman and both of them falling over. The laasloyght was spent at the Peppermint Hippo with Nina. Pocahontas was out with Jack and Cinderella was out on a first date with Finbar Knuckleshuffla who was on a break from filming Flatlands Next Top Model made by local production company InbreedIndeed TV.

Sunty 21lbs Maayye

FLATLAND DISTRICT WEEKLY NEWS

The Chumpton-by-Kumberly House of Illicit Beverages has re-opened again following last months explosion. The emporiums Landlady, Gladys Carbunkle, was pleased to be open for business again as this was the seventh explosion this year (*but happily only the fourth to take lives*). Gladys is famed for her ample bosoms, a breasties so huge that she uses them to serve drinks on rather than use a tray. Gladys carry's the churns containing the illicit beverages with her labia majora.

Anyone wishing to use the Chumpton-by-Kumberly House of Illicit Beverages for parties, weddings, christenings or wakes should be aware of the combustive nature of the drinks served. Smoking is prohibited as is starting small fires ... or even large ones.

A spokesperson for the Flatland District Monastic Fire Brigade was un available for comment but his friend was. The friend was quoted as saying "Ner a nickera nor a nackera, ner a nickera, nackera be". Hopefully this will dispel any fears future clientele may have about visiting The Chumpton-by-Kumberly House of Illicit Beverages.

We awoke today to discover that both the ladies had stopped out the noyght and didn't get back home until daaymiddlin. Pocahontas was always more of the concern as Jack had proved himself somewhat untrustworthy around the ladies (*and Nigelle*). Cinderella arrived back shortly after Pocahontas and Cinders was looking smitten. Pocahontas on the other hand was looking tired; Jack it would seem had something of an insatiable appetite and his ability to do sexing more or less continuously was only outdone by his appetite for brutally beating his prisoners at Ropey Police Brigade Station. Sunty was ordinarily a dull day but today was particularly dull. The ladies were in bed asleep and Nigelle was on the road with his Flexit battle bus so Nina and I popped in to the Chumpton-by-Kumberly House of Illicit Beverages and visit my old chum and former dancer Gladys Carbunkle. We arrived back home from Chumptons House of Illicit Beverages just before noyghtmiddlin. I had lost all my clothes, had managed a faecal accident, twice, and had sadly set three fires on the way home. Not sure of the severity.

Moondee 22th Maayye

Today is for sleeping.

Toosdi 23th Maayye

FLATLAND DISTRICT WEEKLY NEWS

Emanuelle Stroker, a handsome woman of Chatterby Fen, is keen for people to know she will be driving Purdybirds about the locale in her three wheeled tractor and trailer. She will be doing so in a bikini (*or garments of similar low clothage*), regardless of Flatland Districts famously inclement weather conditions, to arouse local men and to leave local women feeling inferior and with low self-esteem issues.

Some concern was raised about Emanuelles revealing apparel having Health and Safety issues whilst driving machinery. Flatland District Council sent a H&S elder to visit Emanuelle and her Purdybirds and was pleased to report back that she was "fantastic and lovely"

This mawnin's delivery of our daily newspaper 'The Flatland District Weekly News' was reporting a story of great interest, a welcome distraction to the furore surrounding Jihadi Jeb and the referendum. It was the story of local beauty Emanuelle Stroker. Emanuelle is one of the Chumpton Strokers, noted mostly for her large collection of parrots. She breeds them for local gun and parrot emporium 'Guns & Parrots'. This story has been stirring up sexual tensions within Chumpton and Chatterby marital circles, the ladies of these villages becoming upset with Emanuelle for getting their men "hot n bovvveerrrd" and making demands of them.

Following this story I received a courier crow from Ropey Hospital for the Genetically Impure warning me that there may be an increase in childers being born in the area this time next year. Lots of toe counting to be doing. ☺

Winsti 24rd Maayye

Cranshaw St.John visited today and informed me that they will be conducting opinion polls at the start of Jism to give us a better idea of our standing and how I should direct the Flexit campaign. I mentioned to him that I was surprised there'd been no sign of Mayor Devilman or his campaign for Flemain in either the press or Flatlands TV or even Radio Flatlands AM. I had mentioned several times previously that I had connections there and could arrange interviews and even get features for the Mayor. Cranshaw assured me there was no need as it was all going to be taken care of.

After a bit of toe counting at the maternity ward I called into the Jolly Sphincter in Ropey town centre. As soon as I walked in I was bombarded with questions about Nigelle. Where is he? How is he? When will he be in for a pint next? It was odd. I had three pints of Badgerspizzle and I didn't buy one of them, they were all bought for me by locals I had never even met before. This was because I was Nigelle's campaign manager apparently. Whilst I was sipping one of my pints I heard more rumblings about Jihadi Jeb. By all accounts over 20 dustbins had been pushed over the previous noyght and several doors had been knocked but when the occupants of the houses opened the door there was nobody there. People were afraid to go out, but as I said to the locals, if you stay indoors then the terrorists have won. The conversation remained centred around Nigelle's solution to all problems, which of course was to repatriate all immigrants and ones that had lived here a while could be put on some kind of register.

It was the general consensus of all in the Jolly Sphincter that the pushing over of dustbins and door knocking might be considered nothing more than high jinks and perfectly acceptable in the UK of Great Britain but it certainly wasn't 'the done thing' here in Flatlands. It was starting to dawn on me that the people of the Jolly Sphincter at least saw Nigelle, my nasty, hate mongering buffoon of a housemate, as a possible leader of Flatlands out of the United Kingdom of Great Britain. A scary prospect.

Our new reverend started his job as vicar today, it will be good to discover his take on the referendum business.

No fires today.

Thrisdee 25rd Maayye

Once again Hector the Time Travelling Tortoise had gone missing. Either he had travelled through time in another dimension to be discovered again at some point in the future or one of the ladies had taken him. My day however was well planned out, a bit of prostrate milking followed by an interpretive dancing demonstration for the local ladies at the WI Hall. At daaymiddlin I went to the Peppermint Hippo for a meeting of the Chumpton-by-Kumberly Prostrate Milking Association. Gustav Belcher was the main examiner and was noted for his extraordinarily long fingers, all 14 of them, and he certainly put his amazing finger length and girth to good use today, my prostrate was well and truly milked but it wasn't until I made my way to the WI Hall and started my interpretive dancing with the immigrants I realised that getting my prostrate milked first was probably a mistake. Even though my movement was impeded due to having Gustav's enormous fingers jammed up my botty only minutes earlier, I still managed to have a fabtasticle session with no flatulent onion broth issues.

Frydims 26rd Maayye

As my days performing at the Peppermint Hippo are limited due to my commitments elsewhere and also partly due to poor anal health, I think maybe I shall heed to requests by many throughout Chumpton and surrounding villages within the district and occasionally post provocative pictures of myself taken at various stages through my lengthy and illustrious career as an Elvis impersonator, as well as a pole/lap dancer at various adult entertainment establishments within the district. I popped over to the club to dig out some of my old photos and to show my face.

SatD 27rd Maayye

This mawnin's edition of the Weekly News mentioned that a beautiful little Arforse called Dave has been found. They make fantastic pets and even better lovers according to some of the locals. Beverley Bloater used to dress his up in stockings or tights and charge workmen from out of the district, that would occasionally fix the pot holes, to have 10 minutes slap and tickle with his Arforse called Lucifer.

FLATLAND DISTRICT WEEKLY NEWS

LOST AND FOUND IN CHUMPTON
Found in Upper Fen Drove at Yon end of lower Fen fen is this delightful 'Arforse' that answers to the name of Dave.
If you recognise this lovely animal or know someone who has lost an Arforse then it is currently located at the Chatterby Sanctuary for Indigenous Flatland Creatures. It will remain there until Thrisdee 3th Jism and if it hasn't been claimed by then, the sanctuary will inhumanely destroy the creature and use its carcass for glue products and bizarre Flatland religious rituals.

Sunty 28rd Maayye

Well, St. Jeremiahs Church was packed to the rafters today to welcome and hear the inspirational words of our new reverend Adolph Horatio Ferdinand Globule conduct his first sermon. He staggered up to the lectern, clearly very, very drunk, and stood there for a while trying to focus his eyes and to collect his thoughts. He then vomited over the front of the lectern and into the font. "Oh fuck …. Oh fuck" he said as he fell back slightly causing the congregation to collectively gasp as they anticipated a tumble. He grabbed the side of the lectern and eased himself out of it. He then gingerly sat on the floor, farted and wafted the aroma into his face for his own assessment and appreciation. He then lifted his cassock and scratched his groinal area where it became abundantly clear from the state of his pyjama bottoms that he had a large wee reasonably recently. That was the sum extent of the sermon. Short, but still more coherent and better prepared than any of Cedric's had been in the latter years and Adolph's sermon was on a Sunty too. As people started to get up to leave the church the collection plate was passed around the congregation. It was swimming with vomit and spare Hoooman coinage and some Davey's but the vomit belonged to a significant percentage of the congregation. Chumpton's House of Illicit Beverages had a Sunty happy hour at firsloyght and Gladys had some old stock to get rid of. As we shuffled out of the church the questions all started again about the whereabouts of Nigelle. People were telling me what a great inspiration Nigelle was.

The church congregation had unsettled me and the rest of my day was spent thinking about a strategy to sabotage Nigelle's Flexit campaign. I was now starting to get a bit twitchy about the whole thing so I sent a courier crow to Cranshaw regarding his boss's lack of campaigning. Just to add to the worry, Nigelle and his chums were featured on the Flatlands TV weekly Sunty Noyght agricultural show 'Cundreyphile'. As with previous coverage featuring Nigelle and the Flexit campaign his bigoted, facile unpleasant barrage of lies was shining through. But for the first time it was dawning on me that the people of Flatlands were buying it. At least a lot of them were anyway, and that was my Eureka moment. I had assumed that the locals of Flatland District would see through the lies and rubbish that were being spouted by a halfwit like Nigelle. But that was only because I saw through it all, of course a reasonable proportion of the locals would fall for the gang of three's Flexit plan but how many was a reasonable proportion going to be?. I didn't sleep easily, I didn't sleep at all really.

Moondee 29th Maayye

Mayor Devilman called me on the tefelone and requested an urgent strategy meeting at his house. I started to feel a bit happier that perhaps the Mayor was going to start taking the campaigning seriously for Flemain. Then he said bring you cowgirl outfit and my heart sank. It was becoming abundantly clear that the Mayor was more engrossed in mastybayshun than saving the district from ruin, (*which is understandable mastybayshun is lovely*) but I couldn't understand his lack of interest in saving Flatlands. Surely it was going to affect him as much as it would us.

CHAPTER SIX

DIVIDE AND CONKERS

JISM 1896

Toosdi 1st Jism

I arrived at the Mayors house at close to daaymiddlin and was greeted by some considerable furore going on in the living room. As I waited outside in the hallway I heard lots of shouting and much banging of table tops. I couldn't quite figure out what it was that all the commotion was about but it was getting very emotional in there. It was an emotional commotion.

The doors flung open and out walked an elderly, frail looking man wearing a very posh suit, similar to the ones I saw the people at the BBC wearing during my trip to London last month. He stopped in his tracks and took a long lingering look at me. For the first time I became conscious I was dressed as a cowgirl waiting to go into the Mayor's living room.

It struck me that may have looked a bit odd. When I entered David's living room there was still an atmosphere of great tension in the air. The Mayor was still seething. As I walked over to the wall to plug my boom box in and start my routine the Mayor asked me to not bother with the dance.

He went on to say that we had more important matters to consider. I sat down in the comfy chair and for the first time I realised that Cranshaw St.John was sat in the corner, in the shadows by the curtains.

"Did you hear any of that when you were outside?" the Mayor said.

"Eerm … I think most of Flatlands heard the shouting, but not what was said" I replied.

"That … gentleman … you saw leave was none other than local media Tycoon Rimbit Muldoon. He owns our only daily newspaper the Flatland District Weekly News and he also owns Flatlands TV as well as a few specialist publications. He is … was a very good friend of mine".

"I've never heard of him" I said.

"No, you certainly wouldn't have seen him around Flatlands he lives in the UK and owns many, many things and places" the Mayor informed me.

He got up from his sofa and strolled over to a fancy glass cabinet and took out a bottle of Hoooman whiskey and started to pour us all a glass. "He lives close to London in a place called Hertfordshire and has a very big house … even bigger than mine" the Mayor continued.

"Bigger than yours" I said somewhat amazed that there was a house bigger than David Devilman's.

"Yes, bigger than mine … he is indeed a very wealthy man" he said "thanks to me" he muttered under his breath. I sat for a while trying to take in the amazing concept of a house bigger than the Mayors. Some of the immigrants had really big houses apparently, but not even close in size to the Mayors. So the idea that there was a house bigger still was rather incredible. The Mayor handed us some of the Hoooman whiskey and returned to his sofa.

"all the shouting was because … and this goes no further … Rimbit Muldoon wants us to leave the United Kingdom of Great Britain. He is going to instruct his TV chiefs and newspaper editors to back the campaign to Flexit the UK." The Mayor said, looking confused.

"Why"? I asked, equally as confused.

"That's what I asked him, all he would say is that when he comes to see me he always gets what he wants, when he goes to see the government at the UK they don't even know who he is. That seems to be his reason for wanting to leave the UK" David Devilman moaned. "I'm going for a shit" he said, almost as an afterthought. David

Devilman got up and strolled out of the room and made his way upstairs to poo for a bit.

The room was silent, uncomfortably silent when I remembered that Cranshaw was sat in the corner.

"Oh dear, the Mayor must be very concerned Cranshaw. It sounds like this Muldoon fella wields a lot of sway around Flatlands media" I said.

"You're half right" Cranshaw replied. "He certainly 'holds a lot of sway' as you say, but to be perfectly honest the Mayor isn't too bothered himself if we leave the UK because …" Cranshaw stopped himself from speaking further.

"go on" I said, "No, I really have said enough, let's just say the Mayor wants to remain as part of the UK but has made sure he is well catered for 'if' the referendum goes against us".

I was stunned. The Mayor wanted to stay in the UK but wasn't too bothered if we didn't. Now I was really confused and a little concerned. The Mayors Hoooman whiskey gave me a thirst so once back in Chumpton I called in to see Gladys Carbunkle and her Emporium for some Illicit Beverages to try and make things clearer.

Winsti 2st Jism

I spent most of today on the compooota. I was looking for anything about this Rimbit Muldoon character I met yisdee at the Mayor's house. I could find nothing out about him other than he owned all the media outlets in Flatlands. I'm sure the Mayor mentioned that he had lots of concerns in the UK of Great Britain but I could find nothing about him. Just lots of 'error' messages whatever they are … it's almost as if the compooota wasn't allowing me to search anything about anything to do with the UK of Great Britain.

I inadvertently clicked onto a photo of a lady putting beetroots into her tuppence and spent the rest of the day doing mastybayshun and soon forgot all about the Mayor's house and Rimbit Muldoon until I came to fill in my diary tonoyght.

Thrisdee 3th Jism

Today sees the next edition of my yoof paper of yoof culture the New Mooosicul Expressions. This was one of my contributions to this week's edition of my fab paper. The main article is about the Webb Gospel singers and their forthcoming tour of Flatlands. The Webb's don't just hate the hoooman immigrants; they hate everyone so they should do very well in the more rural parts of the district. Both ladies were out tonoyght with their boyfriends and I am hoping both will return with their dignity and tuppences intact. Nina was out with friends in Ropey town and will catch the late guided bus home.

NEW MOOOSICUL EXPRESSIONS

The Webb Gospel Singers are embarking on a world tour of Chumpton and Chatterby starting tonight at Chumpton WI hall. They will be performing their own unique brand of music and right winged, guilt based, religious politics as well as having an array of knitted merchandise and memorabilia available for purchase after the performance, which will last for approximately 7-8 hours with a 6 minute interlude at the 6 hour mark.

Here we see Denzil Webb with his two wives Bertha and Berther asking the question where will he shelter his sheep. A question I have no doubt everyone has asked themselves from time to time. I have assisted Denzil with his sheep sheltering conundrum with temporary accommodation locally sourced.

On a different note, Peppermint Hippo (Chumptons premier lap dancing and adult entertainment venue) will be having a "speed dating with sheep" night this Thrisdee evening. Get there early so you don't get an ugly one.

Frydims 4rd Jism

Today I spent most of the day in Ropey town, meeting up with Nigelle and his merry band of halfwits to get ready for tonoyghts live debate on Flatlands TV. Nigelle had drunk quite a lot of Badgerspizzle beer throughout the day and was suitably irritating, but sadly I knew this would make him more popular with some of the locals but what could I do.

The debate went well for David Devilman I thought. He informed the viewers that if we remained in the UK then it was very unlikely we would go to war with them and that if we left the UK we weren't sure what might happen. He also said that if we remain in the UK it is also very "unlikely" we will be invaded by aliens from another planet as the Flexit manifesto had claimed. I felt he could have been a bit more assertive on this issue. Perhaps replacing 'unlikely' with 'will not'.

The debate was chaired by Flatland TV's Hillbilly Billy Hill. David looked good in his suit, Nigelle looked drunk, Micky Dove lurked in the background looking "up to something" and Morris Poncen fell of his chair and got his leg caught in the chair legs. It took three people to free him which was a welcome relief from the politics for the audience present.

SatD 5rd Jism

The Flatland District Weekly News landed on the mat with a thud just after firsloyght and the write up for the previous noyghts debate was front page news. The opinion polls had the Flemainers ahead of the Flexiters by 15%. The poll results were: Flexit = 27%, Flemain = 42%, Don't know = 68%

It was the 68% of don't knows we had just over 3 weeks to try and convert to Flemainers as even though we were ahead in the polls they were notoriously unpredictable with their accuracy.

Sunty 6th Jism

We went to Chatterby sands today as it was forecast to be sunny for 20 minutes. Time to get out my mankini and impress Nina and any other ladies that might want sex ... or fall asleep too close me.

Any of my Fenbook lady friends are struggling to get a wide on don't bother with this new "Viagra for ladies" currently being used in the Merica USA.

For your perusal is a photo of me in a mankini which I think I'm right in saying that most of you lucky ladies should have a gusset like a fish fryers cuff after gawping at my physog. You're welcome 😊😊😊

Chatterby sands Mr Universe

Moondee 7st Jism.

A Star in the making

Here is Vladimir Pututin from Ropey Town performing his new single "Check out my package Mr. Postman" at the semi finals of 'Chumptons Got Talent'. He is available for bookings at weddings, stag nights and childrens parties.

Some of the ladies (and a few of the gents teehee) may notice he tends to dress to the left these days.

Tonoyght I was over at the club with Nina and the ladies to watch the heats of 'Chumptons got Talent'. What a noyght, it was just what we needed to take our minds off the referendum. Tonoyghts heat we saw the talents of Vladimir Putitin, a possible winner

Toosdi 8th Jism

Today the tefelone rang thrice; this is normally a month's worth of tefeloning. The first call was from Cranshaw to ask if I had seen Mayor Devilman this mawnin. And odd question I thought but I informed him I had not seen him. The second call was from Sylvia Sylvia from the club to say we possibly had a new dancer to fill my slot. I laughed at Sylvia when she said "fill my slot". Sylvia did not find this funny. She went on to say that the dancer was local girl and flirt called Grisselda Flange and was happy to fill the Frydims slot. I sniggered again. Sylvia Sylvia hung up the tefelone. The third call was from Mayor Devilman. He told me he was going into hiding for a few days as the editor of the Weekly News was running a very harmful story saying that he had been sexually interfering with animals. I failed to see how this would harm his reputation as we were in Flatlands, in the Fens; in East Anglia ... people are more suspicious of you if you don't interfere with animals but he's the boss. I let Cranshaw know that he had been in touch and what to expect tomorrow mawnin in the papers.

Winsti 9th Jism

The TV and Flatland District Weekly News were full of Mayor Devilman and his romantic liaison with a farm yard inhabitant. The Flatlands firsloyght TV news did a vox pop and it was abundantly clear that nobody was that bothered. Later on in the day an opinion poll actually showed the Flemain campaign had increased its popularity by 2%.

Thrisdee 10th Jism

I spent the mawnin in Chatterby teaching some lollypop ladies the mystic art of Kung Fu. I have received a few calls from people enquiring about getting me to teach them

Kung Fu. I didn't understand at first as I have no training at this martial art but the I saw that my tefelone number was almost identical to the Chatterby Institute of Ninja and Punching Folk. I thought it was a good opportunity to earn some more money and popped over on the guided bus route to Chatterby. Guess who the fuck I bumped into!

Travelling back from teaching some Lollypop ladies the mystic art of Kung Fu this afternoon guess who I saw sitting opposite me on the Flatland guided bus. That's right, none other than Beyonce herself. She's a lot slimmer in real life and her voice is a lot deeper than I expected but she is still very nice. She smelt of canned tuna and Badgerspizzle beer and when I asked her for an autograph she told me to fuck off and that she wasn't Beyonce. After asking her 135-137 times between Chatterby and Chumpton she finally confessed she was Beyonce and signed my testicles with a marker pen.

Have any of my Fenbook pals seen anyone really famous today?

Beyonce Knowles

Frydims 11st Jism

Cranshaw St.John tefeloned to say that the Mayor had returned to civilisation and was ready for tonoyghts live TV debate. I went over to Ropey and met up with Nigelle, Micky and Morris. Morris trapped his arm in his coat and fell over trying to get out … twice. I asked Nigelle if he had read any of the papers this week (*I was trying to gauge whether or not he knew about the farm yard incidents*) but he replied that he won't read papers that are full of immigrants and if we leave the UK he will either ban papers or stories about immigrants appearing in the papers. The debate went out live and even though the farm yard encounters weren't even mentioned it was not a good noyght for the Flemain campaign. Morris accidentally appeared on stage after going to the toilet and getting lost. He wandered on to the stage, approached the lectern, unzipped his trousers and began urinating live on Flatlands TV. The studio audience howled with laughter and when Hillbilly Billy Hill interviewed Morris he said he thought it was "Just a really busy toilet". Nigelle blamed Morris's lack of direction on immigrants and the studio audience burst in to applause. Micky Dove even scored points when David Devilman stated that most money experts were fairly certain that leaving the UK would be financially disastrous for Flatlands. Micky said he was fed up being told 'facts' by 'experts' and that we had enough of listening to experts. To my absolute horror everyone agreed with only a few seeming to show concern. Nigelle repeated over and over again that we needed to take control of our borders and stop the UK people from coming into our beautiful district and talking the strange talk and eating their weird food. Every question that Hillbilly Billy Hill asked Nigelle he kept repeating "let's take control of our borders" and that he was going to build a wall and the UK'ers were going to pay for it. He finished by saying he wanted his Flatlands back and he finished to a standing ovation.

SatD 12st Jism

The papers stated that the polls were showing that the Flexiters (*as they were now calling themselves*) had made considerable gains. The poll results were as follows: Flexit = 38%, Flemain = 45%, don't knows = 59%.

The Flatland TV shows kept showing Morris peeing on stage over and over again. It was his bumbling stupidity that was hitting a note with the people of Flatlands. Troubles ahead.

Sunty 13st Jism

We went to Chumpton World of Adventures today and had a lovely day. Light relief from referendum fever. Even in the Flatlands best root crop based theme park it was difficult to avoid seeing the increased support for the Flexit campaign. Somehow they were all wearing T shirted garments (*proper ones like they wear in the UK*) with 'Flexit, Taking our District back' printed on the front. I enquired where they were getting their T shirts from and someone told me to make my way to the Field Bar and "that lerrrrvly Nigelle F`Rage was giving them awaayy". When we got to the Field Bar we quickly found Nigelle, Morris and Micky Dove. Morris was wearing one of the T shirts as trousers and he had also managed to get his hand caught in the back of his shoe whilst trying to put them on. Nigelle was drunk and handing out these very professionally made T shirts. I asked him where he got them from and he told me it was a gift from somebody called Rimbit Muldoon. I of course had to wear one as I was technically Nigelle's campaign manager, even though I had purposely tried to miss-manage the campaign, it was starting to look that was once a foregone conclusion now hung in the balance with the Flexiters making big gains in the polls. We quickly forgot the troubles with the referendum by drinking lots of Turnip Pochine and Beetroot Daiquiris whilst enjoying the attractions and the rides that the best root crop based theme park Flatlands had to offer.

FLATLAND DISTRICT WEEKLY NEWS

Chumptons World of Adventure is happy to announce a new attraction starting soon and available on the 9th Thrisdee of each month. The Frigggg brothers from Norfolkshire which is outside of the Vale of Flatland District and is from the Northern end of the UK country somewhere, will be appearing on the Chumptons World of Adventure Ghost train ride.
Franklin Frigggg (far right in the picture) said he was looking forward to putting the willy's up the people on the ride

The Frigggg brothers

Moondee 14lbs Jism

Moondee and back on the campaigning again. I have decided to start getting my businesses in order in case the unthinkable happens and we actually leave the UK and we start experiencing huge financial hardship that the experts we apparently shouldn't listen to are telling we will face.

After firsdocky I rewrote my advert for the Happy Pauper shop window to let the folks of Chumpton folk aware that I do trepanning. I want to start pushing this as the new 'holistic' treatment for most things. I will also begin promoting my new found skills in gender reassignment and breast augmentation (*although the advert said 'get y' breasties resized' for the locals to understand*) as well as continuing my interpretive dance school and inventing of all manner of fantastic inventions.

Toosdi 15lbs Jism

NEW MOOOSICUL EXPRESSIONS

Flatland ladies! if your vagina's are dry and crusty then treat them to some lubrication with a night in the company of Ropey Town's very own Zachariah Belch. Zachariah will be performing at The Ropey Root Crop Outdoor Arena Sunty next. Zachariah will be performing tracks from his new album entitled 'Beastiality' which charted at No 3 in the Flatland Chart Parade. He said "my new album describes my personal journey .... a journey that took me from Chatterby to Chumpton".

Zach's management have requested that should any locals ladies consider throwing their underwear at him during his performance could they please give them at least a rudimentary cleaning as stage hands were injured at his last live performance at Chumpton WI hall. The weight and odour of the undergarments hospitalised 3 roadies when chucked onto the stage last Jism.

This week's yoof paper will have a lead story on Zach Belch. His album called Beastiality was a fen wide success. The cover picture reminded me of the photo in Mayor Devilman's living room. Zach is very popular among the ladies of Flatland District and has featured regularly in "Flatlands top 103 most eligible bachelors" in 'Fengurl' magazine. One admirer said he'd rank higher than his current best polling of 73 if he washed some of the pig faeces from his flowing locks. The lady didn't specify whether she was referring to his pubic hair or his noggin. We suspect both.

Winsti 16nd Jism

Ropey has been rid of buskers and beggars for many years, thanks in no small part to the unrivalled brutality that PC Jack Wormer of Ropey Town Police Brigade. I can't see these little buggers lasting too long once Jack gets hold of them.

Chumpton-by-Kumberly Informer

A group of genetically modified rodent musicians are reported to be rampaging locally and running amok trashing hotel rooms and driving expensive vehicles into swimming pools.

They are known to be taking drugs and drinking heavily (as all musicians do) before painting the town red and causing rock star like mayhem.

It is very important the public don't approach them (even for selfies) or encourage them by buying their album.

It's very warm isn't it.

Thrisdee 17nd Jism

This mawnin's edition of the Weekly News made it abundantly clear the Rimbit Muldoon was pulling out all the stops in trying to get the population of Flatland District to leave the UK. It announced that it was fully supporting the Flexit campaign and suggested its readers should vote to leave the UK when voting in next week's referendum. It showed pictures of Hoooomans lining up at the Flatlands borders waiting to get into our beautiful district. The picture was clearly faked but I have little doubt that the locals in the Jolly Sphincter in Ropey and the congregation in St. Jeremiahs church were more than happy to believe this rubbish. I went over to the Peppermint Hippo and had a carrot wine and roadkill hotpot for docky at daaymiddlin and some of the locals were in for a bit if light entertainment. None of the performers were in during the day but Sylvia often obliged with some moves of her own to keep the faithful few happy and earns a few extra turnips or Hoooman pennies depending on who the clientele were. Conversation quickly got round to the referendum and it seemed half of them wanted to leave the UK and half of them wanted stay. I made my way home and went on the compooota to see if I could take my mind off things for a while with some pictures of tuppences. I did a quick 1 minute 62 second mastybayshun before Nina returned with ladies from Chumptons WI sewing circle. They returned shattered, they had sewn 27 circles, a new record.

Frydims 18th Jism

Frydims firsloyght firsdocky TV was telling stories about how because of the influx of immigrants from the UK into Flatlands the resources were stretched to breaking point. Apparently, policing was now stretched to breaking point, Ropey Town Hospital for the Genetically Impure was stretched to breaking point, the Monastic Fire Brigade was stretched to breaking point (*although to be fair, I may have contributed to that from time to time*), and by all accounts we have something called Social Services??? And that was stretched to breaking point too. The story went on to say that we couldn't fit another single immigrant autocar vehicle on our section of the A14 or A14/1 and the immigrants had taken all our jobs. This was amazing as none of it was true but I knew that many of my fellow citizens of Flatlands would be taking it all in.

Today's opinion poll results were as follows:

Flexit = 48%

Flemain = 52%

Don't know = 37%

It was looking very close indeed.

SatD 19th Jism

Chumpton-by-Kumberly Informer

LOST: This delightful Fen Kitten has been lost from number 12 Yon Fen fen, Lower/Upper Fen Drove, Chumpton since Sungomooncum last Winsti. Anyone who knows of its whereabouts or has smelled it recently then do not approach it or make eye contact as it hasn't been weaned off Hoooman breast milk yet. Instead please contact the Ropey Town Police Brigade on its emergency number 1789598784612524545492154954849 6548 ext 2 option 4.

The Weekly News once again led on its front page with stories about the referendum and agreeing with Micky Dove's comments about not needing expert advice. It was out of my control now. The last live debate will happen on Toosdi noyght, the noyght before the referendum and I think it may be either make or break for both camps. My thoughts about all the political turmoil was momentarily relieved by this Lost and Found ad in the paper. It has got me thinking about the possibility of getting the ladies a pet. I may have a word with Jack about this Fen Kitten.

Sunty 20nd Jism

My trepanning has always been more than just a hobby; it was always something I wanted to use at some point as another form of income. When I had to raise money to get the club refurbished I proved my ingenuity. I placed adverts locally and today put an old picture on my Fenbook page to let my Fenbook chums aware I am available should any of them wish to have holes drilled in their heads. Unfortunately the contact number I put in the advert was a binary number and doesn't show up on anything other than compoootas.

I am now taking bookings for my Chumpton Trepanning Clinic.
If you have headaches, demons or sexual deviancy caused by brain pressure then trepanning is the thing for you.
Away with the dull drudgery of so called "Doctors" surgeries, away with bothersome pills and potions, come get trepanned at Chumptons Trepanning Clinic.
I am a fully certified Trepanner and plastic surgeon with a sort of qualification from the much respected seat of learning The University of Chatterby.
Booking accepted via carrier crow, homing goat or telephone. The number is 01010101010101010.
Remember book early whilst my trepanning tools are still relatively clean .... ish.

Trepanning with my apprentice Gildroy

fenbook Surch for peeeple and othur things tooooo 🔍   📷 Morton Hoome Feind frends 👥 📷 🕐 🔽

Many thanks to local artist Blodwella
Frangipane who kindly drew one of my
Trepanning classes I took before being
closed down.
I shall be re-opening my Trepanning
clinic as soon as I am allowed back in
Q&B or other Flatland DIY Stores

Moondee 21jr Jism

Today was largely spent sorting out the re-homing and collecting of the Fen Kitten I
saw in the paper on SatD. I spoke to Jack and he thought it was going to be a great idea.
He had it ready and packed in a cardboard box for when I went to collect it from the
Police Brigade Station. The ladies were understandably very excited when Jack and I
got back with it just after daaymiddlin. They opened the box and cuddled the little cutie
and petted it. Pocahontas was given the honour naming the latest addition to our house.
She was unable to speak the name she had chosen because she had put the Kitten's
head in her mouth so she typed it on the compooota. Our new pet is called
P)&h595£$?@. Pocahontas ran around the house for a while with P)&h595£$?@'s head
in her mouth and Nina told her let Cinderella have a turn petting it. Cinderella liked
playing racing cars with the little kitten. The lovely little kitten even made the

screeching sounds like a car as Cinderella scooted P)&h595£$?@ around the living room carpet. As the ladies were playing nicely with their new pet, Nina and I took the opportunity to pop upstairs for 4 minutes and 2 seconds of sexing. On our return we discovered P)&h595£$?@ had sadly passed away from unknown causes although Pocahontas had blood coming from her mouth and Cinderella was holding one of P)&h595£$?@'s legs in her hand. Both the ladies looked guilty. I buried P)&h595£$?@ next to Barry in the garden. I conducted a short ceremony similar to the one I gave Mr Tibbins back in Janeundmary when I thought he was dead. I sang a medley of Kylie Minogue songs and cried for 11 seconds.

Toosdi 22jr Jism

Tonoyght saw the last live debate on Flatlands TV. When I arrived at the TV studio I met up with my old mate and TV producer Gregory Dykesnaffler. Nigelle was already in make up so I had a quick chat to see how drunk he was, sadly he was very drunk. This it would seem, had turned into a winning formula. Any other area of professional or public life it would be a recipe for disaster but it appears these days the Flatlands folk love drunken fascist ramblings.

The debate was similar to the last one but when Hillbilly Billy Hill pushed Mayor Devilman about what would happen if he loses the referendum he said he would send a letter the very next mawnin to the UK of Great Britain governance people stating Flatlands intention to leave the UK. Once the letter was sent it would take about 2 years before it was dealt with (*that sounds a bit like the speed the Ropey Post Office deal with customers*). When Nigelle was asked about whether or not they had a plan for Flatlands to exit the UK they all just looked at each other, sniggered and in unison said "YEAH!" and sniggered again. When pressed about who would be the new Mayor of Flatland District if Mayor Devilman resigned after the vote they all looked at each other quite shocked. Apart from Micky Dove, he just squinted his piggy little eyes and turned away from his colleagues as they stared blankly at each other.

A poll had been taken and prepared for the late noyght news. It was exactly the same as the last Frydims poll except the 'don't knows' had risen by 11%.

Today's opinion poll results were as follows:

Flexit = 48%

Flemain = 52%

Don't know = 48%

I went to bed and wondered what tomorrow would bring.

CHAPTER SEVEN

FLATLANDS VOTES

Winsti 23th Jism

The polling stations would be open from firsloyght all the way laasloyght and it was anticipated to be an unusually high turn out to vote. At the Mayors election only 0.02% of the eligible electorate bothered turning out. Indications are this time it could be as high as 0.04%

I went and cast my vote early to avoid the press but unfortunately not early enough. Some hacks from the Flatland District Weekly News were hanging around outside the Chumpton WI hall (*Chumptons official polling station*). They asked me how I thought the campaign had gone and if I thought that we'd be successful. I nearly gave the game away by replying that I was sure the people of Flatland would see sense and vote to remain in the UK but stopped myself just in time once I remembered I was the campaign manager for the Flexit campaign. Luckily I didn't need to perjure myself as they didn't bother asking how I voted as they assumed it was a foregone conclusion. I returned home and switched on the TV. All the news was obviously about the referendum and at daaymiddlin I popped over to the Peppermint Hippo as we were having a referendum special noyght and it was also where some of the TV cameras would be as the result comes in. The Flexit campaign was having a victory/losers party and I wanted to make sure all the finger food buffet was ready and was almost within its best before date. All the club regulars had been and voted earlier, from what I gathered most had voted Flexit much to my dismay but I had to look thrilled. Virtually all of them said one of the main reasons they voted Flexit was not because they agreed with the policies or because they particularly liked the Flexit gang of three, but because I was the campaign manager. This I found extremely galling, how many others would be voting out of loyalty to me. The Flatlands TV news kept playing loops of Nigelle shouting how he wanted to make Flatlands great again and "We want out district back" sloganeering jingoisms. They would then show David Devilman looking incredibly smug in his made to measure suit, this was Flatlands TV's balanced approach to reporting the referendum.

When the news crews turned up to the Peppermint Hippo there were some incredibly drunk people wandering around the club in varying stages of undress and confusion ... fantastic advertising for my club if nothing else. The TV cameras were all ready to go and all we could do was sit and wait for the polling stations to close. Nigelle, Morris and Micky all turned up shortly before the polls were due to close, in the battle bus and the news crews were there ready to greet them as they stepped off their carriage. The news reporter asked them all as a group how they got on when they cast their votes. The looks on their faces told me straight away that they had forgotten to vote, well at least that was three less votes to worry about. They wandered into the club and ordered themselves a drink at the bar, I told Sylvia to go out to my office and get the very sparkling Parsnip vino. Mayor Devilman was at Flatland District Council offices in Ropey town hall and his news team were set up too.

The monitors were ready and running and the news came through that the polling stations had officially closed. That was it then. We were in for a long noyght by the looks of things. The areas were split into three regions of the district, Chatterby, Chumpton and Ropey and all the votes had been emptied from the swill buckets ready for counting. There were very few people from Flatlands that were able to count to the standard required despite the additional fingers and toes most of them had. To resolve this problem with the counting of the voting slips they asked that the adjudicators were of an incredibly high educational standard. The counting staff had to be able to count to over 100 and able to do writing neat enough that others could understand it. Ironically the only people that easily fit this criterion were the Hoooman immigrants.

As the noyght started to unravel Hillbilly Billy Hill was taking the opportunity to use his unusually large penis as a swing-o-metre to show how the voting was going. The first result came in a bit before noyghtmiddlin and it was from Chatterby region. The result went as follows.

Votes eligible for the region **4111**, votes cast **7**

Votes for leaving the UK of Great Britain – **2**

Votes for remaining within the UK of Great Britain – **5**

This was encouraging news as it was first blood to the Flemainers. I wanted to punch the air with joy but I could only punch Nigelle instead as an expression of my disappointment but still very satisfying. The cameras zoomed in to Nigelle as he was wiping the small amount of blood from the corner of his mouth.

"Mr F`Rage, what is your reaction to the news that Chatterby region has decided to vote to remain within the UK"? the reporter asked.

Nigelle looked straight into the camera and said "it is an outrage quite frankly, and … you know … I wouldn't be surprised if they were all the immigrants, the fuckers … fucking immigrants probably not even eligible to vote in this referendum".

The reporter looked quite startled at Nigelle's response; although I'm not sure why as it was the same reporter that has been covering his campaign so knew his form.

I could see the monitor as they went back to the studio and Hillbilly Billy Hill was gyrating his hips to show the viewers of Flatland District how their referendum was going with the aid of his swinging winky.

At a bit more after noyghtmiddlin the second regions results came through and it was Ropey Town region. The results for Ropey were as follows:

Votes eligible for the region **2955**, votes cast **42**

Votes for leaving the UK of Great Britain – **22**

Votes for remaining within the UK of Great Britain – **20**

That was a win for the Flexit campaign. Once again I punched Nigelle in the mouth. This meant that even though the regions were one a piece the numbers meant it was more or less even with a very slight lead for the Flexit campaign. It was all hinging on the Chumpton-by-Kumberly region results. My own village was going to be the deciding region whether or not we would remain as part of the UK.

A short while later the announcement came through that, even though it had the lowest amount of eligible voters of the three regions it had the highest turn out and after two re-counts Chumpton-by-Kumberly was ready to give the final results. The whole of the Peppermint Hippo went so quiet you would have heard a rickets riddled childers leg brace drop.

The results for the Chumpton-by-Kumberly region were as follows:

Votes eligible for the region **1423**, votes cast **51**

Votes for leaving the UK of Great Britain – **28**

Votes for remaining within the UK of Great Britain – **23**

The monitor sparked into action and we saw Hillbilly Billy Hill swinging his winky with such ferocity that it's starting to get a bit hard. The swing-o-metre was becoming more of a weather cock; maybe he could do the weather forecast after the referendum results. By the time he was ready to let the inhabitants of our district know what the future was going to hold for them Hillbilly Billy Hill was in a state of full sexual arousal. His swinging turned into thrusting and his thrusting became wild. Despite just thrusting into thin air he was getting enough purchase to become very aroused indeed and his visual aid to help the Flatland folk understand their political destiny had descended into a sort of frenzied non-contact mastybayshun, almost a dance, almost interpretive dance.

It became painfully obvious that most of the people in the club, including the reporter, were trying to work out what the result was in their heads. That would've taken a very long time to do so instead we were relying on a local newscaster/celebrity in the news studio in Ropey Town pointing his very large, very hard gun like winky at us, like it was some sort of 'referendum heist'. I didn't know whether to listen for the result or give him my wallet.

Hillbilly Billy Hill cleared his throat and put his finger to his ear and said "Okay, people of Flatland District all the results are in and here they are". He slowed his thrusting right down and looked at the camera for an unusually long pause as he smiled a very strange smile. We all thought he was hearing the results from the production gallery through an ear piece prior to announcing this historic result. However, as the camera panned out a bit it would seem that the end of his winky was dripping sex wee. As the camera zoomed in again further it was then abundantly clear that Hillbilly Billy Hill was having a shuddering moment live on TV just prior to reading out our referendum results. Politics must have been a lot more exciting than I ever gave it credit for. As he regained some of his composure he continued with his announcement. "The number of votes eligible to be cast throughout the region of Flatland District are 8529, the number of votes actually cast are, conveniently 100", another pause, this time definitely for dramatic effect "The votes cast from those wishing Flatland District to leave the UK of Great Britain is 52, the votes cast from those wishing Flatland District remain within the UK of Great Britain is 48. So with 52% of the vote against 48% of the vote, the result of the Flatland District referendum is that we want to leave the UK".

Instead of a huge cheer from all those in the Peppermint Hippo there was a kind of half cheer followed by a muted silence. I looked over to the gang of three cretins and they were all blissfully unaware of what had just happened. The camera man and reporter were bombarding Nigelle with questions but he was quite drunk on Badgerspizzle beer and making even less sense than normal. Morris had somehow managed to get his leg trapped in the toilet door and Micky Dove was away from the crowd rubbing his chin and surveying all that was going on around him through his piggy eyes.

I left the club just before Firsloyght and wandered back to home. I did a huge poo and then went to bed, somewhat thrilled that it was in that order.

CHAPTER EIGHT

A NEW AGE BECKONS

JUULII 1896

Thrisdee 1nd Juulii

As the news sunk in that we had voted to leave the UK of Great Britain I wandered about Chumpton in something of a daze. Everyone was walking about in something of a daze, but that was not unusual in Flatlands, this however was a different daze. Most of the villagers were walking about in a daze worried for the future. Even though there was a very poor turn out of eligible voters everyone had a view on the matter one way or another. Oddly, the split in opinion was approximately the same as the vote, if the locals had manged to find the polling stations or bothered themselves to go and vote I'd imagine the result would've been about the same.

I switched the Flatlands TV news on at daaymiddlin to see that David Devilman was going to resign from his post as the Mayor of Flatland District. My dazed like state was immediately changed to one of utter disbelief and horror. Surely it couldn't be that Nigelle F`Rage was going to be our new Mayor … or that despicable little shit Micky Dove …………… No …. It could never be Mayor Morris Poncen. A little bit of sick came up into my mouth.

The full magnitude of the situation had just fully hit home.

Frydims 2th Juulii

Today I have put up a piece of paper in the Happy Pauper to get a petition going to overturn the referendum result that will see Flatlands leave the UK of Great Britain. I was going to do one on fenbook but quickly realised that there were only 25 compoootas in Flatlands and they were mainly used for looking at ladies tuppences. By daaymiddlin docky time most of the inhabitants of Chumpton that voted for Flemain and could read and write had signed it. Although, there was a considerable number of X's on it but luckily Horatio Horatio, the owner of Happy Pauper, had helped the less literate of the village understand what it meant by reading it out for them and telling them to put a cross in the signature column. Not sure that's allowed but the assistance is greatly appreciated.

Every time the TV is switched on in our house the Flatlands news is churning out lots of different scenarios about what might happen and what might not. Nigelle was wandering about the house happy he'd won but strangely distant. The TV reports were showing Micky Dove being as evasive as ever and Morris Poncen getting his limbs caught in the nearest available thing to get caught in. Nigelle sat at the kitchen/operating table eating stewed carrot's and parsnip chips with a nice Beetroot smoothie. I asked him why he looked a bit vague but he shrugged it off. I also asked him what his plans were now he had won the referendum but he just shouted something about bloody foreigners. I could tell he was concerned and I think I may have hit a nerve, he hadn't thought that far ahead. His incoherent ramblings of the past few weeks were now about to be found out. It was never even a consideration that the Flexit campaign was actually going to win but with the lack of any conviction from David Devilman's campaign they snuck in the victory. Subsequently, nobody had even thought of organising a plan for Flatlands actually leaving the UK. Micky Dove had been on Flatlands news and when he was asked about what the Flexit exit plans were he said that David Devilman should have made a plan, and that it wasn't Flexits fault if the Mayor's office hadn't devised an exit strategy. What a fucking mess.

The day was spent tip toeing about the place as the ladies had accidentally drunk some devils prolapse I had left out for reporters wishing to speak to either me or Nigelle. The ladies regained consciousness and had a terrific headache and as a result would scream every time Nigelle shouted the word "immigrants" (*which was a lot*). Nigelle was clearly agitated and didn't like the thought of more reporters, who only a day earlier where his champions, now asking too many pesky questions.

The exchange rate for root crops to Hoooman moneys has dropped quite dramatically. Yisdee you could buy 1 big bag of onions for fifteen pounds thirty five penceses in Hoooman money or six Davey coins. Now it's plummeted to 1 bag of onions for thirteen pounds. The lowest it has been since 1789, thirty years ago.

SatD 3rd Juulii

This mawnin the Flatlands news had reported that Morris Poncen was the favourite to become the new Mayor of Flatlands. His idiotic bumbling stupidity had appealed to the idiotic bumbling stupidity of the Flatlands folk that had voted for Flexit. This was most galling for the slimy, little shit Micky Dove and although he had publically supported the concept of Morris becoming Mayor, you could almost see it eating away at his insides. He was indeed a despicable, piggy eyed, untrustworthy, little shit of a man. He was the only one of the gang of three who genuinely believed that Flatlands would be better off without the UK of Great Britain. Nigelle was mostly concerned with ridding the area of immigrants (*of which he, as mentioned on numerous occasions was one*), Morris Poncen was just thrilled to have new friends, friends that would assist him when he got trapped in revolving doors, but Dove was the one with the eyes on the prize.

This theory of mine was shown to be true later in the day. The Flatlands gossip mill was alight again when the hateful, vile, cuntbucket Micky Dove, had contacted the Flatlands media circus (*one TV station, a radio station and four local newspapers … five if you include my yoof paper*) to state that he could not in all consciousness support Morris Poncen as the new Mayor of Flatlands in the forthcoming Mayoral elections proposed in a couple of months time for Frydims 25lbs Septicbowel. He also mentioned, almost as an aside, that he would himself be running for the office of Mayor of Flatlands. Morris seemed to take it all in his stride, I don't think he really understood what was going on. When the press went to interview him to find out his thoughts on the apparent skulduggery by one of his Flexit running mates he just smiled inanely as he attempted to get his arm free from the collection draw of the bubble-gum machine outside the Ropey branch of Happy Pauper.

Sunty 4rd Juulii

The next instalment of this ongoing saga continued this mawnin. The previously rarely mentioned fact that the Flexit campaign had no strategy for leaving the UK finally started to hit home, especially regarding what was facing the Flatland District and its future.

With the exception of Nigelle all the people who were planning to run for Mayor were either former friends or ex school chums of David Devilman. Septicbowels elections would be a very interesting time. Whoever gets the position of Mayor of Flatlands would invariably have a poisoned challis as they'd be the person that sends the letter to the UK government of Great Britain advising them we would be officially leaving the UK. This would almost certainly spell financial disaster for the area, at least for the short term but probably for many years to come.

Now the people in favour of Flexit, even the very few convicted enough to exercise their right to vote, were looking rather concerned. The dazed expression of a couple of days ago was now replaced with a blank stare into the abyss.

Moondee 5st Juulii

The onion slipped even further against the Hoooman pound this mawnin and potatoes were on the run too. I was feeling a little low and we all needed cheering up so I decided to take us all to Chumpton World of Adventure to try and take our minds off the impending doom that was awaiting our grey, drab, incredibly flat little district.

As we wandered about the best root crop based theme park in all of Chumpton, possibly even the area, I couldn't relax; I couldn't get enjoy the day. Even several hallucinogenic onion Cocktails didn't shake the melancholy I was feeling. Something was not sitting right at the back of my mind. I was not quite right in my mind. I didn't have a right mind. My mind isn't right. I'm not right in the mind. On the guided bus back to central terminal at Chumpton village, Nina sensed I wasn't right in the head so she did what any caring partner would do to someone with mind problems; she did some mastybayshun on me. A full 5 minutes 115 seconds later I still hadn't done the shuddering. She tried putting my winky in her mouth (*that always does the trick*), but nothing. Luckily the guided bus went over a boulder or something and the jolt seemed to shake my sex wee loose. As I helped Nina clean her hair, sleeve, chin, chestal area, left shoe and back of the seat and the lady sat behind us, it all began making a bit more sense. The other bus users could tell by the look on my face that I had, had a special moment, a moment of realisation.

I am beginning to suspect all is not as it seems at Flatland District town hall.

Toosdi 6lbs Juulii

FLATLAND DISTRICT WEEKLY NEWS

Awww, young lovers Jizelle Ffflapp and Enricho Stabber are the perfect Flatland couple. Snapped in a loving embrace during a "romantic picnic for two" during a visit to Chumtpon World of Adventures.

Professional snapper/paparazzi for The Flatland Weekly News Bailey Davis was strolling through local gardening legend Percival Threwnn's ornate garden homage` to Beetroot known as 'The Beetroot Garden', when he saw these two cuddling. It bought a smile to my face and a lump to my trousers to see such a tender and beautiful display of affection in a public space.

Unknown to us but as we walked around Chumpton World of Adventure yisdee the most famous photoperson in all of Flatlands, Bailey Davis was out and about snapping people doing their thing. Good to see that the world hasn't ground to a halt just because Flatlands has voted to leave the UK.

Nigelle was still unsure what was going on so I gave him a really good trepanning at firsdocky today. I used my extra-large drill and made two very large holes in his cranial bonce cavity to let all the demons out that had been bothering him during the campaign. Afterwards he seemed much more relaxed, very floppy indeed. Due to his floppiness and even more drivelled, dribbly speech I decided to release a statement to the Flatlands media circus. As I was Nigelle's campaign manager, I decided that he was "no longer interested in being a part of the Flexit movement and just wanted his old life back. He wished everybody the best of luck in the forthcoming Mayoral elections on the 25lbs Septicbowel". True to my word, after some hefty trepanning, I gave Nigelle his old life back.

The announcement was met with indifference. The man who only days earlier was the darling of the Flexit campaign was now no longer wanted in the public eye. Instead he was tied to a bath in the basement of my house with two very large holes allowing pressure, headaches, demons and brain matter to gently ease out of the his cranial bonce holes. Once the trepanning has kicked in I will suggest that he goes to Merica of the USA, situated in another part of the world where there were many, many, many racists. He would be in his element there.

Winsti 7st Juulii

Nina was out and about in Ropey town and I was busying myself at the maternity ward in the Hospital counting infants digits and limbs. As I left the hospital I saw Nina across the road standing outside the 'Dykes' public house/Discotheque. It's one of several pubs in Ropey but this one was attracting a large number from Flatlands ever increasing LBGT community (*something that has become much more popular since the influx of Hoooman immigrants*). As an erotic drag dancer I obviously welcome allsorts into our community but many within Flatlands don't share my enthusiasm for our LBGT chums. When I visited London the other month I saw plenty of Gay men and ladies everywhere, all very much in love and nobody batted an eyelid. Flatlands is a bit more behind with the times, this annoys me. I shouted loudly for a few times to attract Nina's attention but I was too far away and it was windy so she probably couldn't hear me. Then to my amazement I noticed several ladies around Nina all getting very flirty with her and gently stroking her hair, like I do with sleeping people. She then kissed one of them followed by a very big hug. I couldn't quite tell if it was a friendly hug and kiss or whether it was a bit more sexy … like I do with sleeping people.

Thrisdee 8th Juulii

Following yisdee's revelation that Nina was possibly just as keen on the ladies as hot hunks of love like my good self I have started wondering if she might benefit from my skills as a gender reassignment surgeon. It would be my opportunity to try and change a lady into a man.

The onion has stabilised against the Hoooman pound which in turn has set both Flatlands and Fenbook alight with Flexit voters convinced that we will be better off after all, (*ignoring the fact that Flatlands council haven't even sent the letter to the government people of the UK of Great Britain yet*). Norfolkshire and other parts of East Angular have said they'd be happy to continue trading with us so everything will be fine then. I'm not so sure. My petition to have another vote so I can get the result I want is filling up quite nicely. I'm up to 3512 signatures now … well I use the term 'signature' very loosely. Some Flexit voters found out about my petition I secretly posted in the Happy Pauper and are insistent that democracy has spoken and Flemainers are just sore losers.

I have not seen anything of Hector the Time Travelling Tortoise for some time now and thought it would be an idea to see if it was in the ladies bedroom, like it was last time. I wandered into their bedroom only to discover Finbar and Cinderella on the bed passionately engaged in each other's company. Cinderella was on her back with her legs over Finbar's shoulders and she was doing some colouring in, in her Disney colouring in book, apparently oblivious to what was going on further down her torso. Finbar was noshing away at her tuppence like a tramp at a free buffet. Ordinarily this would be an awkward situation to say the least, somebody walking in on such an intimate moment between two people. This however was more concerning as what I saw, what I smelled nearly made me heave my docky up (*Turnip sandwiches followed by potato cake*). Cinderella's 'vagina' as us doctors call it when discussing doctoring things at doctors parties an such, was in quite a state. It would seem that the surgery was not a complete success after all. How Finbar managed to remain in such close proximity to the lump of heavily decomposed flesh without vomiting was amazing, and a tribute to his poor sense of smell and devotion to his courting Cinderella, but clearly something had to be done.

After daymiddlin I went to Ropey Hospital to do the paperwork for all the toe counting I have done recently (*blooming red tape*). I popped in and saw one of the consultant paediatricians called Billy S'vile. He had a famous twin brother in the UK of Great Britain that worked at the BBC, the same BBC I visited. I did enquire about Billy's brother on my recent trip to London and the BBC but I got stony faced reactions so I'm guessing nobody has heard of him. There was always something not quite right about Billy but he was always approachable and helpful when I asked him about techniques regarding my gender reassignment surgery.

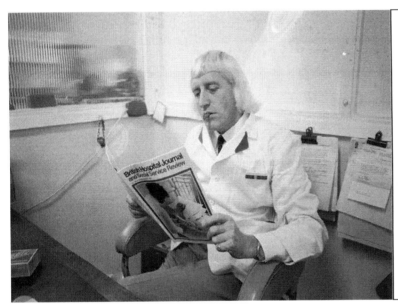

Here is Doctor Billy S'vile, my doctoring chum and great help in advising me about gender reassignment surgery. It was him who got me into wanting to have a go at doctoring in the first place and put me in touch with the University of Chatterby to take my online doctors test to allow me to do surgery on ladies breasties and tuppences and chaps winky's.

Frydims 9th Juulii

I examined Pocahontas and Cinderella's tuppences for any remedial surgery that might be needed. After Nigelle's Firsdocky trepanning I decided that Pocahontas's gender reassignment had gone reasonably well but Cinderella's tuppence needs a major overhaul.

Business at the club has been steady and I have had some repeat orders for some of my inventions. The money is okay but now the referendum is out of the way I must try and concentrate on getting myself sorted before we leave the UK. I have not heard from David Devilman since the referendum. I am surprised and relieved to be Honest.

SatD 10lbs Juulii

Tonoyght I shall be trying out a part time job to get some more money rolling in to add to our nest egg ready for when the local economy goes arse up. Since the referendum result I have been shocked, dazed, happy, sad, accepting, denying, all manner of emotions but there is still something nagging at the back of my mind that I can't quite put my finger on.

Tonoyght I shall be starting my new part-time job as a sheep. The winter months at The Peppermint Hippo can be sparse and once the district has left the UK of Great Britain we may be in for tough times. It's always handy to have a back up career ... even if it is as a sheep.

The farmer I'm working for has assured it's easy work and he'll come and visit me about noyghtmiddlin for a cuddle. It sounds like he really cares for his sheep.

Do any of my Fenbook chums have any tips on being a temporary sheep.

Sunty 11jr Juulii

Things got quite unpleasant last noyght dressed as a sheep so tonoyght it's a different farmer, different outfit. I am hoping for a better, more respectful outcome, less anally painful.

My local friendly farmer Grunty Crowboiler was a bit friendlier than was entirely necessary. Grunty reminded me of my relationship with 'Rowenta', one of his sexually promiscuous sheep, and said I looked a bit like Rowenta now. It was at this point it all started to get a bit out of hand … although what wasn't out of his hand for long was his winky. The cundreysoid can be a strange place to live some times.

Quite frankly last nights try out as a sheep was a disaster. Farmer Grunty Crowboiler came to visit late last noyght and made advances that I have only ever previously experienced whilst serving custodial sentences.

Suffice to say my career as a temporary sheep was a short and somewhat painful one. An experience I am looking forward to put behind me.

On a more positive note I am trying out as a Cock (see picture) over the next few days. I am confident nothing could possibly go wrong this time. I am regularly told I'm a Cock so thought I'd use these lovely compliments to good use. Wish me luck Fenbookers

Moondee 12nd Juulii

This mawnin I made some important decisions concerning the ladies gender reassignment. Pocahontas seems to be holding out well despite some early setbacks with her vagina falling off every now and then. Cinderella has had problems with infection in her tuppence and after the consultation with fellow doctoring expert Billy S'Vile, I will be doing some emergency remedial surgery today. On SatD noyght I was doing some part-time work as a sheep. Sadly one of the sheep had passed away earlier in the noyght when it had been attacked by either a Finnitechygobbit on its way to terrorise local childers from their slumber or it was a local lad … on its way to terrorise local children from their slumber. Either way there was a reasonably freshly dead sheep so I helped myself to its vagina before the local young folk, eager for a covert sexual encounter; hear of the dead sheep's whereabouts. I gave Cinderella some sleepy drink and removed her old tuppence that I had fashioned from her winky when she was a chap. I put that on the draining board and attached the sheep's vagina as per some of the drawings Billy S'Vile had done for me on a beer mat a few days earlier at our doctoring conference in the Jolly Sphincter. To avoid infection from the sheep's tuppence (*thus avoiding doing all this for nothing*) I had soaked the sheep's tuppence in the purest, quadruple distilled 764% proof Turnip Pochine to make sure that it was completely free from dirt and bugs and stuff. I triple fixed the sheep's vagina to Cinderella's tuppence slot with Selotape, stitches, and staples.

The remedial surgery was a huge success. The only down side was when Finbar came round to visit Cinderella for a 'welfare visit' he sucked on her tuppence when nobody was looking. Due to the extremely high alcohol content in Cinderella's vagina Finbar is now completely blind.

Notice how I haven't mentioned fires for a while now ☺ ☺ ☺ ☺ ☺ ☺ ☺ ☺☺ ☺ ☺ ☺☺ ☺ ☺ ☺☺ ☺ ☺ ☺

Toosdi 13ᵗʰ Juulii

Cinderella is recovering well, Pocahontas has been helping her do some colouring and kitten strangling in order to try and take her mind of the unbearable pain she must be suffering. Jack came around after daaymiddlin and took Pocahontas out for a stroll and a good fingerblasting.

Tonoyghts laasdocky we had turnip soup for 'beginners course', we had roast turnip and turnip mash and turnip chips with some kind of road kill for the 'mainly course' and for the 'enders course' we had turnip crumble with turnip ice cream. It was a great way of using all the turnips we got from Chumptons World of Adventure last week.

I asked Nina what kind of roadkill she had used because it had a strange taste. She replied that she thought I had bought it from the Happy Pauper yisdee. I told her I hadn't been to the Happy Pauper yisdee. It was then that I realised that the meat she had used was Cinderella's old tuppence I had left on the drainer during surgery. I didn't tell her the truth, I just pretended I had forgotten "oh yes, that's right I did go to the shop in the mawnin before anyone was up" I said. I spent the next hour trying to be sick and brushing my teeth.

No fires today.

Winsti 14th Juulii

My interpretive dance class was very interesting. Gary, my London driver whose daughter PC Wormer held hostage, approached me after the lesson to say he was unable to make it to the next lesson. I told him that was fine but he seemed terrified that Jack would find out and do something to his daughter again. I gave him my word he'd never find out and he seemed really grateful. I told him I was really grateful to him for taking me to London.

"I had a great day out with you, even if I didn't get the job as a signer for TV" I said.
"As long as you're certain I'm okay not to come for the next lesson" Gary said nervously.
"Of course not, don't worry I won't tell Jack, he does exactly as I tell him to, don't you worry about him".
"Really … he does as you tell him to"? Gary said, now a lot more thoughtfully.
"Absolutely, I know things about Jack that means he does as he's told. Besides he is seeing one of my ladies so that makes him my friend …. I guess" I continued.
Gary cautiously said "I have booked a weekend in London for my wife and I to celebrate our wedding anniversary … I can cancel if you really want me to attend".
"Honestly don't worry about it. PC Wormer won't go anywhere near your daughter, I'll make sure of it, oddly he's actually pretty good with kids" I said. Gary didn't seem convinced. He was however very relieved and grateful.

Thrisdee 15st Juulii
More money making ideas are flooding my noggin and bonce area. I'm struggling to find local ladies that either fit up chimneys or willing to do it nakedly.

fenbook | Surch for peeeple and othur things teoooo 🔍   👤 Marton Hoome Foind frends 🔳🔳🔳 🔳▾

HELP! HELP! HELP ! HELP !

I have started a new business venture called "The Naked Lady Chimney Sweeping Service" and need some of my lady Fenbook pals to help out with some cover shifts.

I will pay top dollar, in human money not root crops, and offer free trepanning and/or lessons in interpretive dance as an incentive as well as remuneration for time worked and chimneys swept starkers.

If you're a bit concerned about he whole nudity thing because your lady regions need a trim, I'm starting another service which is trimming ladies naughty bits plummage with scissors. Both ladies in the picture had a substantial anal beard, as you can see, thanks to my other business (The Chumpton Lady Gardener) they are both now free of spiders legs/clock springs etc.

Frydims 16lbs Juulii

Tonoyght we saw the first ever shift from one of my new performers, Griselda Flange. She knocked em dead with some of the punters buying extra packets of Klappers Tummy Wipes from Sylvia behind the bar. The floor looked like it looked after a prostrate milking meeting.

Latest attraction at the Hippo

Meet Grisselda Flange, a local lass who will be appearing at Peppermint Hippo (Chumptons premier lap dancing/pole dancing bar) every Frydims noyght. Our latest lovely will be working the pole and also private dances. So come on lads, if you want to see this lovely in a skimpy bikini or even less then its got to be Peppermint Hippo.

She? Is appearing at my club courtesy of the recently held auditions noyght.

SatD 17st Juulii

This mawnin I had a very considerable poo just after firsloyght before firsdocky. It took a large amount of concentration and squeezing out, so much so I forgot to give Nigelle his first trepanning of the day. Later on he was less floppy because of it. As he was less floppy he was a bit more talkative than usual, normally a bad thing. Today though he was telling me that Morris Poncen went to school with Mayor Devilman. This I already knew, but what I didn't know, that Nigelle managed enlightened me with, was that the school was in London and that he and Mayor Devilman didn't even come from Flatlands. I'm not sure I believed Nigelle my feeling of uneasiness was getting worse.

Sunty 18th Juulii

After the upheaval of recent times and the uncertainty that remains within our community we have been clutching at straws for good news. Anything that the local community can celebrate with a couple of gallons of Potato wine or Badgerspizzle beer is looked upon as a blessing lately. A wedding is as good an excuse as any to down a substantial quantity of alcohol.

FLATLAND DISTRICT WEEKLY NEWS

The Flatland community would like to extend its best wishes to Jeremiah Katkiller and his beautiful bride Jemimah Katkiller who were married last week on Toosdi last at Daymiddlin. The happy couple were wed at St.Jeremiahs Church. The reception was held in a nearby field and several people attended.

Fortunately Jemimah's maiden name was also Katkiller due to a crazy quirk of fate, and also because she is a distant relative of Jeremiah. She is his sister and second cousin.

Here we see a photo of the happy couple taken shortly before they retired to the bridal suite/barn. Jeremiahs father, also called Jeremiah, said it was "a booodiful daay".

Moondee 19th Juulii

The club was busy this laasloyght. Nigelle ventured out of into the Peppermint Hippo for the first time since I announced to the press that he was leaving the Flexit movement. The TV was on in the bar and Flatlands TV news was on when we walked in. I was just about to ask Sylvia to turn it off or change channel when I saw the lead story. It was all about the Mayoral election campaign that was taking place over the next few months. It was announcing the candidates that were currently running. They were the terrible twins, Ian and Duncan Smythe, who both went to school with Mayor Devilman. Another was Morris Poncen, who went to school with Mayor Devilman, Theresa Posh-Farquharson, who didn't go to school with Mayor Devilman and Micky Dove who was a vile, piggy eyed fuck-twat who very little was known about his schooling. It put a bit of dampener on the noyght but we still managed to drink too much distilled root crop juices.

Toosdi 20st Juulii

I have been easing off Nigelle's trepanning lately. His demons have been making him more coherent and because he and the gang of three had spent so much time together on the battle bus it was becoming clear that he had learned a lot about his two running mates.

As Nigelle's demons took hold it made him easier to understand the few interesting snippets of information he divulged. Maybe something to remember for future trepanning ~~victims~~ patients that fewer holes drilled in the cranial bonce cavity can sometime create greater lucidity.

Nina was asking about getting more of the roadkill meat from the Happy Pauper like we had last week. I didn't know what to say but I certainly couldn't tell the truth now. Perhaps I could find some more scraps of body parts ready for the incinerator at Ropey Hospital and see if Nina notices the difference.

Winsti 21lbs Juulii

Still no word from David Devilman, not even for private dances. I can only assume he is busy getting his affairs in order before the new Mayor of Flatlands takes over the role. He did say in his resignation speech outside Ropey Town hall the mawnin after the referendum that he was going to steer the ship until he passed on the baton to the new Mayor. Rumour had it he was spending lots of time in London so I can only assume he was helping pave the way for Flexit negotiations. Perhaps he was trying to talk the Government of the UK to allow us to keep exporting root crops to the UK without export taxes. I can't help feeling the Mayor … soon to be ex-Mayor hasn't been entirely honest.

I was at the hospital this mawnin and chatting to Billy S'Vile about the vaginal transplant I did for Cinderella. He seemed very impressed, although he did have the same look on his face that David Devilman has when he's stroking his Growler and he kept thrusting his groinal area against my knee. The more I mentioned the surgery the quicker the thrusting got. Dr S'Vile loves talking about surgery.

Maybe Billy has bought his dog into work with him. A bit unhygienic if he has though. Anyway, I managed to sneak a few limbs ready for incineration into a carrier bag to see if Nina noticed the difference between that and the roadkill we buy from the Happy Pauper in Chumpton. I will keep the limbs in the shed for a few days so they can get the same level of decomposition that Cinderella's tuppence had at the point of surgery.

Thrisdee 22nd Juulii

NEW MOOOSICUL EXPRESSIONS

Here is the very first promotional photo of Indie darlings The Maccabees. Taken before Orlando Weeks was the main vocalist the band enjoyed the singing delights of Jerebiah Jerehiab from Chatterby. His services were no longer required after he had arrested for the attempted sodomisation of local Toy salesman and naturist Feldman Hagar. He was later found inserting pieces of lego into a fox cubs anus. The rest as they say is history.

Today's edition of my yoof paper is out in the shop, ready for the hip and happening youngsters of Flatlands to purchase and enjoy. My yoof paper has been an unexpected success and each week it has sold out every copy in Chumpton. I went to Chatterby this mawnin, just after firsdocky, and spoke to Zachariah Beelzebub the franchise owner of the Chatterby branch of Happy Pauper about selling the New Mooosicul Expressions. He agreed to stock them on a sale or return basis so I left a happy chappy. My Naked lady Chimney Sweeping service has taken a bit of a tumble due to the aesthetically unpleasant qualities of the ladies I have provided the clientele with, not to mention their poor chimney sweeping abilities. Oh well not every idea can be a winner.

Frydims 23nd Juulii

Chumpton-by-Kumberly Informer

FOUND IN CHUMPTON
A young Finnitechtygobbitt (guessing no more than 120-130 years old) was found wandering bewildered and confused between lower fen Fen and Yon End on Thrisdee this week.
I'm guessing this young calf is no more than a F3 generation mutation and is currently being kept at Mrs Migginsworths B&B (room148) until the rightful owner claims ownership or responsibility.
You can ring Police Constable Jack Wormer on Tel No 999 9999 999 to arrange collection. A cage will be needed.

This mawnin in one of the local papers there was a story about what may have been the Finnitechygobbit that killed the sheep the other weekend when I was trying out as a 'temporary sheep' on Grunty's farm. There is still no sign of Hector the time travelling tortoise but I still have plenty of stuff left over in my inventing shed to make another one. Maybe Edith's cat fancy's doing a bit of multi-dimensional time travelling.

SatD 24nd Juulii

Today we visited Chumpton World of Adventures and I saw Morris Poncen. He had somehow managed to get stuck on the zip wire ride that goes between the Turnip groves to the Beetroot gardens. He waved at me and smiled and I asked him if he was okay. He said he was but he was a bit hungry and could do with a drink and a wee as he'd been stuck up there since Frydims daaymiddlin. I asked him if I was the first person he'd seen since becoming stuck but he informed me the place had been alive with people. I wondered why nobody had helped him but on further investigation it transpires I was the first person he'd mentioned it to that he was stuck up there. I notified one of the members of staff that Morris needed helping down and they thought it was just a publicity stunt for the forthcoming referendum. When I explained the referendum had happened a month ago they seemed quite confused. I'm guessing that level of stupidity means they would've voted for Flexit.

My interpretive dance class was a little later than usual. It was well attended as usual thanks to PC Wormer standing at the side menacingly slapping his noyght stick in his hand.

This seemed to put some of the students off their stride a little so I asked Jack to leave, thanked him for his help and closed the WI hall door as he left. I turned round to my class and could feel a huge collective sigh of relief sweep across the students, none more so than my star pupil Gary the driver. As the class began dancing interpretively to Black Laces 'Gangbang' song Gary began dancing his way over to me.

"Hey there Gary, how was your weekend in London" I enquired
"Really, really lovely thank you" he said. "Look I just wanted to say on behalf of everyone here thanks for getting rid of that fucking brute of a so-called Policeman, he is just so intimidating".
This made me feel a little bit guilty about using him to pressgang people into coming now.
"Look" I said "I'll ask him not to come anymore, I'm sorry I did in the first place to be honest … and if you guys and girls don't want to attend any longer I totally understand".
"No it's okay, it's quite good fun" Gary said, "Look, if you need giving a lift anywhere again you only have to ask" he continued.
Good to know if I need to go anywhere in the future.

Sunty 25th Juulii

Chumpton-by-Kumberly Informer

Local girls have been gasping with sexual excitement as news filters through the village that one half of the Crakdigga Quads (Jeremiah and Jeremiah pictured below, left to right) will be crooning their melodies at the Chumpton WI hall next Frydims.
You may recognise the boys from the appearance they made on the Hooomans TV program X Factor. Of course that was filmed shortly before the other two brothers (Jeremiah and Jeremiah) were sentenced to a custodial stay at her majesties pleasure following and incident with a traffic cone, some duct tape and a sexually submissive Cringewarbler from Chatterby. It was to be the last time they appeared as a foursome (or Quintet as it's known in the music industry).
They will be ably supported by Jebwould, a local duo of no discernible talent.

Jeremiah and Jeremiah Crakdigga

The local ladies are all frothed up and speaking in a very sexually provocative manner at the news that one half of the Crakdigga quads will be playing the WI hall next Frydims. Even Nina has admitted to doing some Mastybayshun with several carrots whilst looking at the poster advertising the event. Once again this has put our house in hot water with the proprietor of the Happy Pauper.

Sadder news has been filtered back to me that Cinderella's beau, Finbar Knuckleshuffla, has been attacked by the Theltwells Dykebumma that has been roaming between Chatterby and Chumpton lately. He didn't see the attack due to Finbar's blindness caused by performing cunnilingus on Cinderella's new pickled sheep's tuppence shortly after her vaginal transplantology. The high alcohol content of the tuppence was to assist with resisting organ rejection and Finbar's cheeky flange snaffle got him blind drunk, literally. By all accounts he was looking for the Happy Pauper and accidentally wandered beyond the village boundary towards the Chatterby timeline and was interfered with by the wild beast.

PC Wormer of Ropey Town Police Brigade said judging by the state of the "entry wound" it was almost certainly a Theltwells Dykebumma or possibly Jack Flickerbean from Flickerbean's abattoir. Neither would have been a very pleasant experience. Finbar will be buried on Winsti if his condition doesn't improve.

Moondee 26lbs Juulii

This mawnin I skinned the rotting flesh I have stored in my inventing shed so that Nina can make more roadkill stew without the expense of the roadkill. She was thrilled when I handed her the mangled decaying flesh and placed it in a pot ready for the hob. As she informed me she was preparing it for tonoyghts laasdocky. I told her I'd be eating at the Peppermint Hippo as I was auditioning new performer. I wasn't but …… well, you know …

I caught the guided bus to Ropey and popped into the town hall to see Mayor Devilman about getting my company registered. The Mayor wasn't in his chambers but I saw Cranshaw St.John and he agreed to sign the necessary paperwork for me. He told me that Mayor Devilman hadn't been seen much since the referendum. I said I thought he was supposed to be steering the ship until we have a new Mayor.

Cranshaw chuckled and assured me that he was definitely steering his ship and continued laughing as I left the town hall. I registered my new company and it was called **ZONCO**, a catchy little name.

When I got back to Chumpton I remembered that Nina was cooking roadkill stew so called into the club as I said I would. I noticed that Flatlands TV news was still showing the footage of Morris Poncen hanging from the zip wire at Chumptons World of Adventure. It turns out that Morris used the zip wire three more times and got stuck every time. Sylvia asked me what I wanted to eat, I thought if they were having roadkill stew at home then I could have it here as I noticed it on the menu … just my one would be made with real road kill and not … well … not hospital waste.

The stew was okay but tasted as strange Nina's to be honest. When I mentioned the unusualness to Sylvia she told me to take it up with Nina as she cooked it, she said that Nina came over with plenty as she'd cooked too much at home and mentioned I might be in later for a bowl of stew. I was sick in my mouth again. I may have started a small fire on my way home from the club. Number 36 Lower fen Fen at yon end of Upper drove were the unlucky burnees but they were on holiday at Chatterby sands so only the dog burned a bit.

Toosdi 27st Juulii

This mawnin I had a visit from the Monastic Fire Brigade. I feared that perhaps someone had witnessed last noyght's indiscretion but they were just passing and wanted to borrow the toilet for one of the older monks. Nina went to Ropey on the guided bus to see some friends at the Dykes Discotheque. I was beginning to wonder about her possible need for gender reassignment but for the time being I think she's better of as a lady.

Winsti 28th Juulii

Today dear diary I called into the club on my way to catch the guided bus to Ropey and Sylvia asked me to ask Nina if she can make any more of the roadkill stew. Apparently they'd sold out and could've sold five times more than she had. This worked out rather well as I was going up to Ropey Hospital to have a doctoring conference with Dr Billy S'Vile about the best way of turning a lady into a chap. My talk with Dr S'Vile was very enlightening and he drew me some ideas this time on a piece of toilet paper he kept in the top pocket of his shirt. After the doctoring talk I popped down to the skip near the incinerator and found plenty of spare body bits just going to waste. Even better some of it was already decomposed so Nina could get cooking tonoyght.

Thrisdee 29lbs Juulii

Crimp Fen inhabitants' hearts were pounding like racing rats at the annual Flatland racing rat Derby. All of this was because local pop act 'Hick' were playing a concert there. I featured it in this week's edition of my District wide Yoof Paper.

NEW MOOOSICUL EXPRESSIONS

This is "local" band Hick.
Hick are about to embark on a world tour of Chatterby, Crimp Fen, Chumpton and Ropey Town, beginning this weekend at Chatterby Womens Institute. There will be a special guest appearance from Jerediah Snufmoovee who will be playing his Pigs Bladder Flatland Bagpipe.
If attending the Crimp Fen gig please make sure that you have checked you have the correct currency, Chumpton Post Office are offering very good exchange rates at the moment. 3 onions equals 1 double headed chicken.

Frydims 30st Juulii

I have had more orders in today for my Badger CB's and a couple of enquiries about my Childers Dream Catcher. My portable lovers are doing quite steady business but the dog wigs and naked chimney sweeping never took off really. The club is doing nicely but although the onion has stabilised against the Hoooman pound, things were still jumpy among Flatland locals. Many now wishing they had voted for Flemain. I have placed an advert in the Happy Pauper and put one in the Peppermint Hippo asking if anyone was interested in coming to work for me as an inventor's apprentice. Just before laasloyght I received a tefelone call from Sylvia at the club saying somebody was interested in coming to do some work for me helping me build my inventions. I nipped over and took a few washing up bowls full of Nina's roadkill stew.

The chap in question was a local chap called Jim Bob Von Hornyrimmer. The Von Hornyrimmer's are an old Flatlands family that date back to when the Flatland District was drained by the Dutch and noted locally for their usefulness with their hands due to the extra fingers. He starts in the mawnin and he'll be out looking for baby Badgers for hand held CBs and a couple of Biguns for CB base units. This is his photo for his ID badge

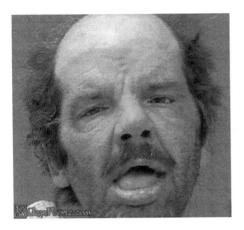

SatD 31nd Juulii

Today Jim Bob came round just after firsdocky to start his first day at new job and he had a bag full of the loveliest, cutest, tiny baby Badgers, all freshly strangled. The parents were in another bag and to my utter amazement they were strangled too and not shovelled. To say Jim Bob had impressed me was an understatement. A fantastic start to our working relationship.

Later I got him making my multi smokers. This is an idea I had a while back allowing people to smoke two, maybe even more cigarettes at once. Not only had he made them by laasloyght but he'd taken them to various outlets for sale and distribution. Jim Bob is a real asset. I have put adverts out in the local papers. I have a feeling that with Jim Bob on board **ZONCO** will go from strength to strength and I will be able to weather the economic uncertainty that is about to follow once the new Mayor sends the letter to the UK of Great Britain governance people advising them we are formally leaving the UK of Great Britain. Once the District has its independence who knows, maybe things might be better for us. What I do know is that with all my businesses I'm in a better position to ride any forthcoming economic storm.

Sunty 32st Juulii

First invention to come out of my new partnership with Jim Bob is the Dou Smoker, allowing you to smoke a couple of ciggies at once. Needless to say I was thrilled at seeing my invention in this mawnin's edition of the Weekly News.

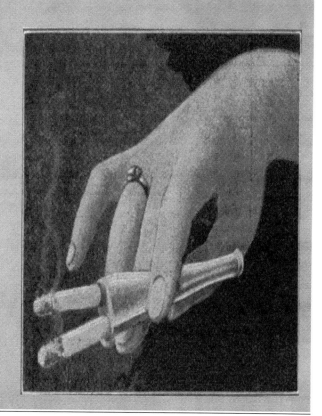

FLATLAND DISTRICT WEEKLY NEWS

DUO SMOKER by Zonco
The "Duo smoker" is a superb device for those who find smoking two ciggies at once either uncomfortable or socially awkward. Currently on sale at all Flatland branches of Happy Pauper this handy device is perfect for new smokers or childers just starting out on there smoking careers.
ever wondered what to get your childers at Chrimtaaas time or Biirrffdees? Then wonder no more, Duo Smoker not only looks cool but also allows double the smooth, cool smoke intake through it's revolutionary "Double fag holder" design. Zonco's world class designers and engineers have spent the last 20 minutes meticulously inventing this marvellous advance in tab paraphernalia.
Don't be uncool and stupid, smoke tabs with Zonco's Duo Smoker today

After daaymiddlin I went for a stroll around the witch dunking pond with Nina to try and walk off the huge stuffed Turnip roast we had for docky. I asked her how her friends were up at Dykes Discotheque in town. She became quite defensive and then when I pressed her for more information she became quite aggressive. She is definitely up to something so I may hire the services of PC Jack Wormer once more to be a bit of a nosey parkering and find out what she's up to.

CHAPTER NINE

N'ER A FAIRER NICKERER, NOR A POORER NACKERER N'ER A NICKERER NACKERER BE

AUTISM 1896

Moondee 1st Autism

FLATLAND DISTRICT WEEKLY NEWS

Introducing the Zonco MULTISMOKER

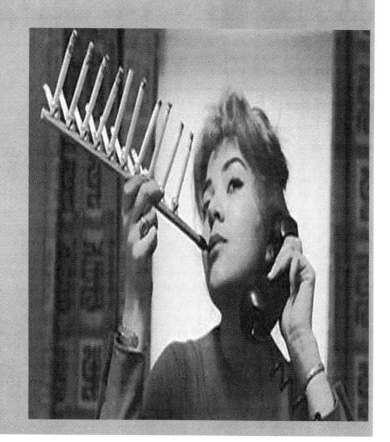

Do you find smoking several ciggies at once whilst trying to speak on the phone to your doctor or respiratory specialist both tiresome and even more tiresome?

Do you struggle to get the full nicotine kick from just smoking one tab at a time yet find the fabulous Zonco Duo Smoker not quite enough bang for your buck?

Then try Zonco's Multismoker. This highly engineered wonderment is specifically aimed at adults and older childers (over the age of say ... 11) who know their tobacco requirements. Perfect for smoking many fags whilst driving the kids to school or simply waiting in the doctors surgery.

Don't be pathetic smoking just one ciggie at a time, smoke loads with Zonco MULTISMOKER

Today the Daily, Weekly News carried another advert promoting another collaboration between myself and Jim Bob for even more smoking paraphernalia, this time for the Multismoker, for hardcore smoking fanatics. I am quite happy at the way I'm conducting my business affairs however, other parts of my life aren't running so smoothly.

Toosdi 2nd Autism

Now I have finished all involvement with the referendum it means what was once the campaign headquarters can now either return to a bedroom/dungeon space or keep it as an office space for further inventing, conducting my business affairs and (*if I can move my compooota to it*) a place for mastybayshun. I made a start on clearing space and generally tidying stuff up and started going through old boxes of stuff, some of it for keeping, some of it for chucking out. Lots of things found I had completely forgotten about and lots of old memories sparked. I even found a very old photo of me as a tiny little hoooman childer. I often forget that I am originally a hoooman and that it was fates fickle finger that bought me to Flatland District.

Aaaaw

Here is a lovely photo of me as a little boy. It was taken in 1905 by family friend and UK broadcasting legend Stuart Hall prior to my abduction to Flatlands.

He asked me if he could photograph me showing him my cock and he'd give me a ciggy for my troubles. I duly obliged and here is the resulting photo. Uncle Stuart seemed frustrated, I can only assume that the thing he had in his pocket was hurting his leg.

I wonder what he's doing these days?

It's one of the few photo's I have left of my life as a Hoooman.

I consider myself to be very much a Flatlander, and have done since not long after my abduction, but I often wonder what my life would have been like if I had stayed in the UK and remained a hoooman. The distant memories I have of my family are mostly of my grandad. I remember he used to say "N'er a fairer nickerer, nor a poorer nackerer, n'er a nickerer nackerer be". We had him put in a home when he started coming out with shit like that, but interestingly it's a saying I have used in Flatlands from time to time and most folk seem to understand what it means.

I have embraced all the traditions and values of Flatland life but occasionally I am aware that I'm very different to my fellow Flatlanders. I'm aware that I can read and write better than most Flatlanders (*I'm aware that I can read and write*), I am made aware many times about my equal number of toes and fingers … and limbs. I am made aware that even though I have picked up many of the local colloquialisms I still use hoooman language mostly. I was made aware I was different as soon as I arrived here all those years ago.

I was made headmaster of our local primary school at a tender age due to my prodigious literacy and numeracy, although to be fair I was an average student in the hoooman world but this made me special 'round these parts'. The fact that my parents seemed happy to leave me in the care of complete strangers told me all I needed to know about their feeling for me. Clearly they had little or no affection for their son, but the people of Flatlands, the odd, strange, peculiar and downright weird people of this drab little district in East Anglia (*or Eesangulaa as they call it here*) took me to their hearts and treated me as one of their own.

Sadly they don't treat their own particularly well, but they clearly they had more concern for me than my own flesh and blood did and that was good enough for me. On reflection, having recently spent a day in the UK of Great Britain's capital city I'm quite glad things turned out the way they did.

Although I do sometimes wonder what my parents and old hoooman friends are doing.

Winsti 3th Autism

Just after daaymiddlin I met Nina off the guided bus from Ropey as she'd been visiting her friends at Dykes Discotheque again. I thought she smelled of tuna. Cinderella had been to visit Finbar Knuckleshuffla's grave. I'm glad to report that Finbar didn't die but it was considered prudent to dig him a grave just in case. It was nice she had somewhere she could take him now his bottom hole had scabbed over a bit and he could walk properly again. Pocahontas was out for a very special day with Jack and Nigelle was playing with his toy cars in the living room.

All was quite tranquil. Just after laasdocky the back door flung open and in strolled Jack and Pocahontas. Jack was beaming as he turned to me and asked "as the guardian of this beautiful lady, I would like to ask your permission for her hand in marriage". I was gobsmacked but was happy to say yes and happy he had asked for permission, how old fashioned. Pocahontas looked happy … well confused really, but happy enough.

Nina said she would start making arrangements and asked jack when he planned on having the big day. Jack said he planned SatD 21st Octerrible at St. Jeremiah's Church once he'd spoken to Reverend Adolph Ferdinand-Globule and confirmed details.

Jim Bob said he could make the wedding dress and the bridesmaid dresses (*is there no end to this man's talents*) and Nina was saying she could make her roadkill stew for the wedding meal (*I'd better get some bin liners ready for my next visit to Ropey Hospitals incinerator skip*).

A wonderful end to the day. No fires.

Thrisdee 4lbs Autism

Thrisdee means a weekly boost to yoof culture. This week's main feature is about legendary crooner and deviant Fred Dickens. Fresh from serving a custodial sentence at HMP Ropey he'll be touring near you soon.

NEW MOOOSICUL EXPRESSIONS

Excellent news for the lovers of "Fen Rock", the support act for the Webb Gospel Singers world tour of Flatland District is none other than Chumpton singing sensation Fred Dickens.

Fred will be singing all his favourite hits from his latest album "Sheltered in the arms of God", such as his wonderful hit single "Nonce".

He will also be performing many of his fan base faves from his previous album "May the Lord taste my Cheese" which had such memorable ditties as "3 extra finger to dual my banjo", and who could forget the timeless classic "I'm blessed with 5 more nipples for feeding my piggywiggy's".

During a recent interview Fred was asked about his unique vocal style which he attributes to asthma and cystic fibrosis, but one things for sure, it'll be his faithful legion of female fans that'll be left breathless once this rocking fenland legend has opened the show.

Frydims 5th Autism

I had a very busy mawnin counting toes at the Hospital. In total I counted 156 toes and 198 fingers. This meant that in the last few days 5 new baby childers had been born or had hatched (*if they were old world childers*) in total. I took the opportunity to start collecting some used bandages again as Jim Bob had requested some white material for Pocahontas's wedding gown. I paid a quick visit to the incinerator but 'the cupboard was bare' so to speak. I later found out that the Dr Jekyll Hyde, the hospital's chief amputating doctor, was on holiday in Chatterby sands so I'll come back next week when he's been busy chopping limbs off locals.

I managed to get back in time for opening at the Peppermint Hippo. Tonoyght was the latest craze from the UK called speed dating.

It's Peppermint Hippo's speed dating night tonight, just 25 new Hoooman pence to get in.

SatD 6st Autism

Jim Bob has almost finished Cinderella's wedding gown, specially crafted out of the bandages I took from the bin outside the rare tropical diseases unit (*they had slightly less bleeding on them*) whilst I was at the Hospital. Jim Bob modelled it for us and he looked stunning, it bought a tear to my eye.

I was having a quick pint of Badgerspizzle (*or pizz as we call it*) when I felt a tap on my left shoulder. It was Morris Poncen, he had his foot trapped in the rest plate of my bar stool. As he was manoeuvring to free his foot his shocking blonde hair was flapping about like a broken sail.

"Hellllo" he said, beaming a broad grin shortly before falling over after accidentally releasing his foot from the grips of the Bar Stool.

"Hello Morris, how are you?" I replied, he beamed a toothy but vacant grin and said that he was very well.

He had with him a very sexy young lady who he introduced as Davina Kraye. "Eeeerrr … this is Davina. She's going to be running in the Mayor's election thingy too … I'm not anymore … Micky Dove sort of stitched me up on that one …….. I thought I could trust him" Morris looked sad.

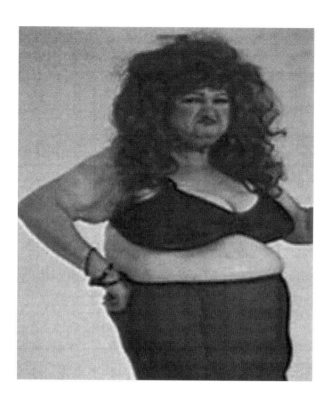

It was abundantly clear to me that if Davina had designs on becoming the new Mayor of Flatlands she was going to try and win the election on beauty alone. Morris handed me a dishevelled photo of him at some school with a bunch of chaps. They're all dressed in top hats and tails outside some posh looking school, one of chaps was an unmistakeable but very young Mayor David Devilman. My attention was diverted from the photo as Davina's magnetic beauty was drawing my gaze. As Davina smiled at me the music in the club seemed to take a hold of her and she began swaying to and fro, fro and to. She had natural rhythm and stunning good looks."Eeeerrrm …. Anyway … I, well WE were wondering if you had any jobs going for a dancer in your superb establishment" Morris spluttered, almost apologetically."I always have room for fantastic looking ladies willing to grind the pole and shake those fine buttocks" I replied. Davina giggled. Morris interrupted and said "Actually I meant … me". I was stunned and at a loss for a reply when Morris started laughing. I never knew he had a sense of humour. My attention was diverted back to the beautiful Davina. "How about going up there now and having a try" I suggested. Within minutes of Davina setting foot on the stage and wrapping her shapely sexy legs around the pole Sylvia behind the bar had sold out of Klappers Tummy wipes completely. I had to get some toilet rolls from out of the cleaners store cupboard to sell. This is Davina our new dancer and possibly new Mayor.

Sunty 7nd Autism

At daaymiddlin we had our Sunty roast. It was Potatoes, Parsnips, roast Parsnips, boiled Parsnips, fried Parsnips and Badgers spleen. It was a feast fit for a king. Nina said she was thinking of making it for part of the wedding menu as the vegetarian option. I asked her about the Badgers spleen and pointed out it was hardly vegetarian. She said that she thought badgers were vegetarian but if not she reckons if she covered it with black pepper they wouldn't notice. Or simply remove it off the plate I suggested, but she was adamant that it would be better to smother it in Black pepper.

As we sat and let our food settle Nina mentioned she was going to catch the guided bus to Ropey. She didn't even offer a reason why she was going to town but I had a pretty good idea why. Once she'd left I called Jack on the tefelone and explained my predicament. He said he was going contact a friend of his who was a private dick … that sounds like a good job. Jack said his friend with a private dick would have results from his private dicking next week sometime. I put the tefelone down slightly relieved but also quite sad too. Jack suggested we met up next week. I suggested Winsti at the Peppermint Hippo.

Moondee 8st Autism

A busy day building Badger CBs and portable love dolls. Jim Bob is quick and good, I even had enough time to cobble together a couple Childers dream catchers.

Tonoyght was a lazy noyght watching TV. My favourite program 'the only way is Chatterby' was on but I was watching it on my own as Nina was elsewhere. She didn't say where, but I'm guessing it's Dykes Discotheque in Ropey.

FLATLAND DISTRICT WEEKLY NEWS

TV GUIDE

THE ONLY WAY IS CHATTERBY

A new series of 'The Only Way Is Chatterby' is back on our screens on the second Thrisdees of each week at laasloyght on Flatlands TV.

This series kicks off with Zacoriah (pictured below) making a surprise visit to the Chumpton Tanning Parlour to top up his dyke water tan ready for the Ropey Town Tractor pull.

Excitement mounts when Russia invades Ukraine and Blodwin enlists in the 2th Battallion Flatland Fusiliers, concerned that Flatland district is next on Vladimir Putins game plan to reconstitute the USSR to its former glory.

Blodwella Klittt finds a carrot and several strands of straw leading to her suspecting her father of having an affair.

Toosdi 9nd Autism

I was at the clock tower just after firsloyght, I intended to catch the first guided bus to Ropey to start my shift early at the Hospital in order to give me more time to collect severed limbs and offal to store and cure ready for Pocahontas's wedding docky.

To my surprise Gary, from my interpretive dancing class turned up in his car, he pulled over and asked me where I was going. I said I was waiting for the guided bus to Ropey and he very kindly offered to give me a lift. I very kindly accepted. I did warn him that the road wasn't in the best of shapes and to look out for pot holes and we drove slowly to Ropey. Gary heeded my warning as it was still dark and quite foggy so the visibility was poor. I thanked him for picking me up and talked about my part-time job at the hospital. I asked him what he did for a living and he told me that he worked for a big 'software' firm based in London and he was an IT engineer. I decided to show off my compooota knowledge and told him that IT stood for 'Intelligent Talk' and he laughed. I think he was surprised at how tech savvy I was. He went on to tell me he works a lot in London doing his compooota intelligence talking.

"How often do you go to London?" I asked

"Twice a week sometimes more, do you leave the area very often? People in the village never seem to leave the area very much. They seem to go as far as Ropey or Chatterby and that's about it" Gary said.

"It's too much hassle arranging border passes and everything" I replied. Gary laughed again; I stared at him with a puzzled look, what was funny about that?

"You can come with me some time if you want"

"That'd be nice, although not the BBC again" I said

"Ha-ha okay … not the BBC. I can take you and show you some of the sights if you like".

"I take it you rarely leave Flatlands then, have you ever wondered what is going on in other places other than the Flatlands area?" He continued.

"District, you mean district" I corrected him, "I was not born in Flatland District, I was kidnapped when I was only a small childer … I mean child … boy, when I was a small boy child. I was held hostage after some swamp mules found me when they strayed too far. They asked for a ransom and my folks refused so I ended up stopping in Flatlands". Gary stared at me with a look of disbelief. "You're fucking kidding me" he barked. I remained silent. "WOW" he said.

"It's perfectly fine" I said. "Not the bit where my folks wouldn't cough up the ransom but the fact that Flatlands folk looked after me, that's fine. I sometimes wonder what would've happened if I hadn't been abducted but I'm fine with everything else. I've done okay for myself"

Gary was shocked by what I'd told him, I could tell by the look on his face.

"So what do you do apart from the dancing thing and working part-time at the Hospital then"? He asked.

"I have lots of businesses. I own a lap dancing club called the Peppermint Hippo in Chumpton, I have my own inventing company called Zonco and do some surgery as I am a fully qualified doctor and I like to do some trepanning too" I replied.

Gary's mouth opened again, I'm beginning to wonder if he has a breathing problem.

"What medical school did you study at to become a surgeon"?

"Chatterby University" I answered.

Once again Gary was doing the mouth open thing.

"Oh … oh … I didn't realise Chatterby had a uni, it just looked like a rundown little village to me, well there you go, just goes to prove that you can't judge a book by its cover. I hardly ever go into Chatterby or Chumpton … or Ropey come to that, as you've mentioned the roads are a bit … Ropey … hahaha" he quipped.

"You're missing a treat Gary, you should come to my club one noyght, I can introduce you to the performers and you can have a complimentary pack of Klappers tummy wipes and access to a mastybayshun booth, all free of charge" I told him.

He declined by shaking his head with his mouth open.

"Why are you going to Ropey"? I asked.

"I wasn't" he replied, "I was working through the noyght and got back earlier than I thought. I wasn't tired so to avoid waking the family up I decided to go for a drive … and that bought me to Chumpton and saw you at that odd monolith …" "The clock tower" I interrupted "… I saw you at the clock tower. I've hardly been to Ropey so it can't hurt to take a drive up there".

"There's a market on today" I remarked.

"Then I can take a walk around town, look at what's at the market and I can give you a lift back if you like". I took him up once more on his kind offer and thanked him.

As we pulled into Ropey the market was well under way and several people were milling about carefully arranging their vegetables on their stalls. Gary parked his car and we went our separate ways.

There had been very few babies born lately so toe counting didn't take long and as Doctor Jekyll Hyde was still on holiday looking for amputated wedding fodder lead to sparse pickings, just some offal. This meant I returned to Gary's car before he did. As I hung around waiting I happened to notice on his back seat was a newspaper called the 'London Evening Standard'. I never gave it anymore thought. When Gary returned a short while later we got in the car and started making our way back to Chumpton. From our chat I could tell he wasn't too impressed with Ropey and quite pleased to be travelling home. I mentioned the paper on his back seat and asked him where it comes from. He informed me it was a daily paper from London and that I could have it if I wanted. I agreed and Gary passed me the newspaper, I rolled it up and took it home with me when Gary dropped me off.

Winsti10th Autism

Once again I was first up and made myself some firsdocky and a cup of onion cosh tea. As I sat watching the Flatlands TV I remembered that I had Gary's UK newspaper still in my jacket pocket. I went and retrieved it, sat down in my comfy chair and plonked the London Evening Standard on my lap. The first thing I noticed was that the date on it said "Monday 8th August 2016", I did chuckle to myself. These so called clever clogs from the hoooman world can't even spell the date right.

I flicked through the paper as I would a comic as much of it was adverts for things I'd never even heard of let alone seen before. The UK of Great Britain was certainly very advanced with its gadgetry but did it have a time travelling tortoise or device to harvest childers dreams. In fact all the stuff they had was pretty much the same as ours only smaller or flatter. Their fashion sense was quite funny too; I think if I were to open a branch of Fenwear in London I could show the hooomans of London the joys of hessian and swamp boots. The hooomans names were much weirder than ours too, they had names like Darren, Mike and Gary, in fact whilst perusing the paper I saw two other people called Gary. Gary must be the Hooomans equivalent to Jeremiah or Jebediah here in Flatlands. Actually, it was this attention to the funny, various names that meant one name I saw I instantly recognised. It leapt off the page at me and stopped me in my tracks.

The name I saw on the index of the business section was none other than someone called David Devilman. Surely it was a coincidence I thought; surely it couldn't be the same David Devilman so I turned to the page that featured the article about this 'David Devilman' character. Before I could even look at the page the back door opened and in strode Jim Bob with another sack of baby Badgers ready to have their insides scooped out and solid-state shortwave frequency electronics fitted into them. I quickly bundled the paper away as if I were hiding something illegal such as counterfeited hen's beaks or other such highly prized Flatland currency.

Jim Bob was in his usual cheery and industrious mood as I poured him a nice cup of tea and as he sipped his delicious onion based beverage I folded the paper up and placed it under the cushion for later when everyone had gone. Nina came down stairs the same time as the ladies and said she was off to Ropey, no surprises there then. This time she was taking the ladies with her and Nigelle was out with Morris and the delightful Davina canvassing for the Mayoral election. Jim Bob was going to be busy gutting baby badgers, which left me lots of time to read Gary's paper. As I waved Nina and the ladies off on the guided bus I called into the Happy Pauper to get a pint of Grimbles Dykeklunger milk as Jim Bob had used the last drop in his onion cosh tea. As I was standing in the que I noticed that Horatio was starting to do something called "Top ups" for mobile phones??? And in the refrigerator there were several cartons of cow's milk ... cow's milk! Horatio was "catering for his new client base" apparently when questioned about these fancy new products adorning his shelves.

Once home I could hear Jim Bob busy in the inventing shed so I took out the paper and returned to the article I nearly got to read about half an hour before. Not convinced I was going to see Mayor Devilman but another, different David Devilman I turned immediately to the page the article was on. As I opened the page I was confronted by a photograph of Mayor Devilman sitting on the deck of a big fancy looking boat called a Yacht (pronounced yot) sipping a wee coloured drink from a fancy glass. Sat next to him was none other than Cranshaw St.John, also drinking wee from a tall glass. The headline read "Devilman brokers another huge land deal". The drink was wine apparently although it was clear, you could see straight through it, not like Flatland wine then ... odd. As I read the article I became numb. The Mayor of Flatlands had bought land several years ago without any building permission, so he bought it very cheaply and as soon as it got building permissions he sold it to developers to build the fancy houses on that the Hooomans were buying up.

There was talk of new roads being built and all manner of fancy-Dan ideas about airports and distribution depots. I was confused about how he got the planning permissions from the Elders, unless of course the Elders were in on the deal too. As I continued to read the article my disbelief became stronger, my despair deepened, my anger grew. The Mayor had another very large house in a very, very posh place called Stevenage as well as a yacht (*the one pictured*) and a villa in Spain. It turns out that he is highly regarded in somewhere called the 'City' which is inside London, how does that work? Even though he has had investigations made into his previous dealing by some people called 'The Inland Revenue'. There were whispers that he used his influential friends to wriggle out of his troubles.

As my eyes scanned down the page I saw the very same photo that Morris Poncen showed me in the club at their posh school. It said at the bottom of the photo "here is David Devilman with his Eton school buddies, including the Prime Minister". Devilman never mentioned he was friends with the Prime Minister of the UK of Great Britain, but then neither did Morris (*although in all probability Morris probably didn't know*). As I read further into the article I saw that David Devilman was born into wealth but was also a self-made man in his own right as a property developer. The article went on to say "he had sold lots of cheap land already and new houses and second homes for the well healed professional had been built several years back". These must have been the houses that Gary and his friends live in.

It was the next part of the article that made my blood run cold.
"Future development will involve new roads, distribution depots and even possibly an Airport. Although, much of this is on hold until the compulsory purchases of the many run down dwellings in local villages near the market town of Ropey have been issued to the residents. Devilman is confident he will secure the necessary permissions and cut through any red tape to ensure that the Flatlands region of East Anglia is prepared for its modernisation".

"Tea boss ... TEA!" Jim Bob bellowed "Do you want some onion cosh tea?" I was jolted from my train of thought from contemplating the future, or lack of, for Flatlands to whether or not I wanted tea. I told Jim Bob I needed something considerably stronger. We both called it a day and set off the Peppermint Hippo for a pint or six of Pizz for Jim Bob and a couple of bottles of Turnip Pochine for me. As far as getting drunk was concerned both Jim Bob and I achieved excellence. I slept at the table we were drinking at.

Thrisdee 11 Autism

Thrisdee is my shot in the arm of yoof culture with the ever increasing sales of my weekly Mooosicul extravaganza. To be honest after yisdee's revelations I was still in something of a state of shock. I hadn't told anyone, not even Nina (*not that she was ever there to tell these days*). I had hidden the paper under the sofa ... as if it were some kind of illicit photo magazine of ladies in undress like the kind sold in Ropey town newsagents.

The featured artiste in this week's edition was the Faith Tones, truth is that they were mooosiculy inept but had used their good looks to pull in the crowds. They were also known locally as 'gad abouts' that enjoyed gentlemanly company more than was considered polite.

After daaymiddlin I sat in my office and went on the Compooota to see if I could find out anything more about David Devilman and his dealings. I typed his name into the 'Ask Jeremiah' search engine and all that came up was information on the Flatipedia site and that just mentioned about his Mayoral role within the District of Flatlands. I'm beginning to think that there is some kind of block on the Fen Wide Web that monitors and stops anyone from finding out anything about the UK of Great Britain ... or perhaps I'm being paranoid. I bet the hooomans of the UK of Great Britain don't have people monitoring their online time. After some searching of my considerable memory I thought I remembered Gary had a phone that was able to get online, maybe his had a different search engine and I'd be able to use it to do some research. I would be seeing him on SatD at the interpretive dance class. I'd ask him.

NEW MOOOSICUL EXPRESSIONS

Finally, Flatlands answer to the Pussycat Dolls, The Faith Tones release thier first album. Its called Jesus Use Me ... a sentiment we have all felt when in the company of these Flatland beauties.

Frydims 12lbs Autism

Thrisdee is 'old age free money day' in Flatlands. This means the public houses and illicit alcoholic beverage sheds of Flatlands are jam packed with pensioners disappointed they haven't yet succumbed to life's dull drudgery of a persistent banal existence in a drab district of a drab region and still, still they draw breath. Their need and compulsion to escape the reality of living means they consume enormous amounts of hallucinogenic (*and occasionally poisonous*) locally brewed concoctions. This often results in carnage throughout the District every Frydims mawnin as detritus from the previous noyghts extravagances are easily found. This mawnin was no exception as I left my house to catch the guided bus to Ropey I discovered evidence of drunken behaviour in my back garden.

Getting a bit fed up with people throwing empty tins of hallucinogenic drink in my garden. Found this one this mawnin as I left for work. I have thrown it into next doors garden, their dog seemed quite happy playing with it as I left. You spend good money on dog chews and toys and they prefer an old empty can of drink. I hope it doesn't cut its lip on the ring pull. — feeling annoyed.

SatD 13Mr Autism

The UK of Great Britain Bomb squad were in the area asking questions about the neighbour's dog being blown up by eating something called a 'hand grenade' yisdee mawnin. There are some truly callas fuckers about, what kind of person feeds a dog explosives? The word around the camp fire is that the UK of Great Britain police squad think there may be an involvement of a group of people called ISIS … or 'so called ISIS' according to Hillbilly Billy Hill on Flatlands TV news. Jihadi Jeb and his brand of root crop extremism are also in the frame.

Interpretive Dance School of Chumpton-by-Kumberly have been asked by the Peppermint Hippo club (*Chumpton's premier pole/lap dancing noyghtspot/adult entertainment complex … owned by me*) to perform a nativity routine for the locals at Chrimstaaas time. We had our first practice today but I forgot my ghetto blaster so we did it without the Black Lace backing track. To be honest I think I have happened by chance on something rather special, and I shan't be using music again, we'll be 'silent freestyling' interpretive dancing from now on.

After the class I approached Gary and mentioned his London Evening Standard paper he gave me and the article about David Devilman.
Gary expressed some surprise "I didn't know he was in that paper but he has appeared in a lot of articles lately. He was accused of some dodgy dealings and people think he used his connections in government to make the accusations disappear".
"The article said he had already sold lots of land for housing" I said
"Yes that's right, there are 1000 houses built with another 3000 planned. It's called 'New Chumpton'. We live in the part called Devilman's acres, it's handy for the road. There are other developments too, like ours they're private estates, some cost a fortune"
"Did you know they plan on knocking down the old village?" I asked.
Gary didn't answer, he didn't need to. His look said it all.
My look of disappointment must have spoken volumes too. "I'm sorry, I should have said something, I didn't know what to say … and you did hold my daughter hostage" Gary explained. "Look I'm sorry I didn't tell you … if there's anything I can do you only have to ask"
"Actually Gary there is, do you have access to the Fen Wide Web on your phone gadget?"

"You mean the World Wide Web" he said. I must have looked confused. "I'm sorry, yes I have access online why do you ask?" he continued.

"Well I was wondering if I could do some research on it. My search engine, 'ask Jeremiah' seems to lock me out". Now it was Gary's turn to look confused.

"Look" he said "Why don't you come to my house one day next week when I'm not working and you can use my laptop or desktop if you prefer".

I didn't have a fucking clue what he was talking about. Laptop and Desktop??? Anyway, it seemed it was the best way to research this further and we arranged to meet up next Winsti.

Sunty 14th Autism

Tonoyght I was on my own again, Nina was out … you know where, the ladies were out with their gents and I was tucking into some delicious roadkill stew (*that wasn't Nina's recipe*). About an hour after laasloyght Pocahontas and Jack returned from a noyght at the local pub in Chumpton called 'The Rancid Armpit'. It's not a nice place and I was only happy for Pocahontas to go in there because she was with the most violent and unpredictable man in the district, our very own PC Wormer. As Pocahontas made her way upstairs to her bedroom, Jack took me to one side and let me know that "Sometime tomorrow a package will be arriving from my Dick". I seemed to have spent a lot of time this last week with a confused look on my face and now was no exception. "Okay" I said with a certain degree of caution and a frown in the middle of my bonce. "My detective … the chap I've got doing you know what … about you know who" he said with a knowing wink. It was much clearer now so I nodded in the affirmative "So I'm off upstairs with Pokie now so don't come barging in the room" he said with a cheeky grin. "Ah … okay, understood" I replied knowingly. I didn't barge in anywhere.

Moondee 15rd Autism

Jim Bob was turning out the childers dream harvesters in the inventing shed like there was no tomorrow and I was doing some early mawnin mastybayshun like there was no tomorrow. Jim Bob asked me to "go somewhere else to do that" so I went up to my office. Not two minutes after I sparked the Compooota into life (*to look at some breasties and tuppences's*) and removed my trouserage, that I heard a knock at the door. I sprinted down stairs and answered the door to a tall, rather spindly, creepy looking gentleman. He didn't give his name and to be honest he seemed more interested in my lack of trouserage and fully aroused winky rather than telling me who he was and what he wanted. It was my secret package that Jack had told me about last noyght. I thanked the chap but he didn't seem to want to shake my hand … rude.

I hurried back to my office with the envelope and opened it with a certain amount of foreboding. It was as I suspected, Nina was enjoying the company of ladies at Dykes Discotheque. There was an extensive report saying when she visited and who she was with. It also had a photograph of her kissing a woman called Natalia Chopyakokov as well as other pictures of them with their arms around each other. It all looked very chummy; I shall pick my moment and confront Nina about it all, see what she has to say.

Toosdi 16rd Autism

Here's me performing at a private local function for a "Hen Party".

My theme for the party was Meatloaf and the Hen was thrilled. I gave her a very intimate private dance and enquired if she wished to insert my trusty sack of root crops into my anus. She reliably informed me she'd do anything for love but she won't do that.

I was paid and left the party like a bat out of hell.

Sylvia from the club came to see me this mawnin to tell me that there had been an enquiry about a possibility of me performing at the Peppermint Hippo tonoyght for a hen party. She wanted the party to be themed and the theme was someone called

Meatloaf who is popular in Merica of USA, a morbidly obese fella with bags of confidence, how tough could that be, ☺ I said yes.

Winsti 17rd Autism

I was up early this mawnin doing my chores before making my way to the clock tower shortly after firsdocky to await collection from Gary. It was a typical Flatland mawnin with large grey clouds drifting slowly and lowly across the district. I didn't have to wait long before Gary came and collected me in his autocar and whisked me away to his humble abode to do some much anticipated research to try and discover what is going to happen to Flatland District.

We headed out of Chumpton along the old fen drove road and then along a dirt track I didn't recognise, to a T junction situated along a hedge in a field. We turned left onto a new road I had never seen before and it was less than a few minutes' drive from Chumpton village. I was confused, how come I didn't know this road existed and yet it was only a few miles from the village where I had lived since I was 10 years old. Gary informed me this was the road he took to leave Flatlands to go to work but he would normally travel in the other direction. I was confused and slightly disorientated now.

In what was only a mile or so along the road I didn't even know existed we came to a small wooded area and turned right into what the sign said was a 'Devilman's Acres private housing estate'. Gary's house was number 11, it was a very new looking house (*the sort you see when watching hooomans TV channels*) and very large. It had 5 bedrooms and was very luxurious, almost as posh as the Mayor's house but Gary's was a fair bit smaller and much newer. We went into the kitchen through the back door via the rear garden. It was lovely with a very nice pond and a large raised rockery area in the middle. I wondered how many tramps you could bury in the raised area in the middle, plenty I bet. As we went into the kitchen Gary's wife and their daughter left and get into another, different autocar. They had two autocars … an autocar each … fuck!

Before we entered into the kitchen I couldn't help noticing a large crack in Gary's outside wall, going right the way to the top of his ground floor and some way into the first floor. He made me a cup of coffee made from real coffee beans and it was delicious, he made me some jam on toast and it was delicious. I looked around his kitchen and everything in it seemed to look delicious. I peeked into his living room and noticed the biggest TV I had ever seen. This was definitely the high life.

As we ventured upstairs I saw two toilets, both with extensive washing facilities (*including something called a bidet which is used exclusively for washing your sphincter .... I know ...... mad ....*) as well as the one I saw downstairs, that made three in total. We went into Gary's office, which was about the same size as my office but much better furnished and equipped. I saw some machines like this at the BBC the other month and wondered how much they cost as well as how they worked.

I handed Gary the copy of the London Evening Standard he gave me, he said I could keep it but I declined, it's best we don't get caught with such literature I told him. He sat down at his compooota (*which is actually called a computer but is pronounced the same way*) and logged on as I pulled up a swivel chair next to him. Gary felt it was better to get it all out of my system so he sat patiently whilst I spent five minutes twizzling round, first one way, then the other. Once I said I'd finished Gary suggested we start. I noticed him smiling, my twizzling must have amused him. He went on to his search engine, his was called Google and when he typed things into the search bar its results were immediate. The search engine on my compooota is called Ask Jeremiah and takes upwards of five minutes to search.

My mind went completely blank when he asked me what I wanted to search for, I was dazzled by it all. The blank expression on my face must have told Gary this.
"You mentioned David Devilman at the weekend, about his dealings in the property market" Gary hinted.
"Are yes" I said, "that's right, the article mentioned he had been under investigation for something, I wanted firstly to know what it was he was investigated for".
"Well I can tell you that without the computer" Gary replied, "you're sitting in it"
I must have looked even more confused than I had only moments before.
"It was the land these houses are built on Morton; he was under investigation for buying green belt land very cheaply and selling it on to developers with planning permission very, very expensively. The planning permission was granted by the District Council, his District Council. It would appear however, that any accusations of dodgy dealings were quickly swept away once his old school chum, the Prime Minister, became involved. Of course none of this was ever proved ... it seldom is".
"The permission to build must have come from the Elders ... but why would they do it?" I said.

"For the greed of money I'm afraid" Gary replied.

"No, you don't understand Gary, why would the Elders grant planning permission on this land. I know its green belt and should only be used for set aside or agricultural use, all us cundreyfolk know that. The reason why this is green belt though is because it's black soil" I said. Now it was Gary's turn to look confused.

"Black soil is the best growing soil in the land Gary, superb for root crops and not so good for grain, but it's absolutely fucking useless for building on unless it's been properly checked out".

"I wouldn't mind betting that small crack in your office wall over there, lines up quite neatly with the sodding great big crack you've got in your wall outside" I said.

We walked over to the window nearest the internal crack, opened the window and looked outside. Sure enough they lined up almost perfectly. Gary walked back to his desk and slumped rather worriedly into his chair. He didn't seem in the mood for twizzling … I did. Gary looked at me with concern, "So do you think…"

"Your house is subsiding? Yep" I said as I gave myself one last big push for a triple twizzle.

"Holy fuck, what am I going to do?" Gary asked.

"What are you going to do? Ha, they're thinking about flattening all the villages in my area" I replied.

"Okay … what are WE going to do then" Gary retorted.

As we wandered back to the kitchen Gary took the opportunity to check out the crack in his outside wall. He returned from his garden with an ashen face and poured us both a very large whiskey each. It wasn't even daaymiddlin yet but who was I to refuse. Gary sat down at the table and stared blankly at his kitchen wall, his superbly plastered, beige painted, large cracked wall, and he sighed.

"You're right" he said, "I think I've got problems but you might be losing the entire district as well as your home". All was quiet for a few moments … even in my head … as we sipped our drinks and stared at Gary's cracked kitchen wall.

"What are we going to do?" I asked.

"What can we do?" Gary replied, "We're completely buggered".

"Not completely … there may be a way" I said thoughtfully, "I don't do much exotic dancing these days but I do dance for special occasions. Occasions like hen parties, special community days … or … or when the Mayor asks me to do private dances for him".

Gary looked shocked, "The Mayor gets you to …".

"Yup" I said "and he'll often leave me alone whilst he washes Growlers saliva from his hand … or my poo from his chin".

Gary looked like he was about to say something but he didn't.

"If you can do some digging about Gary, I can re-establish contact with the Mayor and hopefully start dancing for him again. If you can let me know what to look for I'll have access to either his chambers or his house sometimes, maybe we can find something that not even being 'chums with the Prime Minister of the UK of Great Britain' can bail you out of".

Gary looked interested. "Maybe" he said and paused. He looked up and said "Let's go for it, we've nothing to lose, either of us … and by the way it either the 'UK' or 'Great Britain' … not really both" he smiled and winked at me.

We spent the rest of the day looking into David Devilman's movements and Gary showed me how to use a computer. I learned so much about Great Britain and the outside world it was starting to boggle my mind a bit. As the day wore on I began to realise that a lot of what the Mayor and council Elders had told us was untrue and I strongly suspect their sole reason for keeping us in the dark ages was to simply exploit us. Gary explained to me that if you keep people uneducated then they can't fight back or stand up for themselves. Indeed, it would seem that if you own the media you can make them think what you want them to think, although Gary informed me this is even worse in the rest of Great Britain than it is in the Flatland District. We manged to discover a bit more about David Devilman but it turns out that nobody really knows who the Elders are, so that can be my first job. Find out who the Elders are. Gary took me back to the village in the aftynune (or afternoon as it's called in the UK) and we agreed to keep in touch regularly to update each other about our progress. We both realised we didn't have that much time to act as the Mayor leaves his job in a few short weeks, after which it's highly unlikely that we'll ever see him again. I went and sat in my office with a cup of tea made with 'tea bags' with tea in it, not stewed onion skins and it was also made with cow's milk. I had tasted a bit of life now and I wasn't going to look back. Nina wasn't back when I got home but I wasn't bothered, her indiscretions and possible gender reassignment operation would have to take a back seat now, I had more pressing issues to worry about.

Did a 5 minute 92 secund mastybayshun … to relieve the stress … it worked.

Thrisdee 18nd Autism

This mawnin, after yisdee's concerns and I have to say it, 'excitement', I was dragged straight back down to earth with the day to day workings as a local entrepreneurism and businessmanism. After setting Jim Bob to work with more portable lovers and some childers dream catchers I went over to the club to meet with the district council health and safety officer to get the final signing off for the club after its refurbishment.

The H&S officer is a chap called Augustus Angulgrinda, an austere man of some considerable height and width. Like our local policeman, he didn't bother too much with prosecuting people but he was very keen on violence to get stuff done. This meant he got stuff done. Augustus was also keen on a few pints of Pizz and a shot or two of Pochine. I started formulating a plan. As he sat at the bar talking to Sylvia I asked him how we faired in his inspection. He was very complimentary saying the place had improved considerably since I took over ownership. His only concern was the lack of ladies sanitary towels. I said we had a communal sanitary pad that was changed fortnoyghtly but if the lady patrons or performers ever got really stuck we could supply them with an empty crisp packet and some duct tape. Augustus informed me that although it was an ingenious temporary measure to a blood filled tuppence I had to install a machine that dispensed fresh pads (*literally health and safety gone mad, not to mention something of a ladies luxury item*). Fortunately I'm close friends with Lady Klipp Klapper of Klapper Rags Ltd, makers of quality waterproof feminine hygiene napkins. I can call in a favour and get my H&S certificate signed off.

As Augustus sat drinking heavily at my bar I told Sylvia to keep the Pizz coming and it was on the house. After a couple of hours drinking he was quite drunk so I sneaked the certificate out of his case that he'd pre-prepared earlier and threw it away. When he got up to leave he obviously couldn't find the certificate, I told him not to worry as I would be in Ropey tomorrow and I'd call in and get it from the town hall. Augustus told me if he was out on a job (*and by out on a job he means at the Jolly Sphincter necking more Pizz*) to just ask an assistant to get one of the Elders to sign it. I knew this would be the case.

When I returned to my house I went on my compooota and looked at some of my old pictures from yesteryear. I found one with the aforementioned Lady Klipp Klapper and posted it on my fenbook page for my fenbook chums to peruse and marvel at my manly physique.

fenbook | Surch for peeeple and othur things tooooo | 🔍   🧑 Morton   Hoome   Foind frends

A performance to remember

here I am singing Robbie Williams "Angels" at last years Flatland charity event for a Hosspiss.

It was a beautiful moment for all those privileged to see it being performed with such tenderness. The young lady I was straddling was none other than Lady Klipp Klapper (later renamed Shorty McShortface following an online competition to rename her) who is best known for her family business Klapper Rags makers of water proof feminine hygiene napkins for swamp donkeys and other drainage dyke based occupations.

Even though Lady Klipp Klapper had the title "Lady" in her name this was rather misleading. She was far from a lady, in fact she was known locally as a friendly lady that used her diminutive stature to give oral satisfaction to gentlemen callers without causing any undue wear and tear on her knees or the gentleman caller's wallet. I will contact Lady Klipp tomorrow and get a machine installed in the club. She also made the favoured brand of tummy wipes and since Davina had been employed at the Peppermint Hippo we had nearly sold out of Klappers Tummy wipes.

Frydims 19th Autism

This mawnin I was due to count toes at the Ropey Town Hospital for the Genetically Impure so I took the guided bus up to town with Nina, much to her annoyance as I kidded her on that I was going to come for a drink with her in Dykes Discotheque. She relaxed when she realised I was in fact going to work at the maternity ward and then had some business to attend to in the town hall.

After toe counting I popped in to the council offices to collect my H&S Certificate. I saw St.John Cranshaw and he agreed to get one of the Elders to sign it. I asked him what the name of the signatory actually was on his return. He looked a bit wary of my question and asked why I wanted to know. I said it's just a squiggle really, and just wondered what the name was. I went on to say I had met the Elders several times but never actually knew who they were. He told me that the Elder who signed my form was the Right Honourable Council Elder Jackson Spangler. When I coyly asked who the other three were I was told to fuck off because "I'm toooo busy to be idling chit chat with the likes of you". Fair enough.

I didn't even bother looking on the compooota at home, I'd need Gary's computer to find out the others and I'd be seeing him tomorrow at the interpretive dance class nativity rehearsals. I did however, call into the library in Ropey town and had a look at the official register of council officials. Mayor Devilman had been the Mayor for just over 40 years and was made the Mayor after his sixth Birfdeee. Yesterday's time spent with Gary taught me a lot of things and one such thing I learned was this is not politically normal. Research proved that he was made the Mayor by the previous Mayor, namely Nick Devilman, his father. 'Old Nick' as he was known throughout the district, had backed his son in the elections and magically he won. The odd thing was that when I looked for Jackson Spangler's name on the official register, it wasn't there. In fact none of them were there and the even though the register had been kept up to date in all other aspects it was missing the names of the Elders. The last entry for the names of any of the Elders were 42 years ago when David Devilman took the office of Mayor in 1726, but then just one year later in 1943 it was left blank. It had remained blank ever since.

I returned home to discover Jim Bob "road testing" one of my portable love dolls, the roaming ram to be precise. He had begun his congress next to Barry's grave and ended up in Edith's garden. Edith had developed amorous feelings and had pinched our table leg again for some mastybayshun. It was all a right kerfuffle and both parties looked suitably embarrassed.

SatD 20st Autism

I spoke with Gary this aftynune (afternoon) and he told me that he had a friend, who is a surveyor, come and look at his house and he is pretty certain that it is, as we suspected, subsiding. Furthermore he said that several other houses were showing signs of subsidence too. A little bit further up the road heading out of New Chumpton the soil was a bit more clay based but still not ideal for building on. Gary said his house might be repaired with some underpinning but things were looking bad. Apparently the building company should have built some test houses (*just brick shells*) and left them for a least a few years to see if subsidence was a problem. As I mentioned to Gary last week, the houses should never have been built there in the first place.

I also mentioned about Jackson Spangler and my finding the previous day. Gary said he would look into it and we arranged to meet up again on Winsti again.

Sunty 21th Autism

Today I decided to confront Nina about her liaisons in Ropey at Dykes Discotheque. At first she denied any wrong doing but then I showed her the photographs that had been taken of her kissing another lady. I asked her if she was a thespian and she denied it.
"Who is this woman you're kissing then" I asked.
"She is jost a frennd" she insisted, "she is jost greeting mee, dis is how we greet each other baack home, it's a sort of duuble kiss". Double cross more like I thought to myself. She had a very guilty look about her, I pressed further.
"This is your one chance to tell me the truth Nina" I said, raising my voice slightly.
"She's jost a frennd, her name is Natalia" she mumbled.
"I know what her name is, it's Natalia Chopyakokov …" I started to say, and then it all started to fall into place. "Just like your … name … is …" the penny dropped "your name is Chopyakokov …"
"She is sistuur" Nina confessed rather angrily. I asked her why she was so cagey if the lady was just her sister. Nina began to sob "she not allowed out of our country because of charges against hur, she wudd haf gon to preeson. She came over here in back ov lorrrrrry … she he-ore illegally".
"What did she do wrong?" I asked her gently, aware she was now very vulnerable and finally telling the truth.

"She norss like me … she not so compassionate as me tho, that is oll I want to say about it" she whispered as she began to weep.

I was surprised at that last bit, not as compassionate as Nina. I reckon Natalia and Jack would get on like a house on fire.

We took the guided bus to Ropey and Nina introduced me to her sister Natalia, in Dykes Discotheque and just as Nina had said, I was greeted with a double kiss. "Aaghh, you are my sistuurs boyfrennd, she tell me oll about you … you are very strange man she say". I think Natalia and I will get along just fine. We had a few drinks in Dykes Discotheque and collected Natalia's belongings and we all boarded the guided bus home. That noyght a very happy Nina, and a very happy Natalia and I all got into bed together, it was a squeeze but it made for a very happy Morton. We were all very, very happy.

Moondee 22th Autism

This mawnin I introduced Natalia to Jim Bob. Jim Bob was a bit smitten I think and he started showing off by running up and down the waste land outside my house shouting "Natalia … look how fast I can run". She smiled and then ignored him. Jim Bob carried on running up and down for another 20 minutes, even though nobody was watching him, until he vomited through exhaustion. Lovely old Jim Bob.

PC Jack Wormer came in mid mawnin to see Pocahontas and his policeman instincts kicked in straight away as he began asking about the new face in the house. I decided the only way to deal with this was with the truth, after all Jack owed me more than a few favours. I explained to him Natalia's predicament and that she was a wanted woman in her own country. Jack looked very uncomfortable with the information I was giving him. I was just about to start playing hard ball with him when he asked me what she had done. When I explained it was to do with the brutality she had shown her patients Jack's demeanour changed. "Well that's different then, of course we will have to change her last name and give her a new identity. I'll get her a Flatlands passport sorted out and you'll have to collect it tomorrow from the town hall, I'll need to get one of the Elders to approve it but that won't be a problem" Jack said.

That last sentence of Jack's jogged my bonce matter into action.
"Jack, do you know the names of all the Elders out of interest?" I asked slyly.

"Of course I do" he said beaming, "not many do though; it's a bit hush hush".

"Could you write them down for me please Jack" and I slid him a piece of paper and a pencil across the kitchen/operating table. He scribbled down all four names, one of which I already knew, and passed the paper back to me.

"Can I ask why you want to know the names of the Elders Morton?"

"No!" I replied sharply. Jack looked a bit surprised and, dare I say it, even a little hurt by my response, but I couldn't risk telling him just yet.

"Look Jack, I'll tell you what I know very, very soon but until I can confirm the suspicions I have are true, trust me, it's best you don't know". He seemed a little bit happier now.

With that, Jack stood up and made his way to the door. As he went to open it he paused, turned and looked at me and said "If you're in any kind of trouble you would let me know wouldn't you … you can count on me … you know that don't you". I smiled and nodded at him. He closed the door behind and left. I was left feeling a little bit more confident now, Jack is a brutal man, but I suspect, a fair one. I looked out my front room window and Jim Bob had started sprinting up and down the bit of waste land again, still nobody was watching him. Silly cunt.

CHAPTER TEN

THE DEVIL'S IN THE DETAIL

SEPTICBOWEL 1896

Toosdi 1th Septicbowel

What a lovely start to a new month. On my arrival at the maternity ward this mawnin I discovered that my one of my neighbours, Blodwella, had given birth to her offspring. The gender is as yet undeterminable but he/she has a healthy number of fingers and toes totalling 63, possibly going to be a fine banjo player later on in life. Whilst at the hospital I enquired about the possibility of getting Natalia a job but none were available for the foreseeable future, possibly try again after Chrimstaaas time once Billy S'Vile retires so he can concentrate on his charity fund raising.

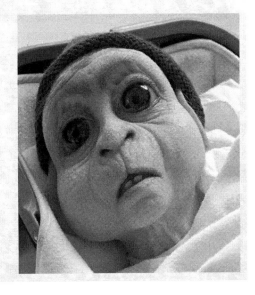

Chumpton-by-Rumberly Informer

Finally, the happy arrival has been announced Jebdah Blodwella, the son/daughter of Blodwella and Blodwin Blodwella. He/she was born at 7.00am on Thrisdee and again three days later. The happy parents, brother and sister, are hoping to collect their childer from Ropey Hospital for the Genetically Impure some time soon where they can return to their home in Lower Fen fen, near Fen End at the top of Lower Fen Drove.

I popped into the town hall and collected Natalia's new passport and identity, Jack had outdone himself this time. There was a new passport and all the supporting paperwork to allow Natalia to start a new life with a new name. From this day forward Nina's sister would be known Natalia Goebbels, and with the anonymity of her new surname nobody would suspect her occasionally unpleasant, cruel and sadistic nature.

Winsti 2th Septicbowel

Once again I find myself waiting for Gary by the clock tower, this time armed with my names of the Flatland Elders, and once again he arrived shortly after I did. I remembered the journey this time and seemed to recall playing around here as a yoof, before roads and houses were built. As we drove the short distance to New Chumpton Gary told me that when he tried to contact the building developer that built the first phase of New Chumpton he couldn't reach anyone because they had gone out of business recently. When we got to Gary's house his wife was present this time and was busy getting their daughter ready for her first day back at school after the summer break (*The kids of Flatland don't get a summer break, or a summer*) She still wasn't over friendly but she was a bit more approachable than before, I think she was still a bit angry with the whole kidnapping of her daughter thing the other month. We had some more of the posh coffee and went to Gary's office. I deliberately didn't mention the crack in the wall this time. I presented Gary with the list of Elders of the council and read the names out to him.

"Well Jackson Spangler we know about" I said, "Freddy Fingerstein, Blair Deville and Blaize Craphammer are the others".
As I read the names out Gary typed them into his Google thingummy and pressed the enter button and hey presto up they came on his screen. As we went onto the first few options available to us it became obvious what the connection was other than the Flatland Elders (*which incidentally didn't show up on Gary's search at all*). All four of the names on Jacks list were all Company Directors for building development business called Hellscape Development Corporation.
Over the next hour Gary did internet checks on all of them individually and they all went to the same school as David Devilman, Eton it's called, and apparently the wealthy hooomans consider it to be better to send their young childers away to live in a

castle and learn stuff there rather than let them live at home and learn who their parents, family and friends are … odd.

It would seem that the company was dissolved very recently and this didn't look too good for Gary getting his repairs done. It was obvious how David Devilman managed to get his planning permission sorted and it was also clear how Hellscape managed to build them without any of those bothersome tests and building regulatory visits. The registered offices were in Ropey.

The next hurdle however was to formulate a plan that would bring the evil n'er do wells to justice, save large chunks of Flatland District from being demolished and turned into a huge distribution centre. As we sat sipping tea in Gary's kitchen (*with a delightful biscuit called an Oreo*) wondering how we can formulate this plan Gary went to a cupboard and pulled out a box. In the box was a mobile phone. He switched it on and gave it to me. He said that if the tefelones (*hooomans call them telephones, they've almost got it right*) are being listened into then I would need to use this so I can get in touch with him. We spent the next hour using the phone and he showed me all of its functions. It was like a tiny version of the computer he has in his office.

I could use the google engine like he can and also call him if I need to. He had it as a spare phone in case his phone ever got lost or conked out. The lavish life style these hooomans lead is a real eye opener. After my instruction on how to use the mobile phone Gary gave me a lift back to Chumpton and dropped me off at the clock tower. As I walked through the village I looked about the place, everywhere seemed slightly differently. These last few weeks had changed me a lot, I felt, and much for the better too. I had learned so much lately, I had learned new words, new ideas, I had learned much about myself too and how resourceful I can be when I really have to. Also, Gary had taught me loads about everything, about computers, about the UK and about the people we call hooomans or immigrants. I'd realised that they were a little bit different from us, better in some ways, not in others but I had learned we are all pretty much the same. I had learned that the people who controlled our little district are greedy and corrupt cuntbuckets and are keen to exploit our ignorance for their own gain, Gary assured me this was true in the rest of the UK and the whole world too.

Thrisdee 3rd Septicbowel

I was pleased to see this in one of the local newspapers. After having spent a bit of time lately with Gary and my recent trip to London I have sampled the delights of posh coffee I'm pleased to see Chumpton has now got its very own posh coffee shop.

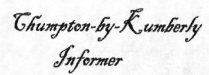

Chumpton-by-Kumberly Informer

Chumpton has finally got itself on the upmarket coffee shop map thanks to Cedric Fingerbottom and his aptly named "Cedric's Colombian Coffee Bean Emporium" that has opened this week down Upper Fen Drove, Upper Fen fen at Yon End by the dyke pump.

A mere 3 Hens Beaks (or equivalent value in root crops) will buy you a delicious mug of Happy Pauper Value Blend instant coffee with a sprinkling of Cedric's own secret chocolate coloured topping. When I asked Cedric about his secret topping he just smiled, farted, dribbled a bit and pointed to his dog (*also called Cedric*), who whimpered whilst trying hide under the counter. I think he was hinting that not even the dog knows the secret of his special blend coffee topping.

Although most of the village is now connected to the National Grid, sadly Upper Fen Drove, Upper Fen Fen at Yon End by the dyke pump isn't, and not due to be connected before 1978 or maybe the year after 1852, so for the time being the coffee is served "chilled" or iced as the Hooomans immigrants call it. Whether your celebrating a significant event or you simply fancy a cup of Cedric's special blend why not pop into "Cedric's Colombian Coffee Bean Emporium" to start your day with a bang.

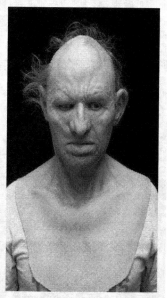

Cedric Fingerbottom

I have spent most of the day getting used to Gary's spare phone he's leant me. I have learned about many of its functions and also discovered that the amount of tuppence photo's (*or pornography as the hooomans call it*) is mind boggling. Despite our community facing the peril of extinction from ruthless developers and learning of methods that our councillors have used to hoodwink us into avoiding social development along with the rest of the UK, I have in all honesty spent most of the day doing lots of mastybayshun … lots and lots of mastybayshun. I have never seen so many tuppences and breasties and chaps with big winky's having lots of sexy time with ladies that have no pubic hair and breast augmentation that is worse and more obvious than my first two attempts on Pocahontas and Cinderella.

My office carpet will be like sand paper tomorrow mawnin. Tomorrow I will continue on our quest to save Flatlands from oblivion. Today though, I shall be playing with my winky a bit more. Hopefully Nina and Natalia will be feeling a bit fruity and I shall be doing a threesup. Some of the pornography I watched today gave me some great tips on what the ladies like when involved in extreme rudeness.

Frydims 4st Septicbowel

As Jim Bob continued our cottage industry of Zonco, 'inventions and useful appliances for the local community' I was trying to find cover for the Peppermint Hippo as Davina Kraye was required to attend something to do with the Mayoral elections due at the end of this month. If push came to shove I could cover the shift myself but apart from being busy saving the world (*or at least a very small part of it but the part I live in*) I had tried out Cedric's Columbian Bean Coffee Emporium and my bottom has been squirting out a liquid that was not too dissimilar to the liquid I consumed at Cedric's coffee shop. I took a photo of the state of my toilet and the state of my sphincter with Gary's phone he leant me. Unfortunately it's linked to some kind of cloud, a cloud that his daughter has access to and Gary asked me if I could avoid 'uploading' photos of my anus and it's recently excreted contents. His daughter hasn't stopped crying since.

SatD 5th Septicbowel

Not only did I cover Davina's shift last noyght but I will be doing so again tonoyght too. She has been in some pretty high brow meetings with the Elders and will continue to do so throughout the weekend. I'm not sure what's afoot but she was seen buying a lot of Vaseline and Bonjella from the Happy Pauper before being picked up by one of the Elders shoooofa driven autocars and whisked away to the town hall.

Luckily I didn't suffer any drastic consequences following my visit to our local coffee shop yisdee and my performance was faecal free. I even came out with a record haul of root crops in my thong. Plenty of stew this week then. Davina was sorely missed and she has been an asset to the Peppermint Hippo in her short while working here.

Natalia informed me that I should start referring to my winky as a penis from now on. It is more professional and gives an air of intelligence and authority. I agree, I shall be trying to use it much more in every day conversation. I do know the correct anatomical terminology for all sorts of body bits as some of it was in the questions for my online doctoring test I took in order for me to start doing gender reassignment surgery. I was hoping I would have had a few more people take me up on my sex change operating but alas no. maybe if I start using the word penis a lot more then people will see me as someone who could easily be trusted to irreversibly change their lives with some penis removal or vagina penis shaping.

Well I'd better stop writing my diary and get over to the club and wow some locals with my dancing and occasional use of the word penis.

Sunty 6lbs Septicbowel

Well, dear diary where do I begin? Last noyght was both a massive success and also a huge surprise too. I did the first stint on the pole and shortly afterwards I was called into a booth for my first private dance of the noyght. When I entered I stopped in my tracks. The surprise almost left me speechless; it was none other than Mayor David Devilman.

"Hello Mayor Devilman" I said warily.

"Not for very much longer teehee" he slurred, he was clearly the worse for drink. As the music began thumping (*Art Garfunkel's 'Bridge over Troubled Water'*) I started my routine. Devilman immediately unzipped his trousers and started massaging his ~~winky~~ penis and couldn't keep his hands off me. Tonoyght I was dressed in my Brittany Spears latex school girl outfit and quite frankly I was rather pleased I chose it. When I saw what the Mayor was up to I was pleased I chose latex, easier to clean. The Mayor was very brief before he ~~did his sex wee~~ ejaculated, although it was something of a disappointing amount, barely clearing his foreskin and dribbling down his fingers. He was making the same noises I heard his faithful hound "Growler" made when I was dancing at his chambers. You know, on reflection I'm beginning to wonder if there ever was a Growler. He playfully smacked my bottom and asked me to sit with him.

"I suppose this is goodbye old chum" he said hardly able to keep his eyes open.

"Really? Why? … I mean I know you have resigned as Mayor but where are you going, surely you'll stay within the area" I enquired slyly.

"Well I have property elsewhere but yes, yes I'll return from time to time".

"Then I'm sure I can dance for you at your house occasionally, as long as you give me some notice I can make arrangements, anyway you have at least four more weeks until the Mayoral election" I said.

"Well that's the thing old chum, I don't" mused the Mayor.

"Eeerm sir" came a familiar voice from the shadows.

"Jeeez Cranshaw, I nearly shit myself ... and not in the way you like it either" I said winking at the Mayor. He giggled drunkenly. "How come you always managed to lurk in the corner somewhere".

"It's what I'm paid to do" Cranshaw replied, smirking at me.

"Well anyway, I meant to say this needn't be goodbye just bye for now" I said chirpily.

"Au Revoir you mean" the Mayor giggled, "Exactly that" I replied pretending that I knew what he meant.

"Well you'll be needing to find a new dancer I'm afraid old bean, your lovely Davina will be very busy next week, and week after, and the week after that" the Mayor said rather cryptically. Cranshaw gave him the 'you've said too much look' and the Mayor took the hint.

"How about just one more for old times' sake" he giggled.

I once again began thrusting and gyrating my hips to the grinding rhythm of the local sensation 'The Faith Tones' covering Jesus want's me for a Sunbeam. As I turned and faced the Mayor he was struggling to stay awake but the sight of my red latex pants thrusting into his face seemed to wake him up. He didn't do any mastybayshun this time I noticed a wet patch in his groin. To be honest the state he was in it could just as well have been piss as ~~sex wee~~ semen.

"Do you like my penis ... my PENIS ... yes you like it don't you" I said as suggestively as I could. I turned for one last erotic lunge and as I ran my gloved hands down my legs to slide my school girl stockings down I peered between my legs to see he had now fallen asleep. Cranshaw and I covertly removed the Mayor from the club placed him into the backseat of his autocar and he drove the Mayor away into the noyght. I texted Gary to let him in on the noyght's events and wondered what he meant about Davina.

Moondee 7Mr Septicbowel

This mawnin the Flatland news was alive with analysis and comment from anyone and everyone in the District. Micky Dove, the twins Ian and Duncan Smythe, Morris Poncen, and Theresa Posh-Farquharson have all dropped out of the Mayoral election race stating various reasons for no longer wishing to be considered. The favourite reason seemed to be that they wished to spend more time with their families. This meant that Davina Kraye was by default the last one standing and therefore was the new Mayoress of Flatland District. Well these are odd times, we have voted to leave the UK and now we have an unelected, and some might say unqualified, Mayoress to preside over some very difficult times in the forthcoming future.

As Davina stood on the steps of the town hall, in front of the Flatland press and TV cameras she was dressed (*almost*) in a see-through chiffon dress that could easily be mistaken as a noyght wear and sporting lots of make-up, the tiniest of knickers and no bra (*showing her breasties for all to see*) she began her speech about what a shrinking violet she was and was not a showy type of person. This is the lady that has packed out my club recently and made a name for herself as the queen of root crop tipping by performing the kind of gratuitous sex acts during private dances that gets prostitution a bad name. Now she's telling everyone that she's not much of a show off. Maybe I was just a bit annoyed I was losing my best dancer but either way last noyghts events with David Devilman are beginning to make sense now.

FENLAND DISTRICT WEELKY NEWS

Are you at a loss wondering what to have for laasdocky tonoyght or simply can't be bothered to cook after a difficult day at the office. Well wonder no more residents of Chumpton and pop on down to the villages latest fast food emporium "Herpes Pizza". Local lad and renowned foodie Jerebediah Shagsista has opened this "little piece of Italy" near the clock tower and hopes to introduce villagers to continental cuisine with such delights as the house special the "Herpes shankerscab meat feast" a pizza designed by the owner himself as well as "12 inches of Jerebediah" which is mostly salami with a squirt of Mayo.
As an opening special offer for six months only, all meals are half price if you can manage to keep it down for 25 minutes. Come on people of Chumpton, support local business with a visit for some lovely Herpes ... stuff.

The day's events had been tough to take in so for laasdocky I decided to treat everyone to a takeaway. The new one that's opened in the village is run by Jerebediah Shagsista who was a frequent visitor to the Peppermint Hippo when Finnders Dastardly owned the club. Sadly Jerebediah had infected most of the performers and nearly all the patrons with some very rare sexually transmitted fungal infections and skin complaints. It'll be interesting to see how he fairs as a restaurateur. I saw his ad in the daily rag so we'll give it a whirl.

Toosdi 8st Septicbowel

FLATLAND DISTRICT WEEKLY NEWS

FLATLAND FLORA & FAUNA - **THE LESSER HAIRED FLATLAND GRATCH**
A picture of tranquility as a Lesser haired Flatland Gratch is pictured Fettling it's calfpups. The Gratch calfpups are believed to be a full F5 generation mutation (show standard). These rarely seen Fen creatures are almost exclusively found around the Chumpton vicinity but have occasionally been found as far a field as Chatterby.
They feed on primarily Swans and sometimes genetically modified turnips but do not make good pets due to their almost constant flatulence and spiteful temperament.

fatpita.net

Today has been spent largely vomiting and projectile pooing. Lord knows what we have caught but it seems to have gone through us all during the noyght. It has been a desperate time as we only have one toilet with a house that has five people and a Nigelle living in it. Luckily we had the basement bath to use if the toilet was in use. I'm not sure what could have caused this sudden onset of illness but we all got it and have all got the same symptoms together. We're too ill to cook so we'll be having another takeaway from Herpes tonoyght I reckon. I haven't had much time to devise a plan to save Flatlands today, but I'll have to come up with something soon as the Mayor has now left office. At least I managed to get a bit of information from him before Cranshaw whisked him away. When Jack called this aftynune he said the Mayor hadn't been seen at the town hall and wasn't at his house either when he patrolled it earlier. Jack asked if I knew anyone who could possibly re-home a Gratch that had been found. I had seen the story in the weekly news this mawnin but I didn't have the room. He did divulge though that St.John Cranshaw (*Cranshaw St.John's other half*) had spent most of the day in floods of tears. Jack reckons they may have had an argument but I think Cranshaw left with the former Mayor and hasn't been seen since.

Winsti 9nd Septicbowel

Today was my weekly Winsti meeting with Gary. As usual he collected me at the clock tower and we went to his house. By the time we got there his daughter had already gone to school and his wife had gone to her job in Cambridge (*which is not far outside Flatlands and much posher than Peterborough .... Imagine that ...*). We sat at the kitchen table, both stumped at the events that had occurred this week. Clearly they were very specific events that had happened from decisions taken for a specific reason but we had no idea what or why. Neither of us was sure if this was a good thing or bad, but both of us were certain that we were running out of time. Something had spooked David Devilman to make him jump ship early but what. I thought I'd lighten the mood by asking Gary about any developments regarding his crumbling and cracked house. I could've possibly chosen my words a little better as he sighed and slumped back in his chair.

"My pal the surveyor is making enquiries about getting compensation for the work required to put the repairs in place. It would need a huge amount of underpinning to stop it slipping any more than it is because of the soil structure. He seems to think we have a good case for total compensation.
I called a residents meeting the other night and informed them of what had happened and advised them to seek expert guidance". I felt very sorry for Gary.
I told Gary about the unusual meeting I had with the former Mayor at the Peppermint Hippo recently. Gary seemed very disturbed by it all, especially the bit were he tried to squirt his ~~sex w~~ ejaculate all over my latex clad buttocks. For all his modern ways Gary is a bit of a prude when it comes to pleasures of the flesh and prostrate milking etc.

"Of course, I could've always had a nosey about his house whenever I go there to dance and do private dances for him in his living room. I've often been left in there for long periods of time whilst he went and wiped my runny poo off his arms and occasionally face" I said … Gary had that disturbed look again.

" … yes … it's a shame he won't be about much very often, it may have been worth having a look at paperwork, maybe receipts or ledgers, if he had any company ledgers" Gary wistfully pondered.

I tried to lighten the mood with a glimmer of hope, "well he didn't say he was leaving completely just yet and I can always get access to the town hall easily enough now that Pocahontas is marrying …." My ideas light bulb was flashing bold and brightly. Gary could tell by my expression I had something, "What … what is it" he said. I mulled it over a few moments longer and then hit him with it.

"You really aren't going to like this … I mean really, really aren't going to like this" I said rather tentatively.

"Go on, we're kind of in a corner here so I'll listen to any ideas you have" Gary said.

"Well … one of my ladies that lives in my house … a former patient of mine … well she's been dating recently and is now engaged to be married and that person can be of huge use to us".

Well that's great" Gary said, "why wouldn't I like that?"

"It's PC Wormer of Ropey Town Police Brigade, he could …) that's as far as I got "NO FUCKING WAY!" gary bellowed. "That animal is a complete fucking psychopath Morton … I mean you're odd but friendly enough … him though". I took being called odd as something of an insult.

There is nothing odd about trepanning people to help them rid themselves from demons and head pressures, nor is there anything odd about assisting people to live their lives in the body they were meant to have. I said nothing though as I could understand his reluctance after us kidnapping his daughter and all.

I let Gary calm down a bit by repeatedly telling him that it was okay and we'll think of something else. Finally Gary realised that there wasn't a "something else" or a plan B and he was more inclined to listen to what I had to say. This calming down period also gave me a few moments to try and plan what I was going to say and how to say it without sparking another tantrum.

"Let's start by saying that when Jack looked after your daughter" I whispered hesitantly "Emily" Gary interjected tersely, "okay … when Jack looked after Emily the day you took me to London it was at my request, I didn't know you then like I do now and I needed to get to London. I know you're annoyed, you have every right to be, but you should be just as annoyed with me because I was every bit to blame as Jack … more so in fact. We have resolved our differences and I strongly suspect you could do the same with him" Gary slowly nodded in agreement.

"Not only does PC Wormer have access to the town halls but he also patrols the Devilman estate every noyght while he's on duty. He can get me in either place, if you can show me what it is I'm looking for then we can get some evidence and possibly go to someone with it. We can then save the world", Gary looked a bit surprised at my last part of the statement.

"… save the wor … whatever. Look is PC Wormer trustworthy?" Gary asked.

"Yes, that bit I can guarantee, and I own him … I mean he owes me … well both really. Don't you worry about Jack, I'll speak to him and you tell me what I need to look for and where it might be kept".

We discussed a plan of action and what it was I needed to look for and we agreed to keep in close contact. I suggested that Jack comes to out next meeting but Gary wasn't keen on him coming to his house, in case his daughter Emily saw her former captor again. We settled on the Peppermint Hippo next Thrisdee and I gave Gary directions. Gary returned me to Chumpton in his car, as we approached the village road he let me drive the last bit as I'd never driven an autocar, or just 'car', before. It was great fun. As I walked up the main drove back to my house I was thinking about everything that had been said today … it was feeling like we were on a proper adventure with maybe even a hint of peril added to the mix too.

Thrisdee 10nd Septicbowel

This mawnin I saw an advert in the Weekly News about abandonment. Obviously this hit a chord with me and made me wonder about why my parents abandoned me.

FLATLAND DISTRICT WEEKLY NEWS

If you have been raised by a family of Cranes don't suffer in Silence. Call the 'Crane abandonment Help line' on (01487845745454632125488845621984514) 345 ext 2 call option 3

Frydims 11nd Septicbowel

News filtered through that after having only just opened Herpes Pizza, Jerebediah had been ordered to close down by our old chum Augustus Angulgrinda from Ropey Town Health and Safety Department. Apparently the relish that Mr Shagsista was purporting to be an onion dip, as a pizza topping was in fact 'gentleman's relish' fresh from the lusty restaurateur's loins.

Nina suggested that we could sell some of her road kill stew and open up our own fast food place. I said it was certainly something for the future but wait until after the wedding when I could get more supplies of road kill. She looked at me funnily and smiled. I asked why she was smiling and she said "Wot, you think I hevn't eaten hoooman flish beforrrrre, things can get tough back hom durrring wintor". I realised she knew my little secret. We shouldn't keep secrets; we have both learned that lesson now. I asked her how long she had known I had been using hospital waste as ingredients of stew and she told me since she first made the stew. She cuddled me and told me to get as much as possible for the wedding and any extra we can sell at the Hippo. She never ceases to amaze me that lady.

Just after laasloyght I popped up to Ropey Town to write an article I'm doing about the local Mooosicul scene for my yoof culture paper New Mooosicul Expressions. It's about the local instrument making clubs popping up and in particular one in Ropey.

SatD 12th Septicbowel

This aftynune I sat down for ten minutes with Jack and made him a cup of tea with the special tea bags (*made with real tea not onion cosh*) that Gary gave me. He enjoyed it and said he drinks it all the time up at the town hall. He occasionally pinches a few bags for the lads at the Police Brigade Station.

As we sat enjoying our posh Typhoo tea like a couple of posh toffs I thought now was as good a time as any to tell Jack about what we had found out. I was very cagey to begin with but quickly realised that Jack had no loyalty to either David Devilman or the town hall. It turns out that over the last few years the town hall had been cutting back on the amount of money they spend on the police brigade and expect them to do the same work.

It also appears that the Elders have stopped paying into the Police Brigade Pension Fund. When I told Jack what had happened and what we had found out he was 100 percent in with our world saving endeavours.

I properly introduced Jack to Gary after our interpretive dance nativity practice and Gary seemed okay. They actually shook hands and when Jack explained to Gary, as he had done to me, about his anger towards the Flatland District Council Gary was looking pretty pleased that Jack was on board.

We agreed to meet up Thrisdee noyght at the Peppermint Hippo and formulate some kind of plan. I was planning and designing some kind of black ninja outfit that was befitting someone about to save the world.

Sunty 13th Septicbowel

Jack and Pocahontas went for a romantic walk along the very, very straight bank of the river Kumber this mawnin. They came back from their romantic walk remarkably quickly after setting off. Jack told me how his bride to be would get so aroused during their passionate times she would positively gush with lubrication. I found this difficult to believe given my knowledge of her previous incarnation. I gave Pocahontas a quick medical check and could see her vagina was scabbed over nicely but I'm guessing that the "lubrication" Jack speaks of is when he knocks the scabs of her tuppence and the pus "Lubricates" Jacks ride. I asked him if she ever said much to him and he said that oddly she has said a lot more just lately and she keeps saying her name is Dmitri and that she wanted to go home now, it spooked Jack a little bit and that was why they had come back so soon.

I told Jack that this was due to her demons playing up and maybe a bit of cranial bonce pressures making her talk the occasional gibberish just like Nigelle used to. Jack said that as the local bobby he was used to people talking gibberish and thought nothing of it. I reassured Jack that I would give her some trepanning and she would be fine. Jack said he was indebted to me, just how I like it.

Shortly before Jack left he mentioned something very interesting. On the Frydims he popped into the Town Hall and bumped into St.John Cranshaw, the other half of the former Mayor's assistant.

He said that Cranshaw St.John had been spending virtually all of his time with Devilman and he suspected the two were having an affair. Of course they probably weren't but the jilted partner of the ex-Mayor could be a very useful contact to have if we needed any information. Jack said St.John 'liked' me and suggested he join our interpretive dance group. I thanked him for this info and asked Jack to try and talk him into attending the next meeting the following SatD.

Pocahontas's trepanning went well. She is struggling to speak now ☺

Moondee 14lbs Septicbowel

FLATLAND DISTRICT WEEKLY NEWS

A fantastic noyght was had by all at the Ropey Town Mooosicul Instermunt Making Club Last Frydims. There were many ingenious home-made instruments at the meeting including these Goatpipes made by Hindred Weaselbumps. Hindred is Ropey Towns official Parish Childer Catcher but his real passion is making musical instruments from animals that have strayed too close to his premises between Chumpton and Ropey Town. Some of the audience present for Hindred's performance with his Goatpipes were surprised and upset that the Goat was not totally dead and was making some screeching sounds that oddly complimented the song being played by Hindred.

Hindred Weaselbumps and his Goatpipes

My piece for my yoof culture paper New Mooosicul Expressions has also made it into today's edition of the Flatlands Weekly News too, for a small fee of course.

Pocahontas was back to dribbling mode today. Jack noticed an immediate difference and thanked me several times. The only noise that could be heard in casa Babeldom this afternoon was the squeaking bed springs of Pocahontas's bed as Jack and "Pokie" as he calls her, enjoyed an aftynune of congress. Jack told me that other than the bedsprings, there was perfect silence during their congress … just how he liked it.

As I made us a cup of tea I noticed a few maggots wriggling on the kitchen/operating table. I thought nothing of it until I noticed some more on the living room floor.

I'm wondering if they have made their way in from the inventing shed were I'm keeping some of the ingredients for Pocahontas's wedding docky.

Toosdi 15 lbs Septicbowel

Tonoyght we will be going to the Klunge Klub in Chatterby to watch the final acts hoping to represent Flatlands at next year's Eurovision song contest. The Eurovision is a contest that gets the very best mooosicul talent that country can offer and they perform the song with a view to being judged fairly and without prejudice. The winners get to appear on Top of the Pops in London. We have sent many, many entrants to appear in the contest but only three have made it out of the country and none of the three made it back. We are hoping at some point in the future that the Flatland representative will be allowed in Paris (*which is where the Eurovision Song Contest is held every year*). Cinderella and her beau Finbar certainly turned a few heads tonoyght in Chatterby. There have only been a few people with dark skin that have ever been seen in Chatterby, sadly none of them survived.

Winsti 16st Septicbowel

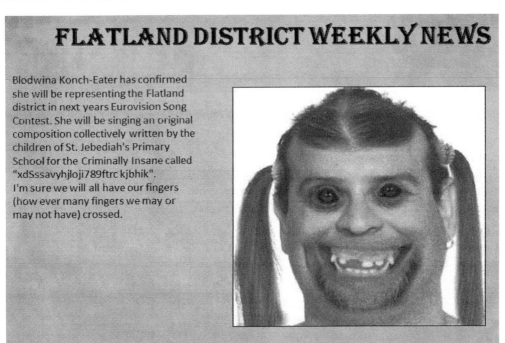

FLATLAND DISTRICT WEEKLY NEWS

Blodwina Konch-Eater has confirmed she will be representing the Flatland district in next years Eurovision Song Contest. She will be singing an original composition collectively written by the children of St. Jebediah's Primary School for the Criminally Insane called "xdSssavyhjloji789ftrc kjbhik".
I'm sure we will all have our fingers (how ever many fingers we may or may not have) crossed.

Blodwina Konch-Eater won last noyght's contest and will be accompanied on the three key piano (*it has lots more than three key but only three work*) by none other than Lanita

Eversole who I featured in The New Mooosicul Expressions some months ago. Let's all keep our collective webbed fingers crossed and hope that they make it far as Paris or at least Peterborough.

Thrisdee 17rd Septicbowel

This mawnin I did a vaginal check on Cinderella and discovered that there was a small infestation of maggots in and around the tuppence cavity. This would explain me finding a few maggots the other day. They were infested from the bottom part all the way to top part where the kleetris is. The kleetris is the thing the ladies stroke when they are doing mastybayshun and is very sensitive. They should only be attempted to be touched by men that know exactly what they are doing, sadly many don't. As a doctor I am fully equipped to stroke ladies kleetrises and I have often been asked to do so in the past by some lady villagers that have their men folk incarcerated in HMP Ropey.

At just after laasloyght, I went over to the club and Jack and Gary were already there. They seemed to be getting on okay and I ordered myself a glass of Pochine. Gary came to bar and offered to pay for it but obviously I don't pay for drinks at the Peppermint Hippo as I own it. I told Sylvia that Gary and Jack were to drink on the house all noyght as my guests. I liked doing that as it made me feel important, Gary seemed impressed. He was drinking the Turnip Pochine and said it was tangy but okay. Coming from someone who has bags of Typhoo tea in his house, I took this as big thumbs up. I have drunk some pretty decent whiskey before now, the hooomans immigrants UK people liked there fancy drink and I can honestly say that a well brewed batch of Turnip Pochine is alright. I warned Gary about drinking too much of it as it could make him go blind. I think he thought I was joking until moments later when we returned to their table, Jack gave him the exact same warning. We enjoyed a drink and a brief chat and we retired to my office/store cupboard so we can speak openly in private without prying ears. As we made ourselves comfy, Jack produced from a bag a small cuddly toy. It was a stuffed Kangaroo he had bought from Ropey town market earlier that day. Jack handed the toy to Gary.

"I would be most grateful if you gave this to Emily" Jack said looking rather embarrassed.

"Thank you Jack I will" Gary said grinning at what was, to those observing (*me*) quite a touching moment.

"Although it is very highly flammable and the eyes are a choking hazard so … you know … be careful" Jack advised.

"I'll put it on her book case then, thank you very much"

With the soppy moment of reconciliation out of the way we got down to business. Gary had taken some screen shots (*look at me with computer terminology*) of the kinds of things I would need to look for. With enough evidence of the suspected wrong doings of our former Mayor we could give it to the right authorities and re-open the enquiry into his business affairs and also include the four Elders. Gary had plenty of things for me to look for from receipts, ledgers and ideally there computer records.

"I'm fairly certain that they have passwords on the computers Gary" Jack said.

"Don't you worry about that Jack, I work in IT I can soon bypass that, if you can get us in there Morton can look for the paper trail and I'll hack into his computer, I could do it remotely but it's easier, quicker and less risky if I'm actually there". This was the first time that Gary had indicated that he actually wanted to get involved in the whole 'breaking and entering' part of our adventure. I was rather impressed.

"Devilman's assistant's life partner, St.John Cranshaw, is still awfully sore at the way he's been treated, perhaps he would be good for some gentle questioning about information that might be useful to us" I suggested.

"I'll have a chat with him soon and see how he's bearing up" Jack said.

"See if you can find out how much funding they get from Central government each year and how much actually get spent on the community. That would include the amount of money for benefits and social housing and the roads, hospitals and the like" Gary chipped in. Both Jack and I were now very, very confused. What was he on about with benefits and social welfare and housing? We asked him to clarify what he meant.

"If you find yourself out of work you can claim benefits, you can get all kinds of assistance if you're ill or find yourself in difficulties. The hospitals and many other public services like the roads are all paid for by central government"

"Central Government?" both Jack and said together, "What do you mean Central Government? Flatlands council is central government" I asked. "What do you mean roads?" Jack asked.

For the next hour Gary told us that the government would have given lots of money, millions of pounds in fact, each year to the council to help with the upkeep of the community. Things like the police and the rubbish collection was paid for by something called council tax. This was the first we had heard of this. We explained to Gary that we had recently held a referendum and we had voted to leave the UK. He was amazed. He then spent the next hour explaining that we were and always will be part of the UK and we didn't have an 'opt out' possibility. Gary thinks that the referendum was nothing more than a distraction from what was really going or maybe a ruse to prepare the folk of Flatlands for some incredible hardship to soften them up for something, possibly compulsory purchase orders. It would also seem that there "has been a misappropriation of public funds on a monumental scale" as Gary put it. "I wondered why everywhere was so run down, why nothing was up to date and seemed to be so far behind with the times. When I wandered around Ropey the other week I thought to myself then that it all seemed to be from another era" Gary said.

It was now beginning to dawn on us that our own council, the people who are paid to look after us have been deliberately keeping us in the dark ages and have been doing so for decades. The money the government give the council has been going somewhere but we haven't been seeing very much of it. We hadn't been paying any council tax but then we had to get rid of our own rubbish on Spunky Cartwrights trailer that pulled about by tractor once a week. The police brigade it would appear has been funded by the council but then they use them like a militia (*another Gary wordism*). The hospital and schools were very, very underfunded, Gary seems to think that they'll be put out for tender to a private company if the new land deals go through. The enormity of this was quite overwhelming. Gary could see we were quite shaken so said it was time to call it a noyght. He would go away and start getting the software ready for hacking into the council's computers and breaking into David Devilman's house. We would all need to come up with plans and try and glean as much information from people as possible before we strike. Even something that may not seem significant might possibly be vital at the right time, we all shook hands and the meeting was over. As we walked out the office/store cupboard back into the club to my amazement there, dancing on one of the poles, to the thrill and delight of all in the Peppermint Hippo, was the last person I expected to see. Gary looked on in amazement, "who the fuck is that?" he gasped. "That Gary old son, that is none other than Davina Kraye, Flatland Districts new Mayoress" I informed him. Gary's jaw dropped as he turned his head to me and exclaimed "Fuck off". I smiled, Jack laughed. We stood for a few moments longer and Gary decided he needed another drink so we made our way to Sylvia for more Pochine.

Gary left his car in the car park and Jack drove him home in his police brigade car.

Frydims 18th Septicbowel

This mawnin Natalia and Nina took the ladies out for elevenses after Cinderella had her vagina disinfected to try and get rid of the maggot infestation. We had struggled to find any more baby Badgers so Jim Bob was in the inventing shed knocking up some kitten radios for the childers at the primary school and I was enjoying a nice cup of tea with cow's milk. I was still trying to get my head around the fact that everything I had known was a lie, everybody I knew was being lied to and we were all being made fools of by people who couldn't give a shit about us, Mind boggling. My thought train was jolted back to reality by a knock at the door. When I answered it I was greeted by a big daft grin from a big daft man. Morris Poncen was stood before me. He held out his hand and asked if I could count on his vote to become Mayor in the forthcoming Mayoral elections. My heart bled a little bit.

"Come in Morris" I said and closed the door behind him. "Morris, we already have a new Mayor, well it's a Mayoress actually … I thought you knew. They made the announcement a while back now and they said that you had all decided to drop out of the election due to personal reasons such as spending more time with your families and stuff". Morris looked broken. He grinned his big goofy grin at me but I could tell he was choking back the tears. "Oh well" he said "at least I don't have to knock anymore bloomin doors, I have managed to get lost quite a few times and also got my hands trapped in quite few letterboxes … so who's the lucky lady then?" he said with his impeccable posh English accent. I told him about the announcement as well as all the other stuff that had been going on, I'm not sure he understood it all but he nodded his blonde mop of bonce hair a lot and grinned. I made him a cup of tea and we sat for while whilst he collected his thoughts.

"Of course I blame that bloomin David bloomin Devilman, he was always a rum un, even at school he had to have his own way" Morris said with an air of some considerable disgruntlement.
"He used to make me do things … things with his willy"
My ears pricked up, "really, what do you mean?"
"Well I promised not to tell, and it was a lot of years ago but as everyone seems to have told me lots of fibs lately then I don't see the harm in telling a bit of truth, nobody would believe you if you told them anyway but that bloomin Devilman fella, when we were in our dorms at school would make me put his willy in my mouth and I'd have to make oinking sounds like a pig … bloomin disgusting".

"Pig sounds ... of course" I whispered.

I sat and chatted with Morris for an hour or so before he eventually got up and left. I immediately got on the mobile phone to Gary and told him of my chat with Morris, about his school days with the Mayor at Eton and the piggy blow jobs. Then I divulged the significance of the pig sounds.

"When I was doing some private dancing for David Devilman at his house I noticed a photograph on his table of him cuddling a pig. I thought it was a bit strange at the time so when I went and had a look at the table I noticed it was in an incredibly thick frame with a wire connected and it was making a noise. I'm pretty sure it might be a hidden camera. If it is then I know Devilman used to hold fairly highbrow meetings in there because he had a slanging match with that Rimbit Muldoon character that owns the Flatlands weekly news and TV station"

"Wait a minute" Gary said "Rimbit Muldoon is a huge media mogul, he has lots of other outlets too, this gets deeper and deeper, maybe we are saving the world" Gary chuckled.

We chatted for ten minutes or so and I said I'd fill Jack in when he got here later to take Pocahontas out for a meal ... or take her up the arse in in her bedroom ... either or really. Gary was surprised Jacks fiancé was called Pocahontas.

SatD 19jr Septicbowel

Well dearest diary, in a week of surprises the biggest was saved for today. This aftynune at the weekly practice for the nativity interpretive dance class Gary turned up with Emily, his daughter that Jack and I kidnapped a few months back, and his wife came to watch too. That was a surprise in itself but the biggest surprise happened during the warm up procedure. As we were stretching off the doors flung open and in walked a figure dressed in grey sweat pants and a Franky Says T shirt. I didn't initially recognise who it was but as the figure drew closer I saw it was none other than PC Jack Wormer, Ropey Town Police Brigades finest. Jack made his way to Gary and his family and joined in with the limbering up. They had clearly all settled their concerns about Jack and oddly, his daughter seemed positively thrilled to see him. The session went well and after Gary and his family had said their goodbyes and made their way home, Jack and I went for a drink at the club.

Sunty 20jr Septicbowel

The Sunday edition of the Flatland District Weekly News was leading with this story about the Great Chumpton Bake off. After the near death experience of the chief judge Meryl Berrell last year it'll be interesting to see if she samples the contestants wares herself or brings in an official taster like her colleague, fellow judge Paul Deepin-Derwood has.

FLATLAND DISTRICT WEEKLY NEWS

The final of The Great Chumpton Bake Off is happening next Toosdl at Chumpton WI hall/arena.

Last years winner was Edwina Kunscracher who made a fantastic Turnip and Onion cake washed down with some of her own Turnip and Onion smoothie. The chief judge, Meryl Berrell said the standard was not what she expected and hoped to have recovered in time for this years competition. Speaking from her hospital bed she went on to say "I never knew that root crops were such a diverse food source".

Edwina said her secret ingredient was a well guarded family recipe which was an aromatic blend of cleaning solvents and cat urine. If you think you can give Edwina a run for her money then why not enter the contest and try your luck.

Footnote; following last years controversy it has been decided not to allow any form of saliva as a binding agent.

Bake off judge Meryl Berrell showing her appreciation of some of the fare on offer

Moondee 21st Septicbowel

Following a conversation held between Jack and I last noyght in the Peppermint Hippo I was going to spend as much time today as I could getting Pocahontas to try and understand how to say the words "I do". The wedding of the century is only a month away now and has taken a bit of a back seat whilst Jack, Gary and I try and save the world. This will be easier said than done as due to some rather heavy trepanning on my part due to Pocahontas's demons saying things like she "wants to go home". She is currently struggling to say anything at all or make any kind of verbal sound. This is perfect for love making but not great for repeating wedding vows. The saving grace is that the service is being presided over by the Reverend Adolph Globule and he likes a drink in my club. I think it is feasible that the Reverend Globule may be so drunk from the noyght before that no one in the congregation would be able to understand the proceedings. This would be in keeping with almost all of his sermons since taking over from the former Reverend Von Ringstinga. I may have to lay off the trepanning for a bit and see if Pocahontas's demons can get her through her big day next month.

Toosdi 22rd Septicbowel

I think there may still be a slight problem with Cinderella's maggot infested sheep's vagina. Finbar Knuckleshuffla, Cinderella's gentleman caller came down stairs from the ladies bedroom with a few maggots in his hair. Although he isn't completely blind any longer he still has poor eyesight and fortunately unaware of his delightful lady's tuppence problems.

Winsti 23th Septicbowel

FLATLAND DISTRICT WEEKLY NEWS

If your childers are at a loose end for things to do during the school holidays or at weekends then you could do a lot worse than send them to the Bare Grills Jungle Survival School of Naked Cookery.

Bare (*real name Grunty Homosek*) dreamt of the idea whilst serving a lengthy custodial sentence at her Majesty's Assizes HMP Norwich after an incident with a Fenland Fallow deer (*similar to ordinary deer but with additional limbs*), a washing machine drum and a considerable amount of dynamite turned bad.

Grunty (*unreal name Bare Grills*) was originally from the Polish City of Warsaw, which is much further north of the UK than Peterborough even. He moved to Flatlands when his train pass ran out at Peterborough and kindly local gypsy folk offered him some food in exchange for work and living in a shed. When the Police raided the encampment and let Grunty and his chums out he inadvertently wandered into Flatlands District ... where he has remained ever since ... and continue to do so.

So Parents everywhere, send your offspring to Bare Grills Jungle Survival and School of Naked Cookery.

Bare Grills (Grunty Homosek)

Gary had mentioned he was looking for something for Emily, his daughter, to do locally at the week end. I mentioned Chumptons World of Adventure, the area's finest root crop based theme park but Gary didn't seem too impressed. I think I will cut this advert out of this mawnin's edition of Flatland District Weekly News.Nina and Natalia spent most of the day scrubbing the front door step with a scrubbing brush and some carbolic soap, afterwards they did the same thing for Cinderella's vagina to try and rid her of the maggots.

Thrisdee 24th Septicbowel

I have had a rush of blood to the head and decided to improve my fitness, stamina and standing within the community. I opened my copy of the Chumpton Informer and saw that the Flatland Quarter marathon was happening soon. I cut the coupon out and posted it with a courier crow and entered myself as a contestant. I proudly boasted of my intentions to Natalia and Nina well over an hour ago and they are both still laughing. It's becoming tiresome now, and quite frankly, rude.

I went out for a gentle jog and a few press ups. The gentle jog was all the way to the end of my back garden and that is where I attempted my press up. I gave up after several go's and remained on the ground next to Barry's grave for a few minutes to get my breath back. I returned and had a very big poo. A good day.

Frydims 25lbs Septicbowel

Today would've been the Mayoral election but instead the other contenders dropped out or had the decision to drop out made for them. Once again Davina had called into the Peppermint Hippo, initially for a quick drink prior to an important meeting but she ended up doing a couple of dances and a private dance for the Reverend Globule.

Just before she left I asked her how she was getting on in her new role in the town hall and she told me that she was enjoying it. She continued to say that David Devilman was in regular contact with her and was helping her settle in to her new job. His advice was invaluable apparently; she said several interesting things as we chatted.

I had drunk a few Pochine's and worried I wouldn't remember anything important she might accidentally divulge so I covertly switched my mobile phone voice recording app on, Davina unwittingly jabbering on blissfully unaware. She said that David Devilman was speaking to her on the phone several times a day and that he was going to be back in Flatlands for a few days next week so she wasn't sure whether or not she'd be able to perform much next week. I asked her about the budget she had from the UK Government, Davina said that she didn't have a budget and all monetary dealings were dealt with by the Elders so she didn't have to worry about it. She looked mildly confused when I asked her about it so I have no reason to disbelieve her. She went on to say that there was no money from the UK she was aware of as we had voted to leave the UK so now all our revenue was generated by the sales of root crops. She was amazed, by all accounts, how little money was needed to run the Flatland council and district.

SatD 26st Septicbowel

At this aftynunes interpretive dance class I was a lot more hands on and very vigorous with my movement. I was proper sweating and out of breath, keen to start getting myself in shape to complete the quarter marathon I had entered. The event was not until the end of Novocaine so I had a bit of time.

After the class I played Gary and Jack the recording I made last noyght of the conversation between Davina and me. They all listened with some interest. Gary complimented me on my presence of mind to ask her some questions that may help us and also having the technical know how to use the recording device on the mobile phone.

Jack was impressed I had a mobile phone that recorded things and showed ladies tuppences and breasties.

CHAPTER ELVEN

BEHIND EVERY GREAT MAN ...

OCTERRIBLE 1896

Sunty 1th Octerrible

I have decided to enlist the help and advice of the official Flatland District Witch Finder General, Lofty Mulldoon (*definitely no relation to Rimbit*) to get me in shape for the race I have rather stupidly entered into.

My training for the Great Flatland Quarter Marathon is well and truly under way. Here I am being chased by Lofty Mulldoon the Chumpton Witchfinder General. His diminutive size deceptively masks a cruel and unusual nature, ideal for training athletes in their prime ... such as my good self.
Today i trained for 3-4 hours and covered the distance from Lower Fen fen to Upper Drove Fen. A distance of almost 200-300 Yards.

Look at me go

Lofty has a particularly vicious streak to his character, even for a man whose job it is to torture members of the occult. Perfect therefore to enthuse someone that needs chasing with a sharp stick to get a move, and I did get a move on when Lofty un-leashed his steel tipped triple sharpened crone prodder.

Moondee 2th Octerrible

After yisdee's exertion I can hardly move. Jim Bob made me a cup of Typhoo tea as standing was proving problematic. I haven't had onion tea for weeks now; I have become very cosmopolitan in my tastes lately. I have even started drinking cow's milk rather than the cheaper Grimbles Dyke Clungers milk sourced locally. I have grown quite attached to the mobile phone that Gary has leant me and I also enjoy the occasional tipple of whiskey as a change to Turnip Pochine. None of this means I'm changing as a person but I am becoming more aware of exactly what we have all been missing for many decades, particularly modern inventions that would have made life much more comfortable or interesting.

Especially things like the life-saving medical procedures that are available now in the UK but have been denied to the people of Flatlands for no other reason than the greed of a tiny, tiny handful of people. In the aftynune Lofty came knocking at my door and off we went again, this time we managed 500 yards. I'm not sure how many yards are in a quarter marathons but I can't believe it's much more than 700 or so. I'm anticipating I'll be fully trained by next week.

Toosdi 3th Octerrible

Well, well, well. Guess who called by tefelone this mawnin? David Devilman wanted to know if I was available for some private dance work today. I was but I told him I was busy today but I was available on Thrisdee, I wanted to find out how long he was in the district before he departed back to his luxurious lifestyle in the beautiful and elite town of Stevenage. He agreed that Thrisdee is fine. I could hear Growler having a drink in the background. As soon as I got off the tefelone from the former Mayor I called Gary on the mobile to tell him of the development. He was only able to talk briefly as he was at work but we decided Thrisdee was a good time to do something he called 'a reccy' mission. I asked if that was anything like a reconnaissance mission and he paused momentarily before confirming it was exactly like a reconnaissance mission.

Thrisdee was perfect for checking out things like where he kept his computer and maybe any keys to locked draws in his desk.

Winsti 4rd Octerrible

FLATLAND DISTRICT WEEKLY NEWS

Yesteryearworld Event presents

Locally renown DJ Peat Pong will be playing records in a field near Chatterby on SatD to an anticipated sellout crowd of 30 plus revellers. He will be setting up his incredible lighting show which includes no less than 22 coloured bulbs and 7 laser pens, all flashing at different times.

A selection of hallucinogenic drugs will be available from the Happy Pauper and Edwards the untrained chemist are having a special on Valium and stool softener.

RAVE ON FLATLAND

I saw this advert in the paper today and thought we could all go out for a noyght out. I text Gary (*yes imagine that, someone from Flatlands sending text messages*) and asked if he fancied going after interpretive dance school. A few seconds later I heard a 'wingedy ding pling ding' that told me I had just received a reply. Gary said it would be fine and if he could find a babysitter as his wife would like to come too. He also mentioned in his reply that he was working today in a place called Bristol. I wasn't sure where Bristol was so I went on Google and had a look. I know where Bristol is now.

Thrisdee 5st Octerrible

I arrived at the Devilman house at mid mawnin as requested. The door was opened by Cranshaw St.John, "Are you the butler now Cranshaw?" I joked as I waltzed in. he looked at me with disdain and a certain amount of shock. I was struggling to hold back my contempt for these people so the occasional joke or lapse of self-control maybe on the cards. I handed him my coat as if he were the butler and he placed it on the coat stand in the hallway as a butler would do. He cursed himself for doing it, immediately realising what I had done. I breezed into the living room and saw Devilman adjusting his pig picture so it was pointing towards his sofa. "Good day Mayor … actually I suppose it's just David now isn't it" I said. I was struggling to not show my disrespect again. I had to make a mental note that my contempt can be turned into gloating if we do this properly. I mustn't give the game away I have a job to do here, and not just dancing.

As I began preparing my ghetto blaster to belt out Aqua's 'Barbie Girl' I heard Devilman unfastened his belt and unzip the fly to his trousers. Growler must be in Stevenage I thought. My stomach started rumbling and turning over summersaults due to the triple helping of roadkill stew I had last noyght followed by some Parsnip and onion smoothies I had Nina make with some very out of date ingredients. My tummy was in a fair bit of discomfort but I didn't care, it was going to be worth it. I was wearing my spangled cowgirl outfit with latex thong, a particular favourite of the ex-Mayors; I wasn't expecting this dance to last long. The opening bars of the song filled the living room and I swayed in time to the music. As I turned around I was startled by what I saw, Devilman was on his sofa with his trousers around his ankles (*this I expected*) but next to him was Cranshaw on his knees stroking his employer's semi enflamed winky. As I started to thrust rhythmically towards them both I could see him stiffen significantly. My tummy moaned significantly too. I stopped in front of the pair and made circular movements with my hips. Devilman was struggling to contain himself, "DO IT! DO IT NOW!" he screamed at Cranshaw. With that, Cranshaw put Devilman's penis in his mouth and began to suck it, every now and then he took his masters winky out of his mouth and made oinking sounds before returning the former dignitaries appendage to his gob.

I turned around now fully prepared for my finale. I slowly bent over and lurched forward one final groan from my tummy told me that the chamber was loaded. I ran my hands seductively down my legs and reached my ankle, my involuntary flatulence and anal seepage, the Bain of my professional dancing career was about to become very much voluntary. As the music stopped the ensuing fanfare of farting filled the living room with a deep clapping sound, quickly followed by complete silence.

The silence was broken by a small whimpering sound that I could identify as Cranshaws. I turned around to see both David Devilman and Cranshaw St.John looking somewhat shocked, bewildered and splattered in my dark, smelly, loose liquid faeces. It was liberally covered over Cranshaw's head and Devilman's torso and groinal area (*apart from the head shaped patch where his trusty assistant was*). Nothing was said about the enormous quantity of poo I had generated this time compared to others. They both got up from the sofa and made their way out of the room to get cleaned up. I cleaned myself up quickly by wiping my bum on his curtains and made my move. I removed the mobile phone from my bag and put the video app onto record. Whilst they were out of the room I first made my way nonchalantly over to the table with the pig picture and picked it up as if I were looking at it. I placed it back on the table facing the wall and I began looking around the living room. I firstly followed the cable from the piggy photo underneath the table. There, screwed under the table was a box that the wire was connected to. I then checked the drawers of the desk but there was nothing of any interest.

I made my way quietly out of the living room along the hallway and checked out each room. Eventually I found a room that was obviously his study or office, a bit like Gary's but bigger and down stairs and with no bloody great big cracks in the wall. As I entered the study I opened as many drawers as I could and filmed the contents as I didn't really have time to check stuff out. Every single drawer was open and finally I took a bit of footage of his computer system for Gary to look at. I took one last scan about and returned to the living room. A very short while later Cranshaw returned wearing a white towelling dressing gown. His hair was wet so he must have had a quick shower. He looked annoyed with me, "the Mayor … I mean Mr Devilman says thank you very much, he'll be in touch soon about future performances". I informed him that I was busy for the next few days. Cranshaw told me that was okay as he and Devilman weren't back in Flatlands for at least the next week. That was what I wanted to know. As we went into the hallway we both dithered by the coat stand. I looked at Cranshaw, Cranshaw looked at me and finally asked me what I was waiting for, "My coat" I replied. Now he was starting to fume a bit, "I AM NOT THE BUTLER" he said loudly and abruptly. I couldn't resist one last dig, I smiled and said "no Cranshaw you're right you're not the butler ... you're sooo much more to Mr Devilman than that now". As I walked out of the front door of the Devilman residence I could feel the trusty assistant's angry eyes digging into my back like daggers. It was nothing though, compared to the anger I had for him, his boss and the Elders. I walked into Ropey and caught the guided bus back to Chumpton smiling all the way.

Frydims 6th Octerrible

After yesterday's reccy mission I sent the footage I took at Devilman's house to Gary in a file in an email. Yes you read that right dear diary; I sent an email with a video file in it. I am getting pretty good with technology. It has so many uses in so many ways that I had never even thought of.

Do not watch something called two girls one cup ... it will only make you hungry. I popped up to Ropey to do my toe counting and to acquire some meat from the hospital incinerator bin before it goes to waste so I can get it home and cured in time for Pocahontas's wedding day.

SatD 7nd Octerrible

This mawnin I participated in 'The Great Flatlands Run'. It is a quarter marathon and considerably further than I had anticipated, a full marathon is 26 and a bit miles so a quarter on is ... is ... a lot. It was certainly a lot further than the 700 yards Lofty Mulldoon had trained me for so I was truly shattered by the end. The route was to Chatterby and Chumpton and back, luckily that's the guided bus route too so I managed an amazing time by catching the guided bus back to Chumpton. It was a bit of a cheat I guess but I managed to get to Chatterby (*and that was 3 miles ... oh and that's half the distance so a quarter marathon is 6 and a tiny bit miles ... just worked it out*) under my own steam in just two and a half hours. So I completed an eighth of a marathon.

This aftynune we had our nativity dance practice and all went well, afterwards we made our way up to Chatterby for the rave recently advertised in the paper. I was going on a professional capacity to try and get an interview with DJ Peat Pong for my yoof culture magazine New Mooosicul Expressions. Gary had never travelled on the guided bus before, he looked nervous. His wife was with us, she's nice, she's called Inga and she comes from Sweden. I asked who was looking after Emily, to my amazement Gary told me that Emily's babysitter was PC Jack Wormer of Ropey Town Police Brigade … Ropey's finest. Gary smiled but Inga didn't look so sure.

The rave was heaving with people, there were in excess of thirty people and DJ Peat had the place jumping. He played all three of his records and one of those was a long player too. We went back to Chumpton and had a noyght cap at the Peppermint Hippo. Inga said that the Turnip Pochine was similar to a drink she likes called Absinth, which too could make you go blind. We didn't talk about our plan to save the world. Gary, Jack and I agreed it was best not to let the ladies know anything about our plans. We didn't want to worry them. Also, we didn't actually have a plan yet.

Sunty 8lbs Octerrible

Last noyght was great fun and when we got back home Gary sent me a SMS text picture (*get me*) of PC Jack fast asleep in Gary's armchair with Emily fast asleep on Jack. It was a cute photo considering that Gary's daughter was snuggling up to a man who had held her hostage only a few months earlier and was known by all as the most brutal officer of the entire Ropey Brigade.

Nina and her sister Natalia were feeling a little hung over after last noyght, they over did it on the alcohol a bit. We read the papers lounged about and Jim Bob appeared about daaymiddlin and started running up and down the waste ground outside our house again to show off to Natalia. I was struggling a bit after all my dynamic athletic endeavours yisdee mawnin. With running marathons, running dance classes then tripping the light fantastic at a monster rave in Chatterby I deserved a rest. So I had one.

Moondee 9th Octerrible

This mawnin I made a trip up to Ropey with Natalia and popped into the town hall before going for a quick drink in the Jolly Sphincter. St.John Cranshaw was at the town hall, I asked him if he had seen Cranshaw lately. I think I hit a nerve as he burst into tears and ran away. He left his desk un-attended so I took the liberty of having a sneaky peak at its contents. I saw a piece of parchment stating that the punishment had been agreed for Zechariah Winkytucha for pilfering root crops. People are going hungry it would seem. There should be some kind of bank that gave out food to people that really need it, some sort of food bank … not sure what you'd call it though.

The town (*and Flatlands in general*) is starting preparations for the annual festival period. This marks a series of traditional festivals in the District to celebrate all manner of ancient and bizarre local customs and rituals. Ropey is currently being adorned with decorations to celebrate some of the ancient fertility festivals about to commence. This involves stringing plastic baby dolls from lampposts and signs throughout the town. This is always a rather unnerving sight as you walk about the town centre.

This particular superstition is paying homage to the Flatland goddess of fertility 'Disraelina' and will culminate in the burning of a straw doll and the offering of root crops (*what else*) as a gift to the deity Disraelina.

Toosdi 10st Octerrible

This mawnin I skinned the thigh I have had hanging in my inventing shed for the last 24 days and washed the top maggots from the green, pulsating flesh. Nina had it diced and in the pot with an assortment of locally sourced vegetables, of the root variety, and a couple of hours later it was making its way to the Peppermint Hippo. I have had an idea about unwanted amputated legs and kebab shops. Watch this space.

Winsti 11jr Octerrible

This mawnin we all went to watch local vagabond Zechariah Winkytucha get his comeuppance following his one man crime spree. He has stolen several items of farm produce on no less than four separate occasions and subsequently paid for this persistent pilfering. He claimed in his defence that he was hungry and was pinching the root crops to try and feed his four children, something he has struggled to do since his wife passed away from a particularly harsh bout of swampy's chest cough.

FLATLAND DISTRICT WEEKLY NEWS

FLATLAND DISTRICT COUNCIL of ELDERS

The Flatland District Council of Elders are pleased to announce that the Chumpton-by-Kumberly's petty thief caught shoplifting various root crops and cabbage cheroots from the Happy Pauper shop has been dealt with.

The council of elders held a special court and heard evidence from all parties including the veg thief himself. The turnip pilferer is believed to be Zechariah Winkytucha from Fen Drove at Drove Fen. His defence, a plea of hunger, was discounted out of hand by the elders shortly before passing sentence of neck stretching.

The elders issued a statement "Pilfering and witchcraft will not be tolerated in the Chumpton area and Flatland District in general".
This months witch trials are being held next week and locals are encouraged to attend at the ducking pond near the allotments.

I felt fairly sorry for him but many of the gathered crowd didn't seem very sympathetic, despite them themselves living very close to the breadline. I guess it's a sign of the times and the people we have become.

Thrisdee 12th Octerrible

This mawnin Jack and I went up in Jack's police car to visit Gary. Jack was called away not long after we arrived following a wheelbarrow containing parsnips, potatoes and carrots had overturned on the Flatlands stretch of the A14 causing rush hour mayhem and severe hold ups of two tractors, a hand cart and four sheep. Gary made me a cup of percolated coffee in a special machine. With the lovely coffee we had chocolate biscuits, I don't know if you the reader of my journal have ever tried chocolate biscuits but if not I suggest you save up your money for a few weeks and buy a packet.

As we sat and enjoyed our drink and biscuits (*or biccies Gary calls them*) we discussed our plan of action to save the world. I suggested we obtain an untraceable and illegal fire arm courtesy of Jack or Guns n parrots in Ropey town and hold the Elders and Devilman at gunpoint, get a video confession and then shoot them all at point blank range. We could then take the bodies up to the hospital dismember them and what can't be incinerated can be used for the wedding docky for Jacks marriage to Pocahontas. By the look on Gary's face, eyes wide and jaw open, he didn't think it was a good plan.

"There'll be no killing of anyone" Gary said quite abruptly, "secondly, what's are you on about using body parts as food for Jacks wedding?" … I may have said too much. "Well … times are hard, I work at the hospital and it seems such a waste of perfectly good meat … you're right I'll stop doing it ………. It's just that it's cheaper than buying roadkill from the Happy Pauper" I explained.
"Road kill? The stuff from the shop in the village say's 'Finest Angus Beef' on the label" Gary protested.
"Is the label hand written?" I enquired, Gary nodded "okay then, Finest Angus Beef it is" I lied.
"Will you let me get the meat for the wedding? I have a friend who's a butcher in Cambridge, I'll ask him next week" Gary said.
"That'll cost a fortune" I said loudly "No … I bet it'll be no more than a hundred quid" Gary replied. I found it crazy that Gary thought one hundred pounds in hoooman money was not a fortune, I really need to get used to this. That's an entire pallet of onions or 700 Davey's.

We then concentrated on the topic at hand, world saving. We both agreed that my plan was rubbish and used unnecessary violence which is bad by all accounts. Gary spent half an hour explaining why unnecessary violence is bad and I was sold on the idea that we must try a more peaceful option for saving the world. Gary said he had watched the footage I took in Devilman's house the other day and he is happy that there is plenty he can do but the important thing was to make sure the stuff we needed as evidence was just copied and not taken. This would make sure they weren't alerted to the fact we were on to them and also we didn't want to get done for breaking and entering.

Our next phase of the plan was to hand the evidence over to the people who could actually do something with the information we would be giving them. Gary said he had researched Devilman's recent enquiry into his business dealings and found out who did the investigations and he would hand the information over to them. All that needed to be arranged was a date and time to go and mooch around the Devilman estate. As Jack patrolled the estate he can do the alarms and let us in.

I shall inform Jack of our plan when he returns from the A14 carnage.

Frydims 13th Octerrible

Jack informed me this mawnin that Devilman was out of Flatlands and in his Stevenage palace for the next few days at least. We decided that as we would be all together we could go and get into the former Mayor's abode after interpretive dance class. I text Gary the proposal and he agreed.

I shall take it easy with the booze at the club tonoyght then if I'm burglarising then next day. Frydims noyght is fetish noyght at Peppermint Hippo and I have been known to enjoy a few too many drinkies … and sheep.

SatD 14th Octerrible

After dance class I quickly got changed out of my thong and leotard and tutu and divers mask and welders gloves and incontinence pad and changed into my clean-ish going out underpants and special latex cat burglars outfit I once used many years ago when doing a routine at Chatterby's den of iniquity the Klunge Klub. Jack and Gary found my outfit too alluring and said it would put them off, possibly because it was shiny, sexy, tight and body hugging as well as crotch-less or possibly because it hadn't been washed since I last used it and the odour was overwhelming, especially after and energetic interpretive dance session. I changed into a set of Jim Bob's overalls and put a pair of Edith's tights on my head. It was then when I remembered the yeast infection the last time I used Edith's tights as a sperm catcher. I removed the tights and Jack handed me a balaclava he had spare (*although it's a bit worrying that someone has 'spare' balaclava's knocking about*). Gary was wearing black jeans and black jumper with a black baseball cap and sunglasses, Jack was dressed similarly. Gary said we looked like the SAS; I'm not sure who the SAS are but I bet they looked fantastic when they did whatever it was they did.

We arrived outside the Devilman residence and Gary parked his car a hundred yards down the road out of sight and we walked the rest of the way. We arrived at the front door and Jack let us in with his keys. As jack switched the alarm off Gary went straight to the office and started first of all with the computer. As the computer started booting up he started his laptop up and began opening draws and took photos of the paperwork in each draw. He was working really quickly. I made my way to the living room and went to the piggy picture turned it to the wall and traced the cable to under the table. As I crawled under the table I shone the torch and opened the DVD player draw and removed the disc (*I had spent several hours watching how to do this on YouTube … well in between mastybayshuns*) ready for Gary to copy.

Gary had managed to start Devilman's computer by using a gadget on his laptop that guessed his password. It was called 'Brute force', Jack really liked this idea as he thought it involved punching computers, imagine his disappointment when he discovered it was done by cleverness and not thumping, poor Jack. Gary started downloading files from Devilman's hard drive (*hark at me … and by the way, oh and IT is Information Technology I've discovered*) and made a copy of the disc I handed him. Once that was done I went back into the living room and replaced the disc and returned the picture to its original position. Gary finished doing what it was he was doing about twenty minutes later and Jack made us all a cup of tea. As we all sat in Devilman's living room waiting for Gary's downloads to complete we reflected on a very successful world saving mission.

Gary packed all his gear up and placed it back into his case and spent a couple of minutes making sure everything looked as it did before we got here. Jack washed up and dried the mugs and I went for one of the most satisfying and enormous poo's I think I have ever had. As I was wiping my bott with the former Mayor's expensive bott-wad I heard something of a commotion going on down stairs. As I rushed out I saw Jack and Gary flying up the stairs turning the lights off behind them. "Someone is coming up the drive" Jack said in a frantic and hushed voice, "quick in the bedroom get under the bed". I didn't ask I did as he said. Gary hid in the next bedroom and I squeezed under the bed. Jack, who is slightly svelter than me got underneath beside me but let out a small yelp. It was then when he noticed my overalls were around my ankles, "I hope to fuck they don't find us like this" he whispered. I asked who it was and he informed me it was his colleagues from Ropey Police Brigade doing there noyghtly check.

As the two police brigade officers came in they noticed that the alarm was de-activated, "That'll be that fucking useless twat Wormer again" they giggled "It'll have been off all fucking day" the other one said. Jack clenched his fists but just managed to keep his cool. They went into the kitchen, checked the office and living room and whilst in the living room helped themselves to a glass of Devilman's whiskey. "I'll fucking av' em … the cunts" Jack said in deep and quite audible whisper.

As tense as the situation was it was also clear that the two officers probably weren't going to venture up the stairs. The problem, however came when they left. They set the alarm and went and sat in there police car for a bit and made sure the alarm had set properly. We were stuck under the bed and Gary in the wardrobe in the next room. We had to get from underneath the bed out onto the landing down the swirly staircase through the hallway into the porch area before the alarm went off and alerted the alarm control centre. This, Jack reliably informed us had to be done in 15 seconds of the first infrared beam detecting movement, unlike the 30 seconds allowed from the when the door connection is broken when entering the building.

"You're a fit man Jack, that should be easy enough for you" I said encouragingly. "Well there's a slight problem there" he replied, "I buggered my back up getting underneath this bed, Gary's in the other room and won't have time to come and get the number and get to the panel. You're going to have to do it".

I was not happy as my technical expertise was still in its infancy but Jack talked me through it. Just then the bedroom door opened and in walked Gary, he switched the light on and said "That was close" … the alarm had started to count down. "GO!" Jack screamed. I scrambled from under the bed and ran past Gary shouting "Alarm" as I ran past him. "Shit" Gary yelled and we ran together towards the stairway. It was then that I realised my overalls hadn't been done up from when I'd had a poo and they fell to the ground and tripped me up. This resulted in me falling head first down the stairs. As I ended up in a crumpled heap at the bottom of the stairs Gary sprinted past me, "What's the code" he shouted. "478623 and press enter twice" I shouted back. I heard him get to the panel, before he asked again I instinctively yelled "47…86…23… and press enter twice". The high pitched beeping stopped but could've only had a second or two to go, we all remained still, perfectly still, as if that would've made any difference to the alarm going off. Our perfect stillness was rewarded and we had stayed undetected by the monitoring station. A minute later Jack hobbled onto the landing and we went back into the living room and helped ourselves to a very large glass of whiskey.

Our mission complete we left the building in its original state and reset the alarm. We made our way back to Gary's car and he dropped Jack and me off at my house and he went home. Gary said he'd need a day to check out the files but we should go to his house on Moondee noyght and he'll tell us what he had discovered.

The noyght was proper exciting and the two of us were pretty hyper for a couple of hours afterwards. After jack left I was still buzzing so I went and watched Edith sleep for a bit, unfortunately I also fell asleep and the next thing I knew it was firsloyght outside and Edith was screaming, I was screaming, the cat was trembling, it was mayhem.

I apologised and told her I had got very, very drunk at the club and gone into the wrong house. After she stopped sobbing I helped her clean up her bedsheets and noyghtgown as she'd wee'd herself when she woke up. I assured her it won't happen again and left rather embarrassed. Poor old Edith must think I'm bonkers.

Sunty 15th Octerrible

Tonoyght we all went to have a bite to eat at Fido's. It has opened this week and is the latest eatery in Ropey town, we went after Nina saw the advert in the paper. Pocahontas and Cinderella, Nigelle, Nina, Natalia, Jack and I had a table booked and all went together. We had a lovely noyght and it was nice to forget about saving the world, even if it was just for a few hours.

On our return I trepanned Nigelle as he was talking trash to the waiter in the restaurant accusing them of being an immigrant and wanting to take his Flatlands back. The waiter was Zach Blodwella, the Blodwella's are possibly the oldest and biggest family in Flatlands. Luckily Zach was too inbred and stupid to really understand what was being said to him but I thought it best to give Nigelle a quick drilling on our return.

FLATLAND DISTRICT WEEKLY NEWS

Slinky O'Dullard is pleased to announce he is opening a new restaurant on the High Street of Ropey Town and it's going to be called Fido's.

Fido's is tipping a cap to Slinky's dog, Fido, who Slinky accidentally ate one night when Fido ventured too close to Slinky's dinner plate. Slinky was devastated to learn he had mistakenly masticated his doggy chum, and only realised his error when he got Fido's collar caught in his teeth.

The collar hangs in pride of place above the doorway as a mark of respect to Fido and also as a reminder to customers not to get too close Slinky when he is consuming food.

If you fancy a night of traditional Korean/Fen/Flatland cuisine the pop into Fido's for a "Bite" to eat

Moondee 16th Octerrible

Jack collected me early aftynune in his police car and we made our way to Gary's house. It was a cold miserable day and autumn was blowing in. When we arrived at Gary's cracked house Emily had just got back from school and Inga had prepared some dinner, some beef stew. We had some and it was delicious, roadkill stew will never taste the same after this.

We all went up into Gary's office with the cracked wall and Gary switched his computer on. As it booted up Gary poured us some whiskey, I was getting quite a taste for this immigrant juice.

"Here you go gents, you'll need this when you see what I have to show you" Gary said solemnly, "Especially you Morton" he wasn't smiling.

"These files show some of the accounts and finances that Devilman has been creaming off the Flatland District Council Budget, it is huge amounts of money he and the Elders have been embezzling, huge amounts. The money the government gives the council just for the upkeep of the roads alone is immense"

"What roads?" both jack and I said at the same time.

"Precisely, what roads? The hospital is being run on a fraction of the money it's been given and the benefits and welfare money has never even seen the light of day" Gary continued.

"Wow, how much exactly?" I asked, "well there's the problem, until we can examine the statements from the councils ledgers we don't have any idea, Devilman has rather cleverly exchanged the money the council received from the government into his own currency, the 'Davey' or something. We need the ledgers to have a clue how much has been exchanged and stolen but also, and most importantly, what we need it as proof of exactly what's been going on. We have plenty of other stuff too about the planning permission, but the only way we can prove any of this is to get hold of the ledgers. They'll either be on computer or they'll be on a hardcopy format" both Jack and I looked puzzled at the last bit so Gary elaborated "paper form, they'll be printed for audit purposes, although I'm fairly sure that any auditors will be paid off by the Elders and Devilman not to delve too deep, to make absolutely certain that everything appears normal to central government. They will still need accurate copies of what's coming into the council to make the books balance though. They will be greasing a few palms to keep this going, with the ledgers and what we have here we can prove who has been paid off and how much at the top but we'll probably never know everyone who was on the fiddle other than the main players themselves".

Jack looked concerned "how are we going to get into the councils computers? I'm not sure where they are even".

I then had an idea, "How about we pump St.John Cranshaw for some information?" Jack looked concerned again, he wasn't keen on pumping anyone but when I explained what pumping for information actually meant he seemed a lot less concerned.

"When I called into the town hall the other day St.John was terribly upset about Cranshaw just dropping him like that, I think I could perhaps get him to talk to us … if I'm clever about it" I beamed.

"Alternatively, I could beat the information out of him" Jack chirped in.

"Alternatively Jack could beat the crap out of him" I said chirpily.

Gary didn't seem too keen on plan B but clearly we needed to somehow get details of the whereabouts of either the computer or the printed ledgers for all council transactions.

It doesn't sound so difficult when you say it like that … or really, really fast.

As we went to leave Gary's office I asked him what it was that I wouldn't like, he looked puzzled until I reminded him that at the start of our meeting he said there was something that I wouldn't like. The look on Gary's face told me he had remembered, "Ah … yes, I saw some rather rude footage of you dancing for the Mayor". I told him that was what I did and it wasn't a problem, then I recalled the last dance I did with Cranshaw. I asked Gary to make me a copy that I could put on the mobile phone. He did just that and gave it to me before we left. On our way back to Chumpton I mentioned to Jack that I'd like to learn to drive, pass my test and get a driving licence. He smiled and told me that he could get me a driving licence tomorrow if I wanted but I told him it wasn't what I wanted. It wouldn't teach me how to drive and for once I wanted to do something properly. He smiled again and agreed to teach me to drive.

We went to the Peppermint Hippo for a couple of pints of Pizz and Pochine chasers. We sat at the bar talking to Sylvia and watching Davina sway those fleshy, sexy hips of hers. I watched with some considerable envy as Davina bent over and lunged in a way that would induce a huge botty belch followed by some seepage if I were to try such a move. Davina's lunge was dramatic and sexy, flatulent free, a thing of beauty. She could possibly give her anal beard a slight trim and it would appear she was menstrual … quite heavily menstrual, but apart from that as close to perfect as possible. After Davina's dance Jack and I sat and chatted with her and asked her how she was coping with the Mayoress thing. She was a little bit cagey and seemed reluctant to say too much like before. When Jack pushed her about the election process, or lack of. She made her excuses and left to purchase some feminine hygiene products from the Klapper Rag machine in the car park.

Toosdi 17nd Octerrible

Local legends the Heps will be playing the WI hall on Frydims, I have managed to secure tickets for all of us and Jack. I phoned Gary and he was keen to come too, hopefully it'll be a great noyght out for us all. It could double up as Jacks stag noyght too. What could go wrong?

Cinderella's maggot infestation in her vagina seems to be clearing up and scabbing over quite nicely. I did a doctoring check this mawnin and I was able to get my head within two feet of her lady parts before I vomited. A huge improvement on last week when she had to sleep in my inventing shed for a couple of noyghts as her rancid genitals were stinking the house out.

FLATLAND DISTRICT WEEKLY NEWS

Flatland Promotions is very pleased to announce the confirmed booking of The Hepatitis Twins to play Chumpton WI hall/arena.
They are playing Frydims 20st Octerrible and entry is free with all proceeds going to the ancient drainage dyke preservation appeal.
The twins will be playing their catalogue of hit and are looking forward to kissing as many of the fans (known as the Heps) that are legally old enough to be kissed

The Hepatitis Twins 'rocking it up' at Chumpton WI Hall

Winsti 18st Octerrible

This mawnin I gave Pocahontas a fatherly chat about her forthcoming wedding to Jack this weekend. She seems to have forgotten about her past as a person of the opposite gender, her days as Dmitri are but a distant memory. I still gave her a light trepanning though. Natalia and Nina took her to lunch at the WI hall and she just sat there dribbling and rocking backwards and forwards. She fitted in perfectly.

Thrisdee 19st Octerrible

Following yisdee's trepanning and fatherly chat I decided to ensure all bases were covered regarding the wedding. I caught up with the Reverend Adolph Globule at the Jolly Sphincter in Ropey; luckily he wasn't too drunk as it was only just after firsdocky in the mawnin. I agreed he could have a free couple of noyghts at the Peppermint Hippo if he didn't worry too much about the vows being repeated during the wedding ceremony. He agreed readily.

Frydims 20st Octerrible

After going to see the Heps at the Chumpton WI hall we ended up in the club drinking Pochine whilst Nina and Natalia took Pocahontas and Cinderella home and start cooking the stew with the meat that Gary got from his butcher friend in Cambridge.

Jack was a great stag, you didn't need to spike his drinks with anything as he spiked his own whilst nobody was looking and he could get as daft as he wanted, no one would arrest him, or us, as he was a policeman and no one would provoke him into a fight as he was a brutal policeman to boot. He ended up fingerblasting the Mayoress Davina Kraye after her private dance for him. He got all drunk and sentimental saying that the menstrual Mayoress Davina bled all over his hand and how much it reminded him of when Pocahontas bled too, the first time he fingered her. A little tear welled up in the corner of my eye when I thought back to when I first met Dmitri and how I turned him into a lady with the help of Nina and my Veterinarian anatomy book (*the irony wasn't lost on me that Cinderella did actually end up with a sheep's vagina transplant*). Finally Jack ended up sleeping on the club floor and pooing himself.

 A great noyght.

SatD 21st Octerrible

Dear diary, the wedding day has arrived.

This mawnin the entire house was up at the crack firsloyght. I went over to the club with Jim Bob and started the process of sobering Jack up ready for the church. Nina and Natalia finished the real meat stew and got Pocahontas into her wedding gown that Jim Bob had made from bits of bandage and paper doylies from the Happy Pauper. She looked unlike any bride I had ever seen before. Cinderella and Natalia were the bridesmaids and Jim Bob had made their dresses out of hessian and bin liners. They looked stunning, unlike any Bridesmaids I had ever seen before.

We hosed Jack down in the car park and dried him and dressed him in his best Policeman's outfit, the one he used for conduct hearings and disciplinary proceedings against him. He looked unlike any policeman I had ever seen before.

At just after daaymiddlin we arrived at St. Jeremiahs church and three very short minutes later Pocahontas and Jack Wormer were married. Nina gave Pocahontas away and as I requested the Reverend Globule kept the ceremony short, he got them to stand in front of the alter and then he released an enormous fart and screamed "I now pronounce you man and wife" before simultaneously urinating and defecating himself and collapsing with alcoholic poisoning … again.

We all made our way back to the Peppermint Hippo for the wedding wake and the cabaret was provided by my dancers and local pop duo Jebwould. I made a truly excellent best man's speech by doiing the entire speech using only the medium of 'no music interpretive dance' and alphabet belching. My speech lasted nearly an hour and it was unlike any best man's speech I or anyone had ever seen before. Gary, Inga and Emily said they had a great time and I taught Emily how to say 'Fuck Off' using interpretive dance and later by belching it.

At just after noyghtmiddlin Jack and Pocahontas left for their honey moon at Chatterby sands in Jacks police car. Some of his colleagues had jokingly tied streamers and cans to the back of his car with a sign that said "Brutal Cunt" on it. We all laughed, apart from Gary who was too busy covering Emily's eyes. Shortly after the married couple left the guests left too and we were more or less on our own. Nigelle was busy drinking all the leftovers before anyone noticed and Sylvia, Nina and Natalia were busy tidying the club up. Finally we all staggered home very, very drunk indeed. What a day!

Sunty 22nd Octerrible

All of us slept and vomited all day.

Moondee 23st Octerrible

Still feeling quite rough from SatD. Nina, Natalia and Cinderella lounged about, Jim Bob was in the inventing shed and I took the guided bus up to Ropey. I had a quick pint of Badgerspizzle in the Jolly Sphincter and bumped into the Reverend Globule, I thanked him for a lovely service on SatD and judging by the look on his face he had absolutely no recollection of it. He remembered our deal for free drinking though. After I left the pub I popped into the town hall under the pretence that I was wondering when Jack was back from his honey moon. I wandered into the chambers to see if St.John was there, he was so I asked if there were any Elders in today. He told me there weren't so I asked him if the Mayoress was in today, he said she was but he was only giving one word answers.

"Is everything okay St.John? ... If you don't mind me asking" I asked coyly.
"Well if you must know actually everything is not okay, everything is far from okay. My life partner, the former Mayor's personal assistant, has hardly been home at all in the last few months, since before the referendum to be honest. So I'm sad, very sad" he said very matter of factly.
"I'm sorry to hear that, I'm sorry you're sad". He looked at me intensely, "Aren't you one of the former Mayor's referendum aides? You always used to come here dressed very strangely" St.John said
"Yes I used to do some work for him ... I used to ... well, I used to dance for him"
"Dance for him?"
"Yes I used to be an erotic drag dancer at the Peppermint Hippo, I own the club so I don't dance much now ... too busy" I said.
St.John looked surprised and interested. "You must come and have a drink there one noyght, as my guest" I said as suggestively as I could muster. He was very interested

now I was showing him some attention, attention he hadn't received for some time from Cranshaw. I thought it was time to go for gold and step it up a notch so I stroked his face and asked him if I could go and see the Mayoress to see if she could dance tonoyght at the club. "She dances there too?" St.John asked in amazement, I nodded. I thanked him and ran my hand down his chest playfully. As I relaxed my arm I accidentally, deliberately brushed his rather chubby winky through his trousers. He liked that very much. I am an absolute slut at times.

I popped in and saw Davina and as I left St.John opened the door for me, he was a lot chirpier now. He asked me if I still did private dances, like the ones I did for the former Mayor. I smiled and said maybe. He asked me to perform at his house on Winsti, I agreed.

Toosdi 24lbs Octerrible

FLATLAND DISTRICT WEEKLY NEWS

Mr Cecil Anus and Miss Cecilia Anus are pleased to announce their engagement to be married .... to each other. Cecil (23 years old) and Cecilia (21 years old) met as childers at the house they both lived in and a relationship quickly blossomed into romance by the time Cecilia had reached puberty at 4 yrs old. A quirk of nature means Cecil has never actually gone through puberty but he is hoping to soon so they decided to become wed prior to starting a family.

Cecil (pictured right) is currently a Root Crop Developmental Science Co-ordinator for Chumpton World of Adventure. Rated as one of the Flatland districts best loved root crop based theme parks. Cecil's job involves making various root crops into delicious hallucinogenic beverages for sale in the childer's bar designed to assist youngsters in coping with the dull drudgery of life's futility. His bride to be, Cecilia is one of the bar staff team at Peppermint Hippo, Chumptons much loved adult entertainment emporium which also sells a delightful range of hallucinatory products. They are getting married at St.Bastards church in Chatterby on SatD afore months end just before Daymiddlin. We wish them good luck.

Cecil and Cecilia

More lovely news in the paper this mawnin with the announcement of an engagement in Chumpton, it's Cecilia, one of our bar staff team and the lucky lad is Cecil, her brother. I must still be feeling a bit slushy after the weekends wedding of the year. I phoned Gary and told him of my plans to sex the information out of St.John. Gary seemed absolutely amazed I would go to such lengths to obtain the information he needed to bring Devilman and his cronies to justice and save the district from destruction. I was amazed he was amazed, this is what being a Flatland sex worker is all about. I got my sexiest outfit that was clean enough to use ready for my performance.

Winsti 25r Octerrible

I took the guided bus to Ropey dressed in my suede Lederhosen and gimp mask and carrying my various accompaniments to assist tonoyghts performance in my man bag. When St.John answered the door he was wearing a chiffon robe a small amount of rouge and he audibly gasped at my outfit. He then hurriedly invited me in checking outside as I brushed past him. He asked if he could choose the music I would dance to, I agreed of course. He chose 'I will Survive' by Gloria Gaynor ... a classic.

My dance was very erotic and flatulence free and as I finished with a sharp groin thrust into St.John's face he let out a small "eek" of delight. I could tell be the size of the lump in his robe he was happy with my performance. He wriggled uncomfortably, adjusting his crotch and then cleared his throat before asking if I did 'extras'. Without committing myself I said "that depends, that depends on if you can help me out" I said in my huskiest voice. "What do you want" he asked breathlessly, "I want access to the Mayor's computer, I ... I need to look at some receipts and some ledgers" I said. The mood changed, "Not a chance" St.John replied firmly. I was committed now so a ran my finger down his chest and slipped it inside his chiffon robe and gripped the thing that was creating such a large lump (*That was his penis by the way ... in case you're not following this bit*) and began slowly massaging it, "that is just such a shame" I whispered slowly. St.John stated breathing heavily as I repeated my last sentence and let go of his love gristle. Immediately he relented "okay, okay whatever you want but you have to do something very ... very special for me", "anything" I said.

No more words were spoken, St.John Cranshaw walked to his bedroom, lifted his robe to expose his bare botty and presented himself on all four and 'made himself available' for penetration. This was something I had hoped for, planned for, even before getting on the guided bus. I bought my bag with me and produced some furry handcuffs and a blind fold, he was ecstatic. I handcuffed him to his bedstead and blindfolded him. He was very excited, unfortunately I wasn't, as lovely as St.John is chaps don't "do it for me". This afternoon I recalled Edith using dead Barry's arm as a pleasure stick earlier this year. So out came the spade and I dug up Barry's arm, I covered it with some of the skin from the amputated limbs I had liberated from hospital incineration bin, made a harness to sit it in and I had crafted my very own love truncheon. As I slid Barry's arm in and out of St.John's anus whilst making thrusting motions and gripping his shoulders I could tell, thankfully, this wasn't going to take long. St.John squirted a huge amount of sex wee into a towel on his duvet, I placed the dead tramps decaying limb back into my bag of tricks and then released him from the handcuffs and removed the blindfold.

I lay next to St.John as he got his breath back and once he had composed himself he said that all the council records were on the big compooota in the chambers apart from the ledgers and they were in the safe in his office. It was now shit or bust time, if this didn't work then it was going to have to be Jacks 'plan B'.
"Right, only remember what we were talking about before we … you know … did it" he nodded cautiously "well that's kind of what I need … I need the ledgers".
St.John laughed, "You must be joking, that'll never happen" he said, then he paused "what do you want the ledgers for anyway?"

I spent the next ten minutes telling him everything he needed to know about what we had discovered over the last few weeks. He was shocked and seemed almost ready to agree to help us but his misguided loyalty to his former boss and his estranged life partner was too much for him to overcome. I had no choice but to play my trump card. With as much tact as I could muster I showed him the footage on my mobile phone of me dancing for Devilman whilst Cranshaw sucked on the former Mayor's winky. I stopped the footage before the faecal blasting I gave them both. He was understandably devastated at what I showed him, after some comforting he calmed down enough to collect his thoughts and agreed to give us whatever help we needed. I gave him a hug and left to catch the last guided bus back to Chumpton. I got home and returned Barry's arm to its rightful owner and went indoors. I had 5 showers and 3 baths but I still felt dirty.

Thrisdee 26ft Octerrible

I was lucky enough to be invited onto Flatland pop legend, Micki Minaj's tour bus recently. I was employed to teach her some of my world famous twerking moves. It all went well until another terrible bout of my involuntary flatulence began kicking in.

Micki was very graceful and confirmed she herself occasionally suffered from the similar but more front bum based flatulence problem which her dancers found upsetting and off putting and sometimes lead to unrest.

Shortly after this photograph was taken she had an uncontrollable tuppence fart. This continued on into her stage performance but luckily people just assumed she had a sore throat thus avoiding any embarrassment.

I have been in pensive mood today following yisdee's event's with St.John. I was trawling through my Fenbook pages and came across some older posts. One in particular was when I met Flatland pop legend Micki Minaj, and I got to meet the curvy bombshell on her tour bus. She was luscious ☺

Frydims 27st Octerrible

Jim Bob had been out looking for baby Badgers, kittens or puppies to turn into novelty radio sets for childers. He came back with this fantastically well-endowed bat, too hot to just be turned into a radio or CB. Following winsti's amorous dead tramps arm incident I thought that could will hire him out as a novelty sex toy.

If any of you lovely ladies in Fenbookland are unsatisfied with your love lives, feeling sexually frustrated and would like to try something a bit …. different. Look no further than a discreet new service I'm offering called "sex with Cyril".

Cyril (pictured below) is a bat that was born to love, born to please, born to tease.

Come on ladies, if you want a lover who is hung like a bat then inbox me and I'll arrange a meeting.

SatD 28nd Octerrible

After dance practice I told Gary about my 'meeting' with St.John the other noyght. I gave him all he needed to know but he pressed me on how I managed to get him to agree. When I told Gary the warts n all version of events the look on his face suggested that Gary had never sodomised another man with a dead tramp's forearm before. To be fair it was a first for me too. I told him about Barry and that he was my companion that sadly died of natural causes but I didn't have the finances for a proper burial. I know the Hoooman immigrants struggle with the concept of trepanning so I decided to leave that part of the rendition out.

We agreed that next week would be the best time to infiltrate the town hall to get the last of the evidence we needed to save the world. Jack would be back from his honeymoon and it would give me time to sort out codes for the safe in the Mayor's chambers where the hard copy of the ledgers are kept.

Gary had found out more and more through lots of research and once we had everything we needed to corroborate it all, we would hand it over to the relevant authorities and wait for the developments.

Sunty 29th Octerrible

Tonoyght is the festival of Disraelina the Flatland fertility goddess. It is an ancient ritual dating back fifty years or more and culminates in the burning of a straw effigy and the gift to the god Disraelina of root crops to get on her good side. It is widely believed in Flatlands that when Disraelina is pleased she bestows extra fingers and toes on new-borns and if she's really pleased with the subjects of Flatland District even extra limbs can be gifted. In fact the maternity ward I work on at Ropey Hospital for the genetically impure is called 'Disraelina ward'.

Of course it doesn't take a genius to work out the extra digits and limbs are as a result of inbreeding mutations but of course, there aren't many geniuses in Flatlands. If our plan comes off and we start getting the funding we are allocated from government we can start educating people a bit better and who knows, maybe find the odd genius or two.

Moondee 30st Octerrible

This mawnin we all awaited the return from honeymoon of Pocahontas and Jack Wormer. Just before daaymiddlin Jacks police car turned up outside our house so he can collect the small amount of Pocahontas's possessions. All the streamers had been removed from his police car but Jack had left the "Brutal cunt" sign in the back window. He said it was a 'mission statement' to all potential wrong-doers … it was certainly that.

The departure of Pocahontas from our humble little house to begin her new life was a bitter sweet affair. We were desperately sad to see her leave but Nina and I felt a certain degree of pride that we had not only managed to change Dmitri's gender but her life too. We had managed to do such a professional job that we duped an emotionally starved public servant into believing she was born a female and get him to marry her. We were very proud of ourselves indeed.

FLATLAND DISTRICT WEEKLY NEWS

This years Chumpton-by-Kumberly entry into Crufts is this fine example of a Chumpton Witchwinkler called Witch Finder General 3rd or Jebediah for short.
Chumpton Witchwinklers were, and occasionally still are, used to sniff out practitioners of the occult in Chumpton and the surrounding Flatland areas.
Happy Halloween everyone.

This aftynune we sat down and watched a bit of Flatlands TV. We were watching a program called Crufts, which is all about dogs that have been brushed nicely and dragged across some sawdust. We are all routing for local pooch Jebediah, ordinarily Chumptons entrants rarely get further than the car park, as some of our local breeds are not recognised at a kennel club or something.

Toosdi 31nd Octerrible

Tonoyght is something the immigrants call 'Halloween'. If you want to go out and celebrate it with a couple of Turnip Pochine's and looking for a babysitter/entertainer to look after your childers, you could do worse than Hellbert or 'Mr Smiles as he's known locally. And you can rest assured that his recent custodial sentence has got his drugs and drinking under control, so no worries there ☺

Chumpton-by-Rumberly Informer

We are pleased to announce that Chumptons very own childer's entertainer "Mr Smiles the Klown" has been released from serving a short custodial sentence following an incident with some duct tape, a roller skate and a Blonde badger called 'Boris'.
He was released from Rampton APU last SatD and is once again taking bookings. If you're thinking of having a party for one of your offspring why not give them a party they will never ever, ever forget and hire Mr Smiles the Klown. Prices range from 3 Davey's per hour or equivalent value in root crops or knives and a selection of alcoholic beverages are usually required as a rider prior to each performance. He normally arrives at your premises several hours before the start of the party so he can "prepare" thoroughly. It's always his aim to give the kids a performance they will never, ever, ever forget ... EVER

Winsti 32th Octerrible

I was up at firsloyght this mawnin did a few chores and made my way to Ropey just after firsdocky. As I arrived at the town hall St.John was faffing about as it was apparent he had only just got in himself. I left him to it.

I went and popped into the Police Brigade Station and asked if Jack was about. The young officer looked suspiciously at me and shouted for Jack. He told him there was "someone here to see him", I recognised the voice as one of the officers at Devilman's house the other week. I smiled inwardly.

Jack and I sat and chatted in an interview room ... interview room 3 ... my favourite. I told him about all the developments and that we were going to be paying a visit to the chambers to have a look in the Mayor's safe tonoyght. Jack seemed concerned that I had divulged as much information as I had to St.John but I explained I had little choice. I accidentally let slip about Barry's grave in my garden, Jack asked me to clarify this. I explained that Barry was a homeless person who lived with me and he had cranial bonce demons and he needed some hefty trepanning and he died of natural causes. Then Jack remembered Barry from one of his raids at my house following nosey neighbours complaining about the screaming. Oddly, that was the end of the conversation. I pointed out once again to Jack that there was nothing I could have done for him and Jack nodded in agreement. He went on to say that he would recommend any other vagrants that might need trepanning to my practice. When I jokingly mentioned that I would need to buy some new drills Jack said "Drills?" it would seem that he's not certain what trepanning involves. Jack changed the subject by saying he had booked a table at Fido's for him and his new spouse. I told him it was okay that he didn't need to be there as St.John new all the combinations.

Just after laasloyght Gary collected me from my house and we went to St.John's place in Ropey. We parked Gary's car nearby and walked to the council offices. St.John opened up the Mayor's chambers and wrote down the combination to the safe and retired to his office to leave us to it. As the safe opened there was a quantity of paperwork and a huge amount of money. Gary and I gasped at the wads of fifty pound notes all bundled up. It wasn't what we'd come for so as tempting as it was to take a couple of fifties we set about finding the ledgers. St.John entered the room and pointed Gary straight to a thick pile of paperwork. Gary took them out of the safe and spent the next half an hour photographing the paperwork before returning it to the safe, just how it was before we arrived. As he went to close the safe his hand hovered over a bundle of money, he picked up a wad turned to us and said "this would pay for the work needed to repair the cracks in my house". I smiled and said take it but Gary rightly pointed out that this would make him no better than them. These immigrants sure are funny people.

St.John locked everywhere up and we sneaked out keen not to be spotted by anyone. Gary dropped St.John off at his house and took me back to Chumpton, he dropped me off at the clock tower and he said he would call me the next aftynune once he'd had a chance to look at all the evidence and bundle it together.

I called into the Peppermint Hippo for a quick drink and was pleased to see Nina and her sister sat at the bar. They asked where I had been all noyght and I told them I had been giving Gary some private interpretive dance tuition as he felt he was lagging behind the others. They seemed to buy that. Davina Kraye was strutting her stuff and root crops were being thrust into her underwear with alarming regularity, at the end of just one dance she had amassed enough tips to make two decent sized stews. Her gusset was hanging down to her knees by the time she staggered off stage, struggling to keep hold of her carrots. She had inserted a few parsnips into her 'vag patch' to make additional space for all the tips. All of a sudden the idea of an inviting bowl of warm vegetable stew was slightly less inviting. The parsnips looked much cleaner on exit than going in though.

Thrisdee 33th Octerrible

Gary text me to say he would meet me and Jack at the club 'early evening' (or *laasloyght as we call it*) after 'dinner' (or *laasdocky as we call it*). I agreed and went to collect my sex bat from Marjory Meninges from Lower fen Fen at Yon end which is just outside Chatterby. She had the look of a satisfied woman, a woman that had just been serviced by very well hung Flatland Bat, I think there'll be plenty of repeat orders from Marjory as her husband, also called Marjory, is serving a lengthy custodial sentence in HMP Ropey for a sudden and unexpected outbreak of morale during the Sunday Service at St Jeremiah's church. God, it would seem is not a laughing matter.

When I eventually got to the club I was running a little bit late and Jack and Gary were already there. Gary was tremendously excited about what he had found.
"It will take quite a while to sort through everything we have found on the computer, on the receipts and in the ledgers but this is huge. They have been skimming tens of millions off the pot for years. Once I hand this over to the authorities it can't be ignored" Gary said excitedly. It was then that Jack pointed out that if this is true, then as soon as the shit hits the fan we will be in a great deal of danger. For the amount of money being talked about they will not take kindly to being ratted out and will definitely stop at nothing to either make it go away, or exact revenge. For the first time since this little adventure started I felt quite worried and more than a little bit vulnerable. We agreed that we needed to send the information anonymously. I thought we should have a backup plan but Jack and Gary assured me that as long we covered all our tracks then we would be perfectly safe. Gary asked jack if he could erase the CCTV footage of each time we went into town, jack informed Gary that Ropey doesn't have CCTV but would check that there was no link to us and our recent slinking about. We needed to be clever about this.

CHAPTER TWELVE

SMOKE AND MIRRORS

NOVOCAINE 1896

Frydims 1th Novocaine

The news this mawnin dear diary, on Flatlands TV and in the paper, was all about the letter that Mayoress Davina Kraye was going to send to the UK Government (*telling them we were no longer wishing to be part of the UK*) could not be sent until all the council officials, the Mayoress and the Elders had agreed about its content. I would imagine that the 52 people who voted to leave the UK (*or Flexiters as they were now being called*) would be hopping mad.

Of course I knew that the whole referendum was nothing more than a scam to take people's eyes off the ball from what was really going on. During the campaigning people had been told by Rimbit Muldoon's media circus that there might be some hardship in the forthcoming years but it would all be worth it in the long run. Of course because it was all lies nobody could quite say how it would all turn out okay, just that it would.

SatD 2th Novocaine

Very little work was getting done as everybody was still chinning about yisdee's scandal regarding not sending the letter to the UK government until we know how it's worded. It was therefore a blessed relief to get to my interpretive dance class. Most of the students were press ganged some months ago by Jack to attend, so nearly all attendees were hooomans and not effected or really aware of our little vote way back in Jism of this year. After the rehearsal we chatted outside whilst Inga was 'vaping' …. not a fucking clue what that is, but the device she 'vapes' with looks similar to the stoner device that some of the yoof use when inhaling dried out Jabberinlafter plants (*mildly illegal*). Gary made sure he was out of earshot and told me that by the time he had gone through everything and made sure all our tracks were covered it would be at least 10 days before he would be sending it to the authorities to act on. This gave us plenty of time to cover our tracks totally he said, "Or devise a plan B" I replied but Gary just laughed at me. I was a little bit annoyed.

Sunty 3th Novocaine

This mawnin I had a knock at the door from a couple of buddies of mine Jezmee and Dezmee Blodwella. They were travelling through and thought they'd pop in for a quick cup of onion tea and a go on my toilet. The Blodwella family are a very large and well established tribe indeed and some branches of their family tree are very heavily mutated. Jezmee and Dezmee are possibly F3, maybe even F4 generation mutation. Their appearance has often been mistaken for makeup and poorly constructed theatrical costume design but closer inspection would show that this is how their bodies are constructed. They were better known locally as 'Sigmund and Ray, magicians extraordinaire' noted for making entire beet nests disappear before your very eyes. They once made a John Deer tractor disappear live on Flatlands TV.

Whilst they were pooing in my WC I quickly made some calls on the tefelone and within a few minutes I had arranged a world tour of Chumpton and Chatterby. They were delighted and as a special thank you they said they would dedicate a trick to me. I didn't have to see it at a show but I'd know it was their trick when it happened. I was thrilled to see them and once they had gone Natalia and Nina came out from hiding in the basement. Nina said they were in league with the Beelzebub, old Nick, Lucifer himself.

I wasn't sure what they were on about but I did know they got a bit of help with the bigger tricks by worshipping the Devil.

fenbook   Surch for peeeple and othur things tooooo   🔍   Morton Hoome   Foind frends

These two charmers are Jezmee and Dezmee Blodwella, or the terrible twins I call them. They are perhaps better known in Flatlands by their professional names "Sigmund and Ray". They are close personal chums of mine and they'll be appearing at Peppermint Hippo performing their magic act as well as at Chumpton WI hall and Chumpton World of Adventure. They're masters of magic and some of the Flatland community believe that they use clever illusions with mirrors and diversions to perform their incredible magic tricks. I happen to know however that the majority of the stunts they pull on stage are created by simply being in league with the devil.

It's as easy as that ☺

Moondee 4th Novocaine

Until Gary can complete the paperwork to save the world there isn't a lot we can do with the whole 'world saving' thingummy. Instead it was business as usual at casa Babeldom, Jim Bob was in the inventing shed and I was busy trying to come up with new ideas for inventions. Jim Bob mentioned that we were running low on woodland creatures for radio sets and even kittens were getting hard to come by. I would need to start getting my bonce into inventing mode again.

Toosdi 5th Novocaine

Cinderella's vagina has cleared up an absolute treat. The maggots it generated have been keeping all the local anglers happy for the last week or so. Finbar hasn't been paying her much attention lately as the smell from her transplanted sheep's tuppence was, on occasion, too much to bear. I hate seeing her lonely so I have asked Chatterby

Zoo if they have any spare animals knocking about, ones that are quite robust as sometimes 'Cinders don't play so nice'.

Just after daaymiddlin Jezmee and Dezmee appeared again, this time without knocking the door ... or opening the door, they just appeared without the whole front door knocking and opening furore. They had heard that I needed a pet for Cinderella, not sure how. Nina and Natalia ran to the basement and hid whilst I put the pan on for a cup of onion tea. When I returned they had disappeared but now I had a Fibbersdick Chabblewacka to look after

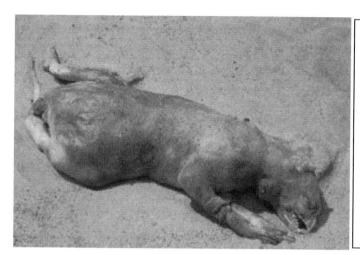

My buddies Jezmee and Dezmee (*Sigmund and Ray*) visited and left a gift for Cinderella. This lovely Fibberdick Chabblewacker has found it's forever home. Hopefully it is quite robust as Cinderella can be a tough master to love and she also has recently suffered from a rancid vaginal smell that many mammals have found unbearable.

Winsti 6th Novocaine

Today Jim Bob and I devised this fantastic, bespoke door opener/TV channel changer. I have taken the two we made today down to Horatio Horatio, the manager of the Happy Pauper, and he is confident that they will fly of the shelves within years. He has said if they do sell he will ask us for more. A very productive day's inventing.

Cinderella is absolutely besotted with her new pet. The Fibbersdick Chabblewacker was, until my magical chums turned up yisdee, thought to be extinct. This was largely because, despite their repulsive appearance they absolutely delicious.

Once the new household addition was settled with Cinders I went and posted my latest invention on Fenbook to see if any of my fenbook chums wanted my funky device.

fenbook | Surch for peeeple and othur things tooooo | Morton Hoome Foind trends

I have designed an automatic door opener/television channel changer (for old style telly's) from some old clock parts and the internal workings of the early prototype of my time machine.

I am looking for chums who will allow me to graft the device into their heads and experiment on them with this latest contraption for feasibility studies. There is a small possibility that this gizmo may contain nuts .... and uranium.

Due to strict Flatland laws no money can change hands but I am willing to reimburse any participants with sexual favours. The sexual favours can be made with or without anaesthetic (*devils prolapse*), depending on preference.

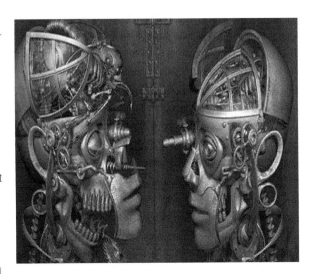

Thrisdee 7th Novocaine

Hmmmm what a day. Absolutely crazy day. Where do I begin? Crickey … not sure I know how to put it into words …

Frydims 8th Novocaine

Edith came knocking at the door today asking if I could possibly get her a ticket for one of the forthcoming concerts for local boy band pop sensation 'No Direction', I of course duly obliged.

She then asked if she could borrow the chair leg again, I of course duly obliged. As I handed her the chair leg she passed a small amount of fartage, not too noisy but extremely smelly, it made a nice change from the smell of Cinderella's vagina. I began wafting it into my face as if I were sniffing the steam off a lovely roadkill stew. Edith

274

looked surprised, frowning as if she were scared of me so I smiled at her to try and calm her. This just seemed to make things worse, she ran to her home next door without saying goodbye or thanks for the chair leg. Strange woman.

FLATLAND DISTRICT WEEKLY NEWS

The ladies of Chumpton-by-Kumberly are waiting with some anticipation at the first performance of local boy band "No Direction". Pictured below No Direction are; (left to right) Jeremiah Clungefudder, Jerebediah Clungefudder and Jeremiahbediah Clungefudder.
The local lads have been rehearsing at the Chumpton WI hall to be ready for their "gig" at none other than Peppermint Hippo (Chumptons finest pole/lap dancing and live music venue) this Frydims. Entrance fee will be two Stoats pelts or various root crops of equivalent value.
They have prepared for their premier performance by getting their hair do's updated in the village at Mason Dicksyline.
Jeremiah Clungefudder said "we're havin one of them there new fangled mullet cuts ... it'll drive the girleeeees crazy. I bet they'll have gussets like fish fryers cuffs by the time we've finished".
The lads are hoping to release their first single entitled "Puuurrdy mouth" on a Winsti some time in Octerrible or Novacaine and are planning a world tour of Chatterby and Ropey Town throughout theses months.

SatD 9th Novocaine

After dancing today Gary gave us an update about how he's getting on sorting through the former Mayor's business affairs. He says he'll probably be done by the end of the week. When he's finished he'll let us know and we can go up to his house for one final meeting. We then need to lay low for a few weeks whilst the dust settles. Jack mentioned that the only loose end is St.John Cranshaw. Jack was concerned that despite having his heart broken he was a liability. I had to admit that I had this fear too but for us to be able to get hold of the ledgers we had to trust him. I hadn't told him who Gary was and as Jack wasn't there the noyght we used him to gain access to the town hall the only person he really knew about was me. Jack offered to have a word with him but I said it wasn't necessary.

When I got home I sat in my inventing shed for a while before going in the house. I needed to have a little think about all possibilities. My gut instinct was telling me that St.John was okay, he was on our side. Truth is I don't know for sure, what I do know is I have had to trust the life partner of a corrupt man we are attempting to discredit and possibly send to prison for a very long time. Cranshaw had betrayed him but then I had, to all intents and purposes, sodomised him with a dead tramps semi decayed arm that he thought was my penis, so he was no angel himself … maybe.

Sunty 10st Novocaine

Trying to take my mind off stuff I decided to once again raid my memory locker and sift through some old pictures in my office. Morris Poncen turned up out of the blue this mawnin and asked if Nigelle was in. I invited him in and went and fetched Nigelle. Mr F`Rage was in fine form and need of a quick trepanning before his demons got out of hand.

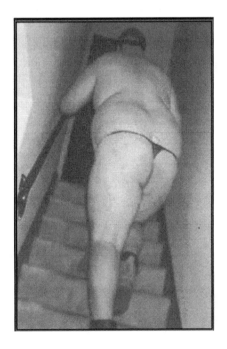

Here I am just about to perform at The Klunge Klub in Chatterby during my ban from working at Peppermint Hippo. This was due to a temporary hold on my sex workers licence by the Flatland District council after an unfortunate involuntary flatulence incident during one of my world famous erotic lunges in a private dance.

pleasant dreams

They went out for a drink and returned a few hours later, on their return Morris asked me if Nigelle could go and live at his house. He told me that he asked his mum and she said it was okay. Nigelle went and packed his belongings into a paper bag and off he went. Another one flown the nest … although nobody was very sad to see him go to be honest. Well then dear diary, I leave you with this alluring picture I put on Fenbook of me at the Klunge Klub last year.

Moondee 11st Novocaine

A man called Leonard Cohen died today, he was a great poet and a minstrel and a very huge loss to anyone who loves mooosic.

Toosdi 12st Novocaine

The Chumpton-by-Kumberly Informer

Local make up lady Briss McHandshandy is available to make you look beautiful for that big occasion when you **just have** to look your best.

Whether it's just make up or a full make over you require, Briss is your gal. whether it's a wedding, christening, wife swapping party or court appearance Briss can you make you look a Hundred dollars (*or equivalent value in root crops*).

Why not remove one of the most stressful parts of "getting ready" for any woman by asking Briss McHandshandy to make up your face. She uses her own home made cosmetics and the ingredients are a closely guarded secret but rest assured, Briss has personally tested them on local animals and a reassuringly significant number of them survived ... over half.

But it's not just the lucky ladies of Flatlands that can experience the wonders of a Briss McHandshandy make over. No, guys can too and for a small surcharge she will happily perform sex acts for your man while you get ready. Just think ladies, no more yelling up the stairs from your fella enquiring "are you bloody ready yet you stoopid cow"? All you will hear is the feral groaning of your fella as Briss does unspeakable things to him and you squeeze into your glad rags at your leisure.

So go on, treat yourself to the Briss McHandshandy Make over experience, because "it's Worth it".

Briss McHandshandy, legendary make up artiste` and prostitute

This mawnin I saw an advert in the Chumpton-by-Kumberly Informer of beautiful Briss McHandshandy. We hired Briss to do Pocahontas's makeup on her big day the other week and true to her advert, whilst Nina put the final touches into Pocahontas's dress n stuff, Briss let Jack have one last pre-nuptial congress. Jack later told me she insisted he took her up the back bottom as the front bottom was menstrual. We both found that pretty hard to believe.

Winsti 13st Novocaine

I received a text from Gary at daaymiddlin saying we should come up to his house tomorrow and he'll show us what he has come up with and how he intends to send it out to the authorities without getting us caught and killed.

Natalia asked me where Nigelle was. I had to think for a while who she was talking about.

Thrisdee 14st Novocaine

Jack and I arrived at Gary's house 'early laasloyght' as requested and made our way to his cracked office. We sat down and Gary fired his computer into action, we could tell he was excited. Whilst we waited for it to boot up Inga came in with tea and biscuits, all this is so far removed from the life I lead just a few short months ago. I knew nothing of computers and mobile phones … biscuits, the snacks I ate were vegetable based … root crop vegetable based to be precise. I knew very little of the outside world, that the UK of Great Britain was actually either the UK or Great Britain but not both.

I have seen a dramatic change in my view of the world and my hopes for the future, I have moderated some of my behaviour and I have not set fire to anything for several months now.

Once Gary had opened up his 'file' from his 'folder' (*see what I mean?*) he began to show Jack and I lots of facts and figures and numbers, lots of numbers. Big numbers … lots of big numbers. He spent the next two hours telling us of his findings and the scale of corruption that had been going on in the town hall. This was only interrupted when Inga bought Emily in to say goodnoyght to her daddy.

As soon as she was out of the room it was back to the coal face again, this time talking about the fruits of his research about the town Elders, much of this we already knew but who were we to deny Gary his moment in the sun, he had after all, worked bloody hard and had taken many risks to get us this far. Gary had more to lose than any of us and seeing his wife and daughter only moments earlier bought that home.

I knew Jack was thinking the same thing. All of them had creamed about 3-4 million a year, each, just from the misappropriation of council funds alone. They had all invested heavily in property, mostly in foreign countries, just after some market that crashed and caused something called the credit crunch about eight years ago.

Gary then went on to tell us how he was going to cover his tracks getting this information to the authorities without getting it traced back to him. This bit really confused the fuck out of Jack and I, it involved things called IP addresses and dark webs and onion browsers or something. We both perked up when we heard the word onion but quickly slumped back into a vail of total confusion when Gary started to tell us how this was virtually untraceable. He said he was going to send it to the appropriate people on Monday (*Moondee he meant*).

Finally, after Gary had delivered his report to Jack and me, we sat for a moment in silence to take all this information in. I asked Gary what he was going to do about his house. He said "That's not a problem because even if I get no joy from the proceeding against them all, and they will have all their assets seized, I have house insurance that will hopefully cover it". I reminded him if it doesn't we know where there is a huge wad of cash and how to get our hands on it. Jack called us a couple of twats when we told him we didn't take any of the Mayor's money.

I asked Gary if I could have a copy of this 'folder' and he plugged the mobile phone into his computer and copied the folder to my phone. We said goodbye to Inga and left. Jack sat in his police car, looked at me and asked if I 2understood a fucking word of what was just said", "Most of it" I replied, although I may have been exaggerating a tad. As we pulled out of Gary's driveway we stopped momentarily and looked at Gary's cracked house and his car. Jack looked sad, I asked him what was up. "If I was a policeman in the UK, outside of Flatlands, I would have a nice house like that and a lovely car like Gary's" he said.

I agreed, although if Jack had been a policeman in the UK he would have been sent to prison a long time ago I thought to myself. As we pulled away Jack was still looking longingly at Gary's car. "It's nice isn't it?" I said, he nodded. "It's easy to drive" I continued, Jack looked at me sternly "when the fuck did you get to drive his car?" he snapped. I told him he let me have a go at driving it a few weeks previously and it was called an automatic, and I did okay. I placated Jack by telling him that I didn't think I would be able to drive a car like his with gears. Jack agreed.

As we got out of New Chumpton and Jack stopped his car, looked at me, smiled and said "Do you fancy having a go at driving this one?" I drove Jack's police car back to Chumpton and don't remember the last time I laughed so much. I stalled the car so many times it would've been quicker to walk. We both were crying by the time he arrived at my house. Jack kindly told me I did okay. He lied. He bid me good noyght and drove away.

Frydims 15st Novocaine

FLATLAND DISTRICT WEEKLY NEWS

The Blodwellas, Chumptons answer to the Osmonds, are appearing at The Chatterby bowl (the Flatland districts premier concert arena) following the huge success of their sellout world tour of Swaffham. The "gig" is on Thrisdee 29rd Novacaine. They will be performing a selection from their latest album, Y'caaaant stop the beet (root), as well as many past hits from their root crop based back catalogue from yester-year.

Tickets are selling fast, 3 have been sold this mawnin, and as The Chatterby Bowl only has a 80 person capacity, tickets are expected to be a hot, hot, hot item. Prices are 75 loom bands or 17 new pence in hoooman money

This mawnin I saw an advert for the Blodwella's (*Jezmee and Dezmee's extended family*), who were going to be performing at Chatterby bowl at the end of the month. Lovely family.

SatD 16st Novocaine

Jack came round with his wife and our ex housemate Pocahontas, for a cup of Typhoo tea made with real cow's milk this mawnin. Pocahontas seemed confused about where she was and was dribbling profusely; it was just like being at a Chumpton WI meeting Nina commented.

Jack took me for drive in his police car to talk about the forthcoming events. I was as worried as he was but we re-assured ourselves that Gary was clearly a very clever man and would never put his family in harm's way unless he was confident about what he was doing. Jack told me he was not going to be unprepared and that he had a gun in the back of his police car and one in his house under the sink. I asked him where he got them from but he just smiled and winked. I guess if you're a police officer then you occasionally meet some bad people … either that or Guns n Parrots in the High Street. Once out of the village we swapped seats and jack let me have another go at driving with equally hilarious results, although I didn't stall as much I did make it jump like a Kangaroo.

Sunty 17st Novocaine

This aftynune Jim Bob came to the house to do a spot of prep work for our Door opener/TV Changer gadgets. He was going to make some more as he was expecting there would be a huge demand for them. He also took the opportunity to run up and down outside again to show Natalia his sprinting prowess. I didn't have the heart to tell him that Natalia was out with Nina and Cinderella.

Moondee 18st Novocaine

At just after firsdocky (*or breakfast as I have started calling it … thanks Gary*) I heard the mobile phone go off to tell me a text had arrived. It was Gary, he was at work in a secret location and had just sent the Folder containing files to the person who headed the enquiry into Devilman, and also sent it to leading media outlets.

I waited all day and well into the noyght but nothing was coming up on Flatlands TV (*to be expected*). Gary texted and told me to be patient. Trying to but it's tough.

Toosdi 19st Novocaine

After my mawnin mastybayshun I checked on Google to see if there was any news. Still nothing so I did some more mastybayshun. Jim Bob asked if I could go somewhere else to do it again but I quite liked the inventing shed. Eventually I went into the living room and switched on the TV there was nothing on the news. I checked google again an hour later and still nothing.

I caught the guided bus to Ropey and went and counted some toes for a bit, collected some hospital waste for the 'roadkill hot pot' at Peppermint Hippo and wandered over the road to see Jack. Once again the officer behind the desk was the lad who was at Devilman's house the noyght we broke/let ourselves in. He had bruises all over his noggin and was walking with a limp.
"What the hell happened to you?" I asked, quite startled by his appearance.
"I attended a burglary in progress last noyght and the perps were still onsite, I took a bit of a beating, but all in a day's work" he replied quite proud of the kicking he'd received … all in the line of duty.

As he was telling me this cautionary tale Jack walked in behind him to file some paperwork. The smirk on Jacks face told me all I needed to know about who the 'perp' was that gave the young PC his beating. Although he was none the wiser that the man he insulted at Devilman's house was hiding under a bed only a few yards away, revenge it would seem had been exacted.

We went for a drive and this time Jack let me drive around town. I killed nobody and only stalled twice but still cried with laughter.

I went to bed just after noyghtmiddlin having checked the news pages several times. I also checked the pornographic websites just to be absolutely certain.

Winsti 20rd Novocaine

I received an early mawnin text from Gary asking if I was at home, I replied yes and he texted straight back to say he was coming to collect me. Ten minutes later I'm sat in Gary's car heading back to New Chumpton. He told me that the BBC Breakfast news had led with the story that East Anglian businessmen from an area of the Fens called Flatland had been questioned by police about irregularities regarding financial dealings at the town council. This was it. We sat in Gary's living room watching his TV on the BBC 24hour news channel. Information was sketchy the presenter said and details were going to follow later in the day. Gary had called into work saying he was sick and we sat and watched telly for the rest of the mawnin. It was interesting watching the news channel about all the rest of the world. Apparently Merica of the USA had just voted a chap to become their Mayor and he was called Donny Trump. Gary said he was the most dangerous man on the planet, clearly they had not met Jack hahaha. From what I could see from the news, Nigelle would fit right in with the Mericans.

Gary told me to keep checking the phone for updates and we must keep in touch with each other. He also mentioned the phone bill and to go easy on the porno sites. He went on to tell me that the phone was mine now, I said thank you lots and lots of times. He would continue paying the bill as long as I didn't over do the mastybayshun sites. We sipped posh coffee and felt nervous. Later on today Jack joined us saying that there was lots of activity at the town hall. He said that there were people he had never seen before crawling all over the place and Davina Kraye was walking about looking very concerned, she'd even put a cardigan on.

We returned back to Chumpton and had a quick drink in the club before we went to our homes. Jack told me that now was to be careful and mention nothing to anyone. This I already knew.

Thrisdee 21rd Novocaine

On my phone this morning it said on the BBC news that Blaize Craphammer, Blair Deville, Jack Spangler and Freddy Fingerstien, known as the Elders of Flatlands, had all been arrested and charged, although the details of the charges hadn't been released just yet. An arrest warrant had been issued for David Devilman but there was no sign of him at any of his UK residences. It would seem we had done it. The police would catch up with Devilman eventually as his face was all over the news. Oddly nothing was mentioned on the Flatlands TV News about any of this, but then Flatlands is behind with current affairs … by about 50 years.

Frydims 22rd Novocaine

Today's updates are that Devilman is believed to have fled the country as his yacht has been found in Spain and there has been sighted several times in the last 24 hours. There hasn't been any news yet on what the charges are but with the evidence that Gary had supplied maybe it's a lot more complicated than we thought. I have tried to occupy my mind with a bit of inventing and some sexy time with Nina, then myself, then Nina again.

SatD 23rd Novocaine

I concentrated all my efforts and energies on some pretty hardcore interpretive dancing. Gary was out of sorts and Jack and I were a bit concerned. We had a chat with Gary after the class. Gary told us that it was looking like the only charges that were going to be bought against the Elders and Devilman was for the dodgy green belt land sales and building deals. This was good news for Gary with regards to getting his house repaired but it was annoying that all the other stuff was getting overlooked. I pointed out to Gary that maybe the corruption in Flatlands was so deep that it was going to take some considerable investigation to work out who is responsible for what. Gary sort of agreed and wondered if the corruption went back up the trail too, much higher than Devilman and the Elders of Flatland. It made sense because for this to work for as long and as well as it has without detection would probably mean that there were people who worked for the UK government had to turn a blind eye for their share of the money. We shouldn't forget that the charges that have been made against them all would currently lead to some fairly hefty jail time, albeit in a nice cushy open prison somewhere, but jail time all the same. We all went to the Hippo and had a few drinks as a way of celebration of hopefully saving the world. Nina, Natalia and Inga weren't sure what we were celebrating but they were all aware something had been going on this last couple of months. Inga possibly had a better idea than Nina and Natalia but was keeping quiet if she did.

Sunty 24rd Novocaine

It was a quiet and hungover mawnin this mawnin. Finbar Knuckleshuffla was out with Cinderella. He was back on the scene now her lady/sheep parts weren't infested with maggots and didn't smell like a septic tank any more. He told me he probably wasn't ready to lick it just yet but would maybe give her a rimming instead. I'm not sure why he felt he needed to tell me that and frankly, I wished he hadn't.

Moondee 25rd Novocaine

The story about the Flatlands scandal was now just a lingering side story on the BBC. There were still no more signs of David Devilman but a couple of the sightings in Spain had been confirmed as definitely him.

Jim Bob was in fine form this mawnin. He starting to get really fast at sprinting now and he has stopped vomiting quite as much so his stamina must be improving.

I went to Ropey and did a bit of toe counting and called in to the Jolly Sphincter for a quick pint of Badgerspizzle. Some young lads were in the corner playing a game of guess the bollock. It was a cunning game of strategy and guile that had been played by young Flatland folk for many generations.

The rules were simple; each player took it in turn expose one of their testicles to the other players and the other players had to guess left or right. The girl's version was almost the same but with breasties. The long dark winter noyghts would fly by in our little district.

Toosdi26rd Novocaine

We booked a table at the Chatterby Foodie File for a lovely meal. We will be having the special half price meal deal and have asked that all intestinal parasites are removed as I have an allergy to tapeworm segments. If the majority of the meal is parasite free I am confident of keeping the food down for the required twenty minutes to qualify for the special offer, this is a regular offer in many of the restaurants in Flatlands.

My final entry in my diary today will say with some considerable pride that I was the only person who managed to keep my meal from re-appearing again within the twenty minutes designated by the restaurateurs. Thrilled. We will definitely be dining there again. Noyghty noyght.

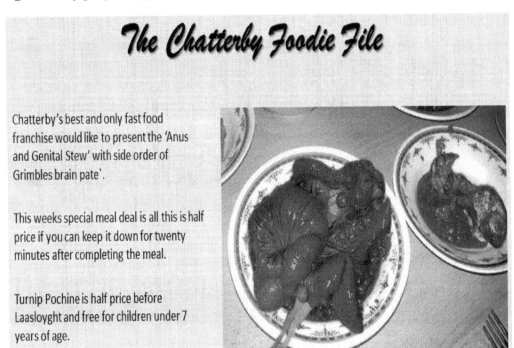

The Chatterby Foodie File

Chatterby's best and only fast food franchise would like to present the 'Anus and Genital Stew' with side order of Grimbles brain pate`.

This weeks special meal deal is all this is half price if you can keep it down for twenty minutes after completing the meal.

Turnip Pochine is half price before Laasloyght and free for children under 7 years of age.

Winsti 27rd Novocaine

Word around the camp fire is that Mayoress Kraye has appointed none other than our old buddy Morris Poncen to the council of the Elders. Morris will have the task of negotiating a favourable exit from the United Kingdom. Morris managing an exit from his jacket without falling over would be an accomplishment. Morris has informed us Nigelle wants to visit Merica of USA to meet Donny Trump. Tonoyght Davina performed, what she told me afterwards, was to be her last stint at the Peppermint Hippo. She was going to need to concentrate on her political career. I found this somewhat strange as it was my understanding that Davina had little knowledge of the workings of council affairs. She didn't realise that we were aware that there was almost nothing for the Mayoress to do as her role was purely as a figurehead. She was up to something I reckon; surely she wasn't still in contact with Devilman. I had no way of knowing but I knew a man who probably would. I think I'll pay St.John another visit on SatD … I might need to dig up Barry's arm again.

Thrisdee 28rd Novocaine

Today, dear diary was a very strange day. I have had plenty of strange days, especially recently, but today was up there with the strangest … no, make that eerie.

Throughout the day I have had the feeling I was being watched. First thing this mawnin I was in the inventing shed with Jim Bob and Nina had taken Cinderella to Chatterby to get her anal beard trimmed. They also give her a really good facial shave with same razor afterwards. Nobody was in the house and only Jim bob and I were in the shed yet I kept seeing things out of the corner of my eye. I went and made us both a cup of tea with real cow's milk and whilst I was in my kitchen/operating theatre I noticed the outline of someone standing in the distance by the bushes at the back of the garden.

I went and sat in my office upstairs and checked my phone for any news yet about Devilman but nothing. As I sat looking out of my office window I saw movement again, this time just a head ducking down. Later I took a stroll over to the club to take a batch of roadkill stew for tonoyghts punters to enjoy. Again, I was aware I was being followed. I dropped off the stew and made my way back home. Still, I had the feeling of being followed. I kept quickly turning round only to see a shadow move. A couple of times I investigated it but of course there was nothing there by the time I'd got to wherever I had seen the movement.

Finally, coming back from a trip to the Happy Pauper, as I turned the corner onto my street and walked the few yards to my front door, yet again I was aware that someone was following me. I walked into my house and shortly after there was a knock at the door. At last, whoever had been plaguing me all day had finally decided to show themselves. I flung the front door open expecting them to run only to be confronted by Gary holding a PC.

"Gary!" I exclaimed, he seemed surprised at my surprise. "Gary, come on in" I said looking past his shoulder at any sign of movement. "I shan't be stopping long Morton. Inga went and bought Emily a new computer so I thought you could make use of this one, seemed a shame to chuck it out. You can use the phone I gave you as a modem and tether it to the computer, that way you can use the web without worrying about the council knowing your business".

We took the PC and monitor and keyboard up to my office and Gary set it up within minutes. He told me that he can set a data allowance and it would only cost him 20 quid a month and he'd have no more unexpected phone bills. I was ecstatic and couldn't thank Gary enough. Now I had a mobile phone and a computer, so as soon as I get home I can tether the phone to my computer (*as Gary showed me how to do my 'hotspot'*) and when I went out I'd switch it off and use it as a mobile phone. I gave Gary some Parsnips that I'd had in the kitchen/operating theatre. I told him they had been up the Mayoress's tuppence … I think he was impressed. As he left the house and I waved him goodbye I turned to go back in and something moved out of the corner of my eye. "FUCK OFF!" I yelled.

Frydims 29rd Novocaine

First thing this mawnin I made my way up to Ropey hospital to toe count. I took the first guided bus to town from Chumpton and I was the only person on it as it wasn't long after firsloyght, and way before firsdocky. I did my duties in the maternity ward and went and watched some of the new mothers feeding their new born childers with their big floppy breasties. I always liked to spend time watching the yummy mummies of Flatlands breastie feeding … and showering … and sleeping, I especially liked watching them sleep. As I walked out of the hospital I popped across town and went to see Jack. I also wanted to pop into the town hall and see if St.John was in tomorrow noyght and see if he wanted 'dead tramp arm bumming' again. Jack had called into the Jolly Sphincter for a couple of beers and he was ordering me one as I said I wouldn't be long. Well I was quicker than that as it turned out. When I went into the chambers I was greeted by a lady I had never seen before, sitting at St.John's desk. I asked if he was in and she told me that he had taken a day's holiday at short notice but would be back in on Moondee. As I walked out of the town hall and started the short walk to the pub to meet Jack once again I became aware that I was being followed. I duck into a small alleyway near the pub and waited a couple of seconds before diving out again. Nothing.

CHAPTER THIRTEEN

THE ROVERS RETURN

DELIVERANCE 1896

SatD 1st Deliverance

Well dearest diary, you know how I said that I had experienced a very strange day recently? Well today was by far the very strangest, most excitingest and at the same time most frighteningest day of my life. Allow me to elaborate.

This aftynune I took my interpretive dance class and was surprised, and a little disappointed, that there was no Gary, Inga or Jack either. All had mentioned in the last few days that they were definitely going to attend and Gary even mentioned he was going to pick Jack up so he didn't have to drive and could have a few drinks afterwards. Although we made inroads with the nativity play and did an entire rehearsal without music or narration, just the raw power of people expressing themselves through the medium of music and random movement, it felt a bit empty without my pals present. I was sure they all had a good reason for not being there, little did I know.

After the class I caught the guided bus to Ropey and decided to call in on St.John Cranshaw. As the bus trundled through the undergrowth, snapping through the poorly maintained vegetation around the concrete guides I checked my phone again to see if they had responded to the text messages I sent Gary earlier but nothing.

I walked through Ropey town centre and made my way to the small terraced cottage that St.John lived in and knocked the door. There was no reply at first but then after the third time of knocking I saw movement through the small frosted glass window. I called out his name and saw him amble strangely to the door. When he opened the door he was bleeding from the nose and mouth and cut quite badly on his forehead. He was holding himself up in the doorway, barely able to support his weight. "What the fuck has happened to you?" I exclaimed. No reply, he just beckoned me in nervously. I followed St.John into his living room, his meticulously kept living room was trashed. "What the fuck has happened?" I said for the second time. "Who did this? Why? Have you reported this to the police?" I asked. St.John just looked at me and broke down in tears.

"I … am … so … sorry" he stuttered. I asked him what he meant and started to feel a little worried now.

"He came back … there was nothing I could do", "Who, who came back?" I asked, "Cranshaw" was the reply.

"I thought he'd gone to Spain with Devilman" I said. "So did I" St.John said. He was still shaking and quite clearly hurt so I poured him a glass of beetroot wine and calmed him down a bit whilst I cleaned the blood from his forehead. After a minute or so he was a bit more with it. I asked him again what had happened.

"Cranshaw came back yesterday and told me he was caught up in all this business with Devilman. I guessed as much and let it go. Knowing he had betrayed my trust was tough but I didn't say anything … until … until earlier today. We argued when he said he was lying low a few days and then try and get to Spain to join Devilman. It was too much for me to take and when I mentioned his indiscretions with Devilman … you know, when you were dancing for him, he denied it and became very angry. I told him that I'd seen the footage, but still he denied it, said it wasn't him that it must have been someone else". St.John sat and stared into the fireplace for a while and then asked if he could see the footage again, just to be sure it was Cranshaw blowing the Mayor and not someone else. I assured him it was Cranshaw but showed him the footage. He crumbled again when he realised I was telling the truth.

"Where is he now?" I asked, "He has gone to get the people who sent the information to the authorities, he knows who you all are … I swear … I swear I did not tell him".

I started to panic, how did he know it was us? I went to check my phone to see if Gary had got back to me, knowing it was unlikely but didn't know what else to do. As I looked at my phone the footage of me dancing for Devilman was still on the screen. It was then when I noticed for the first time that the angle of the footage was from the ceiling view and not the piggy picture. My blood ran cold as I realised that there must be more than just one camera in the living room. I had made a point of turning the picture to the wall when we were sneaking about his house. I did look for anymore cameras and on the ceiling and all I could see was a smoke detector. That has to be where the other camera was kept.

I sat on the sofa and tried to think but I was struggling to focus. St.John said that Cranshaw told him he had been in the area a few days, keeping tabs on people. It must have been him that was watching me recently.
"When did he leave here?" I asked, "about three hours ago" St.John replied looking very anxious.
"I can't be absolutely certain …but I think he has a handgun". I was frozen to the spot with fear. I could feel the panic beginning to rise in me, my mouth was dry and I could only imagine Gary, Jack, Inga and little Emily all lying in a pool of blood. I erased the horrible thought from my mind's eye and realised I had to do something about it.

I left St.John's house and made my way to the police station. Of course nobody was in so I remembered that they left the key to the police station underneath the second plant pot to the left by the front door. I let myself in and made my way to the cupboard where the police car keys and Turnip Pochine stash was kept. I took the keys to the police car parked outside and a quick swig of Pochine for some courage. I switched the engine on, engaged the gear and pretended that Jack was sitting right next to me giving me instruction. I drove out of the yard to the main road and stalled it. Restarted the engine and started making my way out of the town, stalling it several more times. As I approached the town perimeter I remembered I was near jack's house. I made a diversion and let myself in with his spare front door key that was predictably, underneath the second plant pot from the left. Pocahontas was sat staring at the TV and didn't even notice me walk straight past her. I went to the kitchen opened the cupboard under the sink and picked up an object wrapped in a towel I guessed was the gun he'd told me about. Sure enough it was a big heavy, black revolver with a clip of ammunition. It was either this or buying a weapon from Guns n Parrots in town, but that requires a fifteen minute 'cooling off period'. I didn't have fifteen minutes.

I put the gun on the passenger seat, fully aware I had no idea how to use it, and continued my journey. I wasn't sure what I was going to do until I got to Gary's house. I was hoping and praying that I wasn't too late and that the sight I saw wasn't a blood bath. As I started to do mirror signal manoeuvre my phone bleeped. It was Gary, he was texting me telling me to come to his house.

I stopped/stalled the car a few hundred yards from the turn into Devilman's Close in New Chumpton and I walked to the front of Gary's cracked house. I noticed Jacks police car parked at the side so they were all there. I started to sneak, very stealthily down Gary's driveway and looked into his front room window. There was no sign of anyone. I very, very, very, very, very slowly opened the creaky Iron Gate that led to Gary's back garden and slowly approached the kitchen window. There I saw them all; Gary, Inga and Emily huddled and frightened on the floor, except Jack. Jack had been tied to a kitchen chair with some silver tape called ducks tape (*not sure why ducks would want silver tape or if you use it for taping ducks up*). Jack had taken a beating but was conscious and talking to someone I couldn't see but assumed was Cranshaw. As I slowly moved to the other side of the window I saw Cranshaw. He was looking scruffy and unshaved but certainly him.

I tried to think about what I should do next but couldn't. I was completely terrified but I had to do something. As I peered through the window I could see that Cranshaw was holding a gun, thankfully it was much smaller than the gun I had and his was a silver colour, mine was black. I win on the best, most aggressive looking gun. I crept to the rear of the garage out of sight from the kitchen and text Gary to say I couldn't get hold of Jack so I had to walk and I was on my way and that I'd be about another 5 minutes. It was the longest and scariest five minutes of my life. By the time my five minutes was nearing to and end I had the very basics of some sort of plan, a simple, incredibly crude plan but a plan nonetheless.

I walked up the garden path and rang the doorbell. My legs were shaking so much with fear I could hardly support my own weight as I stooped forwards to look through the spyhole in the front door. I could see Cranshaw approach the door and he was holding the silver gun, it didn't look so girly now. I stood close to the door and I pulled back the safety catch on my lovely black revolver and held it in front of me with my upper arm by my side and forearm pointing forwards towards the door. I saw his shadow in the spyhole of the door checking it was me. I tried to look unconcerned and nonchalant as I became aware he was looking at me. Then I heard the latch on the door click and before I knew it the door swung open revealing the villain of the piece, Cranshaw St.John.

I knew I didn't have time to hesitate as I could see that, not only did he have a gun, it was in his hand ready for use. My only advantage was the element of surprise. The moment he opened the door and I had a clear shot I pulled the trigger and shot a bullet into Cranshaw's stomach. I felt the gun recoil in my hand and had the urge to pull the trigger again but decided against it. He sunk to his knees with a look of complete shock and went to point his pretty little silver gun at me. I kicked the gun out of his hand and it span several yards across the polished wood of Gary's hall floor. I closed the door behind me, and punched Cranshaw in the face as hard as I think I have ever hit anyone, even harder than Nigelle. I picked up Cranshaws lady gun and dragged him by his collar into the kitchen. There was a lot more blood coming from Cranshaw than I thought there would be, in the films there never seems to be that much blood. Gary, Inga and Emily all stood up and greeted me with open arms, I felt like a hero. Cranshaw regained a bit of consciousness and started moaning loudly with the pain. Gary immediately released Jack from the kitchen chair as I led Inga and Emily out of the kitchen.

I heard a dull thud and Cranshaws moaning stopped. When I returned to the kitchen Jack told me he looked at Cranshaw's wound and it was not as bad as it looks, certainly not life threatening but he would need a hospital. We loaded the handcuffed Cranshaw into the back of Jacks police car and he took him to Ropey hospital.

I went into Gary's house and tried to calm down a bit. I was shaking still when Jack returned an hour later to do the paperwork and take statements. The one time living in a sleepy little district with its own way's and customs had benefits when it came to officialdom. Jack told us that Cranshaw was going to survive but was now chained to a bed in Ropey hospital A&E with one of the Bobbies from Ropey police brigade next to him with instructions to bop him on the noggin if he gets awkward … or if he just felt like it. Jack had been patched up himself while he was there by the fine A&E nurses. They had used leeches and seaweed bandages as well as a couple mystical ancient Flatland healing chants to aid quick recovery. He had called in to check on Pocahontas and had changed out of his bloody uniform into his civilian clothes before coming back to Gary's house.

What a day, what a day. Who needs to start the occasional fire when you have a gun and get to shoot someone with it? ☺

Sunty 2th Deliverance

This mawnin has been hectic. After firsdocky Jack and I went to check on Gary and his family. They were fine and Emily had slept well. Jack had gone into the station and had filed the paperwork and statements and would file charges once Cranshaw was well enough to be questioned. There was not going to be any involvement from other police brigades like Peterborough as they would ask too many questions about the guns and the other entire goings on. Best it doesn't get too complicated.

Gary and Inga kept thanking me, it wasn't at all necessary but it did make me feel good about myself. In fact since I have met Gary and his lovely family I have started feeling good about myself a lot more lately. We sat down in the living room and I told them all about going to St.John and realising that there was a second camera because of the different angle in the living room. I told them about how I remembered we all had a whiskey after the two bobbies had left and we all would have been on film. I mentioned that I had the feeling I had been followed and watched the previous days, another way Cranshaw would've figured out easily enough who was involved. Jack and I left just before daaymiddlin and we went to visit St.John to check he was okay and to let him know what had happened.

St.John had tidied his house up and was relieved that Cranshaw was now in custody. He told us how Cranshaw had told him on the Frydims that the only charges that would stick to Devilman would be the land deals and building irregularities, we suspected this was the case anyway. All the other stuff about misappropriation of government funds had been "lost" by the enquiry and Rimbit Muldoon. There were almost certainly too many names that had links to them to risk making a song and a dance about it. We said goodbye to St.John and made our way back to Chumpton-by-Kumberly.

We explained to Nina and Natalia about what had happened and Jack told them how brave I had been and that I had saved the world. They were very impressed and when Jack left we went upstairs and all of us had sex three times and every single time they were awake, every single time. ☺ ☺ ☺

Moondee 3th Deliverance

Still no word of Devilman's arrest.

After the weekends excitement I was looking forward to a bit of quiet time but word had got around of my heroics. I was being treated as something of a rock star by the locals in Chumpton. The Peppermint Hippo was absolutely jam packed but very few people were here to watch the dancers they wanted me to tell my tale of daring do and bravado. I explained about how Devilman had planned to buy their houses from them with something called a compulsory purchase order which meant they had to sell them at the price Devilman agreed.

I told them that the referendum was nothing more than a sham and designed to make the economy dive so that everyone would be more accepting of the rock bottom prices Devilman would offer them for their property's and their land. I went on to tell them that Chumpton, Chatterby and Ropey, as well as all the smaller villages, were going to be flattened to make way for industrial units and expensive housing. And then I told them about the dodgy goings on that had already occurred, which lead to me, Jack and Gary saving the world … well our world.

 I didn't buy a drink all noyght long (*which I wouldn't have anyway as it's my club, but still nice to be appreciated*) and subsequently I'm struggling to write in my diary so noyghty noyght.

Toosdi 4th Deliverance

This mawnin I watched with interest and bleary eyes about Cranshaw St.John on Flatland news TV and then met Jim Bob outside in the garden. He had found some puppies that a local farmer didn't want so we made good use and turned them into CB radios. They would make ideal Chrimstaaas gifts for childers.This got me to thinking that Chrimstaaas was only around the corner, the local newspaper was full of Chrimstaaas adverts and it was only the 4th Deliverance. I swear Chrimstaaas gets earlier and earlier.

FLATLAND DISTRICT WEEKLY NEWS

If it's Chrimstaaas or Birfdeees and you're wondering what kind of present or gift to get your offspring then look no further than Chumpton-by-Kumberly's Emporium of Toys.

The picture only shows a small part of our stock, we have double what's shown in the photo.

Whether it's a fire damaged dolls head or a freshly gassed rat we stock the lot.

Picture your childers face on Chrimstaaas mawnin when they open their present to discover they have a newly deceased rodent to play with.

At Chumpton's Emporium of Toys we guarantee our toys will last well over a week before becoming dangerous.

Imagine your youngster lovingly cuddling a parched dolls head on the day of their Birfdeeee.

Winsti 5lbs Deliverance

With Chrimstaaas in the air, albeit prematurely, we went to Chumpton's Emporium of Toys on Upper fen field and yon end of upper, lower fen drove Fen. We got a couple of things for Cinderella and Pocahontas and I bought Emily a lucky dog's tail. It wasn't actually from a real dog but from a Mugwins Chufftickler, this is an indigenous animal noted for its close resemblance to dogs except Mugwins Chuffticklers have two more legs than a dog. They can run quicker than dogs but don't turn corners as well. If I'd thought it through I could have bought her the entire animal but I'm sure she'll love just the tail.

When we returned I went upstairs to do some mastybayshun on ~~Emily's~~ my computer looking at some films of ladies known as MILFs. Before I got a chance to reduce my trouserage and straighten my legs in anticipation of the 4 minutes and 64 seconds of self-indulgence about to ensue,

I heard Nina shout up to tell me Jack was about to come up. I returned myself to my clothed state just as Jack came bounding into the room. "You'll never guess what" he enthused "Devilman handed himself in to the Police in Spain and he's back in London now". I am guessing he realised the games up now his right hand man is in a hospital bed in Ropey Town looking to spend some serious jail time in HMP Ropey, he has decided to give himself up.

I didn't see anything on Flatlands TV news but then Jack told me that it was on Gary's TV at his house. Apparently he's going to spend a few days at his parent's house in a place called Newport Pagnell and they asked Jack if he'd look after the house for them while they were away.

Thrisdee 6lbs Deliverance

This mawnin Nina asked me what I wanted for my Chrimstaaas pressie. Easy to answer that question I told her, have a look on my fenbook page I hinted. It was a no brainer ………….. literally.

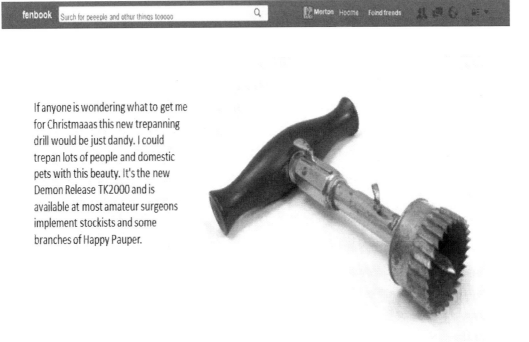

If anyone is wondering what to get me for Christmaaas this new trepanning drill would be just dandy. I could trepan lots of people and domestic pets with this beauty. It's the new Demon Release TK2000 and is available at most amateur surgeons implement stockists and some branches of Happy Pauper.

DemonRelease TK2000

Frydims 7st Deliverance

Dear diary, once again the weirdness creeps back into Flatlands everyday life. This mawnin I went to the hospital to toe count and see if I could talk the bobby looking after Cranshaw St.John into allowing me to speak to him. I counted 159 digits on the 6 new born childers and went to the 'Bernard Matthews ward for hostage situation shot gun injuries' (*it happens more often than you'd think in Flatlands*). The police person on guard duty was fast asleep so I took the opportunity to walk right in. Cranshaw was sleeping too so I gently roused him from his slumber by calling him a cunt and punching him square in the chops.

It worked eventually, I had to slap him several times with increasing force to wake him properly though. The noise also interrupted the police officers sleep and in he came with the speed of a thousand gazelles and asked me to step away from the bed in that nasally tone police officers are taught during training school. Cranshaw waved him away and asked for privacy.

"We meet again Morton" he said almost like a bond villain.
"We do indeed Cranshaw, this time without guns … shame really" I replied in an equally 007 manner.
"You know the Mayor has handed himself in don't you" Cranshaw continued, I nodded "There's only one reason he handed himself in Morton, because he knows he can get most of the charges against him dropped … he won't be in prison for very long". Cranshaw smirked and the smirk developed into a chuckle, again, very Bondesque in its manner.
"Maybe, but you will be, you'll be inside for a very long time" I said.
He didn't comeback with anything but he just started laughing in a very mocking way … a mocking Bond villain laugh. Now the whole Bond villain thing was really starting to piss me off and especially the mocking laugh bit so I stood up, turned to walk out, stopped, turned, walked back to the bed, and punched Cranshaw in the gut … right in the part of the stomach where I shot him. He screamed, I mean really screamed. I missed people screaming. I hadn't heard a scream like that since Dmitri/Pocahontas regained consciousness as I was cutting his/her penis off, and then again when he/she regained consciousness once more when I was re-attaching her tuppence.

I was escorted from the ward by the policeman but as I left I could hear Cranshaw still moaning and shouting in agony. I smiled like James Bond.

I wandered over the market square to the Ropey Police brigade station to see Jack and tell him about my encounter with Cranshaw. The lad behind the desk told me that Jack had been called to the town hall on an emergency. I made way to the town hall straight away and walked into the chambers and was met by St.John, looking somewhat bemused.

"Is Jack here St.John? … What the fucks going on?" I asked.

"Jack is here but you can't go in, it's a crime scene Morton. It's all rather odd but the Mayoress has gone … disappeared".

"What do you mean? Just because she's not here doesn't mean …"

"No" St.John interrupted, "She's taken all of Devilman's money out of the safe and some other bit's and pieces but mostly the money. She's definitely gone".

Jack strode out of the chambers and told St.John that it was to remain off limits to everyone except to the Police. It was money that oddly was accounted for in the council's ledgers. We both popped to the Jolly Sphincter and quaffed a couple of Pochine's. I told Jack about my encounter with Cranshaw and this made him laugh but he was worried about something, he couldn't quite put his finger on it but something was troubling him. As usual there was nothing on the Flatlands TV News about the District Mayoress clearing off but I didn't think there would be.

SatD 8jr Deliverance

Well, well, well diary. Things are getting more and more madder as each day passes.

This mawnin I was in the inventing shed with Jim Bob when Nina came in with a courier crow from Jack at Ropey Town Police Brigade Station telling me to take the next guided bus to Ropey and meet him at the pub. I did as he asked and within half an hour of holding the courier crow in my hands I had replaced it with a lovely tepid pint of 'Noel Chrimstaaas Winter Warmer Badgerspizzle' the Chrimstaaas beer special. It was exactly the same as normal Badgerspizzle except the winter warmer had cinnamon sprinkled in it at sometime during the 45 minute brewing process. We found a nice secluded table in the corner of the smoke room part of the pub, perfect for courting couples or covert spy like types, having world saving meetings. And let's be clear dear diary, this was definitely world saving material, I could tell by the look on Jacks face.

"How's your crime scene going on the Jack" I asked. "You'd better brace yourself for this Morton" Jack replied rather wearily "There is no crime scene anymore mate. It has been returned to a working office, there is no crime apparently"
"What on earth are you on about? Has Davina come back with the money?" I enquired.
"No ... no Davina hasn't come back ... Devilman has though. He turned up this mawnin when I was at the former crime scene. He has invoked a rule, an article in the Flatlands Council of the Elders Charter that states if a Mayor should either die or suddenly resign their post then the previous Mayor can, if possible, hold office until an election can be organised to elect a new Mayor. St.John confirmed it was correct and there is nothing any of us can do about it"
"But how can this be right?" I cried, "how can this be, he should be in prison, he has committed crimes"
"Oh he has committed crimes and he still has to stand trial for them but when you went to school with the Prime Minister of the United Kingdom and you have an unlimited supply of money then you can make things happen. He made bail this mawnin in London, so despite going on the lamb, because he handed himself in to the authorities he is not deemed to be a risk of abscondment". Jack said.

I was numb. On my way home for the short journey on the guided bus I had a mind full thoughts. Good thoughts, bad thoughts, jumbled thoughts but mostly worried thoughts. Thoughts worried for our future, the future of Flatlands and of course my future.

The man I helped expose to the world as a miscreant and crook was now returned to power, almost as though nothing had happened. My cranial bonce was full of these thoughts and it was bouncing round like a moth in a lamp shade for most of the guided bus journey home, although for some of it I pressed my mouth on the window and made fart noises.

Sunty 9th Deliverance

FLATLAND DISTRICT WEEKLY NEWS

It's a lovely sight isn't it! a young fella giving his Lesser spotted Flatland Bilge-Belcher a cuddle. Sadly though it is also the time of year to remind people the a Bilge-Belcher is for life and not just for Christmas. They may look cute when they are still calfs like the one in the picture, but a fully grown one is seven to eight times bigger than the little cutey below.

Jack and I popped up to see Gary this mawnin as he had been away for a few days visiting his parents in a palatial district known only as Newport Pagnell. We thought we would break the news about Devilman's return to him ourselves. We were concerned that he would get away with all charges completely but Gary assured us that was extremely unlikely, but he was concerned for our safety, not in the immediate future but in the long term Devilman will almost certainly want revenge for our little gang pissing on his chips.

Jack had to go and tend to a major incident following reports of carrot pilfering in a nearby field and said he would pick me up later. I sat in Gary's kitchen sipping a cup of tea so I told him about the advert in the Flatland weekly news for Bilge Belchers and mentioned that I was thinking of getting him one for Emily.

I have never seen tea come out of someone's nose holes before.

Moondee 10th Deliverance

Another day in Weirdsville started this mawnin just after firsdocky. I got another courier crow from Jack telling me to come to Ropey again, this time meet him at his house.

An hour later I was in Jack's living room watching Pocahontas dribble profusely whilst staring intently at the wall and Jack sitting in his armchair vigorously scratching his testicles, nursing a hangover. Jack got religiously drunk last noyght on Beetroot wine and looked like he was about to vomit. Jack never returned to Gary's house to collect me so I assumed that the carrot pilfering was out of control but it turns out that he was called back to the station in Ropey. He was unable to come and collect me later as he wasn't allowed to use the police car; this was because he was no longer a policeman. Devilman had sacked him.

I showered jack with the garden hosepipe and got him dressed and we went for a walk into town for a drink, a hair of the dog. We walked past the town hall to get to the Jolly Sphincter and saw St.John Cranshaw storm out of the building clearly distraught about something. We caught up with him and calmed him down and asked him what the problem was. He told us that David Devilman had called him into his office and told him that he was being demoted back to his old position as the 'interim Mayor' had a new assistant. It was at that point that Cranshaw hobbled into the room with a walking stick. We all went to the guided bus stop and made our way to Chumpton and had a noyght in the Peppermint Hippo. Word had already filtered through that Devilman was back in town and his right hand man was also in place, apparently all charges that Jack made against him for holding Gary and his family as well as Jack himself had been dropped by Devilman. Looks like the bad old days had returned. The mood was sombre, not only did it mean a return to the bad old days but I'd need to look for a new dancer, Devilman never danced at the Hippo and he had worse breasties than the previous Mayoress, marginally.

Toosdi 11nd Deliverance

This aftynune I was asked to attend the town hall but this time without any latex or thongs or nun outfits, no dancing at all in fact, I'll felt naked. I arrived feeling nervous as I had a pretty good idea who wanted to see me. As I walked into the chambers I was met by Cranshaw, I so wanted to punch him in the stomach again. He led me into the Mayor's chamber and there sat at the desk was Mayor David Devilman. As I approached the desk, in the dim light I could see the outline of someone else sitting at the desk. As I got closer there sat Gary. I was confused now.

"I believe you two know each other" Devilman hissed. "Gary?" I exclaimed, he looked glum and just shrugged.

"You may or may not know, PC Jack Wormer has lost his job, St.John Cranshaw stormed out of his job, which just leaves you two. Gary here has handed over all the evidence pointing to my indiscretions and the evidence he sent out has been 'lost' or destroyed by the enquiry and also by my old chum Rimbit Muldoon. As we speak now Ropey's finest police officers are at your house Morton, removing the computer that Gary here so kindly gave you. All of the evidence kept in the chambers has been destroyed, all of the evidence at my house has been destroyed, and at my various other houses so there is nothing left to incriminate me to any wrong doing. In return for Gary agreeing to hand over his evidence I can guarantee him and his families safety and we continue as if nothing has happened. You however haven't quite paid your debt, have you?" Devilman said. Cranshaw moved into my eye line, grinning.

"You Mr Babeldom owe Cranshaw an apology. You owe me an apology too. You will also return your licence to sell alcohol from the club, I can't take the club off you but I can take your drinks licence. A strip joint that can't sell booze is no use at all really is it, consider this a warning, if you try anything like this in the future then the consequences will be very grave indeed".

I was fuming; it is not a strip joint! The Klunge Klub, that's a strip joint but the Peppermint Hippo was Chumptons finest pole/lap dancing bar and adult entertainment complex. As we left the town hall Gary asked if I wanted a lift home, I declined, not because I was angry or anything, I totally understood his reasons for giving up the information, but because I just needed a bit of time to think. The bus ride home gave me that time to think. Also time to blow fart noises on the bus window again. I told Gary I'd see him tomorrow. He offered to pick me up, I smiled and thanked him.

Winsti 12ft Deliverance

When Gary picked me up this mawnin Jack was already in the car. Gary had collected him first and me second. We trundled down the cobbled part of the A14 through the field gate and turned right towards New Chumpton. Gary mentioned several times that he was sorry he handed all the evidence over, and each time we assured him we understood that he had more to lose than any of us. The good news was his repairs to his cracked house were going to get done and Devilman was going to be under the beady eye of the authorities now so I'm pretty sure there was going to be no more reprisals for him. I wished I could say the same about jack and me, not to mention St.John of course.

As we approached the turn in for Devilman's Close I noticed that Gary's car wasn't slowing down. I pointed this out and Gary smiled, we aren't going to his house he smirked, we are going for a day out in London. Of course both Jack and I were thrilled at visiting the capital of the United Kingdom but even more so when he told us it was just for some drinks and a tour of the sights of London. He called it a "Jolly".

We parked Gary's car in a place called Enfield and took a tube train into London's middle bit. We went on the biggest Ferris Wheel I have ever seen and then we went to a place where famous people made of wax hang about just doing nothing, that proved very popular. We had a ride around London in a big double decker bus but the upstairs had no roof which was excellent for seeing all around and also proved handy for spitting on people. We had a drink in a pub at a place called Covent Garden and a fantastic meal in a fancy posh restaurant called Subway. They sold the most delicious sandwiches known to the hoooman race. There were lots of people rushing around being very busy and I have to say I liked it. Jack wasn't so keen on the hustle and bustle but I must admit I was quite relieved to be going back to Flatlands by the time we got back to Enfield and started making our way back home. When we dropped Jack off at his house and then me at mine I was very tired. The house was quiet as everyone had gone to bed so I made a Typhoo tea with cow's milk and sat down to contemplate the day. It was a perfect way to try and forget the stresses and disappointments of the last few days.

Except of course it wasn't. It actually made it worse when I sat and thought about the day. The day was fantastic, with great food, drinks and sights, with fantastic company, but it was more than tinged with sadness too. Sadness because it made me realise that many of the things we'd enjoyed today were things that the folk of Flatlands have had denied to them by the greed of the people they voted into power to serve them. There would've been nothing stopping anybody going for a day out in London or even Newport Pagnell. They could have gone to Spain for a holiday instead of Chatterby sands. With better education and better roads, with better facilities come better jobs and better wages. All of this had been stopped by Devilman and his cronies for no other reason than pure selfishness and the more I thought about it supping my tea the angrier I got. I was angry at the way the strange, quirky and sometimes outright weird folk of Flatland District had been treated, I was angry at the way my friends Jack and Gary had been treated. This isn't over dearest diary; you wait and see this isn't over.

I took my mind off being angry by cleaning my trepanning drills and I did a quick mastybayshun before sneaking upstairs and climbing into bed with Nina and Natalia. It did the trick as I slept soundly.

Thrisdee 13ft Deliverance

I have awoken feeling refreshed and significantly more optimistic than I did yesterday mawnin before my surprise trip to London. I had to do something to give Devilman his comeuppance but not sure what yet.

Jim Bob was happy to tell me that he'd been incredibly industrious during my day out yisdee and we now had loads and loads of CB radio's made from puppies, baby Badgers and kittens. So many in fact we now need to do a Zonco promotional drive to start shifting some of them before they become infested with maggots. I'm not convinced that wasn't how Cinderella didn't get her recent infestation of fly pupa but I can't prove a damn thing.

I went into the house and made a quick tefelone call. Before you knew it I had pulled a few strings with old contacts in the biz and arranged this aftynune to be on Flatland AM Radio doing an advert for my radios …. ON RADIO! Do you see?

You cannot possibly imagine the joy that this news bought to good old Jim Bob. It was as though his life's efforts and work had culminated into this one deed this aftynune. This advert was going to make it all worthwhile. Of course I had to take him with me and once we got there I prepared a small amount of spoken speakedness for the ad and realised there was only one person for the job. When I told Jim Bob he was going to be the voice of Zonco's Badger CBs he vomited, he literally vomited with glee.

It went well and Jim Bob couldn't stop thanking me. It was lovely to catch up with some old pals at Flatland AM Radio and when Jim Bob heard his ad on the guided bus radio going back to Chumpton he dry heaved. There were unhappy rumblings at the prospect of Devilman coming back as Mayor now that many of the local folk were aware of his previous chicanery. It made me a bit angry again.

Frydims 14ft Deliverance

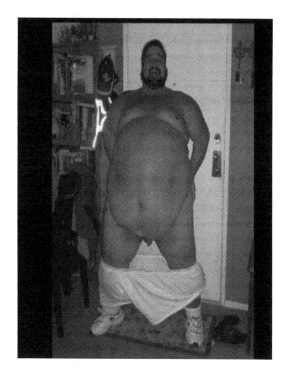

fenbook | Surch for peeeple and othur things tooooo | Q | Morton Hoome Foind frends

As it's fast approaching Christmaaas I thought I would treat my lady Fenbook friends (and some of the male ones too) to my contribution to this years Chumpton Prostate Milking Club annual charity calendar.

You're welcome

Once again I took to the old compooota in my office from when I was the Flexit campaign manager, (*as this was my only source of internet connectivity after Devilman instructed the police to seize my computer*) and despite most Flatland folk knowing all about the scandalous behaviour of our ex and now interim Mayor there was practically nothing on the Fen Wide Web about his return to local politics.

I found my fableearse photo for another calendar I'm featured in and posted it on fenbook to try and cheer people up a tad. This was taken when I had a beard to appear more with it or even more sexually adventurous.

SatD 15st Deliverance

This aftynune we had our last practice at doing the nativity through the medium of interpretive dance. The nativity play will be done in complete silence with the hope of audience participation, although this may prove difficult as ticket sales are slow.

After the practice we sat and had some tea Inga had made and put in a Thermos flask, it was very nice and was called Earl Grey. We chatted about the week's events, our trip to London and the disappointment of seemingly having all of our investigations thrown back in our face. Gary said this type of thing happens all the time in the rest of the UK and although it was sad it hadn't surprised him.

As we sat around the rickety old wooden table Nina commented about how she wished she had bought a camera to get a photo of us all. Gary said it was time for a selfie so I began undoing my trouserage, Inga grabbed my arm and shook her head. Clearly I don't know what a selfie is then. Inga took her mobile phone out, held it at arms length and took a picture of us all around the table and we all dutifully smiled. She put her phone back into to her bag and we all returned our faces to their normal look. All apart from me, I continued smiling, beaming in fact. As we all went our separate ways I was still grinning and Gary asked me why I hadn't stopped smiling since Inga took the photo a few minutes earlier. I reminded him all the information he'd had to submit to Devilman last weekend was still on my mobile phone. Gary was smiling as much as me now. Of course neither of us knew who we were going to give this information to but at least we still had it. See, it always pays to have a plan B ☺

Sunty 16th Deliverance

I saw this small article in the paper this mawnin, I have discovered that this sort of thing happens all the time in the rest of the United Kingdom but obviously not so much in Flatlands. It raises a few eyebrows but if you're lucky enough to fall in love you can't help who it is you fall in love with. Just be glad that you have.

FENLAND DISTRICT WEEKLY NEWS

Chumpton residents are celebrating it's first gay marriage. The happy couple are Jerebediah Flobbweasel and his husband Jeremiah Flobbweasel. Despite their surnames being identical they are not brothers, but merely first cousins. Their union has caused some controversy among the Chumpton's church going community as Jeremiah had originally been betrothed to Jerebediah's sister and Jerebediah to Jeremiah's sister in an arranged marriage that was drawn up by the family prior to Chumpton being connected to the National Grid, last year.
It transpires that once electricity began surging through the village and light bulbs started taking the place of the more traditional earwax candles favoured by the elders, it became apparent that Jeremiah and Jerebediah had been dating each other unwittingly due to the poor lighting and the incredible likeness each bore to their siblings.
They will be honeymooning in Chatterby Fen pursuing their favourite hobby, dredging the drainage dykes of the A141 looking for discarded body parts of car crash victims of yore.

Moondee 17th Deliverance

Well the news today is remarkable if not unsurprising. The Flatlands TV news this mawnin was awash with Hillbilly Billy Hill telling the folk of Flatlands that the interim Mayor was holding a snap election. The aforementioned presenter had interviewed Devilman in his house, in the very living room where I danced for him whilst he was fellated by his confidante and right hand man Cranshaw St.John. I noticed the picture of the pig was no longer there. The election will be this Frydims and currently there was no other candidates expected to stand. He went on to say that he intended to see through the referendum result by taking Flatland District out of the United Kingdom and kept repeating Flexit means Flexit. He said it over and over again but, because he has been out of the district for some time now he didn't realise most people knew it was just a sham, a ruse. Most of the Flatland folk were going to be pretty angry.

He continued saying Flexit means Flexit even when asked what the plans were for leaving the UK. The news carried on running the story relentlessly throughout the day and was becoming annoying. I had to think of something to stop this catastrophe but it knew I was running out of time. I'm pretty certain Devilman wouldn't make such long term plans unless he knew something we didn't about his impending court case.

Jim Bob was still walking on air after becoming a radio star with the adverts for our Badger CBs and it seemed to be doing the trick as the weekend sales were very good but we still had plenty left and not long to Chrimstaaas now. Maybe it was time for a call to some old chums at Flatlands TV for some telly selly time.

Toosdi 18lbs Deliverance

I was up early this mawnin and was greeted by Jack knocking on my door not long after firsloyght. He was looking a lot happier with his lot than the last time I saw him. He still had no idea what he wanted to do but I suggested that he could come and work at the Peppermint Hippo as door staff/occasional dancer. He was happy with door staff but not so sure about lap dancing. I told him that the doorman's position would be the easiest in the world as I was going to have my liquor licence revoked soon by the incumbent ex-Mayor (*soon to be Mayor again*).

Jim Bob came in and had a cup of tea just as Natalia came into the kitchen for some firsdocky. Jim Bob asked Natalia to *"Come out to the garden and see how strong I am picking up the wheelbarra full o` horse crap"*. Natalia smiled and agreed and Jim Bob beamed. I like Natalia. As soon as he'd finished picking up the wheel barrow full of manure he began doing star jumps followed by a bit of sprinting out the front. Natalia came back in by then telling Jim Bob she'd watch him from the window. She didn't.

She asked Jack what he would be doing no he was no longer a policeman, Jack shrugged. She suggested he look after people's houses in the district while they were away, "Loike secuurrity gord" she said. Jack agreed it would be well worth looking into and was even cheerier now.

I tefeloned Flatlands TV station and spoke to an old chum that works there and asked if I could have some air time for my Zonco Badger radio's TV Advert. That was all sorted; all I needed to do now was make an advert. I called Jim Bob in from his sprinting and asked him if he'd be interested in becoming a TV advertising star now as well. He readily agreed and so we'd need to set about recording and advert.

Jack was the camera man on my mobile phone and Nina gave Jim Bob a make-over with lipstick and plenty of rouge to make him look alluring. We shot the advert in one take as there were very few words for Jim Bob to remember and we were good to go. I agreed to drop it off on Thrisdee and I spent the rest of the day making a newspaper advert to put in all of the daily and weekly editions of the Flatlands rags.

Winsti 19nd Deliverance

This mawnin we had an emergency. I was first up as usual followed by Jim Bob coming in for a cup of tea before beginning a hard days inventing and also readying himself mentally for the special trials and tribulations in becoming a TV advertising star, due to occur only the next day. Then Nina came down followed by Natalia five minutes later. As Nina started preparing firsdocky she asked what time Finbar Knuckleshuffla came round. I looked very confused and asked why she thought Finbar had been around and why so early. Nina turned quickly with a look of great concern and said that Cinderella was not in her room. I told Jim Bob to sprint the 200 yards or so the Finbar's house to see if she was there. Natalia said she'd be watching him from the window to see how fast he was and Jim Bob left like an express train out of the front door and bounded down the street. I went outside and started shouting her name like she was an escaped puppy (*in many ways she was*) and Nina and Natalia put their wellies on in preparation to start searching if Jim Bob returned with no news. Jim Bob returned with no news.

We searched in opposite directions, Nina and I headed towards Chatterby fen and Natalia and Jim Bob headed towards Ropey. I tefeloned Jack and asked him if he would help by looking around Ropey and he happily agreed. For several hours we tramped up and down the road/mud trail between Chatterby and Chumpton, paying particular attention to the drainage dykes but we found nothing, it was a fruitless search.

As we trawled through the reeds along the bank of the drainage dyke known as the River Kumber I saw something on the bank ahead. I feared the worst as I approached the object. As I got closer to the object I could see it was a body and my heart sank. Cinderella must have fallen in and washed up on the bank of the dyke sometime after drawing her last breath. We could bury her next to Barry in my garden, I could wear my latex vicars outfit again … it makes me feel sexy. Just then the body moved slightly, it straightened its leg and passed a slight guffy fart. In double quick time I was close enough to see the body wasn't Cinderella but Davina Kraye, our former Mayor. She was very sleepy. I noticed the vast number of empty bottles of turnip daiquiri and beetroot Pochine lying about the place. I also noticed a really nice holdall with the word Adidas written on it. I thought that would come in handy for carrying baby badgers for any future badger CBs we might want so I took the bag and left Davina where she was.

It was not looking good; Natalia asked if she could have Cinderella's room if she has died. Maybe a bit soon but I said yes.

Just as it was starting to get dark, just before laasloyght there was a knock at the front door and it was Jack with Cinderella. We all felt huge relief; apparently she had spent the entire day riding the guided bus between Chumpton and Ropey. We were all thrilled to see Cinderella again … apart from Natalia as she had to start moving all her stuff out of Cinderella's room.

I decided that it was best for all concerned if I gave Cinderella a good trepanning to release the demons that made her wander. Nina went to the cupboard under the stairs and returned with a box neatly wrapped with Chrimstaaas wrapping paper. "Yo might ass well hef dis den" she said in her lovely gruff Eastern European accent, with a glint in her eye. I opened it up and it was the Demon Release TK2000 I wanted for Chrimstaaas. I welled up slightly … so did Cinderella when she saw it … she could probably see how happy I was happy.

I gave her some devils prolapse for sleepy time and treated her to a thorough trepanning. The titanium teeth and easy grip handle cut through her cranial bonce bone like it was butter. As we waited for her to regain consciousness Jack asked if it would help if she came and lived with him and Pocahontas, he said it would be great company for his bride, and I think he quite fancied a threesup after I had been telling him about my escapades with the Chopyakokov sisters. I agreed it was for the best and help him load Cinderella into the guided bus luggage compartment and we all waved goodbye.

Everyone was thrilled apart from Natalia who had to change bedrooms for the third time that day. When Finbar came calling a short while later to take Cinders on a date we didn't have the heart to tell him she was living in Ropey now, so we told him she'd gone missing, that we couldn't find her and she had probably died in a drainage dyke. He was very upset but it was for the best.

I received a text from Gary saying he would pick Jim Bob and me up nice and early ready for Jim Bob's big day in becoming a TV star.

Thrisdee 20th Deliverance

What an unusual day dearest Diary, what a very strange and wonderful day indeed.

Jim Bob was at my house just after firsloyght and Gary turned up shortly after. He came into my kitchen with his new laptop (*as Devilman had is old one*) and a VHS video recorder with a funny adapter gizmo hanging out of the back. We loaded the advert of Jim Bob extoling the virtues of my inventions and his handy work and loaded it onto a VHS video tape. Gary just kept saying "Badger CB's?" inquisitively and smiling whilst shaking his head.

We went off to Ropey in Gary's car with everything we needed for placing our adverts on Flatlands TV to sell the last of our clobber for the last minute Chrimstaaas rush known as 'Black Frydims'.

We met my old chum Gregory Dykesnaffler the celebrated Flatlands TV producer, he led us through to a small studio and offered us a warm cup of onion tea. Gary tried it out of curiosity but I think his tastes are more refined than hours and he did well to keep down the one gulp he took. As he took us through to the editing suite, which consisted of five chairs of varying make and colour and three VHS video players, also of varying make and colour. As we sat down Gregory showed us how to insert the tape and left us to it.

"You do know that with today being the Mayoral Election Day that we'll all be very busy with the coverage from town hall and the various interviews with Mayor Devilman, can you cope with running your own advert as we have no technicians to help, just remember to press play when you see that big red light come on" Gregory instructed us shortly before leaving us in the booth.

We waited for about ten minutes and then the red light blinked away, we all smiled and I pressed the play button. The screen in front of us showed us our advert as it went out, we all sat watched with interest.

The advert showed a grinning Jim Bob walking into the inventing shed in my garden holding one of our Badger CB's.

"Are you stuck for ideas this Chrimstaaas? Are you wondering what to get the person who has everything? Then we at Zonco might just be the answer to all your solutions. This Badger CB is perfect for keeping tabs on your childers so you know they're safe with just a 'come back good buddy' away …… or …. Or perhaps you'd prefer to know what your former Mayor has lined up for you after today's Mayoral Elections. Perhaps you'd like to know that not only did he sell the land to build New Chumpton, but also, he intends to flatten your houses and buy your farm land with something called a compulsory purchase order which means you have to sell at the price he offers. Perhaps you would like to know that he has ideas to turn Flatlands into nothing more than an industrial hub for distribution and luxury homes, making him and his cronies millions and millions of hoooman pounds whilst leaving us with nothing and in most cases homeless. If you want to enjoy more Chrimstaaas's in this wonderful, unique little District then maybe you might want to come into Ropey today and let him know how you feel … bring the family … bring your anger".

It then switched from showing Jim Bob in the inventing shed to showing a close up of Devilman in his living room whilst Cranshaw sucked his winky and made strange oinking sounds as music was playing loudly in the background. A portly, but very sexually attractive dancer with his/her face pixelated out, writhing to the music. Then it cut to a heated discussion between Devilman and local media tycoon Rimbit Muldoon arguing over the his cut in the land deals and threatening to influence the Flatlands electorate into voting Flexit in a referendum. Then Devilman laughed and said he could do what he wanted because the referendum was a waste of time anyway, purely designed to scare people into accepting any offer made to them in the face of a failing economy whether we remained or left, it was irrelevant.

Finally it cut a private meeting between Cranshaw, the Elders and Devilman. It was a brief clip of them all laughing as Devilman loudly boasts that "I'll bring this poxy little district to its knees and when I do I'll fucking flatten this shit hole".

It then looped on the "I'll fucking flatten this shit hole" several times to fade.

It was done. We waited to be asked to leave but nobody had noticed our little advert/information film so fifteen minutes later the red light started blinking again. We rewound the tape and pressed play again and watched our handy work once more. Three more times the red light blinked before Gregory stormed into the suite as the bemused station workers realised what had been rolling in the breaks.

"GET OUT, GET OUT!" Gregory bellowed as he slammed the door behind him. I apologised for my deed but mitigated it by saying something needed to be done. Gregory smiled and informed us all he had seen it the first time it aired, he did the best he could to distract his colleagues but could only let in run another three times. We thanked him and he wished us luck then open the door and shouted "AND FUCKING STAY OUT!"

We left the Ropey TV station and made our way to the market square just outside the town hall. Already thirty or forty people had gathered, some with placards, some rather worryingly with pitchforks. All three Ropey Police Brigade officers were doing their best to not look concerned. By early aftynune there were three maybe four hundred people milling around the market square occasionally breaking into a chant but they were all chanting different things so it was largely undecipherable, but chanting nonetheless. The three police officers had disappeared only to re-appear ten minutes later, out of uniform and carrying placards of their own complaining about cuts to police budgets (*Spelt budgies*). By late aftynune there were possibly a thousand people or more had arrived, most arrived on foot but some on back of mules, some on tractors, some in wheel barrows but all came with an axe to grind. One of the police officers went into the police station and got hold of a megaphone and handed it to Jack.

Jack made his way to the steps of the town hall and Gary and I followed. Jack switched the megaphone on and called for calm and a bit of quiet. After several attempts a degree of order was achieved and he handed the megaphone to me. I was surprised to say the least as I didn't really know what to say so I improvised.
"Thank you all so much for coming out and fighting for your community. To the Mayor …" someone from the crowd interrupted "He ain't no Mayor of ours" and a cheer went up. I continued "To the Mayor we are nothing more than an inconvenience, an obstacle, something that has served a purpose and is about to be discarded and tossed to one side like … like … like a used baby childers nappy … that's full of poo and been on the childer for a few days and you've had your money's worth out of the nappy but it has

to go now … so it's thrown out … into the bin. Well, that's you that is, you are the nappy full of childers crap and tossed into the bin" (*perhaps not the best simile but, as I said, I wasn't expecting to make speeches today*) oddly, an enormous cheer rang out and the thousand strong crowd burst into applause.

"The Mayor's conspicuous by his absence don't you think?" I continued, but this was met with complete silence, the word conspicuous must have thrown them, so I tried again. "It's noticeable how the Mayor hasn't come out to address you" this time a large cheer rang out across the square.

"We will go in and see what he has to say for himself, if we aren't out within 20 minutes, will you come in after us?" I cried. This got the biggest cheers of all.

We walked into the town hall as three chaps with a purpose and our purpose was justice (*I wished I'd said that outside now*). There was nobody on the front desk so we strode defiantly into the chambers and through into the Mayor's office. The office was empty. I then noticed a small door slightly ajar in the corner behind the entrance door; I'd never seen this door before as it was cut into the wooden panelling. Jack went through the door and came back a couple of seconds later to inform us that the door led to a small alleyway at the rear of the building. Clearly Devilman and Cranshaw had scarpered. We returned out to the throng in the market square and Jack once again handed me the megaphone, this time we didn't have to ask for quiet as the crowd fell silent autonomously. At the front of the crowd I noticed St.John Cranshaw, smiling at me and gave me a little wave, very camply, for some reason I waved back in an equally camp manner.

"Well as you can probably guess by our quick return that the Mayor and his side kick have disappeared out the back of the building. Hopefully we will never see them darken our district ever again" another massive cheer ensued. "Maybe now" I continued "Maybe now we can have proper elections and elect someone who has OUR best interests at heart, and the elections can be held every few years or so, what do you think?" this sent the massed gathering into a frenzy and hats and cats and a couple of chickens and even a goat got thrown into the air. Once they settled I was just about to start waffling on again when St.John Cranshaw shouted out "WHY DON'T YOU DO IT MORTON?" More cheering was followed by a chant of "Morton for Mayor" as I turned around I noticed that Jack and Gary had both joined in the chanting too.

Once the crowd calmed down again I agreed to do it for the next few months and then we can hold proper Mayoral elections where everyone who fancies having a go can at being the Flatlands Mayor can put their case forward and try to get elected.

We stayed in the market square a bit longer and had a few drinks. The crowd got merry and eventually dispersed and made their way to their homes. On our journey back to my house Gary kept teasing me by referring to me as your highness. When we got into my house and told the girls what had happened they were absolutely beside themselves with excitement.

I think it goes without saying I am expecting some excellent sexing tonoyght.

Frydims 21lbs Deliverance

You will not believe how much sexing I was allowed to have with Nina and Natalia last noyght. A lot if you were wondering, and some of it quite rude and ALL of it whilst they were awake. ☺

I took the guided bus to Ropey and made my way to the town hall. I entered the building to find it still derelict as it was the noyght before. I sat down at the front desk and wondered what to do. Just then door swung open and in walked St.John Cranshaw "I saw you come in, I thought you might need a hand" he said with a big broad grin. I agreed and made my first job as interim Mayor to appoint him as my assistant. My next job was to send a courier crow to Jacks house telling him to put on his uniform as he was now in charge of the Police Brigade of Flatland District. He was there within twenty minutes, another man beaming.

I went through Devilman's old desk but most of the contents had been removed and the compooota and survva had been smashed. Gary phoned me on my mobile and said he was popping in this aftynune as he had some news for me. Jack set about tidying the place up and St.John went and got some Typhoo tea and cow's milk for refreshment. Mid aftynune Gary arrived and came and sat in the Mayor's office, bowing his head as he entered. The news he mentioned earlier was that he had a friend who lived just up the road from him in New Chumpton. He was an accountant that had retired and was willing to help us out as a temporary measure. Gary said he could also install a couple of servers and a super duper computer and could supply computers throughout the district. He reckoned within a couple of years he would have lots of computers in the district, in the hospital, in the schools, even in people's homes.

We will need ~~new~~ roads between the main villages and Ropey town, not to mention plenty of new medical equipment for the hospital. Better equipment for the Police Brigade and certainly better buildings and more properly trained teachers for the schools. There are lots of things to be getting on with and do for the future that will take time. Gary left and I said I would see St.John on Moondee and Jack tomorrow for the nativity at the Church. Jack gave me a lift home and said he would finish teaching me to drive so I can take my test and have a car and drive myself next year. Jim Bob was keen to look after all of the Zonco stuff and Nina and Natalia would be in charge of Peppermint Hippo for the next six months whilst I was interim Mayor.

Today was a very good day.

SatD 22nd Deliverance

Fantastic day yisdee and once again plenty of rudeness between myself and the delightful duo Nina and Natalia. Three times thank you for asking and two for them they were fully conscious and mostly consenting. The last one they were very drowsy so I took the opportunity to try it up the botty. That woke them up … but only briefly, my winky is not as big as it was in my youth. Chumpton-by-Kumberly Interpretive Dance School sponsored by Peppermint Hippo was assembled at St. Jeremiah's Church ready for the big performance. Some members mentioned the revealing and transparent nature of my leotard and questioned its appropriateness given my role as Mary, who was the mother of the baby Jesus. I reminded them that it was only make believe and also that I'm now the Mayor. We started the performance very well until Floella Nipsy (*an erotic dancing legend almost on a par with my good self*) who as you may recall, has incontinence issues had a sneezing fit that created scenes of great unpleasantness for those seated in the first three rows back from the font. It is always sad to see childers cry, especially ones that have been sprayed with the urine of a celebrated erotic dancer, but I know some of their fathers that frequent my club often pay good money for this kind of treatment on Fetish noyght every Frydims. The rest of the performance went off without a hitch. We all went and had a celebratory drink back at the Hippo and some of the school childers even tried to have a go on the poles. I decided to get up and show them how it was done but sadly the involuntary flatulence returned and some of the cast sat near the front saw more than they bargained for when my costume malfunctioned.

Sunty 23st Deliverance

A quiet day today. Time to reflect on the events of the last few months and certainly yisdee. Jim Bob has been honing his taxidermy and I saw a nice couple of adverts in the weekly paper this mawnin.

I saw Jack briefly this aftynune. I asked him how Cinderella was settling in at his place and he said "She's doing fine Morton, hardly says a word, just like Pocahontas … although last noyght as I was cleaning my gun she momentarily lost that distant stare she has and grabbed my arm, looked me in the eye and said 'shoot me … kill me now, I beg you', which was a bit odd". I think I may need to continue with the course of trepanning to ensure no more outbursts or attempted escapes like last week.

fenbook | Surch for peeeple and othur things tooooo | Morton Hoome Foind frends

Good Mawnin Fenbookie pals. I have began getting ready for Chrimtaaas which is only several days away now. I am taking orders for my trusted employee, Jim Bob to indulge his skills as a taxidermist of Flatland creatures. I have pictured for your perusal this Friblles Jizzswapper that met with an unfortunate end after local school master Jerome Kidwhippp mistook it for an errant child that had asked for more food. They are perfect toys for the kids or great ornaments for loved ones.

Chumpton-by-Kumberly Informer (Christmas edition)

This is Jebs Cabs, Chumptons very own taxi service. Don't drink and drive during the festive season, ... the rest of the year is fine. If you are leaving Peppermint Hippo or had a few Turnip pochines at Chumptons World of Adventure and finding difficulty in remembering your name then call Jebs Cabs via Fenbook, courier crow or tefelone on (std 01487796539755645321969885) 13

The Chumpton Warbler, "specially" bred for Chrimstaaas. Not sure if you want white meat or cat flesh? Why not treat you and your family to both with a Chumptons Warbler. Is it a cat? Is it a bird? Who cares, it's tasty and that's what matters on Chrimstaaas day.

Moondee 24nd Deliverance

Today is Chrimstaaas eve and I spent it at the town hall with Gary's friend the accountant called Douglas. He is a nice man and drinks lots of tea, he bought some biscuits with him. Douglas is always welcome. We spent the first hour or so just getting to know each other. He was telling me that he was an accountant for a big accountancy firm in London when he was a working man. He told me he retired when he was 55, 15 years ago now. He has spent many years of his retirement travelling the world with his wife, they moved to New Chumpton a couple of years ago to settle down now their travelling days are behind them. I told Douglas about being kidnapped at 10 and my life as a local lynchpin within the Flatlands community and treated him to some of interpretive dance as well as a short display of my erotic dancing, but without any flatulent lunges. He looked a bit uncomfortable so I stopped. I think he was probably becoming sexually aroused.

We went through what was left of the council's paperwork and looked at the ledgers we had downloaded and photographed when we broke into the offices a while back. Douglas, it's fair to say, was as gobsmacked as Gary was at the scale of the corruption and wholesale thievery that had been going on for decades. He warned me that to pull something off of this magnitude, lots of palms would have been greased and told me to be careful who to trust. He kindly agreed to do the books and be in charge of accountancy for the six months I had agreed to be the Mayor of Flatlands. This aftynune I had a visit from none other than Morris Poncen. He flounced in with his blonde mop of unkempt hair, still flailing like a broken sail, and asked St.John if he could see me. He came into the office and for the first time I sat behind the Mayoral desk. A couldn't help notice that the carpet was filthy underneath the desk and it positively crackled when you passed your feet across it. I bent down and ran my hand over the dirty patch and it was like sandpaper. Then I remembered this was where Growler used to sit, that's why it smelt so bad. Morris was here to ask about his job and if he still had one. I asked him if he would be interested in a new role as his previous job of negotiating Flatlands leaving the UK was not really needed. He looked confused. I explained that the whole referendum wasn't real, that it was merely an exercise to scare the folk of Flatlands so Devilman could implement any deal he wanted and make even more money. Morris still looked confused so I asked him if he would like to in charge of tourism in Flatlands (*of which there is obviously virtually none*). Morris was thrilled. We finished just after daaymiddlin as it was Chrimstaaas eve tonoyght and every one would want to get home early to be with family or the men would need to do their Chrimstaaas shopping. The last order of the day was my inauguration ceremony. Jack, St.John and a couple of the cleaners either took part in or witnessed the interim Mayoral induction and I was presented with the daisy chain of office. The interim Mayors ceremony was a lot shorter than the full ceremony and not as frightening. It lasted 7 minutes 2 seconds (*just a tad longer than some of my mastybayshuns*) and then we all went home.

Today dear diary was another good day.

Toosdi 25th Deliverance Chrimstaaas day

Merry Chrimstaaas. This mawnin Jim Bob came over with his Chrimstaaas presents and stayed for the Chrimstaaas docky feast. We feasted at the Peppermint Hippo with some of the regulars, Sylvia and her husband Horatio Horatio from the Happy Pauper. Nina, me and Natalia, Jack and the ladies as well as Gary and his family popped in later for Chrimstaaas drinkypoo. We all had a lovely time and the feast was turkey, which made a nice change from roadkill stew. Later we were joined by the stars from the Chumpton-by-Kumberly Interpretive Dance School and the party really kicked off. We spent the rest of the day drinking and dancing to Wham, as the one of the singers called George had sadly passed away. Noyghty noyght

Winsti 26th Deliverance Boxers day

We have spent most of the day sleeping and pooing and occasionally vomiting. Needless to say that Chrimstaaas was a huge success.

Thrisdee 27st Deliverance

Now then dearest diary, just when you thought this tale of world saving daring do and intrigue had seen its final twist another one comes along.

I went to the town hall and let myself in as nobody was in until Moondee. I walked into the office and immediately noticed that my desk had been opened and the paperwork on top of it was all over the place. As I walked towards the desk to investigate I heard the door close behind me. I quickly turned to discover David Devilman and Cranshaw St.John standing behind me. Both looked dishevelled, unshaven and dirty, both looked quite angry. Devilman was holding a gun, this was not like Cranshaws lady gun but it was a big, dark grey, manly, scary looking gun. My knees buckled slightly as I realised I was in a fair bit of trouble.

"Well hello Mr Mayor … I guessed you'd be in today" Devilman said in his best mocking tone.
"How does it feel to be wearing the big shoes?" he continued as Cranshaw stood next to him sneering.
"What do you want?" I asked, "You seemed to have cleared most things out when you left in a hurry on Thrisdee"
Devilman shook his head and smiled "I'm only here for you, nothing else. You obviously didn't take me seriously when I said the consequences would be grave if you crossed me again" I flinched as he pulled the safety back on the gun.

"I'm here for no other reason than to kill you, you have taken more than you can imagine. So now I'm going to put a bullet in you and leave for a sunny climate before the authorities realise I'm gone. All they'll find is the dead body of a pretend Mayor in a backwater little Hicksville … no great loss".

I sensed he was about to pull the trigger so I tried to buy some time.

"Why did you do it? How did you do it?"

"It was quite easy really, when you go to the kind of school I went to, mix with the kind of people I mix with and bribe the kind of people I bribed. When you have photographic evidence of several highly ranked officials and politicians involved in some very unsavoury practices then trust me, nothing is insurmountable. Why did I do it … because I can, because it made me rich … richer. I would have been out of sight and out of mind if I'd have remained the Mayor of Flatlands but you and your band of merry men royally fucked things up. I was never going to do more than a year in prison anyway but I was assured if I remained out of the way and continued with being the Mayor of this little craphole then I wouldn't even do that" he chuckled. "All I have left to do is exact my revenge on you … then go and live the high life in a sunny country until all this blows over".

I was frozen to the spot, terrified. Devilman raised the gun and pointed it at me. I closed my eyes and waited for the end of my life. There was a loud crashing sound followed by a dull thud as the gun went off. I felt a sharp searing pain in my left arm followed by Jacks voice shouting "Mawnin Boss". I opened my eyes to see that Jack had come crashing through the big heavy solid wooden door, barging it into Devilman just as he squeezed the trigger. Devilman went flying to the floor, before Devilman had chance to squeeze another shot off Jack's policeman reflexes kicked in like the day he punched Nigelle in my garden and, like he did with Nigelle, he punched Devilman square in the chops and rendered him sleepy. Jack then turned his attention to Cranshaw and with one well aimed punch to the noggin rendered him sleepy too. It was one of the finest examples of Police brutality I had ever seen. Whilst they were having a nap Jack handcuffed them together and tied them to two office chairs, back to back with curtain chord and I made a tefelone call home.

There was no jug of water to dramatically chuck over them to rouse them into consciousness but both Jack and I needed to wee so we improvised. They were awoken from there slumber to discover they were restrained and the shoe was very definitely on the other foot now.

"Hello gentlemen, did you have a nice kip?" I asked. It was my turn to be smug now. "We are just waiting for back up and then we can start to get things moving". Devilman was defiant and as arrogant as ever, "Do you seriously think that anyone will believe you if tell them what happened here? Did you not listen to what I said? I have friends in very high places, I may have to serve a couple of years in a nice cushy prison somewhere down south but I'll be out sooner than you think and when I do ..." both jack and I laughed at the same time. For the first time Devilman looked concerned. Cranshaw as usual remained quiet.

"Tell your back up to make sure they have good lawyers because if we are mistreated in any way" Devilman squeaked. I could tell by his voice that he was worried.

At this point the big heavy door swung open again and in walked Nina and Natalia. Natalia came over to me and treated the small flesh wound the bullet caused on my arm whilst Nina approached our captives with a bottle of green murky liquid. Cranshaw finally spoke wanting to know what was in the bottle so I explained to him that it was a drink made from a blend of triple distilled root crops and various fungi, it was called the 'Devils Prolapse' and was used to anesthetise people or for the euthanasia of small animals injured during coitus with ... well ... bigger animals.

I pointed out to them both that because they didn't fund the hospitals properly this was what was used to put people to sleep before surgery rather than the proper drugs used in proper hospitals. Jack administered the drink and despite a brief struggle both men were once more asleep as all four of us loaded them into the back of Jacks police car. I tidied up the chambers and locked everything up before we all left.

Frydims 28lbs Deliverance

Gary came and visited us this aftynune and asked how we were all doing. He noticed my arm was bandaged up but I just told him that I had caught it on a nail in my inventing shed. He had come over to tell me that he had arranged with his company to have servers installed at the town hall and get the existing phone lines upgraded. He had drawn up a plan to ensure that the compoootas were taken out and given to a museum of technology and they were to be replaced with modern computers. We chatted about timescales to try and drag Flatlands into the 21st Century, about how it would take a while but it could be done. I poured Gary a glass of vintage single malt whiskey and we toasted the future. Of course he asked where I got the booze from and I told him I found it in one of the drawers in Devilman's desk. I actually got it from Devilman's house along with a few other things he won't need again.

SatD 29th Deliverance

There was no dance school today so we went to Gary's house. While Nina and Natalia played with Emily and chatted with Inga (*whilst coveting Inga's house*), Gary and I went for a driving lesson. Gary said it would be a good time for me to learn as the roads would be empty this time of year. I reminded him this I Flatlands and the roads are empty all the time of the year, we chuckled away as hurtled down the A14/1 at 15mph.

Sunty 30st Deliverance

We have been preparing the Peppermint Hippo for the very best New Year's party ever. We were going to have live music from Jebwould and some lovely food with real meat from a butchers shop in Cambridge and not some unfortunate Farradays Chuffsnuggler that strayed too close to the guided bus route.

Jack came over and took me out for a drive in the police car, I got on pretty well. I asked him when he thought I'd be ready for my test. He said he would put me in for a test for a full driving licence in the New Year, I'd have to take it in Peterborough so we'd need to do some driving out of Flatlands. Scary.

Moondee 31st Deliverance New Year's Eve

The last day of the year and Gary and his family came over to wish us happy New Year before they set off once again to the much fabled Newport Pagnell to visit their family. We all hugged and kissed, although I may have kissed Inga a bit longer than is considered polite in the rest of the UK (*just over a minute*). We wished them a happy New Year and chatted. I said to Gary that this has been an unforgettable year for Flatlands; he assured me it had been an unforgettable year in the rest of the UK too.

We sat and drank some Typhoo tea with cow's milk and Gary mentioned that when he switched his TV on this mawnin that the main story was about David Devilman and

Cranshaw St.John. Apparently they had done a bunk again and were suspected to be travelling through France. One source had phoned the TV station to say that they had seen the pair on the outskirts of Paris and this sighting had been confirmed by Flatlands Police Brigade. As they were about to leave Emily asked what that funny noise was, I said I hadn't heard anything but Gary said he thought he heard a whimpering sound, like a puppy. I shrugged and they went on their way.

After they left I went into the basement to see how my latest gender reassignment patients were doing. Maybe they needed a little bit more trepanning to help them get rid of any cranial bonce pressure and demonic possession. The chubbier one of the two was called Davina De`Vices, we named her that after one of our previous Mayors and the other was called Clarissa De`Vices … Davina's sister. Both these patients were terribly confused about their sexual identity when they came to our clinic on a couple of days earlier. After a brief settling in period of twenty minutes or so we prepared them for surgery with a quick trepanning and then removed their 'birth genitals' and sculpted them into a ladies tuppence and gave them both some breasties made from some tennis balls we found in the neighbours garden. The neighbours no longer had any use for them as sadly their dog had been blown up earlier this year. Both ladies looked in a pretty sorry state but then so did Pocahontas and Cinderella when we reassigned their gender and look how great that turned out. Nina had dressed them in lovely dresses made from some old hessian potato sacks and bin liners. Both patients were having a course of very, very intense trepanning … very intense.

We changed and went to the club to see in the New Year with a bang. It was a wonderful night and spirits were high. Jack was enjoying himself and relaxing with a glass or two of Parsnip Vodka but couldn't have more than 10 or so as he was on duty. He asked me what I did with Cranshaw and Devilman when he dropped them off the other day, I was stuck for words momentarily until Jack told me that if they had met with an 'unfortunate accident' it was fine with him, whilst winking at me. I assured him both were still alive but will not be troubling us or anyone ever again. He grinned and left it at that. He then said in the next breath "Nina tells me you have some new ladies, patients of yours staying with you, I'm looking forward to meeting them" he said once again winking at me. I told Jack these ladies were more robust than Pocahontas and Cinderella, I said he could be more forceful with these ones. Just after noyghtmiddlin Sylvia asked me if I could to go to my office/store cupboard to get some extra mop heads as Floella Nipsy was about to do an impromptu performance. It was all going on outside, dancing, music, shouting and laughing. The relative quiet of my office was a momentary relief, a sanctuary that gave me time to reflect on the madness of this last year. I had come a long way in this time. I have made new friends and ended up with a delightful young lady in my life and her lovely sister too.

They both like to do very rude things, occasionally consensually, especially when I have saved the world and become interim Mayor, so this means no more trips to Grunty's field to spend time with Rowenta the sheep. I have realised that it's easier to be nice to people than horrible, although being horrible is sometimes necessary … and funnier. I have been to London, twice, became a club owner and the now I'm a local dignitary of Flatland District for the next six months or so until we can organise some proper elections. I have started to learn to drive and tried lots of new things and became aware of lots of things too.

The next year is going to be really tough but I'm looking forward to it. As I sat and reflected on a very strange few months of a very, very strange year, I started to doze off. I hadn't been asleep for very long when a bright light and a crashing sound awoke me. I'm not sure what it was but whatever it was it drew my attention to an object on the table near the office door. As my eyes adjusted I could see Hector the Time Travelling Tortoise, what was he doing here? How odd, I didn't notice him on the way into the office, oh well. Just under the table Hector was perched on I also noticed the Adidas holdall I found next to Davina's very drunk personage when we lost Cinderella the other day.

I had brought it over to the club just before Chrimstaaas and noticed it felt like it had something in it but I didn't have time to see what was in it. I picked it up and opened it to discover ten very bulky wads of fifty pounds notes (*UK currency*) stuffed inside it. it was the money Davina took from the town hall safe when she attempted to scarper. I'm not sure if "finders keepers" is an actual law but this would make my bank balance look very favourable indeed and give the Peppermint Hippo the kind of refurbishment it deserves … I could do a lot with this money.

I could treat my friends and buy a car and have a holiday abroad … or at least out of Flatlands. I could get Gary's house repaired and buy a new computer or a bigger house for myself. Moments earlier I was reflecting on how I had changed as a person and now was my chance to prove it. If I kept this money I was no better than Devilman, Cranshaw and the Elders of Flatlands so this was the perfect opportunity for me to show to myself that I really had changed. Changed in to a better man and all I had to do to prove this was to return the money to the safe, first thing Monday morning. But for now I'll just sit here and stare at the enormous, life changing sum of money.

So all that remains to be said dear diary and any future readers of this account, is to say let's hope for a better year than this one, let's look to the future and hope we have a very, very …

... Happy New Year.

79265104R00191

Made in the USA
San Bernardino, CA
13 June 2018